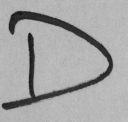

Tell Them
It Was
Wonderful

• • • • • •

Tell Them
It Was
Wonderful

• • • • • •

Selected Writings by

Ludwig Bemelmans

*Edited and with
an Introduction by*
Madeleine Bemelmans

Foreword by
Norman Cousins

VIKING

VIKING
Viking Penguin Inc., 40 West 23rd Street,
New York, New York 10010, U.S.A.
Penguin Books Ltd, Harmondsworth,
Middlesex, England
Penguin Books Australia Ltd, Ringwood,
Victoria, Australia
Penguin Books Canada Limited, 2801 John Street,
Markham, Ontario, Canada L3R 1B4
Penguin Books (N.Z.) Ltd, 182–190 Wairau Road,
Auckland 10, New Zealand

First published in 1985 by Viking Penguin Inc.
Published simultaneously in Canada

LIBRARY OF CONGRESS CATALOGING IN PUBLICATION DATA
Bemelmans, Ludwig, 1898–1962.
Tell them it was wonderful.
1. Bemelmans, Ludwig, 1898–1962—Biography.
2. Authors, American—20th century—Biography.
I. Bemelmans, Madeleine.   II. Title.
PS3503.E475Z477   1985   818'.5209 [B]   84-40365
ISBN 0-670-80391-X

Printed in the United States of America by
R. R. Donnelley & Sons Company,
Harrisonburg, Virginia
Set in Baskerville
Designed by Robin Hessel

For Paul, James, and John, the grandchildren
he so greatly desired but never knew.

Foreword

.　　.　　.

During the forties and fifties, the *Saturday Review* ran a weekly editorial lunch, generally on Wednesdays, at the old Seymour Hotel, to which we would invite authors and publishers, less for an exchange of lofty literary views than the enjoyment of their company. I can think of no one who fulfilled this latter purpose as well as Ludwig Bemelmans. No guest needed less prodding to express himself. He was the only author whose very presence could intimidate Bennett Cerf, then a regular SR columnist, into the melancholy status of silent observer or, worse still, nonperformer.

Bemelmans was the least inarticulate and most delightful personality I ever encountered. When he walked into a restaurant, his unsurpassed knowledge of menus and manners struck terror into the hearts of head waiters and chefs. The snap of his fingers was like a thunderclap or the soft pluck of a harp string, depending on his pique or pleasure. The slightest arch of his eyebrows across a crowded dining room was a mandate from Olympus. He was elegant, ebullient, expansive. He could discourse on writing, painting, food, wine, hotels, and great cities with a combination of overview and minute detail that was the envy of essayists and encyclopedists. He was less tortured by self-doubt (as least visibly) than any writer I know. He was not only the supreme man-about-town but the man at the center of the town, the compleat continental and cosmopolitan, the person for whom the keys to large and beautiful cities were originally invented.

Such a person would have had to be a product of Viennese culture. (You didn't have to be born in Vienna to reflect its cultivated reach.) Such a person would also have had a wide-ranging family tradition of catering to highly developed tastes.

Ludwig Bemelmans, in short, was born and raised to be a cultivated entrepreneur of upper-class fancies, a talent eminently suited to the operation of world-class restaurants or hotels. He could move at ease among the aristocracy, whether represented by cultured achievement or wealth. He had an unabashed aversion to middle-class culture. He was attuned to the elite, and he became its tireless depictor and its gatekeeper. He was also a master of the incongruous; he would convert the slightest implausibility into outrageous merriment.

Such a man, inevitably, would be the toast of the town— whether New York, Paris, Vienna, London, or any cosmopolitan center that had first-rate art galleries, fine hotels, good music, and caviar. Whether he was drawing bright and irreverent covers for *The New Yorker* magazine, or exhibiting his paintings at a Madison Avenue gallery, or writing fey stories or books, he was a prime divertissement and one of the best conversation pieces New York had known in some time. As an author, he turned out more than three dozen books; he was close friends with the editors of The Viking Press, who tried manfully to populate their catalogue with his titles. Their appetite was stimulated by the public response. People loved his droll accounts of life in the great hotels, of improbable characters, of ridiculous conversations and unimaginable predicaments, of high jinks and low life, of dogs that could do everything except card tricks, of mad kitchen battles between waiters and chefs, of plot-and-counterplot in the art galleries, of perennial absurdities in the human situation.

An entire generation has come of age since Ludwig Bemelmans held his readers at bay with his delightful, oddball reminiscences. I have no doubt that current readers will find him as engaging and appealing as did his contemporaries. As I say, anyone who could make Bennett Cerf seem tentative was a phenomenon beyond compare.

I have many favorites in Bemelmania—"The Old Ritz," "Paris" (retitled "La Colombe"), "The Dog of the World" among them. And they are all here, ready for savoring and instant delight. I commend them unequivocally to today's readers.

Contents

• • •

Introduction

. . .

Shortly after Ludwig's death in 1962, his editors at The Viking Press, Pascal Covici and Marshall Best, tried to persuade me to do a Bemelmans biography, but I felt that a recent widow was not the best choice for this assignment. Might she not tend to idealize the deceased or to glorify the role she'd played in his life? Besides, Ludwig had written so extensively of his own experiences that I thought the record was fairly complete.

The *Madeline* books have long been classics and have been translated into many languages. However, as the years passed, the Bemelmans books for adults became more and more difficult to find. Yet I continued to hear from ardent fans, some of whom had an almost cultlike devotion to the author. A woman wrote from California that every word was like "apricot nectar." A man living in Flemington, New Jersey, quoted verbatim passages that I had forgotten.

I began to feel an obligation to these people and to a new generation of readers to make at least some of the material available again. Just about this time I received a letter from Barbara Burn of The Viking Press, urging me to put together a Bemelmans book filled with pictures as well as text. With this encouragement

I started to organize an anthology composed of excerpts from as many of the books as possible. However, when I had finished, the selections seemed too fragmentary and would probably not have been appreciated by readers who did not already have some familiarity with the original works. Almost everything Ludwig wrote was a blend of fact and fiction, and much of it was autobiographical. So in an effort to give the book more structure and more substance, I decided to concentrate on the major segments of his life, as he lived it in those parts of the world with which he was most closely identified. The result, though essentially true, is in no way an exhaustive or accurate autobiography; rather, it is an account of his life and a study of his character, insofar as he chose to reveal himself to his readers.

Ludwig was born on April 30, 1898, in a part of Tirol now known as Merano. However, his earliest memories were of Gmunden, where his father owned a hotel called the Golden Ship, into which the family moved sometime after Ludwig's birth. In "Swan Country," he describes the gracious life he lived there until the age of six.

Though the occasions on which he saw his father had not been particularly happy, and sometimes were disastrous, Ludwig suffered from his father's absence after he abandoned the family. In a letter dated May 31, 1962, Ludwig wrote to his friend Alma Mahler Werfel, "I have forgotten so much of youth and much of it was not experienced. In me a whole portion of it is missing—it is like a floor in a house where there is no furniture." Much as he missed a conventional family life, or perhaps because he never had one, he was quite unsuited to domesticity.

The transition from the elegance of the hotel to the earthy atmosphere of a Bavarian brewery offended his sensibilities. In contrast to his brother Oscar, who was the model for "The Homesick Bus Boy" of the Splendide, Ludwig developed a lasting dislike for Regensburg. On the other hand, his love for Tirol never left him.

When he arrived in New York in December 1914, his father, by then a jewelry designer on Maiden Lane, failed to meet him at the boat. So Ludwig was obliged to spend Christmas on Ellis Island, where he received a necktie as a gift. Eventually, Ludwig went to live with his father in an apartment on the Upper West Side of Manhattan, but they never did get along. After he got a job as a bus boy, Ludwig moved into a furnished room.

Despite his loneliness, he appreciated the freedom, informality, and goodwill he found in America. Though he gave other reasons, unpublished letters show that it was out of a sense of loyalty and in the spirit of idealism that he joined the Army. He was disappointed in his hope of going abroad with the Ambulance Corps, but he served proudly with the Medical Corps at Fort Ontario and Fort Porter. According to a letter written to me by one of his fellow soldiers, Ludwig's reception upon his arrival at camp in a Boy Scout uniform, was unforgettable. "Soon, however," this soldier wrote, "because he was such a regular fellow, he was accepted as one of the guys." Based on a diary he kept at the time, *My War With the United States* (the book in which all the pieces in the "Army" section appear) is Ludwig's own account of Army life and of the misunderstandings created by his German accent and his views on military discipline.

Much as he hated the hotel business, both before and after his Army experience, the patrons and employees were a never-ending source of subject matter for his drawings and stories. Years later, whenever he had an exhibition at the Hammer Galleries, his sketches of chefs and restaurant scenes were great favorites with the collectors.

The early thirties were years of intense hardship, deep depression, and bitter disappointments. However, when I met Ludwig, the future was beginning to look a little brighter. He had just completed his first children's book, *Hansi,* and was decorating the walls of a restaurant that was being financed by a group of advertising men. By the time we got married, I was a freshman at Barnard. Before this, having left the Novitiate of the Sisters of Charity at Mount St. Vincent, I had pursued a brief career as a model. It must have been the incongruity that appealed to Ludwig.

It was great living at the Hapsburg, which Ludwig was managing, but he entertained so lavishly that the other stockholders rebelled and voted to buy him out. With the money from his share of the stock we were able to afford passage on a one-class ship that docked in Antwerp and to spend some time in Bruges, where Ludwig found the inspiration for his second children's book, *The Golden Basket.*

When Barbara was born the following year, the financial situation was precarious. But somehow the means were always found to satisfy Ludwig's wanderlust. One day while waiting his turn in a dentist's office, he read in *National Geographic* that in Ecuador orchids grow on trees. Within a week, we were on the S.S. *Santa Clara*, a Grace Liner, bound for Guayaquil. It was the first of several trips to South America.

In 1943 Ludwig went to Hollywood to work on a screenplay based on one of the stories he had sold to MGM. His experiences as a Hollywood writer inspired the novel *Dirty Eddie.* The character Ludlow Mumm is a composite of himself and a friend with a social conscience and Communist sympathies. The hero, Dirty Eddie, is a talented pig, who has an important part in the movie on which Mumm and a collaborator are working. Moses Fable, the head of Olympia Pictures, is really Louis B. Mayer. After the book came out, he issued the following order: "Never hire that guy [euphemism] again—unless we absolutely need him."

During World War II, Hollywood and Beverly Hills were havens for British and European notables—novelists, poets, musicians, and the wealthy—with or without titles, and an invitation to Lady Mendl's was a special mark of social approval. The rapport between Ludwig and his indefatigable hostess was instantaneous. *To the One I Love the Best* (in which appeared "Invitation," "The Footstool of Madame Pompadour," and "The Visit to San Simeon") celebrates their friendship. The title is taken from the inscriptions on the tombstones of each of Lady Mendl's favorite poodles. Ludwig was on as good terms with Lady Mendl's husband as he was with her. Sir Charles Mendl did not resent being portrayed as a comic character in Ludwig's work; in fact, after publication he sent a cable from Paris that read: MUCH PLEASED WITH BOOK AND WHAT YOU WROTE ABOUT ME. DON'T BELIEVE ANYTHING TO THE CONTRARY. MUCH LOVE, CHARLES.

Ludwig's love affair with Paris began in 1946 when Ted Patrick, the editor of *Holiday* magazine, asked him to do a series of articles on postwar Europe. From that time until his death, Ludwig was a regular contributor to the magazine. In 1947 we all sailed together on the S.S. *America,* but after a summer abroad Barbara decided that her horse was more interesting than grand hotels. When a suitable person to stay with her could be found, Ludwig and I would start off from New York together, or I would meet him later at some convenient airport. As Ludwig spent more and more time in Europe, it seemed sensible to have a pied-à-terre in Paris, which would be a repository for his personal effects and art paraphernalia when he took off for England, Ireland, and various spots on the Continent. And since he loved to entertain, what better solution than a bistro with living quarters overhead? Of course, he never anticipated the headache La Colombe would become. Fortunately, disasters sometimes make good stories.

Ludwig's fondness for boats dated from his early days in New York, when he traveled around Manhattan Island in a motorboat owned by his friend Willy. One ambition he never fulfilled was to take a boat down to Florida via the Inland Waterway, but his dream of becoming a ship-owner was finally realized. With the Riviera so overrun by tourists that even the residents of the most luxurious villas could not enjoy peace and privacy, Ludwig reasoned that a sailboat would be the logical solution to the problem of overcrowded beaches. "Ship-Owner" is the story of his Riviera cruise.

Ludwig died in his sleep on October 1, 1962. He had been ill for more than a year with a number of ailments, and it was painful to witness the physical deterioration of someone who had always been so full of energy and impatient of weakness. Though he felt miserable most of the time, he continued his normal activities—painting, writing, traveling, and planning for the future.

Ludwig hated militarism but loved the circumstance attending it. That is why we buried him at Arlington. I am sure he would have enjoyed the folding of the flag draped over the casket, the playing of taps, and the shots fired over the grave.

Ludwig had closed one of his last letters to Pat Covici with the words, "One more thing—I would like to have on my tombstone,'Tell Them It Was Wonderful.'" (It was and it wasn't.)

Childhood

· · · · · · ·

Swan
Country

. . .

As it is now, so it was then, only more so—a setting like the scenery for a Viennese operetta. A place in which, a plot in which nothing violent would happen. The décor was in pastel colors, gay and simple and immediately understood. In it people walked about in lovely costumes.

There was music everywhere. Men in uniforms, women who were elegant. Peasant women in beautifully embroidered silks. The emperor had a villa close by and a joke was told about Franz Josef, who was a serious man.

He had invited the Danny Kaye of those days, a comedian named Giradi, to cheer him up. They sat opposite each other and there was silence and then the emperor said: "Why don't you say something funny?"

Giradi replied: "What could you say that's funny when you lunch with the emperor?"

There was no radio, no television, nothing but music and conversation, and life was comfortable. Like the pages of a children's book, the days were turned and looked at, and the most important objects in this book were the sun, the moon and the stars; people, flowers and trees. Large trees, whose leaves throbbed with color and which reached up to the sky—black tree trunks, sometimes brownish black and shining in the rain, young in spring, and yellow in the autumn, when each leaf in the light of afternoon was like a lamp lit up. Pink and violet clouds, and flowers very clear and close, for when one is small one can put one's face to them easily and breathe in their fragrance, and look at them close. Does one ever see things clearer than as a child? The sky is blue, the gardener's apron is greener than spinach. The eyes of Gazelle are large and brown and kind.

A whistle is heard; a ship approaches. Suddenly it is close and big as a house, alive and floating, snow-white and gold among the lavished wealth of color of garden, field and mountains. The ship's name is *Elisabet*. She turns and in a dead slowdown comes to the dock. The reflection wobbles for a while in the broad waves the ship made when the arrested paddle wheel dragged along. Now the captain waves, and I wave back, and then after a little while the captain pulls a cord. One sees this and a puff of white steam flowing upward, and then the sound of the steamer whistle is heard again. The steamer ripples the water, the floating deck makes a gurgling sound. The "phlop, phlop, phlop" of the paddle wheel has stopped.

When the ship approaches, the swans go this way and that on the water, and when they hear its whistle they leave to make room for the *Elisabet,* and one of them, our swan, stretches, rises out of the water, beats his wings, and then awkwardly runs on the soles of his feet with much splashing, half running, half flying on the water. He finally takes off, with labored flight; he stretches his neck, making a straight long line; he sails overhead and then comes down; he lands with a swishing beat of wings, with his webbed feet stretched out in front of him—bracing himself against the water. He has his wings outstretched still and then folds them, and from a high, standing position he becomes suddenly the beautiful swan in the lake. He comes to our dock and climbs out. He is the most enterprising of the swans.

We eat in summer in what was once a hothouse and is now a dining room. My Papa is an impatient perfectionist, which makes life difficult for him. He has to have everything beautiful at once, and because it takes all summer for the grapes to ripen he has placed glass grapes among the foliage, and put electric lights in them. They hang among the thick foliage in what is called the *vignoble*, for we speak only French in this garden. The vines are dark green at the ceiling and light green along the sides. The swan waits to be fed, making sounds of impatience with his beak, as if he were a goose, sometimes even hissing when he has to wait too long.

The little city of Gmunden, on the Traunsee, in the Austrian province of Salzkammergut, is very cosmopolitan. The Duke of Cumberland has a vast estate there. The Queen of Greece was born there, and in 1953, when I went back to paint Schloss Ort, there was a car ahead of me with number 21 on a blue license plate, and it was she, who had come back to look at the beautiful lake and the scenes of childhood.

My father was a Belgian and a painter who had inherited property in Gmunden. Besides the mansion which, with its trees and park, stood surrounded by water, he owned a hotel called "The Golden Ship."

Its clientele was remarkable for variety and character. There came every year a Russian grand duke who occupied two floors. There were Parisians, Americans, Germans, Greeks—every nationality. I saw Papa rarely, and my mother I don't remember at all in those days. I lived with my governess in the garden on the lake. She was young and French. I could not say "Mademoiselle" then, and addressed her as "Gazelle."

Papa, when he came to the place where I lived with Mademoiselle, was always busy arranging *plaisanteries*. He built me a complete little carpenter shop where I could work and paint alone and in which he never, as normal fathers would, puttered himself. He had his own workshop where he busied himself with modeling in clay, making frames, designing machinery and inventing. He was never without a project. He created the first Pedalo, a watergoing bicycle, which he tried out on the lake. It was elaborate and in the shape of a swan. He had a very beautiful, small motorcar made for me and he presented me with these toys very formally and with an air of apology that made it difficult for me to thank him, or show my enthusiasm in full. I have inherited this and am very embarrassed when anyone thanks me for anything.

Papa sometimes came and sketched Gazelle wearing a helmet or a cuirass. He was fond of armor and collected it. He played the guitar and had a very good voice. The song he liked most to sing was *"Ouvre tes yeux bleus, ma mignonne."* He dressed unlike other people, in velvet jackets, corduroy suits, large black hats, and flowing ties. He wore a mustache and a beard. He had very small feet, a whipping walk and small, nervous hands.

Papa sometimes would paint in the garden. He brought a small easel and a large palette and put on a blue smock But he never painted me; he always looked at me with the curiosity of a stranger meeting someone for the first time. I bowed to him, he bowed to me.

I was presented to him, always carefully washed and dressed. He approved to the extent that he decided to make use of me as an angel during Christmas when I was four years old. Papa gave a Christmas party for the employees of the hotel and for the fishermen, boatmen, and peasants. A large table was in the center of the ballroom of the hotel, with gifts for the children. My golden curls were especially curled and brushed and they had made white wings for me and attached them to my shoulders. Overhead on the ceiling was a pulley, and a hook was attached to some white satin which had been wrapped around my middle, and I was pulled upward on a rope and suspended above the Christmas tree. I disappointed him badly, for the smell of burning wax candles, the pipe smoke, the heat and the fear of falling made me ill. I was taken down and abruptly dismissed. I cried, and Gazelle cried—and we went back to the security of our little park.

Papa surrounded himself with friends who, like himself, were determined to be outstandingly different from the provincial citizenry and the staid aristocrats who lived in Gmunden. Their worries were about the next day's happiness, which they made like the baker his rolls, and always while whistling, singing, or reeling in their fish. They found caves to illuminate at night and gave parties in them. They covered wooden floats with flowers and sailed them on the lake. They sent off rockets that awoke the town and exploded high in the sky and filled the night with a rain of phosphorescent stars that were all reflected in the lake. They gave concerts, sang operas and acted in their own plays, and Papa was the president of a society which was called "Schlaraffia."

The hotel existed merely to cater to these celebrations. The maître d'hôtel, Monsieur Zobal, a very distinguished-looking, quiet, small man, who invariably wore snow-white linen and tailcoat, was busy blowing up balloons, helping Papa gild plaster statues, setting off fireworks and stringing up lampions.

Above all I admired his skill with napkins. After deft and precise folding of the snow-white linen, he turned the napkins with a last twist into the shapes of fans, ships, plants and swans. He also chiseled swans and castles out of blocks of ice. Whenever there was something especially good for dessert over in the hotel, Monsieur Zobal saved some of it for us and brought it across the next day.

In the hothouse where we ate, the meals were gay. We sat facing the lake; there were Papa's dogs who came and the swan. There was conversation and, in two carafes, red and white wine. Gazelle drank out of a glass on a thin stem; I had a little golden mug with my name written on it. Monsieur Zobal brought gifts and the chef sometimes came himself. The swan was sometimes rough in his affection for me and once knocked me off balance and into the lake. Gazelle jumped in and saved me.

We left the house at nine on our daily walk, hand in hand, along the promenade. I was always neatly dressed, my curls combed, my shoelaces properly tied and always with white gloves. I was her little blue fish, her little treasure, her small green duckling, her dear sweet cabbage, her amour.

·   ·   ·

Summer, winter, autumn, spring—there was every day a long promenade with Gazelle, and we always came to a place with thistly bushes, where quinces grew, and then to a garden and a field, rose-colored with the blossoms of heather, and after that to a small inn, where cakes and chocolate were served.

All is still there—quinces, heather, the small inn, all unchanged. The daughter now runs the inn but she has the same smile, the same voice, the same ease and air of comfort and of peace that her mother had.

This intimate life in the small park and the old house on the lake—being bathed, dressed, fed, cared for—was only clouded by such tragedies as having toenails cut or getting soap into my eyes, when the big, clear tears of childhood rolled down my cheeks.

The other person who cried frequently was God. The God of that time and garden in Gmunden was "le Bon Dieu" who worried only about making this life beautiful, and from whom all good things came. He was a beautiful old grandfather, and when it rained it was because people were bad; He had to cry and the tears ran over His cheeks and down His beard and over the lake. Mademoiselle said that the Bon Dieu was everywhere in every flower, animal, and cloud. And therefore one did not need to go to church.

I never was visited by other children. These long years of childhood were spent in the seclusion of the park and the vast house alone with Gazelle.

Monsieur Zobal came over to supervise the cooking, which was French. Papa came also when he needed the hothouse to celebrate in or to rehearse musicians, or when he tied his sailboat to the dock.

One time, when I was six, he wanted to take me on a drive around the country.

Among the few German words I knew was *Pferd,* which means horse; the coachman's name was Ferdinand, and because he had to do with horses I called him Pferdinand.

The coach, like everything Papa had, was an extraordinary vehicle, a shiny black landau, the body suspended on heavy straps of red Russian leather with gilt buckles. Pferdinand in top hat and livery and a bear rug over his legs waited. Two white Borzoi dogs also waited to run after us.

This was to be a family outing and Mama came and sat down in the carriage. I was handed over, with my golden curls squeezed down by a hat held in place with a stinging rubber band. Whenever I was taken from the side and hand of Gazelle, there were tears. I sat and cried as we waited. At last Papa came, looked at me seated in the coach and, lifting his hat, said to Mama that he was sorry but he couldn't come, because it would bore him. "I'll talk to him, later—when he understands—when he is seventeen," he said, and turned on his heel. As on that Christmas night when I had been an angel, I was happy again to be handed back to Gazelle, who cried also, and then le Bon Dieu started to cry—it rained. It rained almost every day in Gmunden—rain that sounded like the water of a shower falling full force on bathwater in the tub. It rained especially when one thought that it would be a lovely day, and when there was a patch of pale blue sky overhead in the morning.

It still rained the last time I was there. I painted the castle in rain. On this voyage I became aware that my palette is still of that landscape in rain.

The colors of houses and landscapes mostly in rain sank into my eyes in early childhood. This time, spent in a restricted place and in solitude, impressed on me the objects in nature which I still see in the shape and colors in which they were.

There was often fog on the lake. The fog was green, blue, violet, gray; it floated into the garden like gauze. It stood sometimes in shapes under trees, then disappeared as it had come. It determined the coloration of water, of the swans, of the eyes of Gazelle and of her hair. And sometimes it was like an immense white shroud, covering all. When the wind tore into it, it moved, and there suddenly appeared again the lake, the *Elisabet,* a swan, the bridge. On my recent visit the old steamer was still paddling "Phlop, phlop, phlop" around the lake.

The seasons passed slowly in my childhood. There were the many phases of spring, with snow melting and running off the roofs, and icicles falling, and the birds drinking in the puddles made by the dripping water, and the sun reflecting in them. One of the many miracles I beheld then was the reflection of the sun in every puddle, even the smallest and dirtiest ones. My favorite season was autumn, the rich autumn of the russet and of all the dark reds and umber, the yellow autumn when all the chestnut trees were lit up with sun, and another phase when the leaves had fallen and the ground was a tapestry of ochre leaves with the trunks of trees turned several shades darker. I remember the smells of autumn, of ripening fruit along the espalier trees, especially of apricots, which were harvested and taken to the chef. He made from them my favorite dessert—dumplings of light dough with an apricot inside and bread crumbs and sugar outside. This dessert is called *Marillenknoedel*—and I was able to eat a dozen of them at one sitting.

Then the last stage of autumn, the park cleared of the ochre leaves, the promenades swept, the trees now bare and the leaves sunk down to the bottom of the lake, shining upward and gilding the water. And, finally, the *Elisabet* was put to bed for the winter on the other side of the lake, tied to a dock next to a tavern. And one day she was covered and went to sleep under a coverlet of snow.

Long hours now were spent indoors with the collection of postal cards of Paris, the Album of Paris, the children's stories of France, the songs written for French children.

And then one autumn the leaves in the park were not raked, the swan stood there forlorn and it was all over—all had come to an end. Papa was gone and so was my governess, and I wished so much that he had run away with Mama and left me Gazelle.

·   ·   ·

I found myself in the arms of a strange woman, my mother, who was twenty-four years old then and very beautiful. She held me close and wept almost the entire journey from Gmunden to Regensburg.

We arrived with a night train. My mother was expecting a child. The arrival was so planned that no one would see. A closed coach took us to the Arnulfsplatz. My grandfather wept and repeated, *"Armes Weiberl, armes Weiberl,"* meaning "poor little woman, poor little woman." My grandmother held me in her arms and looked stone-faced, for she had made the path even and promoted the match. It was also said that among her many lovers had been my father.

For a long time, my mother locked herself into her rooms and never went out. That was because she was the first divorced woman in Regensburg. Except for the scandal with King Ludwig I and Lola Montez, no one had ever heard of a case like this. People were married—men had illegal children with servant girls and provided for them, and all that was accepted, but marriage was a sacred institution. They did not bother to ask who was the guilty party. The woman was marked. My grandfather, who had been very much against the marriage, insisted on the divorce.

In the beginning Mama tried to replace Gazelle; mostly in tears, she dressed me and undressed me. There were no children's books, and she would tell me stories about her own childhood—of how alone she had been as a little girl and how she was shipped off to a convent school in Altötting, which was run by the kind nuns of an order known as the *"Englische Fräulein."* She described the life there—how the girls slept in little beds that stood in two rows and how they went walking in two straight lines, all dressed alike. She was much happier there than at home, for her parents had never had any time for her. This made me very sad. She cried, and I cried. She lifted me up; I looked at her closely, and a dreadful fear came over me. I saw how beautiful she was, and I thought how terrible it would be if ever she got old and ugly.

Lausbub

· · ·

Regensburg is a Bavarian city on the banks of the Danube, and it possesses one of the finest Gothic cathedrals. When I was little it had about sixty thousand inhabitants, first among whom was the Duke of Thurn und Taxis. He lived in a castle which it took fifteen minutes to pass; it stood in a park that encircled the city. The Duke retained the Spanish etiquette at his court; his servants wore livery and powdered wigs; he rode about in a gilded coach cradled in saffron leather and drawn by white horses. He supported several jewelers, the city's theater, a private orchestra, and the race track.

Grandfather's brewery stood on a square facing the Duke's theater, in the oldest part of town. His daughter, my mother, was born in Regensburg. Grandfather loved the city.

My father, who lived there for a time, did not. He called it the cloaca of the world, but with a broader, more Bavarian word, which in Regensburg is used frequently as a term of rough endearment among friends. And so he went to Munich whenever he could escape from Regensburg; and when he could not, he walked out to the railroad station at least one evening a week. When all the other people went to the breweries, he would walk up and down the station platform until the signal bell announced the ap-

proach of the fast train from Paris. This train stopped for three minutes in Regensburg, and in that time my father would lean over the iron barrier and look into the bright windows of the dining-car over which brass letters spelled out the elegant phrase, *Compagnie des Wagons-Lits et Express Européens,* and under which were a coat of arms and the word *Mitropa,* in carved wood. There he hung, drinking in the perfume, looking at the furs, at the few fortunate people who were walking up and down and climbing into the carmine-upholstered compartments. He would wait until the red signal lamp at the end of the train had slid down over the narrowing rails and disappeared around a curve on its way to Vienna. When he came back, he would complain of Regensburg's houses, its people, its way of life.

He was not altogether wrong, for it was a small provincial

town, slow and gossipy. Regensburg went to sleep at nine in the evening, its surrounding country was without much excitement or good scenery, and I disliked it chiefly because I had to attend the Gymnasium there and all my professors came to eat in the restaurant of Grandfather's brewery, so that he was always informed that I would not pass the examinations, that I was unruly, impertinent, never serious, always late, and kept bad company.

At the end of my first year at the Gymnasium I had to repeat, and when this first year came to its second ending, and it had to be repeated once more, it was decided to send me away to a quiet little academy in Rothenburg, privately managed, for backward boys, where even an idiot could slowly be advanced. But even there I failed again to pass. The Rector, a very thorough and patient man, wrote home and asked to have me taken away.

Mother came to Rothenburg. We sat in the Rector's living room under an eyeless plaster bust of Pericles. The Rector, in a shabby green coat, felt his way around; almost blind, he looked through spectacles as thick as the bottom of a beer glass, and in the frames of which his eyes swam somewhere outside of his face, immense and unreal. After he had said "Amen" to my future, Mother started to weep, and we left his room.

I said good-by to my friends. My linen and my stockings and clothes, all neatly marked "51" with the numbers in red on a white tape, were packed by the Rector's wife. We ate at the inn, called the Iron Hat, before we went to the station.

It was a silent trip. I could not find my voice. I wanted to kiss my mother and ask her forgiveness and somehow promise that she should not be sorry, that I would start a new and good life. But at that age one cannot say anything and after a while I played with the long leather strap that hung down from the window of the compartment. Embossed on it was "Royal Bavarian Railway," and I thought how I would like to take my pocket knife and cut it off. It was such a nice strong leather strap and would be useful for many purposes.

There was a stop in Nürnberg, and a buffet on the station platform. "You don't deserve this," said Mother, but she bought me a pair of the lovely little sausages, which are nowhere else better, and a small beer, and then she put her hand on my head and said: *"Es wird schon werden, Ludwig"*—"Everything will come out all right in the end."

The hope and prayer of every German mother at that time was that her boy would at least finish the six years of Gymnasium, which made of him a better-grade soldier when the time came for his military service. He would not be an officer; for that he had to enter the cadet corps. But he was allowed to sleep at home, he did not have to wear the formless baggy uniform issued by the service, the clumsy boots, the cap without a visor. He was marked off, besides having his own well-tailored uniform and a stiff cap with visor, by two little shoulder straps, with a narrow blue and white border. He did not have to stand at attention when an officer passed, hold that position and follow the officer with his eyes until he had passed. He simply saluted. His term of service was only one year instead of three.

It was a disgrace to be a common soldier, mingling in the barracks with the louts that came from the potato-growing country around Regensburg, commanded to do every kind of stable duty, to shine officers' boots, and to be addressed as *"Gemeiner"*—"common one." But this awaited me. Mother had said over and over in the train from Rothenburg: "Disgrace, disgrace, disgrace."

When we came back to Regensburg, to the brewery, I found Grandfather not at all upset. He was happy about not having another "studied one" in the family wasting money. He felt my arms and saw that I was strong.

In his living-room, in the old house next to the brewery, he outlined a career for me that included one year's apprenticeship with a butcher, to learn how to judge meat and cut it and make sausages, then a year with a plumber and electrician, and then going into the brewery and starting there the way his own father and grandfather had done and the way he had learned to make beer himself.

Mother held me all the while and said: "No, Papa, not to the butcher, not to the electrician, and not into the brewery."

Attached to the brewery by mortgages were thirty-seven inns, all over the countryside, in which Grandfather's beer was sold. He had two kinds of beer: one a bitter-sweet, thick, black soupy brew; the other a blond beer, light-bodied, with much snowy foam, and bitter. Every spring Grandfather went on a round of visits to his inns, and my picture of happiness will always be one of him and his hunting wagon:

First the sound of the slim wheels on the gravel in the inner garden; then, the deep liquid "clop clop clop" of the horse's hoofs as the wagon came out of the brewery through the tunnel, over creosote-soaked wooden blocks; and finally the clatter of the hoofs on the cobblestones in front of the house. Grandfather slowly climbing up in front, onto the reed basket seat of the delicate little wagon, almost turning it over on its red wheels, as he puts his great weight on its side.

He wore a loose green coat, with buttons cut from antlers, a brush on his mountain hat, a whip for decoration in his big hands. He made a sound with his tongue, and the trotter lifted its knees up to its chest, and, weaving back and forth, its neck arched in a coy, young pose, it sailed out. From the back seat waved Grandfather's servant Alois, who always went with him. They stopped and drank and ate in all the inns, and bought calves for the butchery, which was part of the brewery. After years of experience Grandfather could drink thirty-six big stone mugs of beer in one evening. He ate heavy meals besides, hardly any vegetables, only dumplings and potatoes, potatoes and dumplings, and much meat.

In consequence of this diet, Grandfather had several times a year attacks of very painful gout, which in Bavaria is called *Zipperl*. Much of the time, one or the other of his legs was wrapped in cotton and elephantine bandages. If people came near it, even Mother, he chased them away with his stick, saying: "Ah, ah, ah" in an ecstasy of pain and widening his eyes as if he saw something very beautiful far way. Then he would rise up in his seat, while his voice changed to a whimpering "Jesus, Jesus, Jesus." He said he could feel the change in weather in his toes, through the thick bandages. But he did not stop eating or drinking.

He had a wheelchair at such times, and Alois had to push him on his visits to the other breweries or restaurants in Regensburg. A kind of track was built for this chair in the backyard of the house; it swung over the roof of the shack where the barrels were kept and came down to the ground in a wide serpentine. Then there were little wooden inclines, to make it possible to wheel Grandfather painlessly over the doorsteps, in front and in back of the house and out into the square.

On the ground floor of the house was a baker, and the stairway and all the rooms in the house smelled of freshly baked bread, nicest on cold winter days. The baker, white of face and clothes, could see Grandfather being wheeled out, and he would say: "The *Zipperl*! Aha! It's got you again, Herr Fischer!" and so said the policeman outside, while he made the streetcar wait, and so did all the other people. Everybody in the city knew Grandfather, and since life was without any other excitement, they had time to say: "Have you seen Herr Fischer? The *Zipperl* has him again!" And Grandfather said nothing but "Jesus, Jesus, God Almighty, ah ah ah, be careful, be careful, Alois. The *Zipperl*!"

I had a small room in Grandfather's house almost up under the gable of the house. It was most beautiful at night; from my window I could see the whole square at once without turning head or eyes, and when it was dark and the theater was lit, after the Duke had arrived, his carriages were driven slowly, just to keep the horses warm, around the circle of plants and trees and the small statue which stood in the center of the square within an iron fence. The rich harness, the liveries of the coachmen and footmen, the lamps, made a magical, lit-up, jeweled merry-go-round.

On the driver's seat of the finest coach, the Duke's, sat a bearded man in pale blue livery, a bearskin cape over his shoulders and a plume on his hat, a hat such as admirals wear, worn sideways with the wide part to the front. I watched this for hours until the play ended, until the circle became a line and the carriages drove under the portico of the small theater and away to the castle.

In the morning Grandfather had coffee at his window, with a canary bird sitting on the backrest of his chair. There was the smell of cigar smoke, of snuff, of coffee and fresh bread. He dipped four crescent rolls into his coffee and looked out over the square, to observe the people and the business of the city. He had a mirror on the outside of the house so he could see who came to visit us. Around him hung more cages with canaries; he fed them in the morning, and trimmed their claws and changed their diet for them, experimenting how to make them lay more eggs or sing better. He marked the results down in a little book, of which he had two; in the other he kept the business of his brewery. So easy and secure was his life.

On the table in front of him was paper, paste, and a pair of big shears. He made helmets with them, out of stacks of large sheets of durable packing paper, which he bought especially for this purpose. They were simple triangular paper hats, with a bush of blue and white crepe paper stuck on at the end, and they were given away. Any child in Regensburg who came and asked could have one. He made these helmets in great quantities, for the orphanage of Regensburg and the surrounding villages. The children of the orphanage and of the dumb and blind institute waved up whenever they passed the house. So that they could fight properly in two armies, he made, for the children who could see, two kinds of helmets, one with a blue bush and one with red. The blue and white were the Bavarian colors; the red, the French.

This work took up a few hours. Afterwards he looked up orders and was very conscientious about filling them, and then, when the rheumatism did not bother him, he took a walk around the park with the brewmaster and listened to his report and told him what to do about the beer.

The brewery also had its own fire department, which always arrived ahead of the city firemen. It consisted of an old beer wagon, painted red and yellow, fixed up with a bell, hose, ladders, hooks, and buckets. It thundered out of the tunnel of the brewery, pulled by the best horses, the skin of their haunches stretched into folds as they pushed the ground away from under them, sparks raining from under their hoofs as they struck the cobblestones. The wagon had to run around the square twice, before it could slow down enough to head into the street that led to the fire.

Next to Mother and myself, Grandfather's greatest trouble was my Uncle Veri; Veri is short for Xavier. He was my favorite uncle; he had the strong dispassionate face of a sportsman; he was so big that the funeral wagon of Regensburg was made to his measure; he was as strong as he was big. When someone had to be thrown out of the brewery—and the men in Regensburg are big and heavy, and can fight—Uncle Veri did it. He would drag the man to the door, go out a little, measure his distance, take a good hold on trousers and coat collar, and throw the man over the iron fence into the bushes that stood around the small statue.

Uncle Veri loved betting. He once made a wager with a city official that he could make a million dots in eight hours. Two brewery hands had to sharpen pencils, and Uncle Veri stuck them between his fingers, four to each hand. The city official wanted to back out, he said it was cheating, he meant it should be done with one or at most two pencils, but finally he gave in. Uncle Veri hammered with both hands at the sheets of paper, while the waitresses, the brewmaster and his crew, the city official and his friends, all counted dots and crossed them off. It was a typical Regensburg form of amusement, for it could all have been calculated in a few minutes, especially since the city official happened to be in the Department of Taxation, who won, of course. But meanwhile they drank and ate and sat there and it helped to pass an evening, and at the end everyone was tired and certain that even Uncle Veri could not do it.

But he could lift the stone in the beergarden that had an iron ring hammered into it, and that with one finger. He did that often and for anyone who asked him; the next strongest man in Regensburg needed two hands to do it. To keep in trim, Uncle Veri carried a cast-iron walking-stick, and an umbrella with a heavy iron bar down its center. He pushed the big brewery horses around as if they were flies; and if he saw a brewery man, anywhere in the middle of the city, groan while lifting barrels, Uncle Veri would say to him: "You make me sick to look at," especially if it was a man from another brewery, and he would hand him his iron walking-stick to hold, and then himself load or unload the wagon, bouncing the heavy barrels on the big leather cushion which is put down to protect the cobblestones. He even slept strongly, sometimes going to bed on Monday night and waking up fresh and rested on Wednesday morning. Everyone had respect for him.

He was bad only with women. All of Grandfather's serious troubles came from that; Grandfather had to pay for the children. When someone looked up from the square, and saw Grandfather busy with stacks of paper hats, and then turned his head and said something to a friend, and both of them smiled, then Grandfather knew that the joke had been told again, that he was busy making paper hats for Uncle Veri's children. Few people, however, laughed up any more, only strangers, because in Regensburg it was an old joke.

Grandfather said that I should start to learn from Uncle Veri how to wash barrels.

Mother cried and said no, she would rather have me dead than be a butcher's apprentice and wash barrels and then be a common soldier and stand at attention while people like the sons of the girls who had gone to the convent with her, and who had studied enough to be officers, passed by. Mother's name was

Franziska, and Grandfather called her Fannerl. "You're crazy, Fannerl," he said. Mother took me by the hand and we went out to visit Uncle Wallner.

This uncle was thin, little, and, for Regensburg, a gentleman. He lived in the best, new part of the town, in a villa with a small park. He was a city father, wore a top hat on Sunday and black clothes and gloves and a golden pince-nez—but even with the golden pince-nez he could not see very well. He was very polite to the proper people in Regensburg; he said it was very important to show reverence and respect to important personages. When I walked with him, very slowly because he took little steps, and we met someone he knew and thought worthy, he would swing his hat almost down to the ground and pronounce the name carefully in greeting.

Sometimes when I was with him and we passed one of Grand-father's waitresses on the other side of the street, too far away for Uncle Wallner to recognize her, or the lady who took care of the public washroom at the railway station, or one of the rough girls that Uncle Veri liked, I would get Uncle Wallner's attention and tell him that was the Frau Direktor across the way, or the Frau Inspektor, or the French Consul's wife. Uncle Wallner would stop immediately and turn and whisper the name across the street and sweep his hat through the air, making a respectful compliment, and he would tell me what a worthy, fine, and gentle lady the washroom woman was. He owned a wholesale grocery business, which was why he was so polite, and, after all, that was a little fun in this stupid city.

Uncle Wallner always advised Mother. He liked to put French phrases into his conversation and speak of a journey he had made to the Paris Exposition in 1889, and to London. *"Mais ça ne va pas, ma chère,"* he said to Mother when she told him about the brewery plans. "A butcher, a plumber, and with Veri as a teacher he would soon turn into a nice little ruffian. No, *ma chère,*" he said, and drummed on the windowpane, and then he sent me out to get him some cigars, so that he could talk alone with Mother.

When I came back, he smiled. He was just showing Mother his new visiting-cards; he had become a Herr Kommerzienrat, a Commercial Councilor of the King in Munich, and had had new cards printed with this title on them, and his housekeeper for two days had already been addressing him continually as Herr Kommerzienrat. "Will the Herr Kommerzienrat have tea now?" she asked, and Uncle said yes. She brought tea and cake, and after this was cleared away, Uncle Wallner drummed on the top of a very beautiful cherrywood table, inlaid with cigar bands under glass. He asked me to sit close to him and Mother and then he started as one does a letter: "Dear Ludwig," and he said that I should think about going to Uncle Hans in Tirol, to Father's brother. Uncle Wallner looked very happy when he said that; he added that Uncle Hans was a very wise man, rich and respected and good.

"He is a good man," Uncle Wallner repeated several times, because up to now I had been told that Uncle Hans was not so good, that Uncle Hans Bemelmans in Tirol was full of *"amerikanische Tricks."*

Uncle Hans Bemelmans, said Uncle Wallner, had many hotels, and hotels are a very fine business. One always has interesting people around, the great of the world; one can travel, see much of life; one eats better than anyone else. In a few years a boy as bright as I was would no doubt be the manager, or even the proprietor, of such a hotel as Uncle Hans had in Tirol. Right there, with Uncle Bemelmans, was the great opportunity. He had not one hotel, he had a chain of them.

There was the Hotel Maximilian in Igls, near Innsbruck, the Grand Hotel des Alpes on the Dolomite Road in San Martino di Castrozza, the Hotel Scholastika on the Achen See, the Hotel Alte Post in Klobenstein, where Uncle Bemelmans had his headquarters, and the Mountain Castle in Meran. In the Mountain Castle even Royalty stopped.

This was wonderful and surprising to me. When Grandfather spoke of Uncle Hans Bemelmans, he called him the "other *Lump,*" the first *Lump* being my father, the painter. The *"amerikanische Tricks,"* Grandfather said, Uncle Hans had learned during several years spent in the United States. The trick which he had brought back from there and which Grandfather told most often was the "Sanatorium Trick"; it went like this:

For speculative purposes, Uncle Hans had bought a piece of ground in Meran, in Tirol. He found out later that he had made one of his rare mistakes. But overlooking his land was the façade of a very fine private dwelling belonging to a Leipzig builder of funiculars. When he realized he had made a bad buy, Uncle Hans offered his land to this man from Leipzig to enlarge his park, but the man said that his park was big enough. Uncle Hans said nothing and went home. The view from the man's balconies was the best in Meran; it overlooked all the mountains as well as Uncle's ground. So Uncle Hans arrived one day with engineers and measuring instruments and a workman who stuck red and white poles into the ground, close to the fence of the rich man, who watched all this from his balcony. A few days later more men came and unloaded sand and bricks and started to dig while others unrolled blueprints on a table under a corrugated shed. When the rich man could not stand it any longer, he came to the fence and asked Uncle Hans: "What's going on here, Herr Bemelmans? What are you doing here?"

Uncle Hans smiled and said: "I'm building a hotel here, the Grand Hotel Tirol. The kitchen and pantry will be right here where we are standing, and the hotel will be eight stories high and look out on that beautiful panorama."

"Oh, a hotel!" said the man.

"Well, not exactly a hotel," said Uncle Hans, "more a sanatorium." He took a deep breath. "The air here," he said, and hit himself on the chest, "the air here is very beneficial for certain afflictions," and he cleared his throat and coughed loudly.

"I see," said the rich man, and he bought the property a few days later. Now he had to pay much more for it, because there were in addition the charges for bricks and sand and surveying and the shack and the labor. He even paid for having it all taken away again. Uncle Hans took care of that too. He had the sand and bricks delivered to the Mountain Castle, his hotel, where he made a terrace out of them for afternoon dancing and tea.

"That," Grandfather said, "was an American trick, well done and complete."

Uncle Bemelmans, Grandfather said, was in possession of the knowledge of every such device, and that was why he had so many hotels. But though he was rich, Grandfather thought of him as another *Lump*, chiefly because he was a Bemelmans.

"They," said Grandfather, "are washed with every kind of soap and water, and rubbed in with slick oil, and they are therefore hard to catch and slippery."

Mother came back with Uncle Wallner, but it was hard to change Grandfather's mind, for he too had friends who advised him, three of them, and they had all agreed that the brewery was the right thing for me.

These friends were the Bartel brothers, people to whose wives Uncle Wallner did not raise his hat. One was called "Cider" Bartel, because he had a cider factory; another was called "Pitch" Bartel, because he made pitch and creosote blocks and the beer barrels for the brewery; and the third was called "Dreck" Bartel. This last had a string of evil-smelling wagons with long tubular barrels on them, and a pumping-machine; attached to the last wagon rolled a low cart, in which lay thick, solid, round pieces of hose that fitted together, and out of these an awful juice dripped onto the pavement of the city. One could tell with closed eyes at what house Dreck Bartel and his two sons were pumping clean a cesspool.

Dreck Bartel did not like me very much. I had written a poem about him in the Bavarian dialect, and was caught with it in class, and had to sit "in arrest" for six hours, and a letter went to Mother about it, and I told Uncle Veri about it, and Uncle Veri knew a tune that went well with it, and in a little while it was known all over the city, and Uncle Veri one night had to throw Dreck Bartel into the park because he became too loud and said he would drown me in a cesspool if he ever caught me.

But finally Mother and Uncle Wallner won.

The old seamstress, who worked in the house all year fixing napkins and torn tablecloths, took the number "51" off all my linen, clothes, and stockings; and with a new traveling bag, Mother took me to the train for Munich, Mittenwald, Innsbruck, Meran.

I was surprised at the first conductor I saw on the Austrian railway and at the stationmaster and switchmen, at their manners and dress. I had learned that only the German is reliable and orderly, and here was proof of it. These men were careless, their coat collars open; they played bowls in a shed next to the station while the customs examination took place. It seemed a remote, disorderly, un-German land, beautiful though it was. When the train started, even the signal sounded strange; the sharp policeman's whistle was replaced by a brass trumpet, its sound was the bleat of a young sheep; and the conductor and the train were in no hurry to start.

I crossed the Brenner and came to Bozen, never leaving the

window of the train; from Bozen the cogwheel railway goes up the Ritten, to Klobenstein, to Uncle Hans's Hotel, the Alte Post. Klobenstein was beautiful; it stood in a ring of distant mountains. The hotel was a lovely, flower-covered, wide, solid mountain house, with thick walls and low ceilings. Uncle Hans and Aunt Marie met me at the station.

From the very beginning Uncle Hans called me *"Lausbub."* *Lausbub* literally should mean "lousy boy," but in South Germany and Austria it is almost a tender word and means something like "rascal." Uncle Bemelmans was comfortably built, but not fat; he wore a beard like the English King Edward's, but on the little finger of his right hand was an immense solitaire diamond, so big that it looked false, like circus jewelry.

He had received letters from Uncle Wallner. It was through Uncle Wallner, because he had traveled and was elegant, that all the Fischer-Bemelmans affairs were arranged. Uncle Bemelmans explained at length why I had come and how I was going to be dealt with. He read me long lectures in his little office, a low, warm, paneled room, decorated with many antiques and heated by a painted white porcelain stove.

In this office there was a carpet on the floor and I could soon draw from memory all the plants, animals, and symbols in its pattern, because I looked at it for such long stretches while Uncle Hans walked up and down over it, back and forth for hours, his hands folded under the seat of his trousers, and over them hanging the square-cut tails of his cutaway.

In the back of the hotel, along with the iceboxes and the pantries, in a stone-floored room, was an old-fashioned ice machine that pounded away in a steady rhythm. Uncle Hans was always listening to that rhythm. He noticed the moment it became irregular and he would let no one else touch the machine. The instant it changed tempo, he would leave whatever he was doing to fix it. During a lecture he would stop suddenly, reach for his hat, and run to the machine, telling me to wait till he came back. He looked very funny then, because he was in a hurry, and hurry did not go well with the dignity of his face and clothes.

He always quoted America, telling me often that in America *Lausbuben* like me sometimes turned out to be very rich men. But in Tirol too, he said, there was bigger opportunity for a *Lausbub* than for a good boy who did as he was told and would perhaps make a good employee but never be rich.

Here in the hotel I found evidence of a lighter kind of life: the cooking was French, without kraut and heavy dumplings; the conversation had more variety, was not so much of buildings, horses, the Bartels, beer, and the *pot de chambre* humor of Regensburg. I was disturbed by a sense of disloyalty to my Grandfather, because I felt I should not like anything else but his house and his person.

I had brought some drawings and watercolors and given them to Aunt Marie. When Uncle Hans saw them and heard Aunt Marie suggest that I study painting, he got very angry. Painters, he said, were hunger candidates, nothing in front and nothing in back of them; besides, if I liked painting, I could always hire an artist, when I became rich by following his teachings. He said I must bury the past and start a new life and be a joy and pride to my poor mother and for God's sake not to become an artist like my father. I would have to start all the way at the bottom of the ladder, he said, like Rockefeller and Edison, and work up from there. There was no reason, he said, why I should not in a few years be a hôtelier like himself, or at least manager of a hotel.

Aunt Marie would come into the little office when the lectures lasted too long, and say: "I think that's enough for today, Hans, let him go."

The first day, when she showed me the lovely room that overlooked the Dolomites and told me the names of the mountains, and looked at my pictures, she asked me what I liked most to eat. I told her "apricot dumplings." We had them for supper, and Uncle Hans complained that the *Lausbub* was being spoiled right from the beginning.

My birthday came soon after my arrival, and Aunt Marie bought me a box of the best watercolors and a drawing pad. I had a week of wonderful vacation and was given a horse on which I rode all over the beautiful mountains. Then one day it was decided that from eight in the morning until three in the afternoon I would be an employee and do all the work that was required of me, and for the rest of the time, before and after, and during the night, I would be Uncle's nephew and eat at the family table, and could have the horse.

The mornings in Tirol are the most beautiful time in all the world. I got up at five, saddled my horse, and rode to the sawmill. It stood on a turbulent brook, flanked by high, straight walls of dolomite granite, among tall trees. Nearby, under the two tallest and oldest trees, stood a little inn, with a garden, a curved wooden bench, and two round redstone tables. There I stopped at seven every morning and drank a pint of red wine, dipping the hard peasant bread in it. I stayed as long as I could and then rode in a gallop back to the hotel to be on time for duty.

The first time I did this, Aunt Marie was up, and Uncle Hans out on his morning walk. He had said: "At least he gets up early, the *Lausbub;* that's something; some of them you can't get out of bed."

Aunt Marie always looked at me and felt my head and said it must be the change in altitude. "He has a fever every morning, and look how his eyes shine." But then they found out about the wine and several other things, and Uncle said that this half-nephew, half-employee arrangement was at an end. He said it would be better to send me to one of the other hotels where Aunt Marie could not help me out of every scrape.

And so I was sent first to the Mountain Castle in Meran, and then in the space of a year I ran through all of Uncle Hans's hotels. Every manager was tried out on me; they all failed and sent me back. The last time was after a very serious offense. Uncle walked up and down again; Aunt Marie cried and said to me while Uncle was with his ice machine: "Ludwig, Ludwig, what is going to become of you? We love you so much and you are so bad. How will it end? What will become of you?" She embraced me and wiped her tears and mine from our eyes.

When Uncle Hans came back he said there were two places for me to choose between. The first was a correctional institution, a kind of reform school, German, on board a ship, where unruly boys were trained for the merchant marine and disciplined with the ends of ropes soaked in tar.

The second was America.

I decided to go to America.

Uncle Hans was very happy. He said that in the United States they would shear my pelt and clip my horns.

He wrote some letters to hotel people he knew, he gave me much advice, and he said that if I ever became a great hotel man,

I would only become so by looking upon all employees as paid enemies; there is an exception here and there, but it takes too long to find out and is too risky to take a chance. Then he said: "Dear Ludwig," like Uncle Wallner, "now we'll forget all about what has happened. I'll find out when a boat sails. Now you have a vacation, ride all you want, and we'll all be happy together." I cried then because I was sorry I was so rotten and always in trouble when they were so kind to me.

Then I went back to Mother, and there it was also difficult, when I saw how she took money for my passage out of envelopes that were marked for other purposes for her own use. We got up early one morning to meet the express to Rotterdam. I was the only passenger from Regensburg on the lonely platform, and Mother said, with her hand on my head, for the second time: "Everything will come out all right in the end, Ludwig."

And that is how I left for America.

Arrival
in America

.   .   .

When I arrived in New York in December 1914, I was sixteen years old.

The quality of my mind and its information at that time was such that, on sailing for America from the port of Rotterdam, I bought two pistols and much ammunition. With these I intended to protect myself against the Indians.

I had read of them in the books of Karl May and Fenimore Cooper, and intently hoped for their presence without number on the outskirts of New York City.

My second idea was that the elevated railroad of New York ran over the housetops, adapting itself to the height of the buildings in the manner of a roller coaster.

Before sailing, the captain of the steamer *Ryndam* persuaded me to return the guns. The shopkeeper in Rotterdam, however, would only exchange them for other hardware, and I traded them for twelve pairs of finely chiseled Solingen scissors and three complicated pocket knives.

On this steamer, the S.S. *Ryndam* of the Holland America Line, was a smoking room. The benches and restful chairs in this saloon were upholstered with very durable gun-colored material with much horsehair in it.

My plan at the time was to have one strong suit made of this material. I reasoned that such a garment would last me for ten years, and in this time I could put by enough money to go back to Tirol and buy a sawmill that stands in a pine forest on the top of a mountain in the Dolomites.

The Hotel Years,
1915–1917

· · · · · ·

My First
Actress

.   .   .

My first job in New York, at the Hotel Astor, did not last long. I filled water bottles and carried out trays with dishes, until I broke too many. So with my uncle's second letter I went to the Hotel McAlpin, where I got a job that lasted a year, at the end of which I spoke passable English, though I was still little better than a bus boy.

Here I wore for breakfast a white suit, yellow shoes, and, suspended in front of me on a thick leather strap, a silver machine, hot and the size of a baby's coffin. For three hours every morning I walked around the men's café, dreaming of Monday and my Actress, with the heavy silver coffin hanging before me. It contained in a lower compartment two heated bricks, and above on a wire net an assortment of hot cross buns, muffins, biscuits, croissants, and every other kind of rolls, soft and hard.

This work ceased at half-past ten, and then I sat for half an hour on the red tile floor in the grillroom and polished an elaborate fence of stout brass pipes which kept apart the waiters rushing in and those rushing out. I could, from where I sat, see the nice knees of a young lady cashier seated on a platform, but I never did, because I was in love with my Actress.

In the evening my hands were as cold as my stomach was warm in the morning, for at dinner, in another white suit and with white gloves and white shoes, I walked around the main dining-room with a silver tray. On the tray rested a thick layer of ice, and bedded on the ice, frosted with coldness, were silver butterchips. I exchanged full butterchips for empty ones.

A small orchestra played—selections from *La Bohème* and *Madame Butterfly,* the "Dance of the Hours," and a Dixie piece that ended in an almost audible "Hooray, hooray!" I wrote requests on little cards and passed them up to the orchestra leader. I asked for tunes from the Merry Widow, music that was allied to my Actress. I would forget then to change the butterchips and would walk around the dining-room, softly whistling and thinking about Monday and the Irving Place Theater, and several times the headwaiter warned me. "Hey, you, wake up!"

I lived on Thirty-second Street in a brownstone house that belonged to a detective, who also owned two parrots, and who sat in the evening with his feet in a tub of hot water while he read the papers aloud to his wife. From her, this Irishman had taken on a German accent. They lived on a diet of sauerbraten and cabbage, and the house smelled of it. They drank containers of beer with their meals.

I had at the time two hundred and fifty dollars. Two hundred were in the bank; fifty I carried in my pocket.

On a bedside table in my room, in a frame, stood the picture of my Actress. It was not her picture, strictly speaking. It was cut out of an advertisement for a railroad, but it looked exactly like her. My Actress had no pictures in the paper. That is why I thought that fifty dollars would be enough.

I had written several letters to her, but I always tore them up. I knew that for an actress one had to send flowers, a little card, an invitation to supper, a *chambre séparée,* a bottle of wine. And at the end of this routine, I reasoned, since it was a simple theater, since she was not well known, being a German actress, I might be able to tell her with fifty dollars.

The rest of my life was very orderly. I kept a small notebook; on the first page was written:

With God, New York, 1916.

On the following pages appeared a strict account of my finances: on one side, income from the hotel and from home; opposite, the outgo. The expenses varied but were about:

Rent	$3.00
Laundry	.68
Fruit	.30
Postage	.06
Shines	.20

Only on Mondays did the page become wild and exciting. Then I wiped away the hotel with a luncheon in a nice place, where they said: "Good day, sir," pulled out my chair, and said: "Good-by, sir." I wore my new suit, smoked a cigar, drank a glass of beer, and in the afternoon walked to the theater to enjoy the buying of the ticket. Perhaps to see her come or go from a rehearsal, to walk up and down awhile and wait for her. Perhaps to speak to her.

There was an additional pleasure at the ticket window: the man knew me by name, he gave me the same seat every Monday, second row on the aisle. "*Grüss Gott,* Herr Bemelmans," he said in Bavarian German.

Over a circle of several blocks around this theater lay, like a vapor, a melancholy, bitter-sweet mood. I walked into it at Sixteenth Street, my heart beating faster, and at Irving Place my hands were moist.

The last Monday I ever saw her, the company was presenting a musical comedy entitled *Her Highness Dances a Waltz.* She was Her Highness.

There was a small orchestra of simple German musicians who looked somehow like their instruments. The flutist was most so, as most flute-players are, thin, long, with all the lines of his face drawn down to the small apron of his upper lip which rested on the wet end of his flute.

The conductor swam over the notes. With the tempo of the music, his rear collar button came out over and disappeared under the edge of his coatcollar. He caressed and scolded the music out of his men. His hair fell in his eyes at the *fortissimi,* and he completely disarranged himself with three mounting rages amidst his instruments when they blew, fiddled, and drummed, crash, boom boom boom, the overture to its one, two, three time ending.

With contempt still on his red face, he turned to the audience and thanked them for the applause. An immense handkerchief waited in his hand to wipe under his chin, over his face, around the back of the neck, inside his collar, while he bowed his thanks to the orchestra, the balconies, into all the corners.

It was fine, honest theater, played in a small house and to a good audience. No one came late. They were plain people, not rich, not poor, and not bored. They wanted to believe, their eyes moistened easily, and they laughed loud and long, and applauded with generous hands. They pointed at things they liked, and at favorite passages they nudged each other in the side.

They left slowly, waiting until some of the lights went out, until the last musician, bent down, pushed his instrument case ahead of him and disappeared through the low door under the stage. They hung around the lobby, hummed the melodies, and said: *"Das war wieder schön," "Schön wars,"* and *"Schön iss gwesn."*

On that last Monday, after the overture, the lights went dim, the ramp lit up, the bottom of the curtain swayed and rose on the first act of *Hoheit tanzt Walzer.* The program said that the scene was an inn on the outskirts of Vienna, the garden of the inn.

The walls of the inn bulged with backstage drafts, the tree swayed; its foliage was a collection of tired, faded green handkerchiefs tied to torn netting. On the backdrop, patched, scraped, and worn with years of service, as was the outdoors in every play of this theater, hung a terrible garden.

To make marble of it, laborious blue worms had been painted into the wide stairway that came down the center of the garden. The stairway was flanked by two nudes, executed with such modesty that it was impossible to decide whether these German ladies stood with their ample fronts or backsides toward the audience. The towers of a castle rose out of the trees, and two fountains with swans in them played to the left and right of the nudes.

An Austrian Archduke, young and sad, had come to the inn to live incognito, to forget his princess who was to marry someone else for reasons of state.

There was one lovely detail in this scene. The Archduke sat at a table in the garden under a tree, and Franzl, the piccolo of the hotel, brought him his coffee, a demi-tasse. The Archduke put one lump of sugar into the coffee, the second he broke in half. One half he dropped into the cup, the other half he threw in the air over his shoulder into the open mouth of the piccolo, who stood behind him waiting for it, like a dog. This had to be repeated three times, so much did the audience love this good piece of nonsense.

After the Archduke had stirred his coffee, the waiter came out of the hotel, and, being an Austrian, the Archduke put his arm around the waiter and told him why he was here. They sang a duet while the piccolo cleared the coffee away. They sang that love for prince and waiter is alike, hopeless and sad.

Then the waiter heard something; he cupped his ear and listened into the back garden, and he said that he heard an elegant carriage with rubber wheels and two horses coming from Vienna. The Archduke disappeared into the hotel.

My Actress walked on. She did not walk, she was there with the grace of a young animal. She stood between the modest nudes; theater and music sank away. She pointed at the tree, lifted a fine white arm, a slim gloved hand, to the leaves, tilted back her lovely head, widened her nostrils, half closed her eyes, drank in the air, said it was spring, and began to sing.

I don't know what she sang, or what the Archduke said to her when he returned and discovered that she was the princess. I just saw throat, eyes, hair.

They sat on a bench and sang of how they loved each other, of how they had loved each other all their lives, ever since, as children five years old, they had first met in the park of Archduke Leopold's castle in Ischl, twenty years ago.

First the flowers, I decided, while he kissed her, and I got up and went out of the theater. A little man in the lobby called a taxi. We drove uptown in a U around Gramercy Park and up Lexington, to Madison, to Fifth, but all the florist shops were closed—light shone only in Thorley's.

There was little left in the way of flowers, shabby pots with single tulips, a few geraniums, hortensias—all flowers for housewives, no single, determined elegant plant. The man finally thought of a rose tree he had in another room. Trained into the shape of a basket, four feet high, decorated with a giant butterfly of a carmine bow, it was very heavy, and worth the twenty-five dollars he asked for it.

I wrote a card, and asked for a large envelope to put it into; we attached it with wire, where it could easily be seen. Back to the theater we drove, so fast that going around corners I had to hold the plant with both feet, and the upper part, with the white roses, with both hands.

The taximan was strong; he carried the rose tree into the lobby alone. From there the two girl ushers would carry it down, after the princess's next song came to its end, and hand it up to her. I went down to my seat in the second row on the aisle.

The second act was half played. The stairway with the nudes was now a ducal park; there was a little mat of artificial grass, the same tree, a bench on the left side of the stage. On the bench sat two small children, arm in arm, a boy and a girl.

The little girl had on ruffled pantalettes and a mauve crinoline; the boy was in white silk breeches, an apricot-colored velvet Biedermeir frock-coat, and lace at throat and wrists. They sang and danced a minuet.

The conductor, with raised eyebrows, pointed lips, kept the music fragile. Carefully, as if holding a fine Dresden teacup in his hand, with his little finger stuck out, he leaned over the flute and counted time for the frail notes. Through the quiet melody, the careful opening of a door in the rear of the theater was loud and disturbing. Then a few voices way in the back whispered: "*Ah, wie schön*," and soon the "*Ah*" was running down the middle of the audience.

The minuet was over; the audience shook the theater with applause and demanded an encore. Tears were in the eyes of all the women. The conductor tapped on his desk and the children started to dance once more. I turned around. My rose tree was wabbling down over the heads of the audience, over in the far aisle; it shone in the darkness.

I unrolled my program. There, under "Second Act," was printed:

SCENE: The Park of Archduke Leopold's Castle in Ischl.
   Time has rolled back twenty years.
PRINCE .... Hansi Pschoor, aged 5
PRINCESS .... Lisl Stolz, aged 6

It was too late to do anything. The "Ahh" was all over the theater now. The rose tree was in the light of the stage, it was tilted past the bass fiddle and the kettledrums, the 'cellist stood up to let it pass and, together with the two ushers and the conductor, to help lift it over the ramp and stand it in the middle of the park in Ischl, twenty years ago.

The waiter came from the wings, and pushed the little girl to the rose tree, and pointed to the card. The little princess hopped from one foot to the other. She looked back at her mama, whose face came out between one of the modest nudes and the tree.

The little princess twisted the envelope from the basket and cramped it tightly in her hand. She made small curtsies, awkward, unrehearsed motions, and threw kisses into the orchestra, the balcony, and back to her mama.

The waiter took the note to open it, to let the little princess read its contents to the audience, to thank whatever kind uncle had sent it. I got up. Leaving the theater, I stumbled and almost knocked over a worried little bearded man who stood in the lobby and with a small silver shovel filled paper bags with little German peppermints. I left just in time.

The waiter had raised his hand. The audience was quiet. The little girl was about to read:

"Will you have supper with me at Luchow's after the performance? I think I love you. Ludwig."

The
Splendide

.　　.　　.

The next day I was fired. But not for whistling, as I had been warned I would be. I was standing miserably, with my tray of butterchips behind a terra cotta column, waiting for the orchestra to play a piece I had just requested—*"Nur wer die Sehnsucht kennt"* ("None But the Lonely Heart"). One of the musicians had gone to get the music for it from an upstairs closet.

The headwaiter came, looking for me, and noticed that I was wearing one white and one yellow shoe. He took me roughly by the arm to push me with my butterchips out among the guests, and I told him to go to the devil. I waited until the orchestra had finished my piece and then went home.

For a week I was unhappy. I visited the Aquarium, the Zoo, and the Metropolitan Museum of Art; I made sketches of the scenery of the Irving Place Theater; and then I looked in my trunk for another letter. The last one was to Mr. Otto Brauhaus, manager of the Hotel Splendide.

The Splendide, from the outside, was a plain building, but its interior was like that of a great private house. It completely lacked the anonymous feeling of the usual hotel, in which one might fall asleep in the lobby, be carried to another hotel, wake up, and never know it was another.

A page in silken breeches, a livery as rich as that of the Duke of Thurn und Taxis and of the same blue, showed me to the office. Under a sign that read: "Don't worry, it won't last, nothing does," sat Mr. Otto Brauhaus, worrying. He spoke to me in German, wrote something on a little card, and then gave it and the letter from Uncle Hans to the page.

The page took me to the dining-room of the hotel, to a thin, foreign-looking man who looked like a high-placed Jesuit. His face in a frame of closely shaven violet beard-stubble, he spoke with controlled, eloquent motions of his head and long thin hands. He never looked at me but kept his eyes downcast as if hearing a confession. His altogether appropriate name was Serafini. He was from Siena and was the assistant headwaiter of the Hotel Splendide. To me he looked like St. Francis in a tailcoat.

In a *hôtel de grand luxe,* such as the Splendide, which is a European island in New York, there is no headwaiter, no captain, no waiter. Everything is much more elegant. The manager of the hotel is *le patron;* and the head man in the restaurant, more important in such a hotel than the manager, or even the chef, is simply "Monsieur Grégoire," "Monsieur Théodore," "Monsieur Victor," or whatever his first name is, and no matter what his nationality. His lieutenants, the captains, are called *maîtres d'hôtel;* and under them the waiters are not *garçons* (that is more the term for a café waiter), but *chefs de rang,* because each one has for his station a rank of several tables. The chef de rang never leaves his tables or the dining-room; he has a young man who runs out to the kitchen for him, and this quick young waiter is a commis de rang. Even the bus boys are called *débarrasseurs.*

Mr. Serafini said very considerately that there was no position for me at the Splendide, since all the employees in the dining-room were obliged to speak French. When I told him I spoke French, he changed the conversation to that language and then asked me to wait.

I waited in the high, oval dining-room for a long time, happily observing the well-designed salt cellars and pepper mills, the fine clean pattern on the plates, the stucco ceiling, and the carpets. Waiters came to set up the room, and they were distinguished-looking men, of better appearance than the guests in the other hotels I had worked in, carefully dressed, quick, capable. Most of them, however, wore spats and pretty shirts. I waited until these had gone and an orchestra arrived and tuned its instruments. Finally, the headwaiter-in-chief, that is, Monsieur Victor, appeared.

Serafini looked down at my hands and whispered to me to come. He placed Mr. Brauhaus's card and Uncle Hans's letter before Monsieur Victor. On Uncle Hans's letterhead were not only the names but also the pictures of every one of his hotels, and Monsieur Serafini said in French: "A young man of good family, he is recommended by the *patron.*"

Without looking at me longer than was necessary to see that I was there, Monsieur Victor said:

"Engage him, put him to work as a commis, see what he can do."

Herr
Otto Brauhaus

. . .

The Splendide had four hundred rooms, a great number for a luxurious hotel. Hotels larger than this become like railroad stations, eating and sleeping institutions. They have to take in anyone who comes along. The staff changes too frequently to give perfect service, to become acquainted with the guests. In the bigger hotels, the manager is usually a financial person, a one-time accountant who leaves actual contact with the guests to a platoon of day and night assistants, a kind of floorwalker with a small desk in the middle of the lobby and no authority except to say good-morning and good-night, a man whose business it is to shake hands and watch the bellboys and be in charge in case of fire.

In a hotel like the Splendide, however, it must be assumed, for the purposes of good management, that every guest is a distinguished and elegant person who, of course, has a great deal of money. The prices are high and must be high; the cost of provisions is probably the smallest item. The charges are for marble columns, uniforms, thick carpets, fine linen, thin glasses, many servants, and a good orchestra. And the management of such a hotel is a difficult, delicate business. It produces in most cases a type of man whose face is like a towel on which everyone has

wiped his hands, a smooth, smiling, bowing man, in ever freshly pressed clothes, a flower in his lapel, *précieux* and well fed.

Rarely does one find in America a hotel manager who has survived the winds of complaint, the climate of worry, and the floods of people, and of whom one can still say that, besides being short or tall, thin or fat, he has this or that kind of personality. Such a one, a real person, honest always himself with a unique character, was Otto Brauhaus, manager of the Hotel Splendide.

Otto Brauhaus was an immense stout man; he had to bend down to pass under the tall doorways of his hotel. Big as his feet, which gave him much trouble, telegraphing their sorrows to his ever-worried face, was his heart. For despite his conception of himself as a stern executive, and strict disciplinarian, he could not conceal his kindness. He liked to laugh with guests and employees alike, and the result was that his countenance was the scene of an unending emotional conflict.

He was a German, from the soft-speaking Palatinate. For all his years in America, he had somehow never been able to improve his accent. Too genuine a person to learn the affected English of

Monsieur Victor, who was a fellow-countryman, Brauhaus spoke a thick dialect that sometimes sounded like a vaudeville comedian trying for effect. He was, in any case, inarticulate, and hated to talk. Two expressions recurred in his speech like commas; without them he seemed hardly able to speak: "Cheeses Greisd!" and "Gotdemn it!"

His friends were all solid men like himself. Most of them seemed to be brewers, and they would have occasional dinners together, small beer-fests, up in the top-floor suite. There they drank enormous quantities of beer and ate canvasback ducks with wild rice. They held little speeches afterwards and ate again at midnight. They spoke mostly about how proud they were of being brewers. Almost weeping with sentiment and pounding on the table with his fist, one of them would always get up and say: "My father was a brewer. So was my grandfather, and his father was a brewer before him. I feel beer flowing in my veins."

Then Herr Brauhaus usually summed up their feelings by rising to say: "My friends, we are all here together around this table because we are friends. I am demn glad to see all my friends here." They would all nod and applaud and drink again.

But things had not been going too well with Brauhaus's friends, these elderly men who ate and drank too well. In one week Mr. Brauhaus went to two funerals. He came back very gloomy from the second, saying: "Gotdemn it, Cheeses Greisd, every time I see a friend of mine, he's dead."

Beautiful was it also when he described his art gallery. Of the Rubens sketch he owned, he often said: "If something happens to me, Anna still has the Rubens," and of his primitives he said: "Sometimes when I'm alone, I look at them, and they look at me, so brimidif, like this," and he would look sideways out of his face, just like his primitives.

He was not given to false conceptions of personal dignity though he insisted on his hotel's being treated with proper respect. Once when he had hung up outside his office, one hour after he had bought it, a beautiful expensive heavy coat lined with mink, and it was stolen, Mr. Brauhaus ran out into the luncheon crowd which filled the lobby and howled: "Where is my furgoat, Cheeses Greisd!" But it was gone and never came back.

On the other hand one day when Mr. Brauhaus happened to be walking through the Jade Lounge, he saw an elderly lady sitting there alone at a small glasstop table, on which were tea and crumpets. She was knitting. Turning to me he said: "What do they think this is? Go over there and tell that woman to stop knitting." He pronounced the "k" in the last word. "Tell her that this is a first-class hotel and we don't want any knitting here in our Jade Lounges." He disappeared into his office.

I was a little afraid to follow orders, for the elderly lady was severely dressed and looked quite able of taking care of herself. I therefore passed the patron's instructions on to Monsieur Serafini, who looked at the lady, went "Tsk, tsk, tsk" with his tongue, and called a waiter. Fortunately, before the waiter could reach her, the old lady packed her knitting into an immense bag and smiled up at a tall man who had come in the door. She was his mother, and he was the new British Ambassador.

· · ·

Brauhaus's goodness of heart, his reliance on the decency of his people, his unwillingness to face them when they had caused trouble, meant that he was always being taken advantage of by the smooth, tricky, much-traveled people who were his employees. "Why doesn't everybody do his duty, why do I have to bawl them out all the time?" he pleaded with them.

But when someone went too far, then Otto Brauhaus exploded. His big face turned red, his voice keeled over, he yelled and threatened murder. The culprit's head somewhere on a level with Brauhaus's watch chain, the storm and thunder of the big man's wrath would tower and sweep over him. Brauhaus's fists would be raised up at the ceiling, pounding the air; the crystals on the chandelier would dance at the sound of his voice: "I'll drow you oud, I'll kill you, gotdemn it, Cheeses Greisd, ged oud of here!"

Fifteen minutes later, he enters his office and finds waiting for him the man he has been shouting at. Brauhaus looks miserable, stares at the floor like a little boy. He puts his hand on the man's shoulder and squeezes out a few embarrassed sentences. First he says: "Ah, ah—ah," then comes a small prayer: "You know I am a very pusy man. I have a lot of worries. I get excited and then I say things I don't mean. You have been here a long time with me, and I know you work very hard, and that you are a nice feller." Finally a few more "Ah—ah—ah's" and then he turns away. To any man with a spark of decency, all this hurts; almost there are tears in one's eyes and one's loyalty to Otto Brauhaus is sewn doubly strong with the big stitches of affection.

Since he could not fire anyone, someone else had to get rid of the altogether impossible people, and then an elaborate guard had to be thrown around Brauhaus to keep the discharged employees from reaching him in person or by telephone. Once a man got by this guard, all the firing was for nothing.

One night it was announced that Mr. Brauhaus was leaving on his vacation. Such information sceps through the hotel immediately, as in a prison. The trunks were sent on ahead, and late that night Mr. Brauhaus took a cab to the station. But he missed his train, and, since the hotel was not far from the station, he decided to walk back. With his little Tirolese hat, his heavy cane, and his dachshund, which he took with him on trips, he came marching into his hotel. Outside he found no carriage man, no doorman, inside no one to turn the revolving door, no night clerk, also no bellboy and no elevator man. The lobby was quite deserted; only from the cashier's cage came happy voices and much laughter.

Mr. Brauhaus stormed back there and exploded: "What is diss? Gotdemn it! Cheeses Greisd! You have a birdtay zelepration here?"

They made themselves scarce and rushed for their posts. Only the bottles of beer were left, as the revolving door was turned, without guests in it, the elevator starter slipped on his gloves, and the night-clerk vaulted behind the counter and began to write. "You are fired, all fired everyone here is fired, gotdemn it!" screamed Herr Brauhaus. "Everyone here is fired, you hear, raus, everyone, you and you and you." He growled on: *"Lumpenpack, Tagediebe, Schweinebande!"* He had never heard or seen anything like this.

The men very slowly started to leave. "No, not now, come back, tomorrow you are fired," Brauhaus shouted at them.

He was so angry he could not think of going to sleep, and as always on the occasions when he was upset, he walked all the way around the hotel and back to the main entrance. There the doorman got hold of him. With sad eyes, he intercepted Mr. Brauhaus, mumbled something about the twelve years he had been with the hotel, that only tonight, for the first time, had he failed in his duty, that he had a sick child and a little house in Flatbush and that his life would be ruined.

"All right," said Brauhaus. "You stay, John. All the others got-demn it, are fired."

But there was no one to protect him that night. Inside he heard the same story, with changes as to the particular family misfortunes and the location of the little houses. They had all been with the Splendide since the hotel was built; the bellboy had gray hair and was fifty-six years old. Mr. Brauhaus walked out again and around the block. When he came back, he called them all together. He delivered them what was for him a long lecture on discipline, banging the floor with his stick, while the dachshund smelled the doorman's pants.

"I am a zdrikt disziblinarian," he said. They would all have to work together; this hotel was not a gotdemn joke, Cheeses Greisd. It was hard enough to manage it when everyone did his duty, gotdemn it. "And now get back to work."

A late guest arrived. He was swung through the door, saluted, wished a good-night, expressed up to his room with a morning paper and a passkey in the hands of the gray-haired bellboy. No guest had ever been so well and quickly served. "That's good, that's how it should be all the time," said Otto Brauhaus. "Why isn't it like this all the time?" Then he went to bed.

· · ·

Besides all of Mr. Brauhaus's other troubles, there was the World War, and his hotel was filled in front with guests, and staffed in the rear with employees, of every warring nation. Whenever this problem arose, he always shouted: "We are all neudral here, got-demn it, and friendts!"

One Thursday afternoon, about five-thirty, I had been sent to the kitchen to get some small sandwiches for some tea guests. The man who makes these sandwiches is called the *garde-manger*. Instead of ovens, this cook has only large iceboxes, in which he keeps caviar, pâté de foie gras, herrings, pickles, salmon, sturgeon, all the various hams, cold turkeys, partridges, tongues, the cold sauces, mayonnaise. Next to him is the oysterman, so that all the cold things are together.

In spite of being in a cool place instead of, as most cooks are all day, in front of a hot stove, this man was as nervous and excitable as any cook. Also I came at the worst possible time to ask anything of a cook, that is, while he was eating. He sat all the way in the back of his department, and before him were a plate of warm soup on a marble-topped table and a copy of the *Courrier des Etats Unis,* which announced in thick headlines a big French victory on the western front.

To order the sandwiches, the commis had first to write out a little slip, announce the order aloud, go to the coffee-man at the other end of the kitchen for the bread, and finally bring the bread to the garde-manger to be spread with butter, covered, and cut into little squares.

The garde-manger was still eating, but since the guest was in a hurry, I repeated the order to him. "Go away," the cook said angrily. "Can't you see I'm eating? Come back later."

I insisted he make the sandwiches now. "Go away!" he repeated. *"Sale Boche!"*

I called him a French pig. Near him was a box of little iceflakes to put under cold dishes; he reached into this box, came forward, and threw a handful of ice into my face. On the stone counter next to me stood a tower of heavy silver platters, oval, thick, and each large enough to hold six lobsters on ice; I took one of these platters, swung, and let it fly. It wabbled through the air, struck him at the side of the head between the eye and ear, and then fell on the tiled floor with a loud clatter. A woman who was scrubbing a table close by screamed.

Her scream brought the cooks from all the departments as well as the cooks who were eating and the first chef. Four of them carried the garde-manger to the open space in front of the ranges. There he kicked and turned up his eyes; blood ran from the side of his face, and skin hung down under a wide gash. They poured water on him, shouted for the police, and everybody ran around in circles.

It was then I put into practice the Splendide maxim I had already learned: Get to Mr. Brauhaus first. I ran up the stairs and found him as usual worrying in his office under the sign: "Don't worry, it won't last, nothing does." I told him my story as quickly as I could. "What did he call you?" said Mr. Brauhaus, getting up. "A *Boche,* a *sale Boche?* Come with me." He took me by the hand and we went down to the kitchen.

On one side of the garde-manger stood all the cooks; on the other, the waiters, most of whom were Germans. But the French and the Italian waiters were also with them, for all waiters hate all cooks and all cooks hate all waiters. In the forefront of the waiters was Monsieur Victor; in the van of the cooks stood the first chef.

One side was dressed in white, the other in black. The cooks fiddled around in the air with knives and big ladles, and the waiters with napkins. They insulted each other and each other's countries; even the calm first chef was red in the face. The garde-manger lay on the floor, no longer kicking; sometimes he gulped and his lips fluttered. I thought he was going to die while we waited for an ambulance.

Everyone made room for Mr. Brauhaus. He waved them all back to work and went into the office with the first chef and me. "You hear me, Chef," he said, "I don't want no gotdemn badrio-dism in this gotdemn hotel, only good cooking and good service is what I want, Cheeses Greisd!" If the cook had done his work, he said, and not called me a *"sale Boche,"* he would not have had his head knocked in; he got what he deserved and he, Brauhaus, wasn't sorry for him. "This little poy is not to blame, it's your gotdemn dumm cooks," he shouted.

When the garde-manger came out of the hospital after some days, he waited for me on the service stairs of the hotel. "Hsst!" he said, and pointed to his head turbaned in bandages. "You know," he went on, "perhaps I should not have insulted you. I am sorry and here is my hand." I shook his hand. "But," he said, pointing again to his head, "it would be very dear for you, my friend, if I should make you pay for the pain. But let us forget that, I will ask you to pay only for the doctor and the hospital. Here is the bill, it is seventy-five dollars."

I did not have that much money, of course, but Monsieur Serafini lent it to me out of his pocket after I had signed a note promising to pay it back in weekly installments of five dollars.

Mr. Sigsag

. . .

One morning I slipped and upset a tray full of breakfasts that
were wanted in a hurry. It was on a day when the German Ambassador, Count von Bernstorff, and his attaché von Papen were
in a hurry to get to Washington. They complained about missing
the train, or going without breakfast, and they complained outside at the front office, which was bad, because it came back from
there directly to Monsieur Victor and could not be hushed up by
Monsieur Serafini. And when Serafini tried to dissuade Victor
from firing me, he was reminded of the Affair of the Garde-
Manger. I was discharged.

But because Monsieur Serafini was my friend and I still owed
him money, he got me a job in the Grill Room behind the restaurant. The Grill was also under the charge of a man named Victor,
but whereas Victor of the restaurant was corpulent, Victor of the
Grill was thin. Fat Victor was German, but thin Victor was Hungarian, and therefore more elegant. They hated each other, never
spoke, and thin Victor undoubtedly engaged me because it would
annoy the restaurant's Monsieur Victor.

Thin Victor was never arrogant to his guests; the bad ones he
would keep waiting with promises, and then hide them behind
pillars. He had a sense of humor, but also theatrical attacks of

temper. When something went wrong, he would wring his hands in front of the guests and call the waiters "criminals"; he would stamp his feet at an omelet that was not fluffy enough, but he was good to work for; unlike the other Monsieur Victor, who fired someone every day, he discharged no one if he could possibly help it.

All the maîtres d'hôtel and all the chefs de rang in front looked down upon the staff of the Grill Room. These men were shorter and fatter, as the room was also lower and the columns at its sides thicker and shorter. The waiters here were mostly Italians, with a few Armenians and Bohemians and a Greek. They spoke bad French and waited on a lower class of people. Pushed away to one side of the Grill Room, which was always full, was a three-piece orchestra whose only function was to drown out the noise of the service, the clatter of dishes, glasses, and silver.

The great Society went in front; back here came musical comedy stars, and millionaires in search of a quiet corner behind a pillar, where they could not be seen while they squeezed the hands of their young women. Here came film presidents, who ate in a hurry and chattered and haggled over the table with knives or forks in their hands; stockbrokers, owners of fur businesses, people who ran fast, risky undertakings, who talked of nothing but money. They spent it freely too, and made few demands except for hurried service. In the lobby, one could separate them: the sheep going to the restaurant, the wolves to the Grill.

My job was to stand in a white apron and help fix up a buffet, to wheel around curries and learn to slice ham and to cut up ducks, chickens, and turkeys. I thus became acquainted with a little Bohemian waiter stationed way in the back of this room. His name was Wladimir Slezack, but since no one could pronounce it, it had gradually become Mr. Sigsag. He was the smallest man in the restaurant, and because he worked very hard and was very fast on his feet, he was a favorite of thin Victor.

Every waiter in a hotel has a "side job." A side job is extra work, other than serving, that he must perform before or after meals; most of it is done in the morning. One man is in charge of filling and collecting all the salt and pepper and paprika shakers and seeing that they are kept clean. Others must get the clean linen from the linen room every morning and check it at night; others collect the dirty linens. Two who write a good hand get out of unpleasant work by writing little menus for special parties and keeping various accounts. Another has to keep the stock of sauces and pickles, make the French and Russian salad dressing, keep clean the oil and vinegar bottles and the mustard pots. This side job is called the "drug store," and it was assigned to Mr. Sigsag.

Mr. Sigsag lived in a little room on the East Side, where he read the works, in many volumes bound in limp green leather with gold stamping, of a man who called himself the "Sage of East Aurora." These concerned trips to the homes of great men, but the biggest book was one entitled *Elbert Hubbard's Scrapbook* (that was the name of the Sage). With these books and included in their total price had come candlesticks, jars of honey, maple sugar candies, and other souvenirs, all in the one package with the volumes. When I visited him he was expecting some new volumes from East Aurora, this time with bookends included to hold his little library together.

Mr. Sigsag studied these books earnestly and drew the lessons from them that he should. They filled him with respect for a life of work and success. He was also a student by correspondence of the La Salle University and had subscribed to several courses, but he told me that what was most important in life was not knowledge, or hard work, but the right connections, also the ability to "sell" oneself, to call guests by their correct names and to remember their faces.

From his library, now lying one volume on top of another, he took a book of which he was very fond, a waiter's bible. After his working hours at the Bristol in Vienna, he had attended a school which the hôteliers of Vienna maintained for the training of new waiters. He graduated from it with high honors. A diploma, a colored lithograph, decorated like a menu with pheasants, geese, wine bottles, and grapes, surrounded his name printed in the center. It was signed by the dean of the school and the president of the Society of Hôteliers, Restaurateurs, Cafetiers, and Innkeepers of Vienna and by the city's burgomaster, and hung in a frame over Mr. Sigsag's desk. So well had he been liked at the school, that the maître d'hôtel principal had had him pose for the photographs that illustrated the manual of the waiter's art, which was learnedly entitled: *Ein Leitfaden der Servierkunde mit besonderer Berücksichtigung des Küchenwesens* ("An Introduction to the Science of Serving, with Special Reference to Culinary Matters").

The photographs showed Mr. Sigsag, a little waiter in a tail-coat, standing in the proper positions for receiving a guest and for recommending dishes from the menu, and also standing incorrectly while doing this. They showed him handing a newspaper to a guest, carrying a tray, lighting a diner's cigar, and demonstrating how to carry the sidetowel, as well as various ways of how not to carry it. There was a list of books at the end of the book, for further study, among them the *Almanach de Gotha* and various cookbooks, and there were color charts of sleeve stripes and collar stars showing the various grades of army and naval officers. One whole chapter was given over to the art of folding napkins in the shapes of swans, windmills, boats, and fans.

Mr. Sigsag spent his free time puttering on a second-hand motorboat which he kept up near Dyckman Street; he asked me to visit him there sometimes. Two weeks from the day I first visited him, he told me that thin Victor was giving a party at a small place outside of the city, along the ocean, in Bath Beach. Several of the maîtres d'hôtel, the head cashier Madame Dombasle, and even the room clerk were invited to it, and so was he, Sigsag, because of his motorboat, in which he was to take Madame Dombasle and her two beautiful daughters out there. After the luncheon he would take all the guests for a little fishing trip, and Monsieur Victor would pay for the oil and the gasoline. A little more work had to be done on the boat and Mr. Sigsag invited me to help him and to come along to the party.

He seemed to have influence. We got days off, with mysterious ease, to work on the boat. These were lovely days. Arriving at Dyckman Street by subway, we put on old pants and undershirts and washed and scraped the little boat as it stood high and dry on the land while Mr. Sigsag talked of the importance of having friends and of working hard, and also of Madame Dombasle's two beautiful daughters.

Mr. Sigsag, who always played as seriously as a little boy, had ordered two uniforms for us: for himself a double-breasted, gold-buttoned blue coat and a white cap with the name of his ship, the *Wahabee,* in gold lettering on it; and another with a little less gold for me. The boat was finally burned off, scraped, and painted and the one hard job after calking it was to get the red paint at the bottom to end in a straight line in spite of the curve of the wide belly of the boat.

Later we went to a little lunch-wagon where we got wonderful ham and eggs, and some beer to take back with us to the boat. Then we lit a lamp, and if one did not look at the big electric powerhouse across the river, this was a scene of peace. The niceness of people could be seen here in their desire to flee from the city; all about us were other little grounded boats, on which men had labored after working hours, quiet, simple men with pipes and old clothes and without much money. The decks of their boats, high above the land and surrounded by grass, looked amusing; on them sat their wives and cooked on little oilburners or gasoline stoves. The boats were of comical design: impossible cabins were built on decks much too small for them and had to be broken up, with half a cabin in the stern and another piece of it stuck on in the bow. On some of them were little roof gardens with flowerboxes, hammocks, easy chairs, and even birdcages. They made up a little city of green, yellow, and blue houses that could swim away. It had none of that impersonal elegance or mass ugliness of manufactured things; everyone had done something with his own hands for his own pleasure. It was all so happy and sad and, above all, good; even the ground was nice, covered with coils of rope, old dinghies, rusted anchors, and green and red lanterns.

As the lights grew stronger in the little portholes and were reflected on the sides of the boats next to them, and the gramophones started to play, and the smell of food came out of imitation funnels, we stopped work and sat in the cabin while Mr. Sigsag told me of his youth.

· · ·

Wladimir Slezack, the eleventh son of a Bohemian blacksmith, was born in a village two hours out of Przemysl. When he was old enough, though still a child, his father paid to have him apprenticed as piccolo at the great Hotel King Wenzeslaus in Przemysl. Here he served part of his apprenticeship and then went on to Vienna, where, his recommendations being of the best, he got a job in a small hotel.

The child piccolo is an institution in all European restaurants. His head barely reaches above the table; his ears are red and stand out, because everybody pulls them. And when he is a man, he will still pull his head quickly to one side if anyone close to him suddenly moves, because he always did that to soften the blows that rained on him from the proprietor down to the last chambermaid; they hit him mostly out of habit.

For the rest the boy learned to wash glasses, to fold newspapers into the bamboo holders and hang them on the wall, to learn the grade of an officer by the stars on his collar, to bow, to chase flies from the tables without upsetting the glasses, to carry water and coffee without spilling, and to know the fifty-one varieties of coffee that are served in Viennese restaurants.

He studied how to make up and write the bill of fare, let the awnings up and down over the sidewalk in the summer, and scatter ashes out on the ice on winter mornings. He also cleaned ashtrays and matchstands, and one could still see his right thumb bent sideways from polishing two hundred of these every day; they were made of a light-colored, very sensitive brass, and the cigarettes burned deep stains into them that were hard to get out.

The boys started to work at six in the morning; they ate standing up, and got to bed at eleven at night. A free day was not provided for, since on Sundays and holidays the restaurant was busier than on other days, serving happy people. The piccolos slept in the restaurant, and Wladi, who was the smallest of them, slept in a kitchen drawer under the pastry cook's noodle board, where it was warm. The others had to sleep in the dining-room on cold benches under which their dirty pillows and covers were stowed away in a drawer during the day.

Little Wladi was fortunate not only in his sleeping quarters, in which he was at least warm, but also in his parentage. So many of the other boys were the chance sons of a chambermaid and a transient guest or waiter, or at best a soldier loved on a bench when the trees were in bloom and all was beautiful on the Prater.

A restaurant in the morning, before it is aired and swept, and the guests enter, is an unhappy place. The stale smells of tobacco smoke, of empty beer and wine glasses, and of spilled food and coffee stay and hang about the draperies and furniture. It is no place for a growing child; this life eventually draws on the faces of these little boys two lines from their nostrils to the corner of their young lips and it makes them pale and brings out the thin veins at their temples. They get to look tired and high-bred; in later years this pallor and nervousness will give them just the right touch of grand hotel elegance they will need for their parts. The boys also learn to repeat the smut they hear from the guests, and to smoke, and to drink themselves to sleep.

Nevertheless, the piccolo was looked upon with envy by the apprentices of plumbers and cobblers; they had the red ears, too, but not enough to eat, and no cigarettes, no drinks, no tips. The piccolo could at least save money. It was the custom in Austria for guests to leave three separate tips. The biggest was for the *Zahlkellner*, the captain to whom one paid the bill and who had taken the order; the next was for the *Speisenträger* or *Saalkellner*, the ordinary waiter who actually served one; and the third, a little stack of coppers, was for the piccolo. These three tips had to be left in clearly defined heaps and far enough apart from each other; for the restaurant law was that all the coins that the first waiter could get within the reach of his outstretched thumb and index finger was his. That is why, in old Viennese restaurants the three tips were always left very far apart from one another, almost on the edges of the small marble tables.

Despite the big hands of the headwaiters, the piccolo was often able to earn and put aside a good sum of money; he had little chance to spend it. His dress coat, a child's garment, he had made by a cheap tailor, or bought it secondhand from another piccolo; his trousers could be dark blue or gray, for in the bad light of the restaurants no one could see below the levels of the tables; finally there was a waistcoat. Under the latter the piccolo need not wear a shirt; a celluloid plastron, like a bosom cut out of an evening shirt, was attached by a button to his celluloid collar, and a tie held the arrangement together. Save for his shoes and socks, the dickey and cuffs, which were stuck in his coat sleeves, the piccolo stood naked in his trousers and frock coat. His hair was plastered down with brilliantine, and kept in order with a greasy comb that he carried in his waistcoat pocket.

He knew all about love and women, and had never played. He looked most unhappy when in the spring he brought ice cream out to the restaurant garden for some well-dressed child with its father and mother, who smiled at him when the music played and the large-grained sand was hard to walk on. And when one sees somewhere in a cheap restaurant, say in a beer hall in Coney Island, one of those old waiters who are known as "hashers" leaning on a chair, with ugly, lightless eyes and a dead face that is filled with misery and meanness, one is seeing that little boy grown old, with flat crippled feet on which he has dragged almost to the end of his useless life his dead childhood.

But little Wladimir was made of stronger material, he survived, he went to school, he saved his money and paid his father back what had been spent to make him a piccolo, and he went to France and England and finally to America. Now he had a job as chef de rang in the best hotel in New York, in the Grill Room of the Splendide, and the maître d'hôtel was his friend. When looked at from Przemysl, this was as great and brave a success as any recorded in the high tales Mr. Sigsag read in the honey and candlestick books of Elbert Hubbard.

After he had ended his story, Mr. Sigsag looked in his little account book; he had set aside a certain sum for entertainment, another for the launching of the boat, for the uniforms and the beer, but we also needed some food to serve on the trip. He promised to show me something tomorrow: how to get a little food without paying for it.

·   ·   ·

The next day, after all the guests had left and the lights were turned out in the Grill Room and the cashier had added up her bills, closed the books, and gone away with the money. Mr. Sigsag led me to the little tiled closet where he prepared his salad dressings. He kept all his sauces, the mayonnaise, and the mustards in an icebox which had a small door, about three feet high and four wide, at the height of his head; he had to stand on a box to reach into it. This mustard closet was built into a huge refrigerator that opened out on the kitchen and had its back to the Grill Room, and it hung like a cage some feet above the level of the kitchen.

Mr. Sigsag made sure no one was around and then started to take everything out of the small icebox. He placed on a table the bottles of chili sauce, A-One sauce, sauce Escoffier, walnut and tarragon sauce, all the vinegar bottles, the chutneys, and the twenty-five French and twenty-five English mustard pots which were in daily use. Then he lifted out the grating on which the bottles had stood, and now I could see the big kitchen icebox filled with cheeses, tubs of rolled butter in ice water, and salads. He brought over a chair and asked me to hold his legs while he reached for a cheese.

"Shh," said Mr. Sigsag, and I looked around once more; there was no one outside. He climbed in and reached down, but he was too short to reach the cheeses. I held his knees, then his ankles, and then his shoes; then I had his shoes in my hands and Mr. Sigsag was down with his face in some Camembert. Also there was a noise. I closed the icebox door. It was the night watchman; he looked in and I polished away at some bottles. The man sat down, lit a pipe, and started to talk; it was a long time before he left again on his rounds.

In the meantime, Mr. Sigsag had been trying to get up; kneeling and standing and sliding and then sitting down again in all kinds of cheese. He first handed out a Pont Lévêque, hard and solid. "There will be trouble anyway," he said, "we might as well take it along." Then he gave me his cold hands, but for some time I could not lift him out. They were smeared with cheese and slipped out of mine. I gave him a napkin, with which he cleaned his face and hands, and finally I could pull him out, his sleeves and trousers full of cheese. He took a shower downstairs, and washed his trousers, but he still smelled.

The next morning, Sunday, I met him very early at the boat, which was in the water now, looking new and beautiful. The sun had just risen and shone warmly on the planks. We put the beer on board, and the cheese, also knives and paper napkins, and then we dressed in the uniforms, scattered around cushions, bought oil and gasoline, and started off, past the electric light plant, and out into the Hudson, under the railroad bridge at Spuyten Duyvil.

The trouble started at about One Hundred and Sixty-Eighth Street—pop, then pop, and poppoppop, and one more pop, and the motor stopped. The boat started to rock and turn around. Mr. Sigsag took a big piece of motor out of the one large cylinder, sandpapered the points, and poured some mixture he called "dynamite" out of a little can into the cylinder. The motor almost flew out of the boat and tiny lightning flashes shot out all over the loose parts. This happened three more times before we reached the Battery, and Mr. Sigsag's uniform was soiled with fingermarks.

"There they are," said Mr. Sigsag and pointed to three women, who were strolling up and down to the left of the Aquarium. Madame Dombasle and her two daughters were very French-looking and sweet in their airy batiste gowns that reached to the floor. Madame carried a fragile parasol and the young girls wore large

satin sashes and bows around their waists and openwork gloves up to their elbows. We tooted the whistle three times and they waved their arms and the parasol.

The entrance to the little harbor at the Battery is hard to negotiate; there are strong currents and only a small opening between high sea walls. We almost made it, were swept away, and then turned and tried again; finally, by keeping the boat, which was almost as wide as it was long, away from the wall of one side with a hook and on the other with our feet, we made the calm square of water, filled with driftwood and a broken life preserver. Madame was helped on board, which was not easy, for she was stout and giggled and did not jump when Mr. Sigsag said "jump." She almost got one foot between the pier and the boat. The daughters, tall, lovely, dark, and young, were easier.

Madame admired the boat, the uniforms, *le petit commandant.* "How many tons has your little liner?" she asked. Mr. Sigsag took them to the roof of the cabin from which they could enjoy the best view of the harbor; there they sat on cushions, under the parasol, and smiled back, a little afraid, jumping when we tooted the horn as a signal that we were off.

I steered the boat while Mr. Sigsag sat in front and explained New York to the ladies, who, having landed in Boston, had not seen much of it—the beautiful bridges, the Statue of Liberty, the ferryboats, the tall buildings. There is a powerful current here; the tide comes in through the Narrows, and it is besides a very much disturbed area of water. There is much driftwood that may get into the propeller, and ocean liners go in and out, fire and police boats, private yachts, the great Staten Island ferryboats making high waves, railroad tugs with strings of cars on long barges. Waves come in from all directions, so that one cannot bother to cut them at the proper angles, and the little boat was tossed high and to all sides.

I noticed that after half an hour we had not reached the latitude of Governor's Island; in another half-hour the prison on that island moved slowly past and ten minutes later the motor coughed and stopped. Mr. Sigsag was just serving beer and cheese sandwiches. While Madame Dombasle and her daughters rose up and down in front, Mr. Sigsag disappeared inside to fix the motor. We lost much distance and were back again near the prison and close to the island; then came a ferryboat and the ladies were wetted to the knees. They shrieked but they were afraid to move, and looked around just as Mr. Sigsag came out of the cabin. The smell of oil and beer and the rocking had made him sick and he bent over the side of the boat. When I saw that, I also got sick. The boat turned again. Mr. Sigsag got up, took a deep breath, smiled at the ladies, and then went in to his motor again.

Then the ladies got sick and held onto each other. In the low cabin were two benches: Mr. Sigsag put the cushions on them and slowly pulled Madame Dombasle back on the narrow gangway, knocking her head as they went in. When she had lain down, Mr. Sigsag offered her some beer, but she whimpered: "No, please, no." The daughters got sicker and the younger one was taken down and laid on the other bench with her long slim legs folded back. The bottles rolled over the cabin top and jumped into the bay.

We crossed over away from the main current and made better speed aong the Staten Island shoreline. Mr. Sigsag felt better and cracked jokes, but in the cabin the ladies were sick again, and seasick women are not attractive. One of the daughters came out for air, her dress wet and ruined; she sat up bravely and leaned into the wind and brushed her black hair from her cheeks where it was stuck in spittle. We forged slowly ahead, and it is a wonderful thing that a boat goes on even when everybody on board is feeling terrible.

We turned past the Arsenal at Fort Totten and went to the right and finally came to Bath Beach, where we tooted the horn again. Thin Victor and his wife, the maîtres d'hôtel, and Mr. Fassi, the chief room clerk, were at the dock to meet us. They all looked strange without their dress coats and stiff shirts, wearing instead gay suits with belts at the back and straw hats with colored bands; but when we arrived there was as much scraping and bowing as at the hotel. The color came back to our ladies' faces; they retired to a room and came down again in good order, with hardly a trace of damage in their clothes and hair. Frenchwomen know how to repair themselves very quickly after a disaster. The trip was soon forgotten and even laughed over.

Built of wood, with white-washed stone urns around it, in which were planted palms, the old hotel gave one somehow a feeling of vacation and freedom. It stood near the shore in a large garden with children's swings in it. The Hungarian chief bus boy had decorated a corner of the dining-room, which was paneled with long strips of dark-varnished wood and contained a piano. There were flowers on the table, and one of the Splendide cooks had been brought out to prepare a very good meal. There was a printed menu and good wines; cigars and cigarettes were handed around; and the maîtres d'hôtel sat about in accented comfort, their legs spread wide apart, smoking with a careless air, and saying with face, hands, and feet: "We are gentlemen today." Also they summoned the old waiter by calling "Psst," something they themselves detested when the guests in the Splendide did it, but here it meant: "See how thoroughly we can be guests."

Madame Dombasle and her beautiful daughters were toasted; then the younger one, Céleste, sat down at the piano and played. The instrument needed tuning, many of the strings rattled in rust, and it sounded as if one were hearing an echo, but she played several salon pieces, *"Ouvre tes yeux bleus, ma mignonne,"* and *"Si j'avais des ailes."* Then there was conversation, everyone sat down, and Monsieur Victor spoke.

As would an old colonel explain delicate tactical problems to his subalterns, so he went over many phases of his career. The talk covered the Continent; it was of glorious dinners, of places and people, of Monte Carlo and Ostende, of the Carlton in London, of encounters with difficult guests of the highest position, of Prince Bibesco, the Kaiser, and other trying cases, and of old King Leopold. Victor told of the time when His Majesty, Alfonso of Spain, came to the Carlton grill, and there was only one table left, reserved for Marie Tempest, the actress, who came in just as the King did. It was a breathless moment. "I don't know how I did it, it came to me from somewhere, the inspiration," said Victor, but he solved the terrible dilemma—simply with the phrase, "The great king, the great actress," and he sat them both down at the same table. A whispered "Ah" went around our table, accompanied by French, Italian, Hungarian, and German gestures of appreciation of so brilliant a performance.

Thin Victor shrugged his shoulders at these expressions of grateful admiration from his maîtres d'hôtel and went on to the problems confronting him now, reviewing matters that had gone badly or very well. The maîtres d'hôtel furnished details, agreed or disputed as to dates or the number of people that had been at a certain table on a certain day or the dishes they had ordered. It slowed up the storytelling, but it brought them closer together. Their eyes hung on Victor's lips.

Next to me, all the way at the end of the table, sat Mr. Sigsag, and when I sometimes asked him a question, he said: "Shh!" very angrily, and listened intently to the head of the table, and laughed at the jokes, and looked dark at serious passages. He let no detail escape him.

Only one man remained aloof. This was Fassi, the room clerk, who had observed a certain distance all evening long. He sat at the right of Victor; smoking his cigar and gazing at the ash, he carried to his table the disdain of the front office for restaurant and kitchen help. Only when Victor told what Mr. Joseph Widener had ordered for dinner yesterday did Fassi stir and say: "Ah, yes, yes, yes, Joseph Widener," leaving the Mr. off, "Joseph Widener, I spoke to him only yesterday, no, Thursday, wasn't it?" and he made it clear therewith that, while Victor took the orders of Mr. Widener, he, Fassi, spoke to the great man about the weather, about horses, and about the general things men talk about.

Most of the time I spent looking at Madame Dombasle's beautiful daughters. Frenchwomen, I think, are rarely beautiful, but when they are they hurt with their perfection. There was dancing afterwards, and the room clerk danced with one of the daughters, Victor with the other, and Mr. Sigsag with the mother.

The party was not without some profit to me, for when I came to change my apron the next day, the Hungarian chief bus boy said loudly, so that all the others could hear: "Guess how many glasses of Tokay I drank last night at Monsieur Victor's party. You saw me there, didn't you?" He had more respect for me from then on as did also the maîtres d'hôtel. Madame Dombasle corrected my French mistakes at her desk, and Victor let me carry his dress coat to his tailor to have a new lining put in. As for Mr. Sigsag, he was soon a maître d'hôtel, and we never heard anything about the cheese.

Art Class

. . .

Shortly after I had paid off Monsieur Serafini, I met an artist named Thaddeus, who ran a school in Greenwich Village. At the time, I was putting aside five dollars a week, and this is what he charged me for the use of the studio and his advice.

Thaddeus was a splendid teacher. Many of his students were poor and paid him no money, but he was equally attentive to all of them. He would go rapidly from pupil to pupil, explaining constructions, pointing out a wrong line, sketching large graphic models of nose, lips, ears, to help them understand. He never made fun of a student no matter how bad the drawing. To a man in front of a sheet of paper containing a scribbly design of a broken stick with five fingers on the end of it, he would say slowly: "Look, it's an arm, its bones are here and there, here they meet; here is muscle; here are veins and ligaments; this is soft shoulder; here is a joint—you can lift a rock with it and throw it, you can scratch your back with it, push the hair back from your forehead, lean on it, you can talk with it and with the fingers on the end of it. Think about all that, and try again." If after all the trying, nothing came of it, and the pupil was not a beautiful girl, Thaddeus told him quietly and definitely to go and try no more, that it was hopeless.

My happiest moment every morning was when I came here from the hotel. I felt as if I had come on a little vacation to the mountains. Thaddeus spoke my language, he understood me and offered me a refuge from the hotel. Here was freedom and integrity and good work. All my troubles would leave me on the ride down to the studio. But also this work was making my other life, the life of the Splendide, tolerable, for I was learning to see.

For in the hotel too there is design; not only in its elegant rooms, not only in the fashionable people, but even more in the shoes of Otto Brauhaus, in our frightened old waiters, in the hands of cooks—fat fingers sliding around the inside of pots buttering them, sitting together on a carrot and slowly feeding it to the chopping knife. There is color in the copper casseroles and in the back of Kalakobé, the Senegalese Negro who scrubs them in a white, tiled scullery.

All this I was learning to see for the first time as I spent my mornings in the studio, and that is all I did there. For I never drew a line in that art class. I couldn't. I saw my picture clearly, simply; I saw it finished with my line and with my colors; but the moment I started to draw, a paralysis overcame me; the fear of doing it wrong made a knot of me inside.

Thaddeus understood this; he had looked at all my work before I came to his school; he knew my inner problem, the only one life that I could take seriously, and he said: "Just sit and look, drink it up and don't worry. It will form itself. It is finished inside of you. I can't help you much, nobody can. The colors, the design, the line, are all your own, you yourself must get them out."

This was a bitter pleasure, a fragile, glasslike feeling. The urge to give something form would run down to my elbows or my wrists and get stuck there the moment my hand tried to work. But sometimes in the middle of the night, or at a moment when I was not thinking of effort, as when I waited for an elevator in the hotel and was scribbling something simple on the wall—a chair, a table, a shoe, a face, then it was suddenly there, right and good. I needed no one to tell me that it was so. But down in the studio I would be frozen again. Though I watched the model for three hours every morning and could draw her from memory, I was never able to break the spell.

The
Brave
Commis

•   •   •

In the locker next to mine in the waiters' dressing-room hung the
clothes of a young French commis who worked in fat Monsieur
Victor's restaurant. This young man had a dream; for every
waiter, like every prisoner, has a dream. With the older ones it is
about a chicken farm, or becoming rich through an invention, or
various small businesses, or a return home to a little house and
peace; with relatively few is it a hotel or a restaurant—of this they
say: *"Sale métier,* filthy profession." But the young ones have more
daring dreams: becoming an aviator, a detective, a movie actor,
an orchestra leader, or a dancer; and because the French champion prizefighter is visiting America, a certain young blond
commis de rang is going to lead a very healthy life and become a
boxer.

He has the boxer's picture pasted up on the inside of his locker
door; he does not eat stews and dishes that are made with sauces;
when he comes down with his chef to the employees' dining-room,
he brings that man's food, but runs up again for plain vegetables,
cheese, and a cutlet for himself; he drinks no wine and empties a
quart of milk into himself at every meal. He arrives at the hotel in
a trot, his fists at the sides of his chest; he has come all the way
down Fifth Avenue this way after a short run through the park. In

the locker room he makes a few boxing motions—*l'uppercut, le knockout*—dancing and twisting his head and then with a loud: "Ah, burr, bhuff," and: *"Ça, c'est bon,"* he takes a cold shower. He has immaculate linen, fine muscles, and he brings his chest out of the shower as if it were a glass case full of jewels. He takes a shower after all meals, rubs himself down afterwards, and then sits in his undershirt in the employees' barbershop, reading books on boxing and arguing with Frank, the American engineer, about who knocked out whom, when and where.

Up in the restaurant he looks fine, first because he is tall and handsome, secondly because he stands straight and the mess jacket and the long apron look good on him, and thirdly because he is always clean. Victor likes him because he is always smiling and is as quick as lightning. He takes the stairs up from and down to the kitchen—thirty iron steps, of which every other man complains—as if they were built for him to train on. He makes the run up in two seconds flat, pushing four steps at a time from under him and flying past the heavily loaded older men so that he almost upsets their trays. They stop and curse him, but he laughs back over his shoulder, takes a stack of hot plates out of the heater, and worms his way to his station through the crowded dining-room with an elegant twist. To reward him, when the visiting French champion comes to the restaurant with his friends, he is seated at the young commis's station and gets service such as no one else receives.

Victor has also promised the young man a future: he will make him a chef de rang at the next opportunity, then in a little while maître d'hôtel. Men so engaging, so fine-looking, who, moreover, know their business well and are quick-thinking and intelligent, are few. And he is a Frenchman, and so does not underestimate the value of such a future and the advice of Victor. He is, besides, very sober in his estimate of the boxing profession. He will try it while he keeps one foot in the Splendide. If all goes well, if he should be another champion, fine. For lesser rewards, no. Meanwhile he will have had fun, and acquired a well-trained body, which is a good possession, especially since most maîtres d'hôtel and managers are fat, bald, pale, and flat-footed. For one so youthful he shows much good sense in his planning.

He asked me once to go to the Young Men's Christian Association with him. This institution seemed to me far from a benevolent undertaking. The commis had a miserable cell for a room and paid well for it; the walls were covered with invitations to various pleasures and benefits to mind and body, always with the prices clearly marked. The quarters were crammed and so were the pools and gymnasiums. The walls needed painting and the runners were shaggy and worn. The guests were nice clean-cut earnest boys who wished to get ahead, but the atmosphere of the place, I thought, was commercial, unhospitable, and false.

The commis introduced me to the gym instructors with the casualness of an old habitué, and for my benefit he put on a little boxing show with one of them and with a ball suspended from a parquet board, which to me, who understood little, seemed very good. When it was time to get back to the hotel to set the tables for dinner, he took another shower and we arrived at the Splendide in a hurry. I was out of wind and perspiring, but he took his shoulders out of his narrow athletic undershirt and asked me in loud French to tell those others what I had seen this afternoon in the way of *"le boxe."*

The brave commis did finally become a chef de rang with a good station, being jumped over the heads of several older men. He made very good money, but more of it went into boxing, and he became stronger and stronger. Because he was such a good, swift, smiling waiter, he received some of the most difficult guests, and one day during a rush, he had to serve a man who was generally feared for he had had many men dismissed. Mr. Mistbeck, a blanket manufacturer, lived in the hotel. He should never have been allowed in the hotel at all, but he had millions. He was on some kind of diet, and everything had to be cooked for him without salt or sugar; a long list of how his food was to be prepared hung down in the kitchen. Also he had his own wines and his own mustard; he mixed his own salads; and all this, in the middle of a rush, was always difficult. The cooks cursed; there was sometimes delay.

Mr. Mistbeck then became abusive. He knocked on his glass, shouted: "Hey," or: "Hey you," said: "Tsk, tchk, tchk," or: "Psst," and pulled his waiter by the apron or the napkin at luncheon or by the tailcoat at dinner. His wife, a little, frowsy, scared, but kindly woman, would try to calm him. That only made him madder; he spoke so loud that the people at the tables around him looked up in surprise; his face turned red and blue, and a vein on his forehead stood out; he moved the silver and glasses, bunched the napkin into a ball, pounded on the table, and sometimes got up and walked to the door, his napkin in his hand, to complain to Victor.

His complaints always started: "I have been coming here for the last five years, and, goddamn it, these idiots don't know yet what I want, you charge enough in this lousy dump!" Or it would go: "Listen, you"—he held the waiter while he said that—"listen, you old fool, one of these days I'll buy this goddamn joint and fire every one of you swine and get some people that know how to wait on table; now get going!" With that he would push the man loose. During these embarrassing moments, his poor wife would turn red and look down on her plate and behave as if she were not there. When the waiter was gone, Mr. Mistbeck would continue to shout at her, as if she too had kept him waiting or brought him something he did not like.

One of the dreadful things about the hotel business is that it offers no defense against such people. The old waiters who have families just mumble: "Yes, sir. No, sir. Right away, sir. I'm sorry, sir." They insult the guest outside the room, on the stairway down to the kitchen; that is why one sees these poor fellows talking so much to themselves—they are delivering a long repartee and threatening to throw out some imaginary customer and telling him what they think of him. Sometimes an incident will rankle for days afterwards, and they will continue to mumble trem- blingly at a pillar, a chair, or through a window out into the street. One can tell from their faces what they are saying, and it usually comes to an end with the swish of a napkin or the quick folding of arms. It is also then that they don't see an upraised hand or hear a call.

Mr. Mistbeck sat at the station of the new waiter, the former brave commis. He was for some reason even unusually abusive, nothing suited him, and finally he pushed back his chair, threw away his napkin, and, getting up, took hold of the young man's lapels to deliver his usual speech. Now the brave commis could not stand being touched; his hands leaped up in fists. In a second, Mr. Mistbeck had *l'uppercut,* and *le knockout,* and had fallen into his chair with his arms hanging down, his face on his fork, and his toupee on the floor.

That ended the Splendide career of the brave commis. Downstairs he was congratulated by all the waiters; in the barbershop he had to show Frank the engineer just how he had done it; and Victor gave him a good recommendation. But in a week the brave commis came back—in uniform. He had enlisted in the American army.

All the men looked at him with great envy; for a waiter it was so wonderful to be brave, and to be where there were no guests.

I thought of my incident with the French cook, about Mr. Mistbeck, and how much I hated this business. Then one evening there was a banquet at which Marshal Joffre spoke. When he was leaving I helped him on with his coat in the lobby, and, because it was raining, I said: "*Ça pleut dehors.*" He turned, smiled, and said in German: "*Mein lieber Kleiner, es ist nicht 'ça pleut dehors.' Es ist 'il pleut dehors.'*" And because of that, and the brave commis, and other reasons, I enlisted in the American army the next day.

The Army

· · · · · · · ·

THE Hospital in FORT PORTER BUFFALO

Please
Don't Shoot

. . .

Oswego is on Lake Ontario; it is a small town without tall buildings. There is one hotel, the Pontiac, a streetcar, also a theater, in which the Paulist Choristers sang yesterday. The town is very friendly, the air is strong and clear. We are stationed out at Fort Ontario. The grounds of this fortress are spacious; there is an immense parade ground.

The Field Hospital, Unit N, to which I belong, was recruited in New York. The men are all volunteer soldiers and the Officers, doctors. The men are mostly college students or graduates, not ordinary privates; I was assigned to this hospital unit because my ties to Austria and Germany make me ineligible for combat duty. Some of the men are older, and professional; for example, the one who has his bed next to mine in the barracks is a Professor of French at one of the large universities—it is either Harvard or Yale, I believe. His name is Beardsley.

I am very glad of his friendship; he seems to take the whole business we are engaged in as if it did not concern him, as a vacation, never has a serious thought. He takes a peculiar pride in having a very ill-fitting uniform and hat. These military hats are badly enough designed as they are, but he fixes his own so that the rim turns up off his face, which makes him look very ineffi-

The GUARDHOUSE
FORT ONTARIO

cient; also he shaves only when he has to. Mostly he sits on his bed and eats a peculiar kind of small white nuts and crosses his legs.

All this is so fine because he is a man of great culture, and I like him so much because I have to think how unbearable a German Professor would be here next to me. In the evening Beardsley looks like a Mexican bandit. He makes no effort to be assigned to better jobs, to win a promotion—he could even have a commission for the asking. But he is happy, and most so when we push a wagon with bread from the bakery back to the barracks every evening; then he sings and says that this is the best time he has ever had, that he is completely happy. Perhaps he has been in some terrible life and now feels happy because he is away from that. He tells me that Schopenhauer states with authority that Happiness is the absence of Unhappiness, which is so obvious and foolish that a backward child could make this observation, but he says I must think about it. I looked this up and it is right: only Schopenhauer says the absence of *"Schmerz,"* which is pain, and in German the word pain covers more than just pain—it means sorrow, trouble, unhappiness. And so Professor Beardsley is perhaps right.

. . .

The allowed me to bring my dog along. The Major said to the Adjutant back in New York City: "Say, Charlie, he has a dog, can we use a dog?"

The Adjutant asked; "What kind of a dog is it?"

I said: "A police dog."

Then he leaned back and said to the Major: "It's all right with me."

"All right, son, bring your police dog," said the Major. "What's his name?"

I am glad of this, yet I have never seen anything like it. I cannot think of a German Major calling his Adjutant Charlie and asking him about the dog—and all this time the Major sat in a chair and told me to sit down, and the Adjutant had his legs on the Major's desk. The Major smoked a cigar and smiled and then talked to me in German about beer and food; he also said how much he enjoyed a trip down the Rhine.

.   .   .

We drill here all day long, and workingmen are building new barracks and fixing the old ones up. There is a Colonel here from the regular army, a smart-looking old gentleman with white hair and a trim, well-kept body; he wears boots and spurs and behaves like an Officer. The men tell me that he is a West Pointer and that you can always tell them, no matter how old they are.

We are being instructed how to take care of the sick, how to transport men on stretchers, first aid, and how to help in a Hospital.

In our free time we go to motion pictures and entertainments for the soldiers. One is as dull as the other. On Sundays we go to churches, and afterwards people ask us to their houses for dinner. In all these houses is a soft warm feeling, a desire to be good to us, and the food is simple, good, and plentiful. We also take walks together, and Beardsley has pointed out a piece of scenery which he named "Beautiful Dreck." It was a bitter landscape composed of railroad tracks, signal masts, coal sheds, a factory building and some freight cars, a gas tank, and in the background some manufacturing plant, black with soot. Some of the windows of this building were lit by a vivid gray-blue light and yellow flames shot out of several chimneys. "That is," he said, "beautiful Dreck, and we have lots of it in America."

Dreck is a German word for filth and dirt but it also means manure, mud, dirty fingers. It is a large, able word, *patois*, almost bad; it covers all that was before us, and thereby can be seen that Professor Beardsley knows much. He told me St. Louis had a particularly good portion of "Beautiful Dreck," but that the best he knew could be seen in the Jersey Meadows, where it covers almost a whole countryside.

· · ·

One day the Wardmaster of Ward Number Three swam too far out into Lake Ontario and drowned, and I became the Wardmaster. This Ward was filled with oldtime soldiers; they call themselves "Oldtimers" and had recently been with Mr. Pershing in Mexico. They were distinguished from all other soldiers in that they had overcoats and uniforms of what they called the "Old Issue," a cloth of much better quality than the new and also of better color, and they were very proud of khaki uniforms that were almost white from much wear and bleaching. These uniforms of course they did not wear; they hung in their closets. They were middle-aged men, and those in our ward suffered from some amorous diseases which they mentioned with pride, considering those who did not have either the disease or the memory of it not quite complete soldiers. Among my duties was to give them their medicines, to take pulse, temperature, and respiration, and the difficult job of turning the lights out at nine o'clock. They read, played cards, talked, and did not want to go to sleep. All objects they used had to be sterilized; I had to wear rubber gloves most of the time.

The first few nights after I took charge I said: "Lights out" when it was nine, turned the lights out, and went to the room outside, where I wrote out reports. But I could see that they turned the lights on again as soon as I was out of the room. This worried me a great deal, because "Lights out" means "Lights out" and there must be discipline in an army. I could not understand that these men who were "Oldtimers" did not understand that in Germany this would have been unthinkable. The third night I intended to do something about it. I walked into the room and waited until it was nine, then I turned out the light but did not go out. One of the men next to the light said: "Hey, buddy, turn on that light, like a good boy."

I told him that I was not "a good boy," but the Wardmaster in charge, and that the orders were to turn the lights out.

"That's right," said the Oldtimer, "but it doesn't say that you can't turn them on again!"

Then another shouted: "Turn on that light, Heinie"; then one of them came in his pajamas and turned on the light, pushing me against the wall, and they all laughed. When he was back in bed, I turned the light out again, and at that moment every one of them threw something at me, even two glass ducks, which is the name for the watering bottles.

I ran over to the barracks and got my Colt forty-five, strapped it around myself, and then I came back in the room with the gun in my hand. I told them that I would turn the lights out again and the first man who would come near me, get out of bed, or even make a noise, would be shot. I turned out the lights again— it was about ten o'clock. They howled with joy, threw all the rest of the things they had not thrown before, and I shot twice into the room over their heads. As yet I did not want to hurt any of them, but I would have shot the first man who came near me.

There was silence after this and then people came running, nurses, orderlies, patients from the other wards, and the Officer of the Day. He took my gun away from me and told me to consider myself under arrest and go to my barracks. The next day at ten o'clock an orderly told me to come to headquarters and see the Colonel.

Most of the Officers were in his room. I saluted in correct military fashion according to their rank, first the Colonel, then the Major, the Captain after, and lastly two First Lieutenants, each with a click of the heels and a slight bow from the waist, which was both elegant and correct and as I had seen the German Officers do.

The Colonel sat behind a desk; he was the very little man who always made speeches about an irrigation project in some country with malaria which he had been responsible for—I think it was Manila, but we heard this speech so often that I have forgotten just where it was.

He started to say, looking out of the window: "The basic function of a Hospital, Private Bemelmans, is to cure men, not to shoot them."

Then he turned around and laughed, and asked me to tell them how it happened. They laughed loud when I told them and said that after all I had done the right thing, in intention that is; they agreed that discipline is the first requisite of an Army, and when I informed them that either one had to enforce it or leave it alone and let the patients run the hospital, they nodded and laughed some more, and the Colonel said that he thought I would do more good to the service if I were outside the Hospital on the guard, since obviously I was a military man and not suited to ward duty. My gun was on his desk all this time. He gave it back to me and said: "But please don't shoot," and then said that he would take care that I was transferred to the guard.

From then on, he, the Colonel, and all the Officers smile when they see me and it makes me mad.

But apparently there is no room for me on the guard as yet, and Beardsley and I have no particular assignment except to drill with Captain Pedley. He is a fine man, he has a likeness to President Wilson on account of his teeth, and while he is not a military man, he is not altogether so foolish and amateurish as most of the others are when they drill us—particularly the fat Officers who are squeezed into creaky leather puttees, get out of breath, and are unable to get us back into formation once they have given two or three commands. The regular army sergeant has to help them or they dismiss us and make us fall into our "original places." Also they lack that distance which must be in an army, because at rest they talk to the men about all kinds of things, even the movies; and one of them even lay down in the grass with us and picked his teeth while he told us about how he bought a house in Flushing and all the woodwork was painted, and when he had some of it scraped off there was some genuine kind of wood under the paint that is very valuable, and how mad it made him that the former owner was so stupid to cover it up and now he had to have all the wood scraped, it cost a lot of money.

Of course all the men are from colleges or as good as he is, but then they are privates now and he is an Officer. He also spoke to me at that time in German—*"Wie geht es Ihnen?"* he said and a few sentences like that—and he tells us that he has been in Heidelberg and Vienna and that the postgraduate courses in Vienna are a fake, but very fine for drinking and girls. Afterwards we drill again. This seems wrong to me.

None of these Officers can ride, fence, or fight; most of them wear glasses. Only the Colonel is a West Pointer, but he is very old and continually makes speeches, mostly in Oswego, on that irrigation project.

· · ·

We have a Glee Club and there are dances. Beardsley and I do not go out much; but there is one from New York, a very tall man, in fact the tallest of all the men, who takes leaves over the weekend and says he goes to New York. He keeps to himself, has a silver hairbrush, and says he is in Society. He is an architect; but Beardsley, who knows New York and Society, says that he is not in the Register, but that he thinks he has seen him at some parties where everyone can get in.

.   .   .

Beardsley has found a fine way to fool the Officers. At inspection, they look at the bed to see if the linen is clean. We have to wash it ourselves and that is a lot of unpleasant work, so he has told me how one keeps one sheet clean by putting it in paper and carefully away. On Saturday, then, we take the usual sheets and the pillowcase off and we take the clean sheet out of the paper and fold it so that a quarter of it covers the top of the mattress. Then it is turned back, comes up over the blanket as if it were the second sheet, and then the end is tucked in around the pillow and the bed looks snow-white and passes. After inspection the white sheet is carefully folded up again and put back into the locker for next Saturday and the old sheets are used during the week.

.   .   .

We are now on the roster for Kitchen Police and this is a miserable job, particularly as the cook—his name is Lichten—burns the beans to the bottom of two square tin tubs which are as deep as an ashcan. When we have washed them we have to go with head and shoulders to the bottom of these receptacles and with a teaspoon scrape the black crust from the bottom. The water is greasy and not hot and it is a filthy job.

.   .   .

The nurses that came up from New York are not what we thought they would be. The one at the head of them is a crude person with a revolting fat body and the face of a streetcar conductor; she also has a stupid walk and a common voice. She teaches us how to make beds, take temperatures, and change the linen of patients in bed without moving them. All the men detest to be taught this by women and much more so when she does it; they are very clumsy at it and cannot make the neat corners that seem so simple to women. But because they know this, they make us feel silly. There is only one . . . she is young and lithe and has lovely black hair.

On Sunday afternoon they all sit down at the edge of the parade ground and look out over Lake Ontario; from far away they look like gulls at rest in their white dresses. I want to show them that we can do some things that they can't do and also impress the little nurse, and I have arranged to get a horse from the livery stable. Down close to where they sit is a wide ditch and I will ride up, gallop, and jump that ditch. The horse I got is seemingly good enough to do that. I rode along, then let him out when he came to the ditch. He stopped so suddenly that I was thrown over his head, taking the bridle with me; it came off and the horse ran back, jumping over two of the Major's children who were playing in front of Officers' Row. Then he ran down to where our mules eat grass and a quartermaster helped me get him. Next day there is a note on the bulletin board, saying: "Privates will not ride in front of Officers' Row," and it is signed by the Colonel.

Fort
Porter

. . .

I have read on the bulletin board that a Hospital for the Insane will be organized in Buffalo, at Fort Porter. They need attendants there and do not wish to force anyone into this work; men are asked to volunteer for it. I am very much interested in this and only regret that Beardsley will not come along. My transfer is arranged and I leave in a few days.

. . .

The train from Oswego reached Buffalo at six in the morning and I took a streetcar that was filled with very strong-smelling Italian workingmen out to Fort Porter.

The Fort is not a Fort as one might imagine, such for example as Fort Ontario. It has no moat, ramparts, battlements, or any military appearance at all. It is about half an hour's slow streetcar ride outside of the city of Buffalo and is a collection of army buildings, red and a grayish blue. A long house is the most prominent, in which are two large mess halls and kitchens. A smaller group, the non-commissioned Officers' houses, is on the most windy corner of the large ground and faces toward the river, also with an outlook toward the lake. On the corner between these two stands a square building, the Post Hospital.

Workingmen are busy making the houses over into an emer-gency Insane Asylum. The windows are heavily barred, the floors covered with a slippery kind of surface. One large room in the basement of the biggest house is made ready to give treatments in bathtubs that have a continuous in-and-out flow of water that is kept at certain temperatures. With these bathtubs go some kind of canvas covers to tie patients down and in this is the first note of mischief or cruelty.

There is another room down there, a long one with a needle shower at the end that looks like a parrot cage with all the hori-zontal wires taken off. Away from it at the other end is a small marble table, on it a hose which throws a strong current of almost solid water, so tightly compressed is it. It can be shot at the other end, into the cage, as if from a garden hose.

There is cement mixing, carpentering, and hammering all over the place, and people stand around, as on all places where some-thing is being built, and watch and give advice. So far, except for the bathing establishment, it is no more exciting than the build-ing of any kind of a house.

I took a day off and went to look at Niagara Falls. It is perhaps because I took a streetcar out there that I felt they were about half as big as I thought they would be. The thrilling spot is where the water turns down and I made a shade of my hands and looked only on that, shutting out all the scenery. That was a powerful sensation. I am sorry that the Falls are surrounded by what Beardsley calls "Beautiful Dreck." Very interesting was a story that the conductor of the streetcar that took me back told me about the Falls.

A tug belonging to the Shredded Wheat Company, which makes a breakfast food and has a factory nearby, broke its rudder and drifted toward the Falls, helpless. A little way from where the water falls down, the tug got stuck on a rock.

The Police and the Fire Department of Buffalo raced out to help them. This took a long time and the men on the tug looking down could see and hear how the tug slowly moved inch by inch, scraping over the rock, either to be more firmly grounded, or else to go over and down. The Police came in the dark; they tried to shoot safety lines to the tug, but could not reach it. A heavy fog sat on the waters, and not until the sun rose were they able to shoot the line over to the tug. When they managed to get the men off, all of their hair had turned white from horror in this terrible night.

More soldiers are arriving; they know nothing of an Insane Hospital and also nothing of Insanity.

Today, a new group of men have come to us, Nurses, Attendants, and Doctors, and many more soldiers, also a Catholic Chaplain with a studious, earnest face; he is very young.

Many of the men are male nurses from the State Hospitals for the Insane. I observe them carefully—they are all strong, but I expected some sign of their profession on them, just what I do not know—this is, however, not apparent in them. They seem ordinary, normal, healthy people and talk of what anybody else talks of.

One of them, who seems the most important of the group, is a tall Irishman with a shock of flaming red electric hair that stands in a bush, sideway as if the wind were tilting it, or like the comb of a rooster on one side of his head. He has freckles, even on his fingernails, and a way of holding his head as if he were looking over a mass of people and listening into distance up and on one side, to the side where his hair points. He is immaculate; his arms and legs are like oak timbers, so strong they have a curve in them. There is also red hair on his hands, he holds them open at his side; he talks little, eats very fast, walks around the Hospital all day, and speaks a strong dialect, which of course must be Irish. It is an English with which he takes more air than is normally needed to say anything and, while it is loud, he seems to talk in, instead of out, with his breathing. I like him.

We have had several lessons in Anatomy. For this purpose skeletons have been shown, stereopticon pictures of the inside of the body. I attend these lectures with great interest and make drawings of all I see and read; therefore I soon know the names of all the bones, the most important muscles, and understand the body's construction, its contents, the position of the organs; and when I see people walk, or stand up after such a lesson, the solemn wonder of ourselves fills me with a deep respect. I feel that when I see children run, there is much happiness in understanding a small part of this organism. The Doctor who gives these lessons is addressing himself almost completely to me alone, as the others are not very excited about it.

The Insane Asylum is finished and the Irishman is really in

charge. There are Lady Nurses, regular Army nurses of a dreadful caliber, women who look like what we refer to in Germany as *"Canaille."* They are gross and not women at all, particularly not in walk and voice.

Among the instructions we are given is this: never to leave the nurses unprotected or alone in a ward with patients. This seems like one of Beardsley's funny ideas; I am sure they could protect themselves and that no man would do them harm. I have never seen such formidable women, with shoes like those they wear and legs like our barefooted peasants'.

There are more lessons and they are getting closer to the work. Always lock the door behind yourself when entering or leaving a ward. The most important rule is never, never to bring arms, knives, scissors, razor blades, razors, or any other instrument that might be a weapon into the wards. The patients are to be fed with spoons only.

.   .   .

The first patients arrived today. It was late at night, but many people waited outside on the street for the long train of ambulances and cars that came up from the railroad station with the patients and the guards that have been their attendants.

These men, the ill ones, seem stupefied and tired; some are in straitjackets and have a guard each. They are all taken to the basement where the baths are. I am told that they have been transported from Brest and, except for this evening, have not been out of their clothing. I do not know whether this is true, it seems possible. Their clothes are filthy, they have beards, also there is a sickening stench about them and their underclothing is foul.

They are bathed and then assigned to wards.

The Doctors do this. The red Irishman is in the middle of all this. To every ward there is assigned a regular State Asylum trained attendant and a novice soldier. The patients get milk, pajamas and bathrobes, and slippers that give them no foothold on the polished floors, while we have strong shoes with rubber so we can stand our ground when anything happens.

There are rows of solitary cells with what the Irishman calls "the tough customers" in them. They have what we believe to be mad faces, as bad as those that actors, mediocre ones, make when they are in horror plays. From that row comes howling. Some of these men have besides the mental sickenss other vile diseases; it would be best to kill them, says the Irishman, that seems the kindest thing to do.

The night they arrived seemed very crisp with danger and excitement, but nothing happened. They sat on their beds and seemed no different from any other patients; some of them wept and mumbled to themselves.

It is a cruel thing to think, but I was disappointed, as were also all the other new men. We thought they might do some funny things, but the Irishman says to wait, they will, and too much of it, in a little while.

He has a definite, rough, and authoritative way with them; they are absolutely in his charge. He lets them know that by word and gesture and the tone of his voice. His personality seems to have developed out of doing this for years. It is in the way he stands and walks, also in the look in his eyes—they are water-blue and penetrate and are strong.

．　　　．　　　．

The patients have been here for a while now. I have learned to know their faces and many things have happened. They are not funny, but sadder than anything I thought could be and never in the least to laugh at. They are heavy, disturbing cases, mostly locked into their inner selves, their condition to be seen only in their eyes and also when they stand at the barred windows and look out into the trees and the street with free people walking up and down and trying to look in. They pace, and something of their unhappiness and condition jumps over to me. The Irishman says one must never feel sorry for them or understand, or attempt to understand, them and not to talk to them. But the transfer of their misery makes me limp and terribly tired.

The patients have small duties to perform—make beds, sweep, dust, wash windows on the inside. The men in this ward suffer from an illness which makes them periodically dangerous. It can be felt coming on; the unrest and disturbance in their minds gets out of all bounds and beyond their power to control it. They get irritable all at once and refuse to obey, grumble at any instruction given them. Then they have to be watched, and all at once without warning their control breaks, they jump and attack. In rare cases other patients are the object, but mostly the Wardmaster. They seem to go for the men from the back and, since they are soldiers and can fight, it is a great deal of work to overcome them. They are terribly strong once they have a hold, and in this state they cannot feel pain. At the least sign of fighting, the Wardmasters from the other wards come in and help. As many as six men fall on one patient; they choke him and hold him down until the man is blue in the face.

The first time I saw a fight I was unable to do anything but try and stand it. It is degrading and miserable, yet one cannot look away. After the patient is overcome, the men carry him down to the continuous bath, where he is left to soak in water in changing temperatures for, I hear, as much as twenty hours. When they come out, they are without any strength and then there is no trouble for several weeks. I have not heard of patients fighting together. This is strange. In almost all cases the others stand by and look; seldom do they help the nurse.

Those who howl in the solitary cells are left there. When the men go in to feed one of them, they rush in like a football team, almost on signal. One opens the door, the others go after the patient, to bring him food or to clean the place.

There are also two religious cases. One has worn the skin from his knees, sliding on them in continuous prayer. A new case has arrived and been put in with him; I went to see him. I have a passkey and have become careless. I locked the door behind me, but the man I came to visit was around the corner of the room where I could not see him. This Hospital is a makeshift building; in a real Insane Hospital there are no corners around which one cannot see. As I walked forward, he jumped at me from the bed and closed his fingers around my throat.

I felt singing in my ears, not much pain. I could not breathe, I saw the religious patient for a while and he swam away into a darkness that was bluish. I felt a bang on my head and nothing more until I came to in another room of the Hospital. It had to be kept quiet because I had no right to go in there. The fortunate thing was that I fell against the door with the patient, and the loud bang brought the Irishman.

At first the attacks on the patients and the way they were choked into a corner made me hate the Irishman and all the other attendants. But even before the attack on me I already knew it was the only thing that could be done there and then. They are as kind as they can be, but they would be dead if they did not instill fear, and of course they fight only when they absolutely must. Also when the patients get out of the baths, the attendants are as nice to them as they are to anyone.

In this ward are also other interesting cases. There is a glass man. A mattress has to be kept on the floor next to his bed, because he is afraid of falling out and breaking. He moves everywhere with care, he screams when anyone comes too near him and sits down with great apprehension. And there are two men who are like puppets. In the morning they have to be sat up in bed, and they sit motionless. They have to be stood up, and if one were to take their arms in the morning and raise them over their heads, the arms would still be that way at night. Another patient repeats one word, the sound of which he likes, endlessly, over and over in monotone.

The most pitiful of all the men are several cases who suffer from persecution fear. They stuff magazines into their bathrobes and sit in corners; they are certain we wish to kill them, stab or shoot at them. They have to be forcefully fed because they think that all food given them is poison. Or we have to eat a little of it ourselves in front of them or give them the trays of other patients who have already started eating. If they still refuse to eat, we sometimes just leave the food. They do not look at it, or curse and upset it, or smear it on themselves, but when we go out—in most cases it happens the moment we are gone—they ravenously eat everything.

They never sleep; at times they doze off in the middle of the night, but only to rise with horrible shrieks from their beds, and in the night these wards are most unhappy. God have pity on these men or let them die.

Of no use at all is religion or the young Chaplain; he feels that, I think, because he is unhappy himself. It made him mad that one woman who visited her husband here seems to be worried only whether he went to confession before he got insane. Yet I think, with its great promise of miracle and power and its character of mysterium, the Catholic religion would be the one most easy to help these patients; the transfer from their own make-believe horror to the church would be easier. I cannot explain this right, but this religion and their illness have something in common, like the texture of two tapestries, while other religions are not so, they are like linen or paint compared to it.

·   ·   ·

There is one man here who is continually searching for something in the toilet bowl, in a corner of his ward. He has his arm so deep in it that at times we can hardly get it out. He says his friend is down there. Also he talks through the barred window, never-ending poetry without rhyme and yet with a meter. His voice falls and rises with it and sometimes he yells the words. One poem I have remembered:

> The Cigarette Trees bloom over the clouds
> And Mainstreet looks like a melon,
> I am going to paint the battleships with Sarsaparilla,
> Do not forget me, the sun will melt this house.

He helps the Wardmaster in his ward, whenever one of the other patients gets out of hand. They are all violent cases and in this ward are only regular State Asylum men and the strongest. He is very strong, was a sergeant and killed an Officer in Europe. The attendants have allowed him to help in a pinch when they were hard up with two men fighting them, but the Irishman has warned them not to take help from the man with the toilet bowl, to watch that one.

·   ·   ·

The days are very short; the light changes early and at that hour the patients are depressed more than at any other time of the day; then also most of the fighting goes on and all of them walk around.

In this early evening I look out of the window and always wait for a certain little boy. He runs along home under the trees to a house at the end of the road, and in his thin legs and the little pants, fluttering in the wind, that hang down over them is the misery of all the world.

·   ·   ·

One afternoon, as I walked across the parade ground, someone shouted my name loudly and right in back of my left shoulder.

I turned and there was no one there, all around the mile-wide field.

I stood motionless and with loud heartbeat; there was a bitter taste in my mouth and my hands felt loose; so did my arms and my whole body, then hot and cold and wet, and tears came to my eyes.

Then I walked to my quarters and there again I heard my name called by the same voice, as distinct, and again in back of my left shoulder. I turned instantly—there was no one there again.

The barracks in which I live have a hall and a wide straight stairway leading up. This stairway started to turn itself around me in a yellow light. I fell.

Luckily no one saw this; I came to my consciousness again and slowly walked up and lay down on my bed.

In the last month two men in this room have jumped up in the night and become patients. I see them every day in the mess hall; I think they will not come out again.

For two hours I lay straight on my bed and looked at the ceiling. I thought of going to a doctor in Buffalo, but he might only give me away; besides all the psychiatrists are from Buffalo and work here. I would most probably run into one of our own men.

Also would I hold out as far as Buffalo? Now that the mind is loose from its moorings, I think it best to end my life rather than go into the wards. I have formed this plan; if only I can carry it through and hold on that long, because I am afraid to even move.

I know where the Guardhouse is, I know where the guns are. I will walk down the stairs, straight out the door, across the lawn and into the Guardhouse. There are men there, but I will manage to be plain so they will notice nothing, go into the lavatory with a gun that I will take from a holster, and then shoot up into my brain through the roof of the mouth.

I get up and start to walk down the stairs and out of my quarters with my mind fixed on this Must of death and afraid that a second of thinking, of reasoning, of hope, might mean weakness and change of mind.

I go out of the Barracks and fall over a cat and the cat does not run and everybody laughs loud.

An order had been issued the day before to get rid of all the cats, of which we have a plague. Two soldiers collected them all over the Fort and brought them back in their arms, then dropped them into an ashcan that is outside our Barracks. When they thought they had all the cats in there, they went to the Hospital and got four cans of ether and poured them in over the animals, then clamped the lid down, put a stone on it, and left. Some cat friend who did not like this came and took the stone off, upset the barrel, and the cats came out and regained consciousness.

They are wandering around in a stupor, lean against the ashcan, and look cross-eyed. Their motions are so funny, at times like half wound up toys, at others, particularly the black cats, who are wet with sweat and ether, they look like caricatures of cursed souls. None of them can stand up; it is so strange and funny, everyone laughs; so must I, and it seems so silly and useless to think that one might want to die.

Night
on Guard

· · ·

The Flu Epidemic has cost many lives and it is to keep the men that work here well that we are changed from one duty to another.

Yesterday the red-headed Irishman and I were working in the Post Hospital carrying the dead men down to the cellar on stretchers. We wear long white nurse's gowns and a cap, also a pad over mouth and nose and look like ghosts. The cellar stairs turn and are very steep.

The Irishman was in front of me, walking ahead down, when the dead man slipped and his feet went into the Irishman's back. He said: "Sit down or I knock you down!" This kept me from screaming or dropping the body.

Down in the cellar is a room and in this we have brought the corpses. The Irishman takes the feet when we lift them off, I take them by the hair as I do not wish to touch their faces or neck, which is stupid of me, but the hair is better, it is not so dead. The post undertaker now has a lot of work, he has the assistance of several undertakers from Buffalo. I wonder if he has a girl.

· · ·

There are not enough men to mount guard, the posts are reduced, and although I am a Corporal I must stand guard.

The third night I am down in the cellar again, now as a night guard. The dead must be watched, there is a regulation to this effect, they cannot be left alone.

The cellar is dark and lit by a loose gas flame, this flame is on the outside of the room where the dead are. They lie in rows and no one has had time to close their eyes. In the white of these eyes dances the reflection of the gas light. I sit as close to the wall as I can squeeze myself and I am terribly afraid, so afraid that I have taken my gun out of its holster and point it at the dead men. The safety catch is off and it makes me feel safe. If anyone of them will move, I'm afraid I'll kill him; I don't see why they cannot be left alone, or locked up overnight, or why there aren't at least two of us.

· · ·

The Epidemic is much better and almost over; now I have an altogether new duty. I am stationed at the Guardhouse and I see that the men who have been on leave report for inspection before turning in. They come in at all hours of the night. Some of them have late passes, which I have to collect as well.

After all the soldiers are inspected and have gone to bed, when everybody except a few men out on posts are asleep, I have time to myself.

After the reports are in order, I read, mostly Voltaire, Goethe, a little book of Schiller's poems, and on Napoleon.

Later I go out; the air is so cold that it bites inside the nose, and when I come back I am much thinner.

It is also difficult to walk because the roads are icy, and at times I must quickly slide to a tree, or the wind would take me along across the frozen parade ground.

The clouds race past the moon; there are more stars than I have ever seen in America. In the metallic light, the roofs of the Hospital buildings seem to float in the air in one flat green-silver row of tilted panels; under them the Hospital is quiet most of the time. At times there is a scream from the bad section and then the figure of a nurse passes the lit windowpane, but that happens not very often.

Around the Fort is water, lit as the roofs are, and in this scene is a dangerous ecstasy, an elation which begins as the fear does. It swells up in back of me, high and wide, and as if I were standing in front of an orchestra with rows of instruments wildly playing.

In this excitement many doors open to walk out of the house of reason. The mind becomes acutely clear. This goes through the body, as if the brain, the fingertips, all surfaces, were sandpapered and the nerves laid bare to every senation. The mind was a little cup and now it is as big as a tub. This happens every night. First of all I feel years older, and whatever I think seems crystal clear. Also I seem able to do anything.

I have had this feeling mildly before, when coming out of a motion picture in which the acrobatic hero has swung himself on a curtain up the side of a tower and jumped on horseback across the parapets. For half an hour afterward, I have felt like doing the most difficult things in play, to jump, to take hold of anything and swing myself up to the next electric sign on Broadway, to successfully punch anybody in the nose that seemed not worth liking.

.   .   .

The highest joy, and it is always a boundless happiness, is when the sun rises. It remains resting on the horizon for a long while and then frees itself, floats freely. I feel then a sense of the miraculous logic and divine bookkeeping that makes all things in this world a day older—myself, my mother, the sawmill, the patients, the dead grass under the snow, the trees—and for all these things wells up a rich affection, so that I must put my arms around a tree and feel its being. I also feel the sun, where it has been, with unbelievable detail—the shadows it has thrown past the church in Klobenstein, on the Christuses, on Uncle Joseph who is out with his dog, on the ventilators of the ships on the ocean, and here now on the snow past this tree.

Shortly before the sunrise there is a blue light all over, somewhat like in a theater, where they change the light from night to morning too fast. Unreal, humid and inky, and spattered with yellow street lamps; when you squint your eyes, the street lights rain gold over the scene. In this light a milk wagon horse clops up the street and a man who has to go to work early comes out of a house always in the same fashion; he yawns, closes his collar, and lets a small dog out after him. He walks down the steps and sees me and lifts his hand in greeting, and then, and always in this same order, bends down to speak to his dog. The ill-formed, unkempt, many-kinds-of-dog makes a creaky sound, scrapes and scratches, and is beside himself with gratitude. He shows this with all his might, wiggling so that one moment his head looks at his tail on the right side of his body and then on the left. It is his daily morning prayer to his master and for himself to show how glad he is to be alive and how grateful to be a dog.

Then the sun rises, it places light on ice-covered branches and on a young oak leaf that has stuck through wind and winter. It is curled like the webbed claw of a bird and becomes liquid and gilded.

Then the prisoners arrive; they go from the Guardhouse to the mess hall to get food. They are dressed in the wonderful fatigue suit, blue with the lovely large Prison "P" handpainted on its back, and they have the foolish fatigue hat—fatigue is so right for this. They also show their prisonness in their walk. Behind them goes the guard; they all hurry to get into the warm kitchen, to warm their hands. I always follow them and love their walk, their faces, their words. Hat, coat, tray, all speak. They say: "We are prisoners, not bad fellows. We only drunk too much, or fought, and it's nice in the jail, but hurry up, kitchen, so we can get a little coffee and sit by the oven." The guard is much less eloquent.

In the kitchen they look around to swipe something from the cook. They get an extra cup of coffee here. The cook is the thin low-class Englishman, with the lovely London dialect. He is simple-minded, and in all simple people is a securing, restful quality. When he looks in a pot, I can read on his face whether it is clean or dirty inside.

There are some specialists, who have a right, or just a claim of their own invention, to a cup of coffee here early. Their faces appear on the side of the door, and they look at the cook, to find out whether he is in the right mood, if he will give it to them.

In all this, the appearance of the horse, the little dog, the prisoners, and the cook, is wonder without end. In them also are the strongest weapons against illness of the mind, against even just a low mood. There is an ever present quiet humor; one must only sit and listen carefully and look for it, but of course I think one must have been very ill to be so grateful. I am no longer afraid. After breakfast I go over to the Guardhouse to sleep. If the danger comes, it is now controlled. Physically it is the same—quickly changing temperature, fast pulse and respiration, cold sweat and bitter running of water down the inside of the cheeks—but mentally it is much better. It is now about the same sensation I have when looking into a shop window of artificial limbs, or when seeing an ugly child weep somewhere alone.

The Mess
in Order

. . .

I have been given the management of the Mess, that is, under
Lieutenant Doyle. I have no worry with buying food or supplies,
that is the business of the Quartermaster Sergeant. We feed many
patients and soldiers, all together almost two thousand people.
The patients' Mess hall is separated and in another building. The
Mess hall for the men is here close to the kitchen.

The cooks are good men, One of them is English and thin; he
speaks a wonderful Cockney dialect, and says he has to make
himself a "heggnogg." We have lots of cockroaches; they crawl to
the ceiling, so at night the windows and doors are left open and
they freeze to death and are swept out in the morning, but there
are new ones the next day; also again those many cats everywhere.

In other posts there are periodic assignments of all men to
Kitchen Police, but here, because of the nature of this house, we
have a steady crew, men who cannot be used for better work, and
they are difficult.

These men are all friends; they come from the Brooklyn waterfront, were drafted. The worst one is Mulvey.

Mulvey sings all day, so that his song—it is the same one—has
become part of the kitchen, like the cooks and the oven. We can-

not drive it out. It is a dreary piece and he draws it out, singing
mostly into the dishwater. The words go:

> Take me over the Sea—
> That's where I want to be—
> Oh, my, I don't want to die,
> Take me over the Sea.

There is also something about "I want to go home" in it.

His friends join him in that line while they are busy with their
dishes. These come in endless stacks all day long, after breakfast,
luncheon, and dinner.

They love to insult each other in play and call themselves by
the vilest names, all in fun; and at times, while the water is running into the tub or they are waiting for the towels to dry, they
box without touching each other, dancing on their toes and, at

the most, disarranging their opponent's hair. In their free hours they are visited by girls that are as terrible as they themselves are—ragged women, young enough, but with thick ankles, in shoes with blunt toes and sideways heels, with pimply faces, wide hips, and fat lips. With them they sit on a row of benches facing the river. But they are always together and behave toward the rest of us with great condescension, as if they belonged to an exquisite club that is very hard to get into. So far as I have seen, all they do out there with the girls is sing again this song, sit on the benches where they insult each other, and shout the same insults of short words after anyone who passes. Their girls sit with knees far apart and love to be pushed and mauled; they scream with happiness.

The ideas of morality that people have seem so confusing. The men here are all so lonesome; the kitchen gang knows nothing else but to box and this business of which they constantly talk by one word. And after all it is only the itch that is in their bodies which marches in front of the command to have more people on earth, and of course they don't want any children, but it itches them just as hard. But these thoughts always confuse me, and I think of women, of girls I have seen at dances and swimming, and most I think of the muscles that run down to the knees on the inside of their upper leg; they are I think the most exciting part, much more so than any other part of their bodies, in young girls most certainly, in women they become flabby, and of porous texture.

·   ·   ·

When the kitchen gang are through washing the dishes, they have to set the tables in the mess hall. After meals, the three-legged stools on which the men sit are turned upside down and placed on top of the tables so that the floor can be mopped. These stools are taken down; then one man runs through the lanes between the tables and places the plates from a pile on his arm. He does this fast from much practice. The plates dance awhile and then settle down. The next one runs around with forks, another with spoons, knives, and another with tin cups. One can hear with little experience what they are doing without being in the room. There are, of course, no napkins.

For some time there have been complaints that the dishes are greasy. They do not wash them well enough, the same with knives and forks and the cups. The Officer in charge took a clean towel, slipped the end of it between the prongs of a fork, and showed me how dirty it became. He streaked a plate with his glove and, tilting it in the light, the path of his finger could be seen across the plate—it was fatty.

It told this to Mulvey, out in the kitchen. He turned from his tub and looked at me with small eyes; he has a way of making them look perfidious. Also, when he is told something, he assumes a position of great ease, leaning on the edge of the dishwashing tub and crossing his legs, his body as in a hammock, leaning toward me. With his free hand he scratches himself. This performance is chiefly for his friends, who stand around him and have great admiration for such a show of indifference.

After I have told him all this, he has to turn around and go on with his work, and he does it very slowly, looking into the faces of all his friends, taking a deep breath, and he says as if he were very tired: "Oh—well." He spits in the dishwater and continues to wash the dishes in it.

I am sorry I cannot box, but I will not allow him to get away with this. The next day is Saturday and there is a football game; they love football games; their terrible girls always come for them and hang around the front of the mess hall. They hurry on that day and don't sing, and I will teach them a lesson. Before they can go off duty, they must ask me for permission.

The best part of this Saturday afternoon is that, when they have almost finished the dishes and started to set the tables, the top Sergeant, the Polish one, comes in late and eats in the kitchen. They are afraid of him; he has a voice like a bear, can beat them up one and all together, and on top of it lock them in the Guardhouse until their bones ache.

I walked into the dining room after the tables were all set, and one of them came to ask if they could go. Mulvey was already out of the door. Of course they could go if everything was done, but everything was not done, not right. I showed them the dirty forks, and the greasy plates. Mulvey was called back. I made them take all the dishes and cups, the forks, spoons, and knives back, to wash them over again. They still thought they could make the game.

Mulvey used steaming water and raced around the room to help them. The plates danced down again, the top Sergeant nodded to me, the men were mumbling curses, audible enough for me to understand that they were not insulting each other. When they were finished they asked again to go.

I pointed at the tables and stools. "What is this?" I said. "Look at it, what a disorder! And the plates and the forks!"

Mulvey was sent to get a long string and two pieces of wood. The top Sergeant leaned against the door of the dining room and grinned, with his hands in his pockets.

The string came, and with a pencil I divided the first and last table in each row of tables in as many places as there were men sitting at them. Then we put the first and last tables in correct position, laid the string over the row of ten tables on each side, and first of all pushed the tables so that they were absolutely straight. The Polish Sergeant helped by bending to the edge of the first table and closing one eye, like looking down the line of stomachs of soldiers. He gave a signal with his hand for each table until they were quite in line.

Then with the string we aligned all the stools, the plates and cups of each man, also straightened out the knives and forks.

When this was done, I told them now they could go and from now on we would do it like this at every meal. By that time it was time for supper. But they ran out to their girls who had waited.

After supper they again hurried and set the tables. I felt sorry for them.

·   ·   ·

I went up to my quarters to get the leather leggings to go out. We can wear spiral puttees, if we buy them, but not leather leggings. We should, however, according to regulations, wear the canvas leggings which are furnished by the service.

Uniforms we can also have our own; I had one made in Buffalo. There is only the terrible campaign hat; no one is allowed to wear a cap or hat like the Officers have, but I have bought myself a Stetson campaign hat which at least holds its shape and has a somewhat better color. Besides it does not turn up at the corners like a cooked mushroom.

My leather leggings, which are forbidden, I have in a bag and, carrying it under my arm, I leave the Fort. Next to the Fort is a park, and there is a bush where I sit down and change the canvas for the leather leggings, and hide the canvas ones until I get back. I have also spurs in my pocket. When this is done, I wait for

Doris's big car. It is a Pierce Arrow with the front seats apart so one can walk between them from the back seat and sit with the driver. Doris is a beautiful girl I met at a dance held by the Presbyterian Church. Her parents are German and very hospitable.

As I sat down under the bush, a blanket fell on me, and then I was hit on the head by a plank. It was from the kitchen gang. They kicked and trampled with boots and clubs until I was insensible. I woke up in the Hospital and could not see out of my eyes; my head swam and all my limbs hurt.

I sent for the Polish Sergeant and asked him to have the kitchen gang arrested. He gave me a chocolate bar and said No, he would not do that, because I had it coming to me. "It will do you good," he said, "this is America."

Leave
of Absence

.   .   .

Everybody can have a leave of absence in the American Army, if he asks for it. Some men don't ask and just go away, which in wartime is desertion in any other Army and punishable by death.

Here it is different. If he is gone, they wait if he will not come back himself within the short while of a few weeks; if he comes back himself, little happens to him, at the most a few days in the Guardhouse or he is docked his pay or demoted if he has any rank; after six more weeks he is officially absent without leave, then when he comes back himself he still is not severely punished, but he is court-martialed and goes to the Guardhouse for several weeks; only after a long while, I think it is six months, does he become an official deserter, and they start looking for him.

We are given frequent leaves of absence because of the nature of the Hospital. I have saved up my allowance to be able to go to New York. Why I want to go there I don't know, except that, since I landed there and lived in that city first, I have been thinking of it as my home in America, and I think it is the idea of going home, which everybody else speaks of so much, that I feel I need. Besides, I get transportation if I take a patient along, and I have also some money. We are well paid and cannot spend any money, at least not much, because we are always invited. There are very few soldiers in Buffalo and many patriotic ladies who need them for their entertainments.

The house in which I lived in New York belongs to a lovely old lady, German, with a daughter who is very young and pretty. Her name is Ada Bach. The house is on Bolton Road in Inwood-on-Hudson, near the Botanical Gardens and a park. It is reached with the subway and a streetcar; it is old and roomy and peculiar; it was the mansion in an estate. Trees stand around it, and in front is a lawn out of which stick a few rocks. There is a hill to the right, no other houses around, and a vegetable garden in back. I lived here chiefly because I could take my dog for runs in the country and because it was quiet.

Ada sometimes writes to me; I have been thinking much of that house and my room and of Ada, and lately I have thought and pictured how I will try and see if I can make love to her.

The nightly talk of the soldiers in their beds made me of the opinion that the way Mulvey and the kitchen gang do it is the best way, that is, without much ceremony, a few words and gestures, but complete indifference and confidence, as if it were accomplished before one starts. I know the formula by heart, it is simple and does not ask for much effort or imagination. It either works or one knows soon that it doesn't.

After I delivered my patient in New York, I took the subway home, and near the park I had to change to the streetcar. This streetcar passes a riding academy, and I got off to hire a horse to start things right. It is a short ride, and Ada was home, and I managed to ride in and be very much admired. I tied the horse to a tree and we had dinner. Mrs. Bach had cooked something very fine, Ada had on a lovely dress and kissed me, and so far it was very successful. Only during dinner Mrs. Bach asked whether I rode the horse all the way from Buffalo.

Afterwards I had to take the horse back, and it was soon evening. Many relatives came and nothing happened, except that I thought everything would be all right by my first of all being very certain of success. There was one difficulty—Mrs. Bach and Ada sleep in the same bed and in the same room—so I had to think of something different.

The next morning is Saturday, and Ada asks me to go to the

City with her. We ride in the subway, arm in arm, and everybody smiles stupidly at us. We ride very far downtown. She wants me to see her Office and her boss.

This man is a lawyer by the name of Mirror, and he says we must come to dinner at his house that evening.

In the Office I am introduced to another girl and a young man. Ada sits down at the typewriter and writes, and smiles at me to show me how well she can write without looking at the machine, and also chews gum at the same time. The other girl is allowed to see all this and I get a chair. Ada can go early and Mr. Mirror calls up his house and tells his wife that we, Ada and I, are coming with him to dinner that evening.

•   •   •

The house in which he lives is on East 193rd Street; it is called Oxford Hall. Towards the street it has a very imposing façade; around it, two feet away from the building on the sidewalk and sunk into thick concrete posts, are swollen brass pipes. A court opens into the building from the street; in its center is a cement fountain, and left and right of the door are two cement lines.

In an outer hall are rows and rows of names, and the one we look for is written out: "Stanley B. Mirror, Counselor at Law."

The upper part of the foyer is decorated as if someone had smeared an unthinkable material with his five fingers on the wall; up to the chest it is of white marble. In the middle stands a gold painted elevator shaft. A boy in uniform with "Oxford Hall" written on him is inside of it when the elevator comes down.

He takes us up and there is a long corridor. All the way up in all these corridors I see baby carriages; there are four on this, the top floor.

I would like to run away because I am certain I don't like this, but it is too late. At the door is a card, again with "Stanley B. Mirror, Counselor at Law," written on it. The door opens and we step into a long narrow hall at the end of which is the dining room.

The furniture in this room is of a period called Mission; it is so big and the room so very little that we all sit glued to the table. Mr. Mirror is a little man, the table is high, the sideboard is close behind him, and the grapefruit on the table is almost in his nose. His face has no more identity than the grapefruit. It is decorated with thickly rimmed glasses and a small mustache, but that only makes it more like all such faces that I have seen everywhere in New York.

They are good people and it is unkind to not be grateful and polite to them, but I feel a strong repulsion in me, against all this, the house, the furniture, Mr. Mirror, and I would like to get up and tell them that I do not like it and go away. But this is of course impossible.

Mrs. Mirror also has glasses, thin ones with a little chain; she is a woman who is not a mother, not a girl, not a mistress or wife type. She is ordinary, unlovely, and only female in an unhappy sense. Her flesh is white, bloated, and porous; she must be hideous in the bath; her voice is metallic and too big for the room, and her hands are common.

The conversation is mostly of Mr. Mirror's making; he had an argument with the superintendent of the building in the morning, and while he eats he tells how he told that man to see that there was enough hot water or some such business, also about a radiator. He insists on being heard. He says over and over again: "Listen to me, listen to me," at any time when everybody's attention is not his. If that doesn't help, he takes hold of his wife's arm or my sleeve and pulls. He starts every sentence like this, three times mostly: "Then I said to him, then I said to him, listen to me, then I said to him, you know what I told him?"

At one time I turned around to look out of the window, which was behind my chair. Outside was a suicidal picture, millions of bricks, run this way and that and up and down, and they became narrow lines far below; they ended on a metal roof with a skylight; rows of windows were along the shaft. When I looked back in the room he still went on: "He always gives me an argument, that guy." For the rest the conversation here is as if it were written on building blocks that are thrown from one person to another; nothing is ever said.

Ada seems to be at home here; she can join in and say the things to which they answer easily and in which they are versed and secure. Sitting next to me, she eats with one hand. so must I because she has my hand in hers, except when she cuts a piece of chicken. Whenever anything comes to the table she says: "Oh, it's so delicious." In saying this she pauses at the letter L, leaving her tongue against the upper teeth for a moment too long. It sounds:

"Dee–llicious." She does the same with "Beautifu–ll" and to the ice cream she said:

"Oh, I think it's the most dee–llicious thing I ever put in my mouth."

But that is not all; they wish to come tomorrow and visit Mrs. Bach's house. Ada says they will be delighted, and I can't very well say otherwise. Mr. Mirror will bring his camera and take pictures of us, and afterwards we will go to the Botanical Gardens and after that to a movie on 168th Street.

Ada says once more that everything was "so dee–llicious." We leave the house and I am glad of the fresh air after we get out of the golden elevator.

We took a taxi. It was not far from home, and since I no longer wanted it, I could have my way on this first evening. Just to try out their value, I used one of Mulvey's phrases and gestures; she seemed to know it, followed in words and motion, and seemed willing to comply.

But all desire was gone.

The typewriter which she can work without looking at it, Oxford Hall, and Mrs. Mirror have done it. Now there is a relaxed dumbness in her face. She is a sweet-smelling animal without will. The lower lip hangs loose, the line of her neck is clumsy, the ankles are too thick, but my dislike fastens itself chiefly on the "Dee–llicious."

I try to think of Mulvey's terrible girls—they are so much worse than Ada—but that is better, they are at least strong—and I also say to myself: Why be so very choosing, after all it is not a pleasure of the mind. But it is.

Bayonet
School

. . .

The Army needs Officers very badly, and a general order has been issued from Washington to the effect that each post can send one out of a given number of enlisted men to Officers' Training Camp. A board of Officers here gave me a very kind examination; I also passed the physical test, and then I received transportation and orders to report to the command at the Officers' Training School at Camp Gordon, which is near Atlanta, Georgia.

Here blows a different wind. The day is cut up into minutes, and from the early morning to the hour of retreat almost every step is counted. It is almost German. In a short period they must make Officers out of civilians and get as much West Point training into them as possible.

To every eight men a young Officer is assigned. He is like a governess, but a strict one. He has a little book with the names of his men in it—we are called candidates—and he watches us all day. These men, who are Second Lieutenants, are somewhat arrogant, and the only consolation is that in a short while we can hand it on to the next group.

Demerits are called "skins." A button undone, a book on the shelf over the bed out of alignment, a shoe under the bed not laced up (even without the foot in it), or looking down when marching at attention to the faraway drill grounds—any of these things means a skin. Sixty of them is the limit during the training. One more, and the Benzine Board, as they call the Faculty, takes prompt action and throws the candidate back into a Sergeant's Uniform.

I get by and go to the Bayonet School; a berth here is very much envied because we can wear spurs, although we have no horses. Not much happens that is funny, because the work is very exacting, leaving no time for jokes. I have gained weight, feel wonderful, and my only sorrow is that when I drill the men, they sometimes have to laugh. I can shout: "At hease!" so it flies across a whole battalion clear and right. We have practiced this in the woods, shouting commands for days, but I have great trouble in other words; "Attention!" is all right, but "Forward march!" is bad.

Our Major is a compact man; he has hardly a neck and is very energetic. They say he was a ribbon salesman before the war; he doesn't know much about soldiering except that he has enduring drive, and he thinks that to ride a horse well means to ride fast. I see him always galloping. He gives frequent pep speeches, and they have introduced a system of making men mad that is childish. Every candidate has to accompany the execution of a command with a grunt, ugh—"port arms, ugh" "at hease, ugh!" I think it does nothing to improve drilling.

This ribbon salesman Major has another wrong idea. In the evening when we march the men back from the bayonet field, he sits on his horse, takes the salute, and as the companies pass, praises those who have the most broken bayonets. It is to him an indication of good work.

But bayonets are easily broken; I have shown my men how. When charging the dummy, just press the butt to the side; the leverage will snap the bayonet right off in the center. I could march home without a single blade intact, but I don't carry it that far.

The Major is nice and when not in the saddle or on the drill grounds one can talk to him. I have observed how easy it is for men in the service here to acquire the spirit of the military. The young men from colleges absorb it quickly. There is a Captain here who is very young and out of Georgia Tech for a short while; he is every bit as arrogant as a German Lieutenant, bearing, voice, vanity, and all.

The Major addressed the Bayonet School; he said with his face purple: "When you see a German, you are looking at the worst so-and-so that God has created," and he spoke long and bitterly that way. Afterwards he turned to me and out of the side of his mouth said: "You know, I have to do this. This is a war."

He did another surprising thing. We have long latrines with many seats in a row, and there is in our barracks a young man who, because he has an uncle who is a Senator, manages to get leave to go to Atlanta when no one else can go or will, because there is so much to study. In consequence of this leave, he was behind in his work, and of course the Benzine Board would have flunked him even with the Senator uncle behind him; they do not fool. Well, this candidate went to the latrine and sat there with his drill regulations in one hand and the gun in the other, which he polished at the same time while studying in the book.

The Major passed by and shouted at him: "Hold it, hold it, stay there!" and then he ran out, and we who were outside had to come in. "Look at him, you guys," shouted the Major, "ten percent intelligence and ninety percent ambition is all you need in this man's army. Here's an example!" From then on he was the Major's pet.

In the evenings there are social functions of a very disappointing kind. The songs that are sung are below anything I have ever heard sung. One is so embarrassing that in the beginning the men only sang it with half voices; now they blare it out because they no longer think about the words. It goes:

·　　·　　·

I want the Bars, just like the Bars that my Lieutenant wears;
They are the Bars, the only Bars, and so on. . . .

It refers to getting a commission as a Second Lieutenant, who wears little gold bars on his shoulders.

We eat many chocolate bars, and at noon drink a colored liquid called Coca-Cola. In the beginning I hated this drink, but it was the only thing at the stand and I was very thirsty from the sun and the exertion of bayonet drilling. Now it must be drunken, I long for it, and afterwards sit down in a very fine restful ease.

The food is good, the barracks crude but airy.

The landscape is not remarkable, but the climate is. In the

morning when we march out, it is so cold that the men's fingers get numb, and at the halt some drop their guns because of this; at noon it is oppressively hot.

There are Negro labor battalions here, and I have much pleasure watching the colored men that are on guard. They creep along with bent knees as if held up by invisible strings, and they have found out how to carry their guns so that they float without effort over the shoulder. The gun lies on its side, the balance is worked out so that a little more weight is in back than in front and thus the butt holds up the hand. This hand is long, and the last joints of the fingers are pasted to the end of the gun. their eyes are open but asleep; I am always afraid they will fall or walk into a tree; and the most wonderful performance is when they change the gun from one shoulder to the other. They hate to do this and go through the right motions but like in a dream. I am so fond of Negroes because I have never seen one until I came to America and they are therefore rare and interesting.

.   .   .

Since the latrine incident, they call the ribbon salesman Major "Ninety Percent." For some time now, I have observed on his side a feeling of suspicion towards me. At times he stands with other Officers; they speak together and then look at me. Most of them laugh and walk away. I am going to get mad about this laughing one day and tell them a few frank opinions.

The Senator's nephew has asked two of us to come along to a party. They say since the Army is here all the good families have left Atlanta, but a few without daughters have remained and we are to go to a house for a party.

We have not been drinking anything except this Coca-Cola for a long time, no beer, no wine, but at this house are these drinks, also whisky. I drink a glass and it shakes me like a wet dog. But the other two are drinking it; they are more at home with this strong beverage. Spalding, who has been with me mostly on the bayonet field, is soon wobbly, and he says to me: "You're my pal."

But later on he comes again, and says: "You're my pal, but I'm not your pal! Oh, no—I'm not your pal!" and also: "You're going with me, but I'm not going with you."

And again, when I ask him why, he says: "You're my pal, but

I'm not your pal!" and finally he takes his glass, and bangs it on the table, breaks it, and says: "Because you're a German spy."

The Senator's nephew, who can drink more, because he is always going out, told him to shut up.

We went home and I heard for the first time that there was a rumor that I was a spy, but that everybody laughed at that.

I was very angry and went to the Major and told him that, after all, the Germans weren't that stupid. He was sorry and everything seems all right again.

The Hotel Years,
1919–1929

· · · · · ·

If You're
Not a Fool

.   .   .

The war was over. I left the army at Camp Gordon and came to New York. I was on my way to Munich, to study art; I had already bought my steamer ticket.

Then I ran into Mr. Sigsag, and he persuaded me to come out to the shipyard with him, to look over a boat he had just bought. It was a small yacht, with a powerful motor and a little galley. We climbed aboard, sat on the deck, and were soon again discussing my career, just as we had on the old *Wahabee*.

"If you're not a fool," Mr. Sigsag said, "you'll come in with us. Never mind art. A few years of work and then you can study, go to Paris, Rome, and be independent." He painted a picture of the Good Life to be found in hotels, just like Uncle Wallner's picture years ago in Regensburg; and, like Uncle Hans, he also talked about art as if it were an affliction.

He explained how he had come by his new and different position as assistant to the manager of the banquet department of the Splendide. The manager, Joachim von Kyling, had watched Sigsag in the Grill and had asked for him; it was just what the Sage of East Aurora had always said would be the reward of Loyalty, Application, and Hard Work. Mr. Sigsag had been there a year now

and was eager to share his luck with me. "It's a gold mine," he said. "If you're not a fool, you'll come in with us."

After I had received my discharge from the Army, I was determined that I would never be a waiter again.

"That's all right," said Sigsag, "you won't be."

"Do I have to wear tails?"

"No, only at coming out parties. Otherwise you can wear a morning coat during the day, and a dinner jacket in the evening. Let's go to a good tailor right away."

"But my ticket to Europe?"

"You can use it to take a vacation in the summer. Come on. . . . Oh, and we'll have to change your name; Bemelmans is as bad as Slezack. I am Monsieur Wladimir now, and you'll be Monsieur Louis, my associate Monsieur Louis."

And so I became Mr. Sigsag's "associate" in the banquet department of the Hotel Splendide.

The most difficult part of the hotel business is the proper management of its banquet department. A restaurant is a song compared with it. A restaurant is unchanging, its chairs and tables stay in place, its function is to serve two or three meals a day, to a clientele that varies in numbers only little—with the days of the week, with rain and sunshine, summer and winter. The guests do not expect the impossible; they make allowances, and it is easy to adjust complaints.

But a banquet department is an ever-changing business. There are state dinners, weddings, concerts, anniversaries, coming out parties, receptions—every kind of large and small celebration of an important day or event, and the givers of such parties invest much money in them. They have looked forward to the day of it, sometimes for years; they will remember it for the rest of their lives; look at photographs, old menus, programs of it; talk, write, and think of it. It is therefore very important that absolutely nothing goes wrong. If the last and least important guest is offended by an employee, thinks he is being neglected, or finds a piece of china or a splinter of bone in his soup, then the entire party is ruined. The host will forget all that has been good about it and mention only the bad.

Yet there are a thousand things to go wrong. Rooms have to be thrown together into suites and their arrangements set up and taken down with the speed of a circus performance. Employees have to be engaged in changing formations and numbers; one must know their abilities, their faults, their trustworthiness. Silver, linen, china, music, food, flowers have to be ordered, and during Prohibition wines and liquor had to be provided. The business of dealing with bootleggers, musicians, society women, and French chefs demands tact, surenesss, and mostly patience.

All this work requires eight hours a day of solid thinking, and as yet only the preparations have been made. Then comes the conduct of the parties themselves, the actual work of bringing into existence what has been contracted for. And these two kinds of work overlap: while menus are being written and contracts signed in the office for future parties, the music is starting to play and a party is demanding close supervision. The work starts at nine in the morning, and ends sometimes at three or six the next morning. Mr. Sigsag is as pale again as he was as a piccolo. Monsieur Wladimir has not one unoccupied second in the day's long stretch. In his short sleep he twitches and dreams of parties, his lips move, he calls the names of waiters and guests, in joy or in anguish. He wakes up with a jump from the couch behind a screen in the outer room of the Ballroom office, where he has lain down for an hour in the afternoon; he has dreamt that the bower fell on the bride, that the Ballroom was on fire, or that we had only one waiter for two thousand people.

The staff contained an old German bartender, Pommer, his two assistant bartenders, then twenty first chefs de rang who could be made maîtres d'hôtel, a secretary, and about thirty more good waiters. After those came an army of extra waiters, transients who worked in all the hotels and were engaged according to the needs of the party. Their number sometimes went up to three hundred.

The cleaning of the Ballroom and its service rooms was the work of three housemen, who were also reinforced by extra labor. The head houseman was a quiet Italian, next after him was a Swede, and then came a German. There was, besides, a troop of sweepers and cleaners, little men, all of them Portuguese, whom Sigsag referred to as the "Gnomes," only he pronounced it "Genomies." They really were like the little people who live under the roots of trees. They were always together, and always carrying something—a rug, platforms, palms, furniture—and, altogether in character, they ate in a low storeroom under the stairs in one of the ballrooms, and when they worked very late, they slept there on rugs. The Genomies spoke only Portuguese, and their leader translated everything to them out of English, which he understood only after he was shown everything with plans and drawings. The Genomies were also used for carrying wine, and breaking open the cases of champagne and whisky.

Prohibition had taken from hotels the most remunerative part of their business. The bars and wine cellars had to be cleared, and the immense foot-thick doors of the refrigerators, when opened, showed empty storerooms. All that fell into the hands of the banquet department. The hotel was reasonably safe from police interference. The services of the city's most reputable bootleggers were at our command; their trucks rolled up to our door without any pretense at camouflage; and cases plainly marked Champagne and Whisky were delivered in broad daylight. The policeman leaned on the Ballroom door and watched them being carried in; for this immunity not a penny of graft was ever asked; it meant only a few drinks for the police after the parties were over, and a bottle or two at Christmas.

The business was a gold mine, as Sigsag had said. The profits on wine and liquor were of course high; we paid no rent; and the best people in America were our customers. There was no over-head; refrigerators, light, office expenses, telephone, glasses, ice and waiters were paid for by the hotel; and a thick golden stream of profit ran into what von Kyling called "the General Welfare." This was the total sum of money which came together from prof-its in champagnes, from salaries, extra compensation for the long night hours, the generous sums the guests left after the party was over, the commissions on flowers, on music, on a number of lesser things. This then was divided, the largest part to von Kyling, the next largest to Mr. Sigsag, and the smallest third to myself. And along with the profits from the immense turnover of cham-pagne—a hundred cases sometimes being used in some single party—there were of course liberal tips on how to treble that profit on the stock market.

Von Kyling came from Hamburg, but he never talked of his youth, except to mention that once he had done something very foolish. He had served his apprenticeship in Brussels and had worked in Paris and London. He had been manager of a restau-rant on a large German steamer when it was interned in New York, and since that restaurant belonged to the Splendide com-pany, they offered him the post of banquet manager at their New York hotel. He knew his business thoroughly and had an excellent mind. Nothing ever happened while he was in charge that was not foreseen, provided for, or in time straightened out. Brauhaus left him strictly alone, for interference in so intricate a depart-ment would have been disastrous, and besides, under von Kyl-ing's able management the banquet department was the only branch of the Splendide that made money. It made, in fact, tre-mendous sums.

Von Kyling had inborn good manners; he was at ease with the most important guests of the hotel and attended to the arrange-ments for their parties in person. He bowed little, had a good voice, spoke excellent French. He kept between him and the guests a protective distance without resorting to the tricks of puffy self-importance and preciousness employed by the maîtres d' hôtel in the restaurant to defend their persons. His face showed great kindness and humor but he would sometimes punish a sub-ordinate for a mistake by falling into a moody silence and not speaking to him for two weeks. He was strict, but fair and honest.

In the center of all the madness that went on all about him day and night, von Kyling walked steadily and had no temptations to live high. He kept his head in all emergencies and always remained an orderly German citizen. He bought all his personal effects in the mass, watching the papers for sales and buying five pairs of shoes at once. He wore a dreadful kind of knitted underwear, a union suit that covered him from ankles to wrists, with a door in the back, because at a fire sale he had got two dozen of them for thirty-five cents apiece. He bought hats that way, too, and evening shirts in shops along Seventh Avenue that were about to close up. His plain suits were made by a little side street Bohemian tailor. He loved the theater, but he always sat in the top balcony seats and looked at the show through opera glasses that had been left in our lost and found department.

He never played the market. Once when we received a very good tip from the head of a large banking establishment, he bought fifty shares of Postum outright and locked them away. The day after, as he walked through the lobby, he heard a waiter telephone to his broker a selling order for five hundred shares of American Can. Wide-eyed, von Kyling took hold of the man by the coat and said: "You are telling your broker to sell five hundred shares of American Can? Have you that much money?"

"Margin," said the waiter. "We all play the market. I made eight hundred dollars last month."

"Who is 'we all'?"

"All the waiters, the cooks, the pantrymen, the doormen—"

"You all play the market?"

"Yes, even the bus boys."

· · ·

Mr. von Kyling took his cheap hat and ran to his bank and sold his fifty shares of Postum.

Mr. Sigsag had his yacht, in a year I had a Lincoln, but Mr. von Kyling had a motorcycle with a side car. With this vehicle and dressed in a pair of breeches and a leather coat which he had bought at an Army and Navy store, he rode about the countryside. "You sleep best on a small pillow," he said.

He had his life clearly mapped out. He hated the hotel, the guests, and he had contempt for most of the employees, "bowing, scraping, everybody's servants." When the large coming out parties kept him up late, and he was very tired and therefore friendly, he would lean over the balcony railing, and wave his arm over the room full of society eating their supper below him, and say to me: "One more year, my boy, and then they all can scratch my back. One spoon, one fork, one plate, one glass, no guests, no visitors, no entertaining." And after that he would go into his office and look through his farm catalogues. He almost counted the days when he would be out of it. He wanted a small place in the country, a little car, the furniture from his parents' home in Germany sent over, and to live simply and alone.

Von Kyling studied over the plans, looked up dates, and checked everything. Without him, Sigsag in his eagerness would have had two or more parties booked in the same room on the same evening, and only one orchestra on another night to play for three dances. To keep a clear head, von Kyling went home early in the evenings. Mr. Sigsag attended to the parties and, after I had learned the problems, I took charge of the staff.

The Ballet
Visits the
Magician

. . .

The management of the banquet department kept on file the addresses of a number of men who were magicians, fortune-tellers, or experts with cards. One of these entertainers frequently appeared at the end of the small dinner parties which were given in the private suites of the Splendide in those days. Our entertainers had acclimated their acts to the elegance of the hotel, and the magicians, for example, instead of conjuring a simple white rabbit from their hats, cooked therein a soufflé Alaska or brought out a prize puppy with a rhinestone collar. When young girls were present, the magician pulled from their noses and out of corsages Cartier clips, bracelets, and brooches, which were presented to them with the compliments of the host.

Among the best and most talented of our performers was Professor Maurice Gorylescu, a magician who did some palmistry on the side. He came to the hotel as often as two or three times a week. After coffee had been served, he entered the private dining room, got people to write any number they wanted to on small bits of paper, and held the paper to their foreheads. Then he guessed the numbers they had written down and added them up. The total corresponded to a sum he found on a dollar bill in the host's pocket. He did tricks with cards and coins, and he told peo-

ple about the characteristics and the habits of dress and speech of friends long dead. He even delivered messages from them to the living.

At the end of his séances, he went into some vacant room nearby, sank into a chair, and sat for a while with his hand over his eyes. He always looked very tired. After about half an hour he shook himself, drank a glass of water slowly, then ate something, and went home.

Professor Gorylescu earned a good deal of money. His fee for a single performance was a flat hundred dollars, and he sometimes received that much again as a tip from a grateful host. But although he worked all during the season he spent everything he made and often asked for and received his fee in advance. All he earned went to women—to the support of a Rumanian wife in Bucharest, to an American one who lived somewhere in New Jersey, and to what must have been a considerable number of New York girls of all nationalities to whom he sent little gifts and flowers.

When he came to the hotel during the day, he would hang his

cane on the doorknob outside the Ballroom office, ask me for a cigarette, and after a while steal a look at the book in which the reservations for small dinners were recorded. Very casually, and while talking of other things, he would turn the leaves and say something like "Looks very nice for the next two months," and put the book back. It took only a few seconds, but in this time his trick mind had stored away all the names, addresses, dates, and telephone numbers in the book. He went home with this information, called up the prospective party-givers, and offered his services.

There was a strict rule that no one should be permitted to look at these reservations, certainly not Professor Gorylescu, but I liked him, and when I was on duty in the Ballroom office I pretended not to see him when he peeked in the book. I also gave him left-over *petits fours,* candies, and after-dinner mints, of which he was very fond. He waved good-by with his immense hands, asked me to visit him soon at his home, and suggested that I bring along some *marrons glacés,* pastry, nuts—anything like that—and then he left, a stooping, uncouth figure bigger than our tallest doorman.

Maurice Gorylescu lived on one of the mediocre streets that run between Riverside Drive and West End Avenue. He had a room in one of the small marble mansions that are common in that neighborhood. The rooming house in which Gorylescu lived was outstanding even among the ornate buildings of that district. It was a sort of junior Frankenstein castle, bedecked with small turrets, loggias, and balconies. It faced the sidewalk across a kind of moat—an air shaft for the basement windows—traversed by a granite bridge. The door was hung on heavy iron hinges that reached all the way across.

In character with this house was the woman who rented its rooms, a Mrs. Houlberg. She stood guard much of the time at the window next to the moat, looking out over a sign that read "Vacancies." She always covered three-quarters of her face with her right hand, a long hand that lay diagonally across her face, the palm over her mouth, the nails of the fingers stopping just under the right eye. It looked like a mask, or as if she always had a toothache.

Gorylescu lived on the top-floor front and answered to four short rings and one long one of a shrill bell that was in Mrs.

Houlberg's entrance hall. Badly worn banisters led up four flights of stairs. From the balcony of his room one could see the time flash on and off in Jersey and the searchlights of a battleship in the Hudson. The room was large and newly painted in a wet, loud red, the color of the inside of a watermelon. A spotty chartreuse velvet coverlet decorated a studio couch. Facing this was a chair, a piece of furniture such as you see in hotel lobbies or club cars, covered with striped muslin and padded with down. There was also a Sheraton highboy, which stood near a door that led into an adjoining room that was not his. From the ceiling hung a cheap bazaar lamp with carmine glass panes behind filigree panels. On shelves and on a table were the photographs of many women; in a box, tied together with ribbons in various colors, he kept packets of letters, and in a particular drawer of the highboy was a woman's garter, an old girdle, and various other obvious and disorderly trophies.

Gorylescu reclined on the studio bed most of the time when he was at home. He wore a Russian blouse that buttoned under the left ear, and he smoked through a cigarette holder a foot long. One of his eyes was smaller and lower down in his face than the other, and between them rose a retroussé nose, a trumpet of a nose, with cavernous nostrils. Frequently and with great ceremony he sounded it into an immense handkerchief. His cigar-colored skin was spotted as if with a bluish kind of buckshot, and when he was happy he hummed through his nose, mostly the melody of a song whose title was *"Tu sais si bien m'aimer."*

At home he was almost constantly in the company of women. He made the acquaintance of some of them at parties where he had entertained. They brought him gifts, and if they were fat and old, he read their minds and told them things of the past and future. At other times he went looking for girls along Riverside Drive, humming through his nose, and dragging after him a heavy cane whose handle was hooked into his coat pocket.

He went to various other places to find girls. He picked them up at dance halls in Harlem, on the subway, on roller coasters. He easily became acquainted with them anywhere, and they came to his room willingly and took their chances with him. I always thought I might find one of them, dead and naked, behind the Japanese screen, where he kept a rowing machine on which he built himself up. For the space of time that I knew him, love, murder, and this man seemed to be close together and that room the inevitable theater for it.

The Professor gave me a series of lectures during my visits to his room in which he detailed for me the routines and the mechanisms of his untidy passions. He insisted during these long *études* that the most important piece of strategy was to get the subject to remove her shoes. "Once the shoes are off, the battle is already half won," he would say. "Get a woman to walk around without shoes, without heels—she looks a fool, she feels a fool, she is a fool. Without her shoes, she is lost. Take the soft instep in your hand, caress her ankles, her calf, her knee—the rest is child's play. But remember, first off with the shoes." While he talked, he would scratch his cat, which was part Siamese. The lecture was followed by a display of the collection of photographs he himself had taken, as evidence of the soundness of his theories.

When the Russian Ballet came to town, Professor Gorylescu was not to be had for any parties at the hotel. He went to all the performances, matinées and evenings alike, and he hummed then the music of "Puppenfee," "L'Après-Midi d'un Faune," and the various *divertissements,* and was completely broke. One day he was in a state of the highest elation because he had invited a ballet dancer to tea. He wanted me to come too because she had a friend, who would be an extra girl for me; both of them were exquisite creatures, he assured me, and I was to bring some tea, *marrons glacés, petits fours,* and ladyfingers.

I came early and I brought everything. He darkened the room, lit a brass samovar, laid out some cigarettes, sliced some lemons, hid the rowing machine under the studio couch, and with the Japanese silk screen divided the room into two separate camps. On one side was the couch, on the other the great chair. He buttoned his Russian blouse, blew his nose frequently, and hummed as he walked up and down. He brushed the cat and put away a Spanish costume doll that might have made his couch crowded. He arranged the *petits fours* in saucers, and when the bell rang four times short and one long, he put a Chopin record on his victrola. "Remember about the shoes," he told me over his shoulder, "and always play Chopin for ballet dancers." He quickly surveyed the room once more, turned on the bazaar lamp, and, humming, opened the door—and then stopped humming suddenly. He had invited two of the dancers, but up the stairs came a bouquet of girls, more than a dozen of them.

All at once it was the month of May in the dimmed room. The lovely guests complemented the samovar, the cat, the music, and the view from the balcony, to which they had opened the door, letting much fresh air come in, which intensified the new mood. Gorylescu's voice became metallic with introductions; he ran downstairs to get more glasses for tea and came back breathing heavily. All the girls, without being asked, took their shoes off immediately, explaining that their feet hurt from dancing. They arranged the shoes in an orderly row, as one does on entering a Japanese house or a mosque, then sat down on the floor in a circle. One of them even removed her stockings and put some slices of lemon between her toes. "Ah-h-h," she said.

There started after this a bewildering and alien conversation, a remote, foggy ritual, like a Shinto ceremonial. It consisted of the telling of ballet stories, and seemed to me a high, wild flight into a world closed to the outsider. The stories were told over and over until every detail was correct. In all of these stories appeared Anna Pavlova, who was referred to as "Madame"—what Madame had said, what Madame had done, what she had thought, what she had worn, how she had danced. There was an atmosphere of furious backstage patriotism. The teller of each story swayed and danced with hands, shoulders, and face. Every word was illustrated; for anything mentioned—color, light, time, and person—there was a surprisingly expressive and fitting gesture. The talker was rewarded with applause, with requests for repetition of this or that part again and again, and there swept over the group of girls waves of intimate, fervent emotion.

The Professor served tea on his hands and knees and retired to the shadows of his room. He sat for a while in the great chair like a bird with a wounded wing, and then, with his sagging and cumbersome gait, he wandered around the group of innocents, who sat straight as so many candles, all with their shoes off. The room was alive with young heads and throats and flanks.

The Professor succeeded finally in putting his head into the lap of the tallest, the most racy of the nymphs. She quickly kissed him, said, "Sh-h-h-h, daaaahrling," and then caressed his features, the terrible nose, the eyebrows, the corrugated temples, and the great hands, with the professional detachment of a masseuse, while she related an episode in Cairo during a performance of *Giselle* when the apparatus that carried Pavlova up out of her grave to her lover got stuck halfway, and how Madame had cursed and what she had said after the performance and to whom she had said it. An indignant fire burned in all the narrowed eyes of the disciples as she talked.

Suddenly one of them looked at her watch, remembered a rehearsal, and the girls got up and remembered us. They all had Russian names, but all of them were English, as most ballet dancers are; in their best accents, they said their adieus. With individual graces, they arranged their hair, slipped into their shoes, and thanked Maurice. Each one of them said "Daaaahrling" to us and to each other. It was Madame Pavlova's form of address and her pronunciation.

All the girls kissed us, and it was as if we all had grown up in the same garden, as if they were all our sisters. The Professor said a few mouthfuls of gallant compliments, and when they were gone he fished the rowing machine out from under the couch, without a word, and carried it in back of the Japanese screen. Together, we rearranged the room. The *marrons glacés* and the ladyfingers were all gone, but the cigarettes were still there.

The Homesick
Bus Boy

. . .

In a corner of the main dining room of the Splendide, behind an
arrangement of screens and large palms that were bedded in antique Chinese vases, six ladies of uncertain age used to sit making
out luncheon and dinner checks. When a guest at the Splendide
called for the bill, it was brought to him in longhand—contrary to
the practice in most other hotels in New York City—in purple
ink, on fine paper decorated with the hotel crest. The six ladies,
seated at a long desk near the exit to the kitchen, attended to that.
And since there were periods when they had little to do, one of
them, a Miss Tappin, found time to befriend the bus boy Fritzl,
from Regensburg.

Fritzl was not much more than a child. He wore a white jacket
and a long white apron, and he carried in his pocket a comb
which he had brought all the way from Regensburg. A scene of
the city was etched on the side of it. Fritzl's hair stood up straight,
moist, and yellow, and he had the only red cheeks in the dining
room. When anyone spoke to him, his ears also turned red, and he
looked as if he had just been slapped twice in the face.

Miss Tappin was very English. She had seen better days and in
her youth had traveled on the Continent. She detested the maître
d'hôtel, the waiters, and the captains, but she was drawn to the

lonesome bus boy, who seemed to be of nice family, had manners, and was shy. Fritzl did not like the maître d'hôtel, the waiters, or the captains either. Least of all he liked the waiter he worked for, a nervous wreck of a Frenchman who was constantly coming behind the screens and palms, saying "Psst!" and dragging Fritzl out onto the floor of the restaurant to carry away some dirty dishes.

When Fritzl was thus called away, Miss Tappin would sigh and then look into the distance. She called Fritzl "a dear," and said that he was the living image of a nephew of hers who was at Sandhurst—the son, by a previous marriage, of her late sister's husband, a Major Graves. "What a pity!" Miss Tappin would say whenever she thought of Fritzl. "He's such a superior type, that boy. Such a dear. So unlike the bobtail, ragtag, and guttersnipes around him. I do hope he'll come through all right!" Then she would sigh again and go back to her bills. Every time Fritzl passed the long desk, whether with butter, water bottles, or dirty dishes, a quick signal of sympathy passed between them.

The conversations with Fritzl afforded Miss Tappin an exquisite weapon with which to irritate the other five ladies who shared the desk—women who came from places like Perth Amboy, Pittsburgh, and Newark. With Fritzl leaning on her blotter, she could discuss such topics as the quaintness of Munich and its inhabitants and the charm and grandeur of the Bavarian Alps. These beautiful mountains neither Fritzl nor Miss Tappin had ever seen. Regensburg is not far away from the Alps, but Fritzl's parents were much too poor ever to have sent him there. Miss Tappin's stay in Munich had been limited to a half-hour wait between trains at the railroad station while she was on her way to visit her sister in Budapest.

Regensburg, however, she soon came to know thoroughly from Fritzl, who often spread a deck of pocket-worn postcards and calendar pictures on the desk in front of her. These views showed every worthwhile street corner and square of his beloved city. He acquainted her with Regensburg's history and described its people and the surrounding country. He read her all the letters he received from home, and gradually Miss Tappin came to know everybody in Regensburg.

"Dear boy," she would say, touching his arm, "I can see it all clearly. I can picture your dear mother sitting in front of her little house on the banks of the Danube—the little radish garden, the dog, the cathedral, and the wonderful stone bridge. What a lovely place it must be!" Then her eyes would cloud, for Miss Tappin had the peculiar British addiction to scenes that are material for postcards. Into the middle of these flights always came the nervous "Psst!" of the old French waiter. Then Fritzl would lift his apron, stow the postcards away in the back pocket of his trousers, and run. When he passed that way later with a tray of dirty dishes, he sent her his smile, and again when he came back with an armful of water bottles or a basin of cracked ice and a basket of bread. They recognized each other as two nice people do, walking their dogs in the same street.

Fritzl's service table stood in another corner of the restaurant, and near it was another palm in another Chinese vase. When he was not at Miss Tappin's desk or in the kitchen or busy with his dirty dishes, Fritzl hid behind this palm. He was afraid of everyone, even the guests. He came out from behind his palm only when his waiter called him, or when the orchestra played Wagner, Weber, or Strauss music, or when I, his other friend in the hotel, passed by.

By this time I was assistant manager in the banquet department, but Fritzl was not afraid of me. I was his friend because I, too, came from Regensburg. Sometimes when I appeared in the restaurant, Fritzl would lean out from behind his palm and say in a hoarse whisper, "*Du,* Ludwig, have you a minute for me?" Once he put his arm around my neck and started to walk with me through the dining room as if we were boys in Regensburg. When I told him that that was not done, he looked hurt, but later, in the pantry, he forgave me and told me all the latest and most important news of Regensburg.

Another time he showed me a little book he had made out of discarded menus. In this book he had written down what he earned and what he spent. His income was eight dollars a week, and his expenses, including an English lesson at one dollar, were seven. In three years, he calculated, he would have enough money to go back to Regensburg. I told him he could make much more money if he attended to his job and got to be a waiter, and he said he would try. But Fritzl was very bad dining-room material. He was slow, earnest, and awkward. A good waiter jumps, turns fast, and has his eyes everywhere. One can almost tell by watching a new man walk across the room whether he will be a good or an indifferent waiter. One can also tell, as a rule, if he will last.

We sometimes took a walk together, Fritzl and I, usually up or down Fifth Avenue, in the lull between luncheon and dinner. One day, in the upper window of a store building near Thirty-fourth Street, Fritzl saw an advertisement that showed a round face smoking a cigar. Under the face was written "E. Regensburg & Sons, Havana Cigars." From that day on, Fritzl always wanted to walk downtown toward Thirty-fourth Street. He would point up at the window as we passed and say, "Look, Ludwig—Regensburg."

He also liked to stop in front of St. Patrick's Cathedral, because it reminded him of the Dom in Regensburg. But St. Patrick's was not half as big as the Dom, he said, and its outside looked as if it were made of fresh cement, and its bells were those of a village church. He was very disappointed by the interior as well.

Once I took him on an excursion boat up the Hudson. "Fritzl, look," I said to him, "isn't this river more beautiful than the Danube?"

He was quiet for several miles. Opposite Tarrytown, he said, "It's without castles. I have not seen a single castle, only smokestacks." Up at Poughkeepsie, he pointed to the railroad bridge and said, "Look at it, and think of the stone bridge across the Danube at Regensburg. And besides, where is Vienna on this river, or a city like Budapest?" For the rest, he said, it was all right.

I sometimes wondered why Fritzl should love Regensburg, for I knew that he had grown up there in misery. His parents lived on the outskirts of the city and worked as tenants on a few soggy acres planted with radishes and cabbages. The land lay along the river and was submerged whenever the water rose. The Danube rose very often. The place where they lived was called Reinhausen. One came to it by crossing an old stone bridge and walking through another city, which was to Regensburg what Brooklyn is to New York. The people who lived in this small Brooklyn always explained why they were living there—the air was better, the view nicer, it was better for their children, quieter—but they all excused themselves. The place resembled Brooklyn also in that one got lost there very easily and that no cabdriver in Regensburg could find his way there without asking a policeman for directions.

When I asked Fritzl why he loved Regensburg so much, his answer sounded like Heinrich Heine. "Do you remember the seven stone steps," he said, "the worn stones that lead down from the Street of St. Pancraz to the small fish market? The old ivy-covered fountain whose water comes from the mouth of two green dolphins? The row of tall oaks with a bench between every other pair of trees? The sand pit next to the fountain where children play, where young girls walk arm in arm, where the lamplighter arrives at seven, and where, sitting on a bench, I can see, between the leaning walls of two houses, a wide strip of moving water—the Danube—and beyond it my parents' house? There I grew up. There every stone is known to me. I know the sound of every bell, the name of every child, and everyone greets me."

Like a child himself then, he would repeat over and over, "Oh, let me go home. I want to go home to Regensburg. Oh, I don't like it here. What am I here? Nobody. When I told Herr Professor

Hellsang I wanted to come to America, he said to me, *'Ja,* go to America, become a waiter—the formula for every good-for-nothing. But remember, America is the land where the flowers have no perfume, where the birds lack song, and where the women offer no love.' And Herr Professor Hellsang was right. It is so. Oh, I want to go back to Regensburg!"

When we returned to the hotel from an afternoon walk, Fritzl always disappeared into the Splendide's basement, where the dressing rooms for the bus boys were, and changed his clothes. The other bus boys' lockers were lined with clippings from *Là Vie Parisienne* and with pictures of cyclists and boxers. The door of Fritzl's was covered with views of Regensburg.

One evening Fritzl came up from his locker to assist at a dinner party given by Lord Rosslare, who had ordered a fairly good dinner, long and difficult to serve. He was a moody client, gay one day, unbearable the next. When he complained, his voice could be heard out on the street. Rosslare's table was in the center of the room, and next to it was a smaller table on which to ladle out the soup, divide the fish into portions, and carve the rack of lamb. The maître d'hôtel and his assistant supervised all this. Fritzl's waiter was moist with nervousness and fear. Everything went well, however, until the rack of lamb was to be carved.

The lamb had arrived from the kitchen and stood on an electric heater on Fritzl's service table behind the palm. Next to Lord Rosslare stood the maître d'hôtel, who intended to carve. He had the knife in one hand and a large fork in the other. He looked along the edge of the knife and tested its sharpness. The old waiter polished the hot plates in which the lamb was to be served and then carried the stack of them and the sauce to the table. Because the maître d'hôtel was shouting at him to hurry up, he told Fritzl to follow with the rack of lamb. All Fritzl had to do was to take the copper casserole and follow him. To save time, they walked across the dance floor instead of around it. Rosslare leaned back and complained about the slowness of the service. The maître d'hôtel stamped his feet and waved the carving knife. With his mouth stretched, he signaled to the old waiter and Fritzl so they could read his lips: *"Dépêchez-vous, salauds."*

All this made Fritzl nervous, and in the middle of the dance floor he tripped and fell. The rack of lamb jumped out of the casserole. Then an even more terrible thing happened. Fritzl, on all fours, crept over to the lamb, picked it up calmly and put it back in the casserole, licked his slippery fingers, got to his feet, and, to everyone's horror, carried it over to the table to be served.

Rosslare laughed. The whole dining room laughed. Only Monsieur Victor, the maître d'hôtel, was not amused. He retired to his office and bit into his fist. Next day the captain at the station got a severe reprimand. The old waiter was to be laid off for two weeks and Fritzl was to be discharged.

In a hotel that employed hundreds of people, there were always changes in personnel. And fortunately an old Greek who had been attendant in the men's washroom in the banquet department left on that day for his homeland. His job was vacant and Fritzl got it.

In the washroom, Fritzl was his own master. There were no maîtres d'hôtel, captains, and waiters to be afraid of. No one said "Psst!" and "Come here!" to him. He began to be more cheerful. One of his uncles, he told me, a veteran of the War of 1870, had, in recognition of his services, been given the washroom concession at the Walhalla, a national shrine built of marble, like the washroom in the banquet department of the Splendide, and situated not far from Regensburg.

Every morning Fritzl went down to the storeroom and got his supply of brushes, soap, ammonia, and disinfectants. Next he went to the linen room and exchanged his dirty towels for clean ones. Then he put his washroom in order. He whistled while he polished the knobs and handles and water faucets, and when everything was shining he conscientiously flushed all the toilets and pressed the golden buttons that released a spray of water into the porcelain basins, to see that they were working. If any of the plumbing was out of order, he telephoned down to the engineers. At noon he reported to the banquet office and was told whether any parties would take place during the afternoon or evening. If the banquet rooms were not engaged, he was free the rest of the day.

When Fritzl worked, he made good money. He soon learned to brush the guests off and to hold them up at the narrow door so that none escaped without producing a dime or a quarter. In busy seasons he sometimes made as much as thirty dollars a week.

He became more tolerant of America and found that, contrary to the belief of Herr Professor Hellsang, birds do sing here and flowers do have a perfume. Late at night, after he had locked up the men's room, Fritzl arranged his coins in neat stacks and entered the total in his book. He often came into the banquet office, when everyone else was gone, and asked to use my typewriter. On this machine, using two fingers, he slowly composed glowing prospectuses of the hotel—letters that his mother would proudly show around. On the hotel's stationery, he wrote that the Splendide was the most luxurious hotel in the world; that it was twenty-two stories high; that it had seven hundred apartments, any one of which was better furnished than the rooms in the castle of the Duke of Thurn und Taxis in Regensburg; that in these apartments lived the richest people in America; that he was employed at a lucrative income in the Department of Sanitation; and that he would probably come home for a short visit in the summer.

The
Simple
Life

• • • • • •

Bavaria

. . .

I spent the three months of my vacation in Schliersee, where
Mother had a summer villa on the side of a mountain. It was a
hunting chalet, which with some carpentry and the digging of a
cellar had been made into a very comfortable, livable house. On
the first floor had been installed an old-fashioned bathroom, with
a tall oven at one end of the long tub heated by short, neat lengths
of pinewood, and an immense bathtowel, as big as a bedsheet,
hanging over a chair. The oven was heated far ahead of time, and
the little room was then over-warm, the water gushing out in
steam clouds that had to be cooled again; but I loved this bath,
because afterwards, when I sat wrapped up in the big bath cloth,
I had a three-year-old's feeling of complete happiness. A tiled
oven also stood in the living-room, with a bench built around it;
heavy tooled-leather furniture, solid clothes closets, antlers, and a
real Defregger picture filled the wall spaces.

The balcony of the villa looked directly down upon the village
below, yet was still part of it. In the neat German garden grew orderly rows of flowers, and as beautifully kept in line were the
ranks of radishes, kohlrabi, carrots, cauliflower, and rhubarb.
There was, of course, the little ivy-covered summerhouse that goes
with such a garden, and the rose trees that grew up tied to thin

sticks stood under brilliant, luminous glass spheres, in which one could see the scene and one's face and the roses, widened and bent, in blue, in gold, in green, and in a deep magenta. Another lovely piece of foolishness in this garden was the two little gnomes and the two rabbits, of painted iron, the gnomes holding an ear and listening, the rabbits forever sitting up.

There was also a sound of the closing of the gate that I loved to hear whenever I came here. It was just an ordinary falling together of two pieces of wood and an old lock, but it said: "Here is my home, now I am here," and because it was to last for only a few months, it filled me with great happiness. We ate breakfast on the balcony, Mother and I and whatever guests I had. The guests, girls I had met in Munich or Vienna, did not always make Mother very happy; without them, this would have been a mother's paradise.

The walk down the mountainside into the village itself took ten minutes, and it was another three to the lake. Off the shore we had a little private bathing house, completely enclosed. It actually stood in the lake, and was reached by walking over a frail bridge. It had a dressing-room, and, next to it, a room with walls and a roof but without windows and, instead of a floor, the water of the lake. A little stair led down into the water, and in one wall was a door half above and half under the surface of the water; when it was opened, one could swim out through it into the lake. There was no light in this room except the mysterious emerald pallor that hung in all the corners and came from the water below. This water-floor, when the lake was quiet, was a lighted square of unreal green, somewhat like the glass spheres in the garden, and again not so, because it was so transparent. Little fishes, also green but opaque, could be seen swimming through it, and the weaving of underwater plants; and when a cloud passed over the lake outside, or a rowboat, then the color changed to a deeper blue-gray. The sun again filled it with brilliance, and with stripes of golden, sunken dust. I loved to look at a girl's body in this water. There was an ecstasy about it then that it had at no other time, when little silver pearls of air danced up and clung to her limbs; and when she came out and was cold, and oneself was cold, she looked like a leaden nymph. It would make an aching, sinful, wondrous morning.

After this swim we always ate another little breakfast at the Gasthof Seehaus. This was a small inn in Schliersee that belonged to a remarkable couple, Herr and Frau Xaver Terofal. His father, a French émigré, had changed his name from La Forêt, turning it around to Terofal, which sounded almost Bavarian. Like everyone else, he wore the peasant costume: the little silver-gray jacket, the short leather pants, well-worn, the chamois brush on his hat. Mother Terofal had the form of a champagne cork.

Besides running their little inn, they were, with their troupe, Bavaria's greatest peasant actors. The first-floor hall of the painted inn was hung with wreaths of laurel from Ludwig the Second, from the Kaiser, from cities where they had played. Their theater, part of the inn, was not the usual amateur summer theater, a converted old barn, but a real theater, with a real curtain and good scenery. In the auditorium were long, scrubbed tables and peasant chairs; and on the stage were played the dramas and comedies of Anzengruber, Thoma, Schoenherr. At the head of the undertaking were eminent men, such as Conrad Dreher, of the Lustspiel Theater in Munich, a beloved and honored comedian with the title of *Hof Schauspieler,* Court Actor, given him by the old King of Bavaria; the presence of Dreher would sell out any theater throughout Germany.

Terofal was, besides, a butcher, a cook, an innkeeper such as one dreams of but seldom finds. In the evening, between acts and in the costume of his role, he would come running over into the kitchen and stir around in pots, feel dumplings for their consistency, cut fresh schnitzels, and run back through the rooms to greet a few guests. The beer here was heavy, brown, and bittersweet, like Grandfather's; it smelled like a drawer of an old dried-out oaken closet, musty, sun- and dust-cured, velvety, and much better than any champagne.

The male lead of the troupe, Franzl, was a tall young peasant who in the daytime carried the trunks from the station and shined the boots of the guests, and in the nighttime slept with many of the women. His shirt was always open, showing a chest black with hair and brown with sunburn, and he wore a little gay line of mustache on the stage and off. He took his loves without much asking; he attached himself with his lips, eyes, and his strong, able hands, and had little worry except to reach his ends as quickly as possible. He thus served many, and when he took their trunks to the station, they always looked better and happier than when they had arrived. He was part of the cure in Schliersee.

Since no consideration was ever involved, and Franzl had all he could eat and drink at the Seehaus, and since he was healthy and never tired, it was all a good arrangement, for Xaver Terofal, for the guests, for Franzl, and even for the ladies who did not take his fancy, for it gave them much-needed whispering material. To be seen walking with Franzl was to mirror both envy and disgrace in the faces of the people one passed.

In the altitude and latitude of the mountains of Bavaria, in this air, the costume of the men is somehow conducive to love. The arms are bare to the elbow, so are the knees in the short trousers that open wide and easy in front like sailors' pants. Franzl, sitting down, was almost nude, so much of his strong limbs and sun-burned chest and lean abdomen could be seen and felt. He smelled, but good, like a horse, and not of office sweat, but of maleness, of hay, of his strength. His unworried eyes were full of laughter, his regular pulse beat visibly under his shirt collar, and his voice was rich and deep. There were many of him in Bavaria. Nine months after the feasts of patron saints of churches and villages, or any of the many holidays, there would be in every village a new crop of little ones, healthy and strong, and the father had then to be coerced into some kind of responsibility by the village priest, who in all this excitement and celebration sometimes also became a father.

After our swim and second breakfast, Mother and I met in the garden, and then our cook Annerl, a young peasant girl, would come and sit down on the bench with us, her market basket in her hand. "What are we going to eat today?" she would say, and for the next few minutes we worried about that. Then I carried her basket and we bought food, for ourselves and for the little rough-haired dachshund, almost paprika-red and of a mean, stubborn disposition, I had given Mother. He loved Mother but hated me.

Every day I ordered a large bunch of field flowers for Mother, plain, pastel-colored flowers—heather, poppies, bluebells, daisies—and, if they were still on the trees in late June, armfuls of lilacs. A barefoot peasant girl, sweet as the flowers she brought, would come through the gate and put them on the breakfast table out on the balcony, overlooking the lake and the mountains. The sun shone, and in the village below, the older women, when they saw the flowers go by, all wished they had so considerate and loving a son as my mother had.

Schliersee, during the few summer months, harbored most of the society of Regensburg, and when, in Terofal's low dining-room, I saw them studying the card on the side where the prices stood, I would order French champagne and trout and roast goose and elaborate desserts, just to make them mad. They would look over at our table and whisper: "It's Ludwig, the good-for-nothing; the *Lausbub* they had to send away to America. Now he's back, just for a vacation; think of what that must cost! He must be a millionaire! Who would ever have thought it? It's always the bad ones, isn't it?" "You're right, Frau Direktor. My Walter was in the same class with him, and got the highest marks, and what is my Walter today? And he can't be more than twenty-one, that Ludwig A millionaire he must certainly be." Then they would nibble at their mean leg of veal, while Mother drank in their remarks as she did the good beer. Through the village she would often walk six feet behind me and my guest, just to catch up with some Regensburg women when they stopped and said: "That's him, the *Lausbub,* but he's so good to his mother. It's always the worst ones that turn out all right."

I kept a slim little boat, down on the lake, and a bicycle on which I rode around the lake every day. On one part of the narrow path was a sign which read: "Bicycling on this lane is most strictly forbidden. The Police Commandant." The third time I was on this path, as I came round a curve, a gendarme in a grass-green uniform, the one officer that Schliersee afforded, came out of a bush and stopped me.

"It's the white pants, Herr Bemelmans," he said, with a smiling good-morning salute. "If you had not worn these white tennis pants you have on, it might have taken me longer. But I saw the white pants going around the lake for two days in succession, faster than I could walk, and I said to myself: 'That's strange.' And so I stationed myself here early this morning. You do not read signs, Herr Bemelmans? You did not see that sign there, Herr Bemelmans, which explicitly says that bicycling on this lane is most severely forbidden?"

Under his tight helmet, his face had gradually grown crimson with indignation. I congratulated him on his vigilance, and said that I liked bicycling on this path so much that, even if it was *ver-boten,* I would like to keep on bicycling on it, and I invited him to a glass of beer in the garden of the little inn that was not far from where we stood. He accepted, and I pushed the bicycle under the chestnut trees, and he ate a pair of thin sausages with a small heap of kraut under them and put salt on his big slice of black bread.

He asked me how it was possible for me to ignore a sign that was so plain, so newly lettered, so big, and which I admitted I had read. I told him that it was perhaps because I had lived so long in America, where one pays little attention to the police, to their signs and orders, in fact to any orders, and that since I never met anyone on the forbidden tour, I had seen no reason why I should not bicycle on it.

He looked at me as one does at someone with a dangerous fever. Occasionally he said: "Ssso?" Then he told me that this trip would cost me five marks. I said: "Thirty times five marks, that's one hundred and fifty marks, that won't be so bad for a month of bicycling." At that his mouth fell open; then he took a bite of bread, and said out of a full mouth: "It is not as simple as that. The first time it is five marks, the second time it is ten marks, the third time five days' arrest, then it might go up and up."

He refused to let me pay for his food and beer when we left the inn. The next day a court clerk came to the villa, with a summons in a black bag full of papers. He wanted fifteen marks. Why fifteen? I asked. It was five for bicycling on the forbidden lane, and ten for insulting a Bavarian gendarme. I gave the clerk some beer and finally persuaded him to let me look at the papers he had in his hand, from which he had read off my offenses. On five folio pages was described the entire encounter, from the first appearance of the white tennis pants, and the ambush, and the repast in the restaurant, down to my conversation, recorded word for word, including my opinions on the police of Bavaria and America. There were also some general comments in which the gendarme had put down his opinion of me, as a loose person requiring watching, a disorderly subject who might be the cause of further serious trouble. I paid the fifteen marks.

The little gendarme was also at the theater every evening, in his dress uniform with a saber and white gloves. He bowed and smiled when he saw me next and said: "I see you are not bicycling around the lake any more, Herr Bemelmans. *Ja ja,* this is not *Amerika!* What you need over there is a police force!" I took hold of him by the loose button under which was stuck his notebook and I said something that cost me fifty marks the next day.

Sawmill
in Tirol

· · ·

Above Schliersee, on the side of a mountain, is an old tree, its trunk twisted by the wind that blows down from the mountain summit. A bench leans against it, and behind it stands a small whitewashed chapel. The sun shines on the wall of the chapel and the warm air comes under the shade of the big tree. Below are fields of clover and wheat, a road, the lake, and the village, the smoke coming out of all its chimneys. All of it is framed by high mountains that hold up a small ceiling of sky, across which wander sun and moon and fields of stars. In this enclosed space lies the whole world, the beginning and the end of life, from the kindergarten next to the church and the play-yard attached to the school to the little walled cemetery with painted crosses and patches of peasant flowers.

In the early evening, music is played in a pavilion on a small strip of park along the lake. When it begins, heaven seems filled with fiddles and the forest becomes like the sides of a gothic altar with wormholed angels, whose worn, gilded wooden curls hang over their simple devout profiles, and whose eyes look down on the thin long fingers that are folded flat together in prayer.

The men are all volunteer musicians, in their working hours masters of their trades. They arrive with shined but battered in-

struments of comfortable design, and their small sons run along carrying notes. They are perhaps twelve men, but on holidays, feast days, and Sundays there are twenty of them. Each one has a large, gray stone mug of beer beside his chair; the sons run to the inn to have them filled when they are empty. The beer is the musicians' only compensation.

It always takes a long while before they are ready. The conductor puts the clarinet to his pointed lips and takes it away several times before they are all seated comfortably. He waves up and down with it three times as a signal to begin and he keeps on waving the time with it. At important passages, to get more sound or very soft playing, he bends his knees apart as if taking exercises, widens his eyes, and sends his eyebrows up under the brim of his hat.

These men are afraid of nothing, that is, nothing they love to play. They like Weber, Schubert, Strauss, many native composers, marches, folk music; they even play Wagner. They make music the way they work; they hammer and sew the notes to-gether and take much enthusiastic liberty, most of all the flute. This musician, a tailor, will walk away from the music in a happy "dulilululiliu," forget the score for a while, and come back to it when he is ready. Having done enough, he stops altogether, bends down for his beer, looks into the mug, and empties it. Another will see his child and stand up and shout a message for him to take home to his mother. The men with the brasses also stop at any time to turn their instruments upside down and shake spit out of them. Then they slowly get ready again, licking their lips when a favorite passage comes and passing the palm of a hand across the mouthpiece. Then, all together, they play such music as *"Connais-tu le pays?"* and *Mignon*. This they play at almost every concert, and also, though Bavaria is now a republic, the royal anthem. They are royalists, who deserve such a king as they once had, one who actually had to be pushed out of the city during the revolu-tion, who could be seen sitting behind his little sausages and beer, on the same chairs as his people, and who would pull the sleeve of the man next to him and ask him to slide the mustard down and then say *"Dankeschön."*

In a close circle around the music stand the children, their faces lifted up to the light and the instruments. Behind them are young people, their heads to one side, their young mouths and moist, warm lips loose and open, like those of young calves, entirely given up to the music. A few foreigners, not French or English people, but non-Bavarian Germans who come here for their vaca-tions, go promenading up and down in loose-fitting coats. Out on the lake painted boats rest on the water, the oars dripping into them, paper lanterns hanging over them. The music goes out over the lake and echoes among the mountains; a crash of the cymbals comes back softly three and four times. At the end there is a trumpet solo, it tears out over the water like a brassy light without shade. Then the musicians pack up, turn out the lights, and wan-der to the inn for a little refreshment.

Over the mountains late at night rags of clouds collect, releas-ing their waters on the high summits, and in the early morning the peaks are powdered with fine snow, which the sun melts into many brooks that turn into a foaming wild stream half-way be-tween the level of the lake and the mountain top. The stream passes from house to house, turning the heavy wooden mill wheels, and down into the lake and out of it on the south side, bearing the boats from which people fish.

The roosters start to crow while it is still dark; lights, at first two little flickers, spring up in the peasant houses; then a pale, flat orange color fills the little panes of their windows; the lamp is lit, and a shaft of its light swims out of an open door as a man goes over to his stable with the lantern. In the railroad yard below, the small engine is being fired; it is switching freight cars, but at seven-forty it will pull the train of six cars to Munich. The churchbells ring, and little women in black come out of all the streets for early morning Mass.

On the mountainside, horses are being hitched to small-wheeled wagons that are to go up into the forest. In the clearings the branches are lopped off, cut in lengths, and piled in neat stacks of firewood, while the trunks are dragged down to the sawmill to be cut into boards and laid out in a shack to dry. Other horses will later take them to the carpenter in the village, who will make of them wagons, furniture, shingles, rafters, fence posts, doors, and window frames.

The people are in the fields; the cattle are being driven up to the high meadows covered with short, mossy, sweet-smelling grass and hardy little flowers. The children go to school, beds are put out in the sun, the women go to market. Work in gardens begins; the guests at the hotel open their windows, look out, and stretch themselves in their white nightshirts; Sophie, the waitress at the Seehaus, puts red-and-white-checked tablecloths out on the long tables on the terrace. Here is everything that one can find anywhere in the world: Father, Mother, and children, love and death, work and dancing, police and religion, and the four seasons.

There is a cold, cold winter, with the lake frozen over with thick green ice, snow over it, and the tracks of skates. The snow crunches as one walks through it. Icicles, some of them thick as stalactites, hang from the roofs all the way down to the ground. The little children who lick them have their ears wrapped up; they have red faces and mittens on a string, in each mitten an egg-shaped stone that has been warmed in the oven at home. They pull little handmade sleds with bells. Springtime here comes with trembling yellow-green leaves, wet fields, and crocuses; summer with tables outside in all the gardens under great chestnut trees; autumn with dark-brown burnt leaves on all the roads, smelling and sounding warm as one walks through them ankle-deep.

From this bench under the bent old tree, in this godlike perspective, as if one hung in the sky, there is, in a brief yet eternal moment of time, clarity and understanding. It comes at the end of long stretches of thinking, sometimes distorted by my reading, and I have to put much that I like aside, along with my respect for the knowledge and brilliance of the minds that have written the books. I have to say loudly to myself that life is Mother and Father, house and garden, nurse and childhood, play, work, love, and children; that it is not what goes on in the Splendide.

I have to think of the poor man, the timekeeper of our hotel, in his furnished room near the Third Avenue Elevated, who woke me up every morning when his loud alarm clock went off. He would come to the window in the underwear he slept in, scratch his stomach and sides and the back of his neck, then rub his bald head. Later I would see him come out of the house below, in his only suit, and painfully walk up the street with his bad feet to a lunchroom called "Joe's," first buying a paper. He was a brutal, soulless poor old man with a little authority at the door where he could growl at people. He had nothing of his own but his awful room, and all his pleasure came from the outside, like the movies, where he saw for an hour and a half, without ever smiling, other people on yachts, in elegance, in a paradise forever beyond his reach.

I walk down through the cool wet forest, its path covered with needles and bordered by small-leafed sour clover growing together with the ferns, and then out into the light green fields. I look at the flowers and think how benevolent God is, how even without the buttercup we would so lack it, how poor we would be without the shape, the motion, the smell of the horse. There is my dog; I throw a stick and he brings it back. If I throw two, he is confused and picks up neither. That and a few other things he can do, no more. So far goes the flower, it must stand there; so far goes the dog, he can run and bark and carry a stick; and so far we go—no further.

In our closet of gratitude we may hang many things: the flower, the dog, the horse, the performance of an actor, the morning in Schliersee, the little sausages in the restaurant next to the Church of Our Lady in Munich, the arrangement of vegetables in a market, words. I have found peace with myself for a while.

The one complete joy is the children, good and bad, clean and dirty. Their eyes are wide and light, they are barefooted and brown and play in the shallow parts of the lake. Little girls bend down to pick flowers while they watch a small brother in a carriage that has wheels like cotton spools. I think of how, after we are gone, they will love the mountains and the old houses as much as we do. They will feel all that we do, this scene, this music; they will walk the same paths, eat the same, and be the same. They all have the same hearts, lungs, eyes, feet, and hands that we have, and they will always have the same hopes and pleasures. They will be we, we shall be they; I can think of no better hereafter for us, a precise repetition of the earth here about me, with these same horses and flowers, with just such faces, such cooking, such beer, and such music. Heaven is not beyond—it is being here again; in this little boy with brown legs hanging into the lake, there will grow another I, though I am not his father. For the same sun will rise tomorrow and the smoke will come out of the same houses, just as it did in my grandfather's time, and we shall always have to love some place and have a father and mother and children.

All this I thought on so many days, and it seemed so right and logical to me, that one morning I sat a long time at the lake, and I was certain that now, at the age of twenty-seven, I could arrange my life properly. I took the train to Tirol, for Schliersee seemed too worldly for what I had in mind. I went to the sawmill I loved so much up in the Dolomite Valley, where I had been happy as a boy. It was for sale and I bought it. The house and the inn, the mill and all the properties, were faultless. The old miller with the huntsman's beard and face had a wife who took care of the house and scrubbed it all day long. There were beautiful cattle, old worn wagons; the rooms, the furniture, the trees—everything was an answer to my desire for good design, for color, and for rightness. I wanted now to marry a simple woman, more simple even than my mother's idea of a wife, almost a peasant, with a healthy frame and an undisturbed mind, like a comfortable oven, who would cook and sing and be healthy and have children.

I wrote a long letter to Mother, who had returned to Regensburg, telling her to pack up and come and bring with her old

Frau Uhu, a family relic, an old servant she had from Grandfather's house, who answered when she was called "Oohoo" and thus got her name. I wrote that from now on I would be a complete joy and pride to her, live a simple life and walk around with my dog, have a wife and children. Mother packed and took a train, but when she arrived I was gone.

I had become almost ill on the third day. I walked around in the fields and touched the trees, and sat at the stone table where I had drunk my first wine as a boy. On my own face I could see that time had passed; I was the same, but I was now twenty-seven years old. I felt terribly old, and I felt guilty about not being happy here. Here all was perfect, but I could not walk around all day saying: "How beautiful, how beautiful, how beautiful," it was.

In the middle of the night I got up and looked for my passport; I was afraid I had mislaid it. I thought of New York, of the Battery, where the elevated trains come running down to the ferry slip, of the bridges. I thought of the trip I had taken to Montana, of Shoshone Canyon, and of living at the foot of Rising Wolf Mountain in Glacier Park. I thought of the wide prairie, of the smoky color of the mountains, of the weaving evening light on the sagebrush, like a sea of frozen ink with patches of yellow and copper playing over it, of an Indian riding along the horizon, alone on his horse.

Tirol does not allow comparison with the American West. Suddenly this little sawmill in Tirol became a little painted music box, on which pretty-uniformed postmen, costumed peasants, English travelers and the nurses for their children turned about to the music of a zither. It was a travel poster, a mediocre stage set. I became so lonesome for America, for even the ugly gas tank that you first see when you come up the bay in Ambrose Channel, that I left the next morning, took a train from Salzburg, the express to Munich, Cologne, Herbesthal, Rotterdam.

Success
at Last

· · · · ·

The
Old Ritz

. . .

The hotel I have called the "Splendide" was really the old Ritz-Carlton, which stood on the corner of Madison Avenue and Forty-sixth Street. Albert Keller, president of the corporation, appears in the hotel stories as "Otto Brauhaus." He was all I said he was, in kindness and character. Theodore Titze, "Victor," was the maître d'hôtel of all time. He exercised an iron discipline on his underlings and operated with the charm of a Prussian sergeant. There were many nice people and many more awful ones. What was most valuable to me were the models the hotel provided: the most beautiful women, the most powerful men, judges that took gifts, savants who got drunk and turned into idiots. There were figures for every kind of play, in front and backstairs.

The Crystal Room (the main dining room), designed by Warren Whitney, was of a grandeur and beauty no longer possible in New York hotel construction. Tall marble columns supported a concave ceiling. The decoration was in the style of the Brothers Adam. A balcony in four sections ran along the wall.

In my early days at the Ritz, I had to clear the dishes from the part of the balcony that was to the right of the entrance. At the beginning of lunch, when Armand Vesey's orchestra played, and the stately procession of people began, there were naturally no dirty dishes. There was butter to be brought up, and ice water, and rolls. The rolls were delicious and warm, and the butter was the best; in back of the screen that hid the service doors, there was a sideboard with an assortment of sauces. A roll there, with plenty of butter and a squirt of ketchup, was a good thing.

Next to the base of one of the marble columns was a stack of menus, the backs of which offered very good sketching surfaces. The palm there protected me, and I was fascinated by the beauty of ugliness for the first time in my life. Two of the restaurant's most esteemed and demanding clients, whom I called Monsieur and Madame Dryspool, were my favorite subjects.

Another esteemed guest, who lived in the hotel, was a famous cartoonist. He was known for his generosity in tipping and for never looking at a bill. The entire staff from the maîtres d'hôtel to the chambermaids considered him a "gentleman par excellence." Spurred on by a waiter with whom I worked as a bus boy, I decided to become a cartoonist. By 1926, after years of work and countless disappointments, it seemed as if I had achieved my goal. I sat up in the cupola of the old *World* building with a group of funnymen: Webster, Milt Gross, Ernie Bushmiller, and Haenigsen. Walter Berndt, who drew "Smitty" in the *Daily News,* helped me a great deal. There was constant laughter in that cupola.

Unfortunately, there were so many complaints about my strip, which was called "Count Bric-a-Brac," that after six months, during which no syndicate had picked it up, I was fired. It was a bitter time, for I had to go back to the Ritz; and the old cashiers and the maîtres d'hôtel said, "Ah, Monsieur Bemelmans, who felt himself too good for this dirty trade, is back again. *Tiens, tiens* [Well, well]."

·   ·   ·

One day, I looked into one of the many mirrors of the Ritz. I was thirty-one years old. The rosy cheeks were more rosy than they had been when I arrived from Tirol, but this was due to indoor exposure. The capillaries had exploded from too much drinking. I had a stomach. I gasped when I walked up the stairs. Morally, I felt as disgusting as I looked, and I said to myself, "How many more of these meals, how much more of this life before you look like Theodore, the penguin-shaped maître d'hôtel or, what is even worse, like some of the guests? You will be unhappy, useless, a snob, a walking garbage can. Get out, throw yourself into life. All you can learn here, you know."

From the deluxe protectorate and refuge that the Ritz had been, I stepped out into the cold world, where you had to get up on a stand to get your shoes shined, carry your own shirts to the laundry, and eat in places that were Greek, Chinese, Italian, and German.

I had planned my change from fantasy to real life with terrible timing. After two weeks away from the Ritz, everything suddenly slipped out of place. Came the crash of 1929. Nobody bought any pictures, nobody had any money. My friend Ervine Metzl, a commercial artist, sat desolate in his studio, with nothing to do. I could not go back to the Ritz, and, as things went from bad to worse, I moved in with my former valet, Herman Struck, and his wife. They lived in Astoria, on the top floor of a house with a beautiful view of Manhattan and a cellar from which I carried the coal upstairs. We had a *gemütlich* existence together—lived on potatoes, kraut, dumplings, and sausages; looked at New York, evenings, and talked of the "old days." Money, there was none. Frau Struck did the laundry; occasionally, Herman brought home a bottle of wine or a cigar. The Ritz was running very quietly. I walked every day, to the tune of "Brother, can you spare a dime?," across the Fifty-ninth Street Bridge.

I never sold anything—never. And I had reduced my demands to the cost of paper. I sat for a while in a café and tried to draw people, but, when they saw themselves, they shook their heads. I came home, freezing, and with stiff fingers opened the door of the house in Astoria. There was a dreadful hour then—before Herman came home and while his wife was out shopping—when I was alone, just as the light of day waned. I sat thinking on the theme of ending it—how? Gas? No; Herman would come in and strike a match, and the little house would go up with a big bang. Poison? We didn't have any; besides, it's painful. Jump off the bridge? In the summer, yes; but now, into that ice-cold river? Thank you, no. In front of the subway? Messy. If we had a car, then I could put it into the garage, let the radio and the motor go, and die beautifully. But Herman had only a motorcycle with a sidecar—and, besides, the garage leaked; it was made of loosely nailed-together boards.

To hang oneself is always possible, for you need only a rope.

We had a rope. When they redecorated the Crystal Room at the Ritz, all the old stuff was thrown away, or rather, it lay on the floor, and anybody who wanted something picked it up. So there was the old rope that had been used to hold people back at the entrance to the Crystal Room. This now was in the stairhall, to hold onto on the way up. It would be just long enough to go around the branch of the old tree in the yard. A chair to kick from under you was all that would be needed, and you were off to a better world. I thought it would be quite nice to have this last connection with the old Ritz—this soft, elegant, velvet-covered rope, in my favorite color, emerald green. I grabbed it with a feeling of security and friendship whenever I went up or down the stairs.

Herman's ambition had been to be a concert violinist. His father had been a restaurant violinist in Vienna and had given him instruction. But the son had not inherited his father's talent and had no ear at all for music, although he was the only one who did not know this. His favorite time of playing was towards evening. The music, which seemed to be composed by Schönberg, was extremely atonal, or anti-tonal.

I was in my room one evening, nailing a frame together to put some canvas on, when Frau Struck came in and said: "Please, shh! Daddy is playing with the Philharmonic."

Herman was sitting in front of his radio, accompanying the musicians in Liszt's *Hungarian Rhapsody,* when there was another disturbance—a knock on the door. Herr Keller, the manager of the Ritz, stood in the doorway.

"So here is where you live?" he said. The canary answered, "Peep, peep." He looked around, was given a cocktail, and stayed for dinner. At the end, wiping his mouth with his napkin, he looked around again and said, "You might as well come back to the hotel." He meant that everything there—the glasses, plates, curtains, candles, carpets, the rope in the stairhall—was from the Ritz.

Frau Struck resented this a little and said, "All honestly come by, Herr Keller, if you please," and she showed him the chips in the cups, the cracks in the glasses, the rips in the curtains, the cigar-burn holes in the carpets—all neatly repaired.

"*Ja, ja,*" said Herr Keller, "*ich weiss schon* [I know]. Is there any-

thing else you need? Just tell me, and I'll see that it gets broken."
The good friend and benefactor left.

I didn't hang myself with the beautiful velvet rope, nor did I go
back to the Ritz. I made a drawing in pen and ink of Herman
playing with the Philharmonic and, with six other such simple efforts, sent it to the *Saturday Evening Post,* which bought and published all seven of them. That was my first toehold on the shaky
ladder of success.

. . .

In a moment of optimism, I rented a studio in a house on Eighth
Street. Within a few weeks, I again felt like a hopeless failure. A
wave of black depression came over me. Outside my windows was
a miserable view. I pulled down the shades and painted scenes of
the Austrian Tirol on them. A lithographer, by the name of Tom
Little, who had a studio in the same building, saw the shades and
the room—I had painted on the walls as well. One evening he
brought the second Mademoiselle who was to be very important
in my life, and to whom I owe virtually everything in my career as
an artist. She was Miss May Massee, the children's book editor at
The Viking Press, and she said simply, "Do a children's book on
Tirol—make it just like the shades on the windows and the pictures on the walls." She folded a piece of paper several times and
explained, "Here goes black and white; on these pages you
can use color." A few months later I handed in the manuscript for
Hansi. Next came *The Golden Basket* and then the first book for
adults, *My War with the United States.* Meanwhile I had met the
third Mademoiselle, and it was in the pattern of my life that I
should find and marry someone who had intended to become a
nun but had left the convent as a novice. When Barbara was
born, we were romantically poor—the garret kind of existence.
My mother asked for photographs, but we couldn't afford any.
However, I knew a photographer, and in the waiting room of his
studio was a table full of baby pictures. I took one of these and
sent it to my mother, who wrote how very close to me the likeness
was.

At first Mama was not impressed by my success. Writers and
artists were to her forever insecure, and there was nothing one
could expect from them but unhappiness. On a visit to New York,

she was especially shocked by seeing a manuscript of mine that Harold Ross of *The New Yorker* had sent back for corrections. All the way down the margin of every page, it said, "What mean? What mean? What in hell mean?"

It precipitated a crisis and tears again. Mama sat with the manuscript in her trembling hands; it was exactly like many years ago when I came home from the *Königliche Realschule* in Regensburg with my composition all red with professor's ink.

"*O, mein Gott! O, mein lieber Gott im Himmel!*" she sighed, looking at Ross's margin notes. "What does it mean, 'What mean? What mean?'"

"It means that he doesn't understand what I have written means."

However, at long last, she breathed easier. My father-in-law was the president of a bank in Mount Kisco. When I sold my first story to the movies, I deposited some money in a trust fund for Barbara. He was so overcome by this that he made me a director. My name appeared on the letterhead of the Trust Company of Northern Westchester.

I wrote a letter on this stationery to Mama; she carried it in her handbag for years. She had shown it around so much that it was worn off at the edges, and whenever I came to Regensburg, everybody addressed me not as they normally would, as *"Herr Bemelmans," "Herr Poet,"* or *"Herr Painter,"* but as *"Herr Direktor."*

The Isle of God
(or Madeline's Origin)

·   ·   ·

When Barbara was two, we spent the summer on the Île d'Yeu, which lies in the Bay of Biscay, off the west coast of France. I have forgotten why we decided to go there. Most probably somebody told us about it.

The Île d'Yeu is immediately beautiful and at once familiar. Its round, small harbor is stuffed with boats; the big tuna schooners lie in the center; around them are sleek sardine and lobster boats. One can walk around in the harbor over the decks of boats. Only between bows and sterns shine triangles of green water. Twice a day there is a creaking of hulls and a tilting of masts; all the boats begin to settle, to lean on their neighbors; the tide, all the water, runs out of the harbor, and the bottom is dry.

The first house you come to is a small poem of a hotel. It has a bridal suite with a pompom-curtained bed, a chaste washstand, pale pink wallpaper with white pigeons flying over it, and three fauteuils, tangerine velvet and every one large enough for two, closely held, to sit in together.

The five-foot proprietor rubs his hands, hops about, glares at employees, smiles at guests. Madame sits behind an ornate desk in the dining-room, her eyes everywhere. The kitchen is bright and smells of good butter, the linen is white, the silver gleams, the waiter is spotless. Outside, under an awning, behind a hedge of well-watered yew trees, overlooking the harbor, are the apéritif tables and chairs.

The prospectus states besides that the hotel has *"eau chaude et froide, chauffage central, tout confort moderne"*—all this is of no consequence, because you can never get a room there. The hotel has but twenty-six rooms, and these are reserved year after year, by the same people, French families.

Further down is the Hôtel des Voyageurs, sixty rooms, the same thing, the bridal suite in green, the prices somewhat more moderate, the *confort* less *moderne,* but also all booked by April. "Ah, if you would only have written me a letter in March," say the proprietors of both places several times a day from June to September.

Walking down the Quai Sadi-Carnot, you turn right and go through the rue de la Sardine. This street is beautifully named; the houses on both sides touch your shoulders and only a man with one short leg can walk through it in comfort, as half the street is taken up by a sidewalk.

At the end of the Street of the Sardine is the Island's store, the Nouvelles Galeries Insulaires. Its owner Monsieur Penaud will find a place for you to live. Île d'Yeu should really be Île de Dieu, Monsieur Penaud explained, "d'Yeu" being the ancient and faulty way the Islanders spelled "of God." He established us in a fisherman's house, at the holiest address in this world, namely: No. 3, rue du Paradis, Saint-Sauveur, Île d'Yeu.

Our house was a sage, white, well-designed building. Through every door and window of it smiled the marine charm of the Island. The sea was no more than sixty yards from our door. Across the street was an eleventh-century church, whose steeple was built in the shape of a lighthouse. Over the house a brace of gulls hung in the air; there was the murmur of the sea; an old rowboat, with a sailor painted on its keel, stood up in the corner of the garden and served as a chicken coop.

The vegetables in the garden, the fruit on the trees, and the chicken eggs went with the house; included also was a bicycle, trademarked "Hirondelle." It is a nice thing to take over a household so living, complete, and warm, and dig up radishes that someone else has planted for you and cut flowers in a garden that someone else has tended.

The coast of the Island is a succession of small, private beaches, each one like a room, its walls three curtains of rock and greenery. There is a cave to dress in. Once you arrive, it is yours. On the open side is the water, little waves, fine sand; and out on the green ocean all day long the sardine fleet crosses back and forth with colored sails leaning over the water.

There seem to be only three kinds of people: sailors, their hundred-times-patched sensible pants and blouses in every shade of color; children; and everywhere two little bent old women dressed in black, their sharp profiles hooked together in gossip. Like crows in a tree they are, and rightly enough, called *"vieux corbeaux."*

Posing everywhere are fish and the things relating to them. The sardine is the banana of the Île d'Yeu: you slip and fall on it. It looks out of the small market baskets that the *vieux corbeaux* carry home; its tail sticks out of fishermen's pockets; it is dragged by in boxes and barrels. Other fish, the tuna predominating, wander by on the shoulders of strong sailors, tied to bicycles, pushed by pairs of boys in carts.

·   ·   ·

One day I bought four lobsters and rode back to the rue du Paradis and almost ran into Paradise itself. Pedaling along with the sack over my shoulder, both hands in my pockets and tracing fancy curves in the roadbed, I came to a bend, which is hidden by some dozen pine trees. Around this turn raced the Island's only automobile, a four-horsepower Super-Rosengart, belonging to the baker of Saint-Sauveur. This car is a fragrant, flour-covered breadbasket on wheels; it threw me in a wide curve off the bicycle into a bramble bush. I took the car's doorhandle off with my elbow.

I asked the baker to take me to the hospital in Saint-Sauveur, but he said that, according to French law, a car must remain exactly where it was when the accident occurred, so that the gendarmes could make their proper deductions and see who was on the wrong side of the road. I tried to change his mind, but he said, "Permit me, *alors*, monsieur, if you use words like that, then it is of no use at all to go on with this conversation."

Having spoken, he went on to pick up his *pain de ménage* and some *croissants* that were scattered on the road, and then spread aside the branches of the thicket to look for the doorhandle of his

Super-Rosengart. I took my lobsters and went to the hospital on foot.

A doctor came, with a cigarette stub hanging from his lower lip. With a blunt needle he wobbled into my arm. *"Excusez-moi,"* he said, *"mais votre peau est dure!"* I was put into a small white carbolicky bed. In the next room was a little girl who had had her appendix out, and on the ceiling over my bed was a crack that, in the varying light of morning, noon, and evening, looked like a rabbit, like the profile of Léon Blum, and at last, in conformity with the Island, like a tremendous sardine.

. . .

I saw the nun bringing soup to the little girl. I remembered the stories my mother had told me of life in the convent school at Altötting and the little girl, the hospital, the room, the crank on the bed, the nurse, the old doctor, who looked like Léon Blum, all fell into place.

I thought about where Madeline and her friends should live and decided on Paris. I made the first sketches on a sidewalk table outside the Restaurant Voltaire on the quai of that same name. The first words of the text, "In an old house in Paris/that was covered with vines," were written on the back of a menu in Pete's Tavern on the corner of Eighteenth Street and Irving Place in New York. *Madeline* was first published in 1939.

It took about ten years to think of the next one, which was *Madeline's Rescue*. One day, after that was finished and in print, I stood and looked down at the Seine opposite Notre Dame. Some little boys were pointing at something floating in the river. One of them shouted: "Ah, there comes the wooden leg of my grandfather." I looked at the object that was approaching and discovered that in my book I had the Seine flowing in the wrong direction.

Barbara

· · · · · ·

Camp
Nomopo

.   .   .

After the first walk through the city, Barbara came back to the Hotel Metropolitano in Quito with her lips blue and her little fists clenched. Mimi put her to bed and I went out to look for a garment that would shield her against the cold wind that blows down from Mt. Pichincha. There was no snow suit to be had; it's not cold enough for that, and the coats for little girls which I found and brought back to the hotel Barbara waved away. Four and a half years old, she knew exactly what she wanted. She sat up in bed with the first measles spots on her chest and said she would rather freeze to death than wear anything like the samples she had seen.

During the next week while she was in bed, I had to design coats for her. I exhausted myself making a stack of fashion drawings, designs of dramatic coats and hats to go with them, and I cut paper dolls out of old fashion magazines and pasted my coats on them. The design that found favor with Barbara was a three-storied kind of pelerine, a garment such as Viennese fiacre drivers of the time of Franz Josef used to wear.

"This is it," she said. "That's the bestest good one."

As soon as Barbara was well, we went to a tailor with the design. The shop of Señor Pablo Duque Arias faces the square of

San Francisco. It is like an indoor farm. Chickens run around among the sewing machines and over the low podium on which Mr. Arias's chief cutter sits with crossed legs; a cat, a dog with off-spring, and a parrot complete the fauna; the flora consist of artificial paper roses stuck in a dry vase that stands on a small shelf between an oil print of the Madonna and a picture of the Temptation of St. Anthony.

Barbara eyed this *salon de couture* with alarm and suspicion, but she let Señor Arias measure her. He studied my design and then we went to the store of Don Alfonso Perez Pallares to buy the cloth—the tailor, Barbara, Mimi, and myself. We found something that looked like the lining of a good English traveling bag. It was made in Ecuador and it was agreeable to everyone.

The coat was in work for a week, and on each day we inspected progress of the garment. At the end, Barbara looked into a mirror and was delighted with the results. It cost $7.50, not counting my time and talent. The coat was a very warm and useful garment on the return trip to New York in February.

Barbara is one of the seventy-five or a hundred overprivileged children who are allowed to play inside the cast-iron confines of Gramercy Park. Another little girl, equally well fixed, is an earnest, dark-haired, five-year-old whose name is Ruthie. Ruthie played with Barbara one day and they became friends—and at their third meeting, on a day in March, when Barbara was dressed in my creation, little Ruthie said to Barbara, "You look like Oliver Twister in that coat. That's a coat like orphans wear. I think it's terrible. I don't see how you can wear it."

On a visit to Ruthie's house that afternoon, Barbara inspected Ruthie's wardrobe. She did not wear the "Oliver Twister" coat when she came back, but carried it in her arms and hid it in the closet of her room.

She succeeded by a week of ceaseless cajolery and little-girl appeal in wangling a new winter outfit from me when it was already spring and all the Gramercy Park trees were breaking out with small green buds. Of course, it was an outfit exactly like something that Ruthie had, only newer.

Barbara and Ruthie were now bosom friends. They sat together on a bench facing a stone urn, to the left of the statue of Mr. Booth, and there they hatched another plot. The plan was to go to a summer camp together. Little Ruthie had been at this camp the year before and she described the sylvan, rugged beauty of that life to Barbara. Barbara said to Ruthie that she'd love to go but that she was afraid she would be lonesome, that she never had gone anywhere without her parents.

"Oh," said Ruthie, "after the third day you forget you ever had a father or mother."

Barbara came home with this bit of grim wisdom.

The camp we chose took care of a hundred girls. It was in the upper Adirondacks. The water came from artesian wells, the children slept in semi-bungalows and washed themselves at ten taps that spouted cold artesian water. The taps were conveniently located in front of the bungalows, the prospectus said, and the children got up to the sound of a bugle at 7:30 a.m. and did their own housework.

When I came to this part of the booklet I was convinced that nothing was better for our darling than to rise in the upper Adirondacks at 7:30 and scrub herself at a cold-water tap.

Barbara hopped on one foot and on the other and clasped her hands with joy when I told her that she would be one of the lucky members of Camp Nomopo, which in the language of the Indians means Land That Is Bright.

The equipment needed for this simple life had to be marked with the name of the child and was as follows:

Bathing suits, 2	Bathrobe, 1
Bathing sandals, 1 pair	Tennis sneakers, 1 pair
Heavy bathing caps, 2	Handkerchiefs, 6
Cotton ankle socks, 4 pairs	Play suits, 2
Cotton underwear, 4 suits	Bedroom slippers, 1 pair
Pajamas, 3 pairs	Rubbers, 1 pair
Tennis racquet, 1	Bath towels, 3
Tennis balls, 3	Face towels, 3
Toilet articles	Mattress protector, 1
Poncho, 1	Laundry bag, 1
Rain hat, 1	Duffel bag, 1
Riding breeches, 1 pair	Folding knife and spoon, 1 each
Bed sheets, 3	Drinking cup with handle, 1
Pillow cases, 3	Sewing material
Dark blankets, 3	Bible, 1

In addition, there was this special equipment:

1 pair Nomopo gabardine shorts	1 Nomopo green tie
1 pair Nomopo brown oxfords	1 Nomopo green sweater
2 white Nomopo shirts	2 pairs Nomopo ankle socks
2 Nomopo suits	

The whole thing went into a green army trunk and was stowed in the back seat of the car.

The cost of going to the camp for two months was a healthy figure, about what it would take to stay at a good hotel for that time. There was a canteen. There were, besides, provisions for pocket money to buy extra things at the canteen and an additional charge for the materials used in the arts and crafts building of Camp Nomopo.

The camp was full of cheer and gladness when we arrived. The Madame who ran it received her guests with the intense charm and cordiality of a Howard Johnson hostess; the counselors hopped around, and little Ruthie, who had arrived the day before, took Barbara by the hand and led her down to their semi-bungalow, Number 5. I checked on the waterspout which was right next to it. The cabin was a loose shelter built on stilts, open to the north and south, with no windows but large shutters that were held up by pieces of wood. In it stood six little cast-iron cots such as you see in orphanages; birds sang outside and the branches of the trees were the curtains.

In this room the floor was a row of unpainted boards through which, here and there, you could see the good earth. We also inspected the mess hall and the infirmary. The counselor that had Barbara in charge showed her how to make her bed, how to sweep the floor, and how to empty the rubbish bin—three duties that were her part of the housekeeping. Barbara did it all with gusto.

The Madame came around at about 3 p.m. and said, "Please leave before it gets dark. It's easier for the child that way."

So we said good-by to Barbara. She was brave. She said, "Good-by," and walked away with her back to the car, waving as she walked. Halfway down to shack Number 5, at the cold-water tap, she suddenly turned. The small face was streaked with tears and she came back and got a grip on her mother and announced that she would not stay in the camp.

I don't know where I got the courage because my heart was breaking, but I took Barbara, handed her to the Madame, who pressed her to her ample bosom. I got Mimi into the car, and drove off. We called the camp an hour later on the phone and the Madame announced that Barbara's grief had lasted for a quarter of an hour. "Now she's in the recreation hall having the time of her life, the little darling. She's sitting in front of the big fire with little Ruthie, listening to 'Peter and the Wolf.' Don't you worry a minute about her—and please, please don't come visiting her until ten days from now."

The next day, while staying at a hotel, I reflected what a wonderful racket a children's camp is, how much better it is than owning a hotel, for example.

Imagine if the guests of a hotel like the Savoy-Plaza arrived bringing their own three dark blankets and sheets, towels and pillow cases, made their own beds, emptied their garbage, went down to the cold-water taps in Central Park to scrub themselves, and without murmur ate the healthy, strength-giving diet you put before them! If instead of going out in the evening and spending their money in rival establishments, they would quietly sit around the bar listening to "Peter and the Wolf" or do arty-crafty things in the ballroom—all of them dressed in hats, shoes, and sweaters marked Savoy-Plaza!

We came back after ten days in which we wrote nine letters and received four cards written by Barbara's counselor. After a glowing report on how glad and happy and what a fine girl she was, the Madame sent for her.

She came in the rain, between the wet, dripping trees, in the Nomopo rain hat, the Nomopo green sweater and poncho, alone and much sadder-looking than "Oliver Twister" ever was. She broke out in streams of tears when she saw us, and she kept crying even after it stopped raining outside. She blinked red-eyed in the sun that shone above rays of floating mist.

We went out to a playfield, and, at one moment when we stepped aside to discuss what to do, Barbara found herself surrounded by her comrades. Madame looked down at her with reproach, and her counselor, a maiden from whose Nomopo sweater I could hardly take my eyes, said, "You're not going to be a sissy now, are you, and run away from us?"

Barbara was the most complete portrait of misery I have ever seen, not excepting the work of El Greco. She cried, "I don't like it here. I want to go home with Mummy and Poppy. I want to go home; I don't like it here. I want to go home."

We took her into the car with us, and I said in French to Mimi that I thought under the circumstances it would be the best thing to take her home with us. While I spoke, she took hold of the leather straps that are attached to the convertible top of the car as if to anchor herself, and said, "You don't have to speak French, I know what you were saying. You said, 'Let's start the car and push Barbara out and drive away like the last time' "—and then she continued, "I dream about you at night and when I wake up you're not there, and in the morning another little girl next to me cries, and that makes me cry too.

"Ruthie said she cried too the first time last year, but her mother just left her there and never came to see her and now she's used to it, but I won't get used to it because I dream of you every night. And it's so cold in the morning, and I have to empty the pail and sweep."

The washing at the tap she had got around, apparently. She was streaked with dirt and her hair was a mess. She said, "We take a bath twice a week, down at the lake, and the water is cold. I want to go home. I don't like it here. I want to go home with Mummy and Poppy."

A man came to the car and smiled and said, "I'm only the husband of Mrs. Van Cortland who runs the camp, and I can assure you that Barbara's the happiest little girl when you're not here. She sings and plays all day long. I think it would be a great mistake for you to take her away."

I told him that we would take her away. Barbara let go of the straps and the man said, "Well, all I can say is that in my twenty-seven years this has happened only once before."

Barbara smelled of garlic and unwashed hair. They had had meat loaf for lunch. It was dark by the time we had made the decision and we stayed for supper. It began to rain again, and there is nothing more wet and desolate than Adirondack camps in the rain. The meal was served on a drafty porch, a piece of canvas blew in with every gust of wind. The menu consisted of melted cheese poured over toast and a lukewarm rice pudding that tasted like glue; a glass of milk was served to each diner.

We left poor Ruthie behind, and the Madame and her husband assured us again that it was only the second time in twenty-seven years that such a thing had happened.

Little Bit
and the *America*

·   ·   ·

"Look, what a lovely day we have for sailing," I said, pointing my pen toward the lit-up greenery outside the open window. The birds sang in the trees, and the sun shone on a deck of brightly colored luggage tags which I was filling out. Under "S.S. *America*" I had carefully lettered my name, and I answered the gay question of "Destination?" with "Cherbourg."

I was about to fill out a new tag when I noticed Barbara's silence. She was standing at the window, staring at me. I saw clearly the symptoms of wanting something, symptoms long known to me and always the same. I remembered that the day before she had said something about a dog, but I had been called away before I could talk about it at length.

For the most part, Barbara is a sweet and normal child; when she wants something, she changes. The child is then under great stress. A trembling of the lower lip precedes the filling of the beautiful eyes with tears. I am allowed to see these hopeless eyes for a moment, and then, as a spotlight moves from one place to another, she averts her gaze and slowly turns, folds her arms, and looks into the distance, or if there is no distance, at the wall. The crisis is approaching. She swallows, but her throat is constricted; finally, with the urgency of a stammerer, and with her small hands clenched, she manages to convey a few dry words. The small voice is like a cold trumpet. The last word is a choking sound. There is a long, cold silence.

On the morning of sailing I recognized the first stage of this painful condition that overcomes her from time to time. I could tell it by her eyes, her mouth, the position she stood in, the peculiar angles of her arms and legs. She was twisted in an unhappy pose of indecision. Not that she didn't know precisely what she wanted: she was undecided about how to broach the subject.

After the tears, the gaze into the distance, the silence, Barbara blurted out, "You promised I could have a dog."

I steeled myself and answered, "Yes, when we get back from Europe you can have a dog."

An answer like that is worse than an outright no. The mood of "I wish I was dead" descended on Barbara. She stared coldly out of the window, and then she turned and limply dragged herself down the corridor to her room, where she goes at times of crisis. She closed the door not by slamming it, but with a terrible, slow finality. One can see from the corridor how she lets go of the handle inside—in unspeakably dolorous fashion; slowly the handle rises, and there is the barely audible click of the mechanism. There is then the cutting off of human relations, a falling off of appetite, and nothing in the world of joy or disaster matters.

Ordinarily the comatose state lasts for weeks. In this case, however, Barbara was confronted with a deadline, for the ship was sailing at five that afternoon and it was now eleven in the morning. I usually break down after three or four weeks of resistance. The time limit for this operation was five hours.

She decided at first to continue with standard practice, the manual of which I know as well as I do the alphabet.

From the door at the end of the corridor came the sound of heartbreaking sobs. Normally these sobs last for a good while, and then, the crisis ebbing off, there follows an hour or two of real or simulated sleep, in which she gathers strength for renewed efforts. This time, however, the sobs were discontinued ahead of schedule and were followed up by a period of total silence, which I knew was taken up with plotting at the speed of calculating machinery. This took about ten minutes. As the door had closed, so it opened again, and fatefully and slowly, as the condemned walk to their place of execution, the poor child, handkerchief in hand, dragged along the corridor past my room into the kitchen. I never knew until that morning that the pouring of milk into a glass could be a bitter and hopeless thing to watch.

I am as hardened against the heartbreak routine as a coroner is to postmortems. I can be blind to tears and deaf to the most urgent pleading. I said, "Please be reasonable. I promise you that the moment we get back you can have a dog."

I was not prepared for what followed—the new slant, the surprise attack.

She leaned against the kitchen doorjamb and drank the last of the milk. Her mouth was ringed with white. She said in measured and accusing tones, "You read in the papers this morning what they did in Albany."

"I beg your pardon?"

"They passed a law that all institutions like the A.S.P.C.A. are to be forced to turn dogs over to hospitals, for vivisection—and you know what will happen. They'll get her and then they'll cut her open and sew her up again over and over until she's dead."

"What has that got to do with me?"

"It has to do with the dog you promised me."

"What dog?"

"The dog that Frances wants to give me."

Frances is a red-headed girl who goes to school with Barbara.

"I didn't know Frances had a dog."

Barbara raised her eyebrows. "You never listen," she said, and as if talking to an idiot and with weary gestures she recited, "Poppy, I told you all about it a dozen times. Doctor Lincoln, that's Frances's father, is going to Saudi Arabia to work for an oil company, and he had to sign a paper agreeing not to take a dog, because it seems the Arabs don't like dogs. So the dog has to be got rid of. So Doctor Lincoln said to Frances, 'If you don't get rid of her, I will.' Now you know how doctors are—they have no feelings whatever for animals. He'll give her to some hospital for experiments."

I resumed filling out baggage tags. When I hear the word "dog" I see in my mind a reasonably large animal of no particular breed, uncertain in outline, like a Thurber dog, and with a rough, dark coat. This image was hovering about when I asked, "What kind of a dog is it?"

"Her name is Little Bit."

"What?"

"Little *BIT*—that's her name. She's the dearest, sweetest, snow-white, itsy-bitsy, tiny little toy poodle you have ever seen. Can I have her, please?"

I almost let out a shrill bark.

"Wait till you see her and all the things she's got—a special little wicker bed with a mattress, and a dish with her picture on it, and around it is written 'Always faithful' in French. You see, Poppy, they got Little Bit in Paris last year, and she's the uniquest, sharpest little dog you've ever seen, and naturally she's housebroken, and Frances says she's not going to give her to anybody but me."

I was playing for time. I would have settled for a Corgi, a Yorkshire, a Weimaraner, even a German boxer or a Mexican hairless, but Little Bit was too much. I knew that Doctor Lincoln lived some thirty miles out of the city, and that it would be impossible to get the dog to New York before the ship sailed.

"Where is the dog now?" I asked with faked interest.

"She'll be here any minute, Poppy. Frances is on the way now—and oh, wait till you see, she has the cutest little boots for rainy weather, and a cashmere sweater, sea green, and several sets of leashes and collars—you won't have to buy a thing."

"All right," I said, "you can have the dog. We'll put it in a good kennel until we return."

The symptoms, well-known and always the same, returned again. The lower lip trembled. "Kennel," she said—and there is no actress on stage or screen who could have weighted this word with more reproach and misery.

"Yes, kennel," I said and filled out the baggage tag for my portable typewriter.

"Poppy—" she started, but I got up and said, "Now look, Barbara, the ship leaves in a few hours, and to take a dog aboard you have to get a certificate from a veterinary, and reserve a place for him, and buy a ticket."

To my astonishment, Barbara smiled indulgently. "Well, if that's all that's bothering you—first of all, we're going to France; the French, unlike the English, have no quarantine for dogs, and they don't even ask for a health certificate. Second, you can make all the arrangements for the dog's passage on board ship, after it sails. Third, there is plenty of room in the kennels. I know all this because Frances and I went down to the U.S. Lines and got the information day before yesterday."

I stared into distance. At such times I feel a great deal for the man who's going to marry Barbara. With all hope failing I said, "But we'll have to get a traveling bag or something to put the dog in."

"She has a lovely little traveling bag with her name lettered on it, 'Little Bit.' "

The name stung like a whip. "All right then." I wrote an extra baggage tag to be attached to the dog's bag.

Barbara wore the smug smile of success. "Wait till you see her," she said and ran out of the room. In a moment she returned with Frances, who, I am sure, had been sitting there waiting all the while. The timing was perfect.

Little Bit had shoebutton eyes and a patent-leather nose and a strawberry-colored collar; she was fluffy from the top of her head to her shoulders and then shorn like a miniature Persian lamb. At the end of a stub of a tail was a puff of fluff, and other puffs on the four legs. She wore a pale blue ribbon, and a bell on the collar. I thought that if she were cut open most probably sawdust would come out.

A real dog moves about a room and sniffs its way into corners. It inspects furniture and people, and makes notes of things. Little Bit stood with cocksparrow stiffness on four legs as static as her stare. She was picked up and brought over to me. I think she knew exactly what I thought of her, for she lifted her tiny lip on the left side of her face over her mouse teeth and sneered. She was put down, and she danced on stilts, with the motion of a mechanical toy, back to Frances.

I was shown the traveling bag, which was like one of the pocketbooks that WAC colonels carry.

"We don't need that tag," said Barbara. "I'll carry her in this. Look." The pocketbook, which had a circular opening with a wire screen on each end for breathing purposes, was opened; Little Bit jumped into it, and it was closed. "You see, she won't be any bother whatever."

The bag was opened again. With a standing jump Little Bit hurdled the handles of the bag and stalked toward me. Tilting her head a little, she stood looking up, and then she again lifted her lip over her small fangs.

"Oh, look, Barbara!" said Frances. "Little Bit likes your father—she's smiling at him."

I had an impulse to sneer back, but I took the baggage tags and
began to attach them to the luggage. Then I left the room, for
Frances showed signs of crisis; her eyes were filling, and the heartbreak was too much for me. Little Bit was less emotional. She ate
a hearty meal from her *Toujours fidèle* dish and inspected the
house, tinkling about with the small bell that hung from her
collar.

It was time to go to the boat. The luggage was taken to a taxi,
and Little Bit hopped into her bag. On the way I thought about
the things I had forgotten to take care of, and also about Little
Bit. It is said that there are three kinds of books that are always a
success: a book about a doctor, a book about Lincoln, and a book
about a dog. Well, here was Doctor Lincoln's dog, but it didn't
seem to hold the elements of anything except chagrin. I wondered
if Lincoln had ever had a dog, or a doctor, or if Lincoln's doctor
had had a dog. I wondered if that side of Lincoln, perhaps the last
remaining side, had been investigated as yet or was still open.

We arrived with Doctor Lincoln's dog at the customs barrier,
and our passports were checked. The baggage was brought
aboard. In our cabin we found some friends waiting. Frances and
Barbara, with Little Bit looking out of her bag, inspected the ship.
The gong sounded, and the deck steward sang out, "All ashore
that's going ashore!" The passengers lined up to wave their fare-
wells. The last of those that were going ashore slid down the
gangplank. Good-by, good-by—and then the engine bells
sounded below, and the tugs moaned and hissed, and the ship
backed out into the river.

There are few sights in the world as beautiful as a trip down the
Hudson and out to sea, especially at dusk. I was on deck until we
passed the Ambrose Lightship, and then I went down to the
cabin.

Little Bit was lying on a blotter, on the writing desk, and
watching Barbara's hand. Barbara was already writing a letter to
Frances, describing the beauty of travel and Little Bit's reactions.
"Isn't she the best traveling dog we've ever had, Poppy?"

The cabins aboard the *America* are the only ones I have ever
been in that don't seem to be aboard ship. They are large—more
like rooms in a country home—a little chintzy in decoration, and

over the portholes are curtains. In back of these one suspects screened doors that lead out to a porch and a Connecticut lawn rather than the ocean.

I put my things in place and changed to a comfortable jacket. I said, "I guess I better go up and get this dog business settled."

"It's all attended to, Poppy. I took care of it," said Barbara and continued writing.

"Well, then you'd better take her upstairs to the kennels. It's almost dinnertime."

"She doesn't have to go to the kennels."

"Now, look, Barbara—"

"See for yourself, Poppy. Just ring for the steward, or let me ring for him."

"Yes, sir," said the steward, smiling.

"Is it all right for the dog to stay in the cabin?" I asked. The steward had one of the most honest and kind faces I have ever seen. He didn't fit on a ship either. He was more like a person that works around horses, or a gardener. He had bright eyes and squint lines, a leathery skin, and a good smile.

He closed his eyes and announced, "Dog? I don't see no dog in here, sir." He winked like a burlesque comedian and touched one finger to his head in salute. "My name is Jeff," he said. "If you want anything—" And then he was gone.

"You see?" said Barbara. "And besides, you save fifty dollars, and coming back another fifty, makes a hundred."

I am sure that Little Bit understood every word of the conversation. She stood up on the blotter and tilted her head, listening to Barbara, who said to her, "You know, Little Bit, you're not supposed to be on this ship at all. You mustn't let anybody see you. Now you hide, while we go down to eat."

There was a knock at the door. Silently Little Bit jumped to the floor and was out of sight.

It was the steward. He brought a little raw meat mixed with string beans on a plate covered with another plate. "Yes, sir," was all he said.

Barbara was asleep when the first rapport between me and Little Bit took place. I was sitting on a couch, reading, when she came into my cabin. By some magic trick, like an elevator going up a building shaft, she rose and seated herself next to me. She kept a hand's width of distance, tilted her head, and then lifted

her lip over the left side of her face. I think I smiled back at her in the same fashion. I looked at her with interest for the first time— she was embarrassed. She looked away and then suddenly changed position, stretching her front legs ahead and sitting down flat on her hind legs. She made several jerky movements but never uttered a sound.

Barbara's sleepy voice came from the other room. "Aren't you glad we have Little Bit with us?"

"Yes," I said, "I am." I thought about the miracles of nature, how this tough little lion in sheep's pelt functioned as she did; with a brain that could be no larger than an olive, she had memory, understanding, tact, courage, and no doubt loyalty, and she was completely self-sufficient. She smiled once more, and I smiled back: the relationship was established. Life went on as steadily as the ship.

On the afternoon of the third day out, as I lay in my deck chair reading, Barbara came running. "Little Bit is gone," she stammered with trembling lower lip.

We went down to the cabin. The steward was on all fours, looking under the beds and furniture. "Somebody musta left the door open," he said, "or it wasn't closed properly and swung open, and I suppose she got lonesome here all by herself and went looking for you. You should have taken her up to the movies with you, Miss."

"She's a smart dog," said Barbara. "Let's go to every spot on board where she might look for us."

So we went to the dining room, to the smoking room, the theater, the swimming pool, up the stairs, down the stairs, up on all the decks and around them, and to a secret little deck we had discovered between second and third class at the back of the ship, where Little Bit was taken for her exercise mornings and evenings and could run about freely while I stood guard.

A liner is as big as a city. She was nowhere.

When we got back the steward said, "I know where she is. You see, anybody finds a dog naturally takes it up to the kennels, and that's where she is. And there she stays for the rest of the trip. Remember, I never saw the dog, I don't know anything about her. The butcher—that's the man in charge of the kennels—he's liable to report me if he finds out I helped hide her. He's mean, especially about money. He figures that each passenger gives him ten bucks for taking care of a dog, and he doesn't want any of us to snatch. There was a Yorkshire stowing away trip before last; he caught him at the gangplank as the dog was leaving the ship—the passenger had put him on a leash. Well, the butcher stopped him from getting off. He held up everything for hours, the man had to pay passage for the dog, and the steward who had helped hide him was fired. Herman Haegeli is his name, and he's as mean as they come. You'll find him on the top deck, near the aft chimney, where it says 'Kennels.'"

At such moments I enjoy the full confidence and affection of my child. Her nervous little hand is in mine, she willingly takes direction, her whole being is devotion, and no trouble is too much. She loved me especially then, because she knows that I am larcenous at heart and willing to go to the greatest lengths to beat a game and especially a meany.

"Now remember," I said, "if you want that dog back we have to be very careful. Let's first go and case the joint."

We climbed up into the scene of white and red ventilators, the sounds of humming wires, and the swish of the water. In yellow and crimson fire, the ball of the sun had half sunk into the sea, precisely at the end of the avenue of foam that the ship had plowed through the ocean. We were alone. We walked up and down, like people taking exercise before dinner, and the sea changed to violet and to indigo and then to that glossy gunmetal hue that it wears on moonless nights. The ship swished along to the even pulse of her machinery.

There was the sign. A yellow light shone from a porthole. I lifted Barbara, and inside, in one of the upper cases, was Little Bit, behind bars. There was no lock on her cage.

No one was inside. The door was fastened by a padlock. We walked back and forth for a while, and then a man came up the stairs, carrying a pail. He wore a gray cap, a towel around his neck, and a white coat such as butchers work in.

"That's our man," I said to Barbara.

Inside the kennels he brought forth a large dish that was like the body of a kettledrum. The dogs were barking.

"Now listen carefully, Barbara. I will go in and start a conversation with Mr. Haegeli. I will try to arrange it so that he turns his back on Little Bit's cage. At that moment, carefully open the door of the cage, grab Little Bit, put her under your coat, and then don't run—stand still, and after a while say, 'Oh, please let's get out of here.' I will then say good evening, and we both will leave very slowly. Remember to act calmly, watch the butcher, but don't expect a signal from me. Decide yourself when it is time to act. It might be when he is in the middle of work, or while he is talking."

"Oh, please, Poppy, let's get out of here," Barbara rehearsed.

I opened the door to the kennel and smiled like a tourist in appreciation of a new discovery. "Oh, that's where the dogs are kept," I said. "Good evening."

Mr. Haegeli looked up and answered with a grunt. He was mixing dog food.

"My, what nice food you're preparing for them. How much do they charge to take a dog across?"

"Fifty dollars," said Mr. Haegeli in a Swiss accent. There are all kinds of Swiss, some with French, some with Italian, and some with German accents. They all talk in a singing fashion. The faces are as varied as the accents. The butcher didn't look like a butcher—a good butcher is fat and rosy. Mr. Haegeli was thin-lipped, thin-nosed, his chin was pointed. In the light he didn't look as mean as I expected; he looked rather fanatic, and frustrated.

"How often do you feed them?"

"They eat twice a day and as good as anybody on board," said Mr. Haegeli. "All except Rolfi there—he belongs to an actor, Mr. Kruger, who crosses twice a year and brings the dog's food along." He pointed to the cage where a large police dog was housed. "Rolfi, he is fed once a day, out of cans." He seemed to resent Rolfi and his master.

"You exercise them?"

"Yes, of course—all except Rolfi. Mr. Kruger comes up in the morning and takes him around with him on the top deck and sits with him there on a bench. He doesn't leave him alone. There is such a thing as making too much fuss over a dog."

I said that I agreed with him.

"He tried to keep him in his cabin—he said he'd pay full fare for Rolfi, like a passenger. He'll come up any minute now to say good night to Rolfi. Some people are crazy about dogs." Mr. Haegeli was putting chopped meat, vegetables, and cereal into the large dish. "There are other people that try to get away with something—they try and smuggle dogs across, like that one there." He pointed at Little Bit. "But we catch them," he said in his Swiss accent. "Oh yes, we catch them. They think they're smart, but they don't get away with it—not with me on board they don't. I have ways of finding out. I track them down." The fires of the fanatic burned in his eyes. "I catch them every time." He sounded as if he turned them over to the guillotine after he caught them. "Ah, here comes Mr. Kruger," he said and opened the door.

Kurt Kruger, the actor, said good evening and introduced himself. He spoke to Mr. Haegeli in German—and Mr. Haegeli turned his back on Little Bit's cage to open Rolfi's. The entire place was immediately deafened with barking from a dozen cages. The breathless moment had arrived. Barbara was approaching the door, but the dog-lover Kruger spotted Little Bit and said, "There's a new one." He spoke to Little Bit, and Little Bit, who had behaved as if she had been carefully rehearsed for her liberation, turned away with tears in her eyes.

Mr. Kruger and his dog disappeared.

Mr. Haegeli wiped his hand on his apron and went back to mixing the dog food. The chances for rescuing Little Bit were getting slim.

"Where do you come from, Mr. Haegeli?"

"Schaffhausen. You know Schaffhausen?"

"Yes, yes," I said in German. *"Wunderbar."*

"Ja, ja, beautiful city."

"And the waterfall!"

"You know the Haegeli Wurstfabrik there?"

"No, I'm sorry."

"Well, it's one of the biggest sausage factories in Switzerland— liverwurst, salami, cervelat, frankfurters, boned hams—a big concern, belongs to a branch of my family. I'm sort of a wanderer. I like to travel restless, you know I can't see myself in Schaffhausen." He looked up. He was mixing food with both hands, his arms rotating.

"I understand."

"Besides, we don't get along, my relatives and I. All they think about is money, small money—I think in large sums. I like a wide horizon. Schaffhausen is not for me."

"How long have you been traveling?"

"Oh, I've been two years on this ship. You see, I'm not really a butcher but an inventor."

"How interesting! What are you working on?"

At last Mr. Haegeli turned his back on the cage in which Little Bit waited. "Well, it's something tremendous. It's, so to say, revolutionary."

"Oh?"

"There's a friend of mine, a Swiss, who is a baker, but you know, like I'm not a real butcher, he is not exactly a baker—I mean, he knows his trade but he has ambition to make something of himself—and together we have created something that we call a frankroll." He waited for the effect.

"What is a frankroll?"

"It's a frankfurter baked inside a roll. We've got everything here to experiment with, the material and the ovens. I make the franks and he makes the rolls. We've tried it out on the passengers. Mr. Kruger, for example, says it's a marvelous idea. I might add that the experimental stage is over. Our product is perfect. Now it is a question of selling the patent, or licensing somebody—you know the way that is done. You make much more that way."

"Have you tried?"

Mr. Haegeli came close, the inventor's excitement in his eyes now. "That is where the hitch comes in. On the last trip I saw the biggest frankfurter people in America—they're in New York. Well, the things you find out! They were very nice. The president received us and looked at the product and tasted it. He liked it, because he called for his son and a man who works close to him. 'I think you've got something there,' said the old man. I think with him we would have had clear sailing, but he had one of these wisenheimers for a son."

As Haegeli talked he forgot completely about the dogs. He gesticulated with hands that were sticky with hash, using them as a boxer does when he talks with his gloves on. Standing close to me, he held them away lest dog food soil my clothes. He stood exactly right, with his back turned to the spot where Barbara was slowly reaching to the door of Little Bit's cage. It was all foiled again by the return of Mr. Kruger and Rolfi. Mr. Kruger kissed his dog good night and stood waiting while Rolfi slowly walked into his cage. He said to Rolfi that it was only for two more nights that he had to be here, he wished us a good night also, and after a final good night to his dog he went.

"Where was I?" said the butcher.

"With the frankroll, the old man, and the wise-guy son."

"Right. Well, the son was looking at our product with a mixture of doubt, so he took a bite out of it, and in the middle of it he stopped chewing. 'Mmmm,' he said. 'Not bad, not bad at all. But—' He paused a long time, and then he said, 'What about the mustard, gentlemen?'

"I said, 'All right, what about the mustard?'

So the wise guy says, 'I'm a customer. I'm buying. I'm at a hot-dog stand. I watch the man in the white jacket. He picks up the frankfurter roll that's been sliced and placed face down on the hot plate—he picks it up in a sanitary fashion—and he takes the skinless frank with his prong and puts it in the roll and hands it to me. Now, I dip into the mustard pot, or maybe I decide on a little kraut, or maybe I want some condiments or relish. Anyway, I put that on the frank—' He held out his hand.

"So I said, 'What's all that got to do with our frankroll?'

"So Junior says, 'A lot. Let me explain. It's got no appeal. Practical maybe, but to put the mustard on the hot dog the customer would have to slice the frankfurter bun first, and that leads us straight back to the old-fashioned frankfurter and the old-fashioned roll. The frankroll may be practical, but it's got no sizzle to it. No eye appeal, no nose appeal—it's no good.'

"Well, the old man was confused, and he got up and said that he'd like to think about it, and then he said he'd like to show us the factory. Well, you'd never think how important a thing a frankfurter is. There are two schools of thought about frankfurters, the skin frank and the skinless. These people specialize in skinless ones—because the American housewife prefers them without skin—but did you know that the skinless come with skins and have to be peeled? This factory is spotless. There is a vast hall, and at long tables sit hundreds of women, and music plays, and they all have in their left hand a frankfurter, and in the right a paring knife, and all day long they remove the skins from the frankfurters—an eight-hour day. And at the end of the room is a first-aid station, because at the speed at which they work there is a great deal of laceration. The man in charge—"

"Oh, please, Poppy, let's get out of here!" Barbara broke in.

"The man in charge explained that in spite of elaborate safety precautions there was a great deal of absenteeism on account of carelessness. They had people who were working on a machine to skin the frankfurters. 'Now if you could invent a frankfurter-skinning device,' said the old man to me, 'you'd be a millionaire overnight.' Well, we're not licked yet. The beauty of working on a ship is that you have everything on board. One of the engineers is working with us on a skinning machine, and I have another outfit lined up for the frankroll."

The light in Mr. Haegeli's eyes faded. He wiped his hand again on his apron, and I shook it, and slowly we walked out on deck and down the first flight of stairs to A deck. I said to Barbara, "Run for your life, for by now he has discovered that Little Bit is gone."

We got to the cabin. Little Bit smiled on both sides of her face, and she bounced from floor to chair to dresser. There was a knock on the door—the thrill of the game of cops and robbers had begun. Little Bit vanished.

Barbara asked innocently, "Who is it?"

It was the steward. "Did you find her?"

Barbara smiled.

"You got her back?"

Barbara nodded.

"Well, for heaven's sake, keep her out of sight. That crazy butcher is capable of anything—and I got a wife and family."

"From now on the dog must not be left," I said to Barbara. "She must go with us wherever we go, to the dining room, on deck, to the lounge, and to the movies. And you can't carry her in that bag—you have to cover her with a scarf or have her inside your coat."

Barbara started going about as if she carried her arm in a sling. The steward averted his eyes whenever he met us, and he didn't bring any more dog food.

Mr. Kruger said, "The kennel man suspects you of having removed the dog from the kennel."

"We did."

"Good," said the actor. "Anything I can do, I will."

"Well, act as if you didn't know anything about it. How is Rolfi?"

"Oh, Rolfi is fine. You know, he's never bitten anybody in his life except that kennel man."

Mr. Kruger offered to get Little Bit off the boat. He had a wicker basket in which he carried some of Rolfi's things, and he would empty that, except for Rolfi's coat, and in that he would carry Little Bit off the *America,* for the butcher would follow us and watch us closely, and if he didn't find the dog before he'd catch us at the customs.

"Isn't he a nice man—Mr. Kruger? People always say such mean things about movie actors," said Barbara.

Camouflaged in a scarf, Little Bit rested on Barbara's lap during meals. On the deck chair she lay motionless between my feet, covered by a steamer rug. She traveled about under Barbara's coat, and she took her exercise on the secret afterdeck, while I watched from above.

After the morning walk, the next day, the steward knocked. He looked worried. "The butcher was here," he said, "and went all over the room. He found the dish with those French words and the dog's picture on it, on the bathroom floor."

"How could we be so careless?" I said, my professional pride hurt.

"And of course he saw the bag with *Little Bit* printed on it. I said I didn't know nothing about any dog."

We doubled our precautions. Little Bit's mouth was down at the edges with worry. I contemplated what to do. After all, there were only two more days, and if the worst happened we could sit upstairs with Little Bit, the way Mr. Kruger sat with Rolfi. I said to Barbara, "Perhaps it would be best to pay the passage and have it over with."

The symptoms were back. "No, you can't do that. Think of the poor steward and his family!"

"Well, we could settle that, I think, with the butcher. I don't like to cheat the line—"

"Well, Poppy, you can send them a check afterward, if that

worries you, or drink a few extra bottles of champagne, or buy something in the shop."

Knock on the door.

"Who is it?"

"The purser, sir."

"Please come in."

The door opened. Behind the purser stood Mr. Haegeli.

"Just wanted to look and see if everything is all right. Are you comfortable, sir?"

"Everything is fine."

"By the way, sir, we're looking for a small white dog that's been lost. We wondered if by any chance it's in here."

"Come in and look for yourself."

"That's quite all right, sir. Excuse the intrusion. Good evening." The purser closed the door.

"What a nice man!" said Barbara.

The butcher was excluded from pursuing us in the public rooms of the ship; he couldn't follow us to the movies or the dining room. But he seemed to have spies. "What a lovely scarf you have there, Miss," said the elevator boy, and after that we used the stairs. The butcher came on deck in a fatigue uniform and followed us on the evening promenade around deck, during which Little Bit sat inside my overcoat, held in place by my right hand in a Napoleonic pose. We made four turns around deck. I leaned against the railing once, holding Little Bit in place, so that I could stretch my arms; Barbara was skipping rope, and the maneuver fooled him. He ran downstairs, and we caught him as he emerged from near our cabin—he had made another search. We saw his shadow on the wall near the stairs several times. He seemed to be nearing a nervous breakdown. Mr. Kruger told us that he had sworn we had the dog and meant to find it at any cost. There was one more night to go, and the next day the ship would dock.

At ten Barbara would deliver Little Bit to Mr. Kruger, and we would fill the bag in which she traveled with paper tissue, tobacco, soap, extra toothbrushes, razor blades, dental floss, and other things, which can all be bought in Europe but which for some droll reason one always takes along.

Little Bit was fed from luncheon trays which we ordered for ourselves in the cabin instead of going down to lunch.

The steward was shaking. "I don't know," he said, "when that guy butchers, or when he takes care of the other dogs. He's hanging around here all the time. I hope you get off all right."

On the last afternoon on board I became careless. Some passengers and a bearded ship's officer were watching the last game of the deck-tennis tournament, and others were lying this way and that in their deck chairs, forming a protective barricade. Barbara had checked on the butcher—he was busy aft, airing some of his charges.

I thought it safe to take Little Bit out of my coat and place her on deck, so that we all could relax a bit. She had been there but a moment when I heard a cry. "Ha," it went. It was the "Ha" of accusation and discovery, chagrin and triumph, and it had been issued by Mr. Haegeli, who stood with both arms raised. Fortunately he was not a kangaroo and was therefore unable to jump over the occupied deck chairs. I gathered up Little Bit, and we were safe for a few seconds. By now I knew the ship's plan as well as the man who designed her. We went down two decks on outside stairs, entered through a serving pantry, climbed one inside service stair, and then nonchalantly walked to the bar. I sat down and rang for the steward. I ordered something to drink. In a little while Barbara, with her lemonade in hand, said, "He's watching us through the third window!"

I swept my eyes over the left side of the room, and his face was pressed against the glass, pale and haunting. He kept watch from the outside, and ran back and forth as we moved around inside.

We went down to dinner. When we came back I got a cigar. He was outside the bar. As I went to the saloon to have coffee he was outside that window.

"Don't give Little Bit any sugar," Barbara said. "He's watching us."

The floor was cleared for dancing, and we got up to walk back to the library. There is a passage between the main saloon and the library off which are various pantries and side rooms, and it has no window. In a corner of it is the shop, and on this last evening people stood there in numbers buying cartons of cigarettes, film, small sailor hats, miniature lifebelts, and ship models with "S.S. *America*" written on them. Here I suddenly realized the miraculous solution of our problem. It was in front of me, on a shelf. Among stuffed Mickey Mice, Donald Ducks, and teddy bears of

various sizes stood the exact replica of Little Bit—the same button eyes and patent-leather nose, the fluff, the legs like sticks, the
pompom at the end of the tail, and the blue ribbon in its hair.

"How much is that dog?" I asked the young lady.

"Two ninety-five."

"I'll take it."

"Shall I wrap it up, sir?"

"No, thanks, I'll take it as is."

"What are we going to do now, Poppy?"

"Now you keep Little Bit hidden, and I'll take the stuffed dog,
and we'll go into the library."

There we sat down. I placed the stuffed dog at my side and
spoke to it. The butcher was on the far side of the ship, but he almost went through the window. He disappeared and ran around
to the other side. I had arranged the toy dog so that it seemed to
be asleep at my side, partly covered by Barbara's scarf. I told her
to take Little Bit down to the cabin and then come back, and
we'd have some fun with the butcher.

When she came back Barbara took the toy dog and fixed its
hair and combed the fluff. Then I said, "Please give me the dog."
We walked the length of the ship on the inside. The butcher was
sprinting outside, his face flashing momentarily in the series of
windows.

At the front of the ship we went out on deck. I held the dog so
that the pompom stuck out in back, and I wiggled it a little, to
give it the illusion of life. It took the butcher a while to catch up.
He walked fast—we walked faster. He almost ran—we ran. He
shouted, "Mister!" I continued running. As we came toward the
stern I asked Barbara, "Can you let out a terrible scream?"

"Yes, of course," said Barbara.

"One—two—three—*now*."

She screamed, and I threw the dog in a wide curve out into the
sea. The butcher, a few feet away, gripped the railing and looked
below, where the small white form was bobbing up and down in
the turbulent water. Rapidly it was washed away in the wake of
the *America*.

We turned to go back into the saloon.

We left the butcher paralyzed at the stern. He wasn't at the
gangplank the next day.

Little Bit landed in France without further incident.

Hollywood

· · · · · ·

Invitation

.   .   .

Psychologists say that an excessive intake of food and wine is a substitute for happiness. I like pudding, I like wine, roast goose, Virginia ham, shepherd's pie, and lobster stew. I am hungry and thirsty a great deal of the time, which accounts for the fact that I have acquired a reputation as a connoisseur of wines and as a gourmet. If I am hungry, then, the thing I worry about most is that one day all the goodies will be taken away from me. Oh no, not by the Russians, by someone infinitely kinder, but still taken away. I am speaking of the day or night after which a photograph of me, and a bad one, will appear on the most somber page of the newspaper, and under it my name, and a résumé of my career, which was mainly dedicated to the enjoyment of life. At least that is what it will say, for I have also acquired a reputation as a lover of life and a professor of happiness.

I believe in God; to me He has been wonderful, kind, and generous; but I have never been able to convince myself that after I have passed through this magnificent world I'll be admitted to a place even more astonishing, to a paradise of better landscapes, restaurants, horses, dogs, cigars, and all the other objects of my adoration; for such would be my paradise. I cannot imagine myself as an angel, sitting on a cloud, forever singing, and I think it would bore the good God Himself.

For such as I, then, all is here and now, the rewards and the miracles. They are the green tree, the sunrise, and all the things we sing about—the jet plane, the paintbrush and the easel, the cadets of West Point, and especially children, most of all babies with their grave, observant eyes.

In spite of all that, the black moods descend upon me, and consolation is hard to find. I can't be helped by psychiatrists, for, of those I know, several have committed suicide, a dozen have been divorced, and the best of them have the look of the haunted and bewildered or radiate the false effusiveness of the overstimulated. I lie on my own couch, suspended in cosmic gloom, the eye turned inward, and it takes me a while to console myself.

There are two cures. One is to work; all misery fades when I work, but I can't work all the time. The other is to celebrate. I, the confirmed lover of life and professor of happiness, look as we all must at life, and at the approaching day when we can only hope to be mourned for. I get hungry again and have to hurry and reassure myself with another good bottle and a fine meal, and after the coffee I look through the blue smoke of my good cigar. I sit in the melancholy mood that is like cello music and search for the answers we shall never know.

People such as I live by rules of their own. We are not happy with the comforts that the group offers. We are off-horses, misfits, we don't fit into the classes. We are not of the laboring class, the professional type, the manufacturer or salesman group, not even of that indigent company that collects in low bars or the brotherhood of the flophouses. In the design that has been imposed upon humanity we are solitary, self-appointed outcases. Outcast is too dramatic a word; let's call us alonegoers. That also is not quite true, for I seek people and like them, but still in their midst I am alone.

My life has been colored mostly by a period spent in the army, as a medic in the violent wards of an insane hospital. I learned there to block myself against things, to impose a rigid discipline on my own mind and emotions. And to be equally impersonal with the patients, for otherwise I could never have been of help to them. I learned there also to regard death as a generous manifestation, and to love life all the more for this discovery. And for the

good of the soul I learned to step outside of myself, to forget the
"I," which is the key to happiness.

Another detail of my character is that I am contrary by nature
and I always take the other side. Also I hate to order round-trip
tickets; I go one-way, because I hold before me the possibility that
I may never come back. A nonconformer, then, I came to Hollywood, and decided again to be contrary. At that time they gave
money away, and I received a heap of it for the original stories
they bought from me, and also a contract that gave me more than
I could ever have hoped for in the wildest calculations. I've always
been careless with money; it seemed illogical to me to save any of
it when there wasn't much anyway.

Now there was, and it seemed to make sense to be miserly. I
had rented a little cabin, a shack at the beach in Topanga, for
forty dollars a month. I always go the whole hog. I decided I'd
wash my own socks, sweep up and make my bed, shine my shoes,
and work. I wanted to paint. The money I had, and the money I
would save, would allow me to do what I wanted for the rest of
my life—that is, be an itinerant painter traveling across America
in my little car and painting the country. I had bought a second-
hand Ford convertible, and with this I would commute to the
studio. The elegant world of Hollywood, the life of the stars, all
that was to be left to one side.

The studio had engaged a suite for me at the Beverly Hills
Hotel. I stayed there until I bought the car and found the shack.
When I went back to the hotel for the last time, to pick up my
mail and my belongings before driving out to the beach, there
were many invitations, among them one to come to cocktails at
Lady Mendl's. I had heard of her. She was a very old lady and a
decorator, and she interested me. She was outside the things I had
marked as off-limits. I accepted this one invitation. I'm very glad I
did, for since I met her, when I sit and look through the blue haze
of my cigar, there always appears the one creature who gave me
inspiration, who fought the phantoms, who, day in and out, set
me an example that made beautiful sense.

She weighed about ninety pounds without her jewels, and
when I met her she was ninety years old.

When you live here and there and travel a lot, the seasons run
into each other, and the years lose shape, especially if part of the
time is spent in Hollywood.

The war was almost over; I had worked with the OWI and finished a guide for the troops in France. I had written the story for an anti-Nazi film called *The Blue Danube* and for another called *Yolanda and the Thief.* There were plans for producing both of these. There were the usual meetings with the agent and the producer. I was quartered in an office, elegant and air-conditioned, and, as I have said, I got the old car and drove to the Beverly Hills Hotel to move to the beach, and there was, among others, the message which said: "While you were out, Lady Mendl's secretary, Miss West, called to ask you for cocktails tomorrow around six."

I experience an occasional pleasant illusion. It is the dreamlike sensation that in a former existence I was a person of great consequence, one who lived in marble halls, a munificent, benevolent king, marquis, or a prince. (All other people who share this belief find that they were equally well placed; no one has ever told me that in a former life he was a butler, a dishwasher, or a policeman.) In consequence of this, I have a great preference for palaces, magnificent interiors, for faded silvered mirrors, marbles, and antique statuary.

In Hollywood one can find almost anything; but I did not expect to find there the reincarnation of the scenes of a former life and to come across a little palace exactly like the lovely silver and blue Amalienburg that stands in the park of Nymphenburg outside Munich. Nor hope to find therein, reflected in faded mirrors, the fabulous creature who with discipline unmatched defied the eternal fears.

The Footstool of
Madame Pompadour

.   .   .

Because nobody walks in Hollywood, we are now driving along
Benedict Canyon Drive in Beverly Hills, looking for a place called
"After All." The number of the house is 1018. In this latitude it
would be too much to expect that a house whose interior is baroque would have an exterior to match. So 1018 is California
Spanish on the outside. In front is a large sanded place to park—it
looks as if a party were taking place, about a dozen cars are
parked close to the house. We drive around a circular patch of
carefully tended grass, from the precise center of which rises the
trunk of a tall eucalyptus tree. These trees ordinarily are sloppy,
their bark hangs in shreds, like an overcoat about to be cast off.
This one is meticulously groomed.

Under the tree is a green garden table, and at the table with a
file cabinet sits a women of ample proportions. She looks up and
smiles, she has emerald-colored eyes, and, as she gets up, half a
dozen kittens fall from her lap.

"Those are my puthy cats and kitty cats," she says, "and without them I don't know what I would do. And you are Mr. Bemelmans. Welcome to After All. I am Lady Mendl's secretary—my
name is Hilda West."

The arriving guest is protected against the California dew by a

porte-cochère with green-and-white-striped canvas storm curtains. Through a green foyer we enter the house and turn right to
go into the salon. The interior is like that of the castle in Nymphenburg (the illusion of the former existence presents itself for a
moment). The room is empty, there is no party, the cars belong to
Lady Mendl's hairdresser, to Dr. Hauser, to the manicurist, to Sir
Charles Mendl, to the florist, and to a very special electrician by
the name of Mr. Nightingale, who tells me all this while he is busy
lighting a small menagerie of crystal animals in a glass cabinet.

The butler approaches with tremendous aplomb and says,
"Lady Mendl will be with you in a minute."

Even if we only know a person from what we read and hear, we
form a definite opinion. In my mind I had designed Lady Mendl
exactly as she was.

There are statues of saints in Latin countries, especially in
Spain, the most beautiful in Seville, that are carried about the
city at night during Holy Week. They move a little stiffly on
floats, borne on the backs of penitents, and in the lights of hundreds of candles. They are loaded with jewels, in silver robes; they
have flowers of silver in their hair; men with silver trumpets pre-
cede them, and the Spanish increase the mortification of the penitents by throwing glowing cigar and cigarette butts in their path.
The penitents curse, and the statues in the flickering lights seem
to show as much commiseration as Spanish etiquette permits.

As she came toward me, this mood of things Spanish and
churchly was in the room, but only for the eye and the moment,
for as she advanced farther she changed completely. She had on a
severe black dress made by Mainbocher, with a gold fob at the
side as the only decoration. Her legs were like those of a little girl,
and well shod, in low-heeled black shoes that a ballerina might
wear. She pulled the skirt away at the sides and straightened it
out, and then stuck her gloved hands in two pockets and with her
chin motioned to a white couch on which were three pillows, in
deep sea-green satin with letters embroidered in white silk.

The first pillow read: "It takes a stout heart to live without
roots." On the second was: "Never explain, never complain." And
on the third: "Who rides a tiger can never descend." We sat down.
On the right was an onyx fireplace, and on the mantel stood an
exquisite small coral-red clock, the only object in this room not

white, silver, or green. We faced a vast mirror, oxidized, and fogged with age.

She looked at me in this mirror (most of our conversations took place via this mirror) and after the get-acquainted talk she said, "Stevie, I have very clear eyes. I have second sight and instant recognition. We will be very good friends, you and I, such good friends that when Mother talks to you it will be as if she talked to herself."

She leaned against me, took my arm and my hand, and went on looking into the mirror as she said, "Mother has invented a cocktail, made of gin and grapefruit juice and cointreau. It sounds revolting, but try it, you may like it, but if you don't, just tell Mother, and you can have anything else you want. Never take anything you don't want. I'm a wanter, and so are you—I know you very well. You and I, we live by the eye, and that's why we are friends."

The butler passed a tray with the Lady Mendl cocktails on it. She watched my face in the mirror as I tasted it, and she said to the butler, "Take it away and bring him a Scotch and soda"—which was precisely what I wanted.

"But you like this room, Stevie? There is nothing in it that offends you?"

I don't know why she called me Stevie, probably because a war was going on with Germany and she didn't like the Teutonic "Ludwig."

"Stevie, listen to Mother. I was born in an ugly house, in an ugly street, the last of five children. I was told that I was ugly by my parents, by both of them, and the furniture in that house was ugly too, and I always got the dark meat of the chicken. I made myself like it, the dark meat, but that's the only thing I compromised on. 'For the rest,' I said, looking into that very clear, cruel mirror in my room, 'if I am ugly, and I am, I am going to make everything around me beautiful. That will be my life. To create beauty! And my friends will be those who create beauty'—and I have held to that every day of my life. I said to myself, as Dr. Coué advised people to say to themselves, 'Every day I am feeling better and better'—so I said, every day, 'I will make my small niche in the world more and more beautiful.' And beautiful things are faithful friends, and they stay beautiful, they become more beautiful as they get older—my lovely house, my lovely garden. I could steal for beauty, I could kill for it."

A new transformation had been going on. She now had the sharp profile of Voltaire. She kicked me in the ribs with her elbow and cried, "*Ha*! Vulgarity marches on like a plague, and everything is getting cold and ugly."

The butler passed with cocktail food.

"Is it cold out, Coombs?"

"Not really cold, milady, but I'd say fur-coat cold."

"Mother is free tonight, Stevie. Would you take her to dinner? I eat very frugally and I hardly drink."

A maid brought in a very carefully groomed miniature poodle.

"This is Mr. Bemelmans," said Mother, introducing me to the dog, "one of the family. And this is Blue Blue."

Blue Blue had no interest in me; he sat down and stared, immobile as a chameleon in a tree. Mother said, "Dear Blue Blue! He went and bit the wheels of the locomotive, the last time we left Paris—he knew how I hated to leave. I have a house in Versailles, the Villa Trianon, and I was almost done decorating it when the Germans came.

"Speaking of the villa, only yesterday a little souvenir arrived from there, a little part of its glory—a footstool that once belonged to Pompadour. There it is, Stevie, please move it over—there's a little patch of sunlight in the center of the room. Place it there so we can properly appreciate it."

I moved the delicate piece of furniture into the sunlight.

"It's been in storage, it's been lonesome and cold. Mother feels about that, for she has hung her heart on objects like that—and there are so many more locked up and in hiding, and I must go and get them out and finish the villa. But you know, Stevie"—and now I got the second kick in the ribs—"I am a self-made woman, and everything you see here I have bought with my own money, but somehow there is never enough. I never, never have enough money to buy all the beautiful things that I want in this world, and to do all the things I want to do. But never mind that; I always manage. Now let's look at the footstool."

The sun had moved from it, and I had to place it anew. It was mounted on four emerald-colored legs with golden claws. A row of silver nails in the shape of fleurs-de-lis held down a petit-point cover that was as delicate as the illuminations on medieval manu-scripts.

There was the sound of a car outside, and then the door opened. There entered life, in the person of Sir Charles Mendl. He came toward us and smiled with a jolly face that was like a ripe plum lying a little on its side. The plum was festooned with a Colonel Blimp mustache.

"This is my dear husband—" Mother started to say.

As Sir Charles extended his hand, he tripped over Madame Pompadour's footstool and lay on the floor, very still.

"My God, he's dead," said Lady Mendl.

"Nonsense," answered Sir Charles. "I'm not dead. Having played polo all my life, I simply know how to fall. When one falls one remains absolutely still for a minute. Now don't anyone bother helping me up."

He remained quiet for what seemed a long time.

"Are you resting, dear?" asked Lady Mendl.

"Yes, I'm resting," said Sir Charles.

"Well, don't overdo it."

Sir Charles was watching the dial on his wristwatch. At the end of a minute he got up.

Mother put one fist to her hip and stamped her foot. She slapped me on the back hard and said, "You search the world for beauty, for beautiful things to live with; you fill your home with the most exquisite pieces and you place them right; all is perfect, and then in comes your husband wearing that awful coat—that inseparable, impermeable, confounded trench coat—and ruins all the effect so carefully established."

Ignoring these words, his plum face leaning back so that he spoke to the ceiling rather than to us, Sir Charles answered, "This coat was given me on the occasion of my visit to the Maginot Line. The Maginot Line, being French, did not keep out the Ger-mans; but this coat, being British, I daresay, still keeps out the rain—and I shall keep on wearing it. I am as fond of it as you are of your precious antiques, my dear."

The butler had taken the offending garment and also the foot-stool, and Lady Mendl, with a curious smile in which she lifted her upper lip and showed her teeth, said, "This is my dear hus-band, Sir Charles Mendl." The hand was extended a second time, and she added, "Dear Charles, do me a favor—go out and come in again. I love to see you come into this house without that coat." Sir Charles obliged.

Sir Charles had a late paper, and the headline was about Paris.

"Oh, to think that France is free again!" said Mother with a saintly face, clasping the white-gloved hands. "Dear Paris, dear Versailles! I shall see my villa again!"

"Dear Paris," said Sir Charles, "and the French—awfully depressing, especially if you speak the language."

"There are a few things Charles and I don't agree on. They are diet, the French, and beautiful things. For example, this poor dear footstool of Madame Pompadour's. It could have been in this house a hundred years, and if he hadn't fallen over it, dear Charles would never have been aware of its presence."

Lady Mendl then asked him, "I wonder how soon one can fly to Paris?"

Sir Charles was seated. Glancing at his paper, he said, "A plane crashed—fifty people killed."

"Anyone we know, Charles dear?"

"No, Elsie, it was a Canadian plane."

"I know some Canadians, very nice people," said Elsie.

Charles said he hoped that none of them were on board that plane, and then he excused himself and went to his room.

"Dear Charles," said Elsie, "he's such a snob. You know, he has a pain in his right leg, and he insists that it's the same disease that the King has." She leaned over and said in confidence, "He's getting a little gaga, poor dear. He's taking on the prerogatives of children, like running off to his room to sulk. But it's refreshing to have a husband who is still attractive to women and who behaves properly. With all the nonsense going on here, it gives me great pleasure. You know how it is with anyone out here who has a title and is an international figure! He has been to see the Pope in private audience, he's received all the ambassadors and distinguished people, he is superb at arranging seatings at table, and he looks so wonderful against the fireplace. Of course the dear man knows nothing about furniture or beautiful things; he makes faces when he has to look at paintings at an exhibition."

Charles came back into the room. Looking at me, he asked, "I say, where are the oysters better, at Romanoff's or at La Rue?"

I said they were best at Chasen's, because there was a much larger turnover.

Elsie looked at him sharply. "Charles, who are you dining with?"

"Oh, a very ravishing creature."

"Is it as mysterious as all that?"

"No, Elsie dear, but I can't recall. I have to look in my little book."

He wandered off to his room again, and I received the third poke.

"You see what I mean," said Elsie in a deep voice and with the Voltaire face. "Charles is getting old—he can't remember any more."

He came back with the pince-nez on his nose and his little black book open. "I'm not dining out. I'm dining in, with Joan Fontaine, at her house."

"Is she a good cook?"

"I don't know her that well," said Charles and left again.

"Mother is going upstairs for a minute, and then we'll take the car. And may Mother bring a friend—Blue Blue? And where are we going to dine, Stevie?"

"At Romanoff's," I said.

Mother clicked her tongue and made a few faces of youthful anticipation and stamped her feet.

Sir Charles appeared once more. "I'll be back rather late, dear. I'm taking Joan to a concert after dinner. Heifetz is playing."

Mother took a stance again, stuck her hands in her pockets and smiled, and left to go upstairs. Later, in the car, she said, "Oh, those musical evenings! Dear Charles is musical. He sings. They say he has a good voice—he has volume and sings notes within notes. As for Heifetz, they say he is the best, but when I come out of one of his concerts I don't know whether I have been to it or not. It isn't music to me. I could just as well have watched him wind a clock.

"Here is Romanoff's—chk—I like Mr. Romanoff very much. He welcomes dogs in his restaurant."

We had a good, slow, quiet dinner, and two bottles of wine. There was some talking, but also the long silences that usually come only after long acquaintance and friendship. When I said good night to Mother at the door of her house I promised to come back the next day for lunch.

I found that I was happy to be with her. She was as comprehensible to me as if I had painted her a dozen times. She was uncomplicated, she was ageless. I observed her closely and at first with some fear that the perfection of this wonderful living objet d'art might have flaws, but I found out that it was perfect, and for me it stayed so. I looked sharply at her in the first days. Just as she covered up her crepy throat with jewels and her arthritic hands with gloves, so she covered or ignored those things in life that age other people. Her will to live happily, or at least beautifully, was so formidable that it triumphed over nature itself. She was younger than all the starlets, she had reckless courage and a restless, inquiring mind.

In the stages of life that were behind her, Elsie Lady Mendl had graduated from an ugly child to a young woman who became a mediocre actress. Of the photographs of her and the paintings, during the years that followed, one would say, to be kind, that she appeared to be a nice enough person but without any distinction. She had no children, she never spoke of her family. Yet now she was beautiful; at the height of life she had achieved a shining quality.

Her face had the luminous pallor of a porcelain statue, young and alert. She had invented the bluing of hair and wore ribbons, jewels, or golden leaves in hers. She exercised hard and adhered to a rigid diet prescribed for her by Dr. Hauser. She followed all his advice with the exception of black-strap molasses, and this I think she refused because she hated black, and any other mournful shade, in all objects with the exception of motor cars and black dresses.

After her ordinary morning exercises she devoted a daily half-hour to her eyes, exercising them by various routines and by flitting sunlight into them through a large magnifying glass. As a result she had the vision of a bird of prey. She was self-made, she was American. She spoke a schoolgirl French and in English she pronounced furniture "foiniture" and servants "soivants."

She insisted on perfection in the running of her house and she had a passion for beautiful things—and these qualities lent her such strength that those who came near her gladly submitted to the discipline she inflicted on herself. All the bums of Hollywood got off their high-wheeled bicycles and behaved themselves, and the most vulgar women turned gentle in her presence.

In Hollywood at that time everyone's bread was thickly buttered; the restaurants were filled and people stood waiting in lines. All things were intensely purposeful, and the streets and stages were crowded with eager people, all of whom acted one thing while they rehearsed another. Life ran at the speed of a newsreel.

"Only I trail the chiffons of time," Mother said—which was not true. When I tried to adjust myself to her tempo I found that I had to hurry.

My departure from the hotel was put off, for there were always invitations. In the many gradations of friendship, this one ripened fast. "When you are as old as Mother you know who you are with; you see very clearly and instantly, and everything is right."

One day when I came to the house West said, "Well, you are one of the family now. I can always tell. Mother listens only to nice things, you will observe, and when she is very happy she makes a face like a little girl in a new dress; she radiates. When I say that a big bouquet of white lilies has arrived from Mr. Cukor, or when I announce that Mr. Litvak has sent a Chinese silk rug, she smiles happily; and she also smiles happily when I say that you have accepted for lunch or dinner. Although you haven't sent flowers or a rug, Mother loves you."

This revelation brought me great happiness. I went immediately to the best florist and sent Mother a bouquet of his finest white roses.

·　　·　　·

Soon after, at Elsie's invitation, I moved into a little apartment at "After All," the most comfortable place I have ever known.

The Visit
to San Simeon

. . .

At the anniversary party for Sir Charles and Lady Mendl, Harry Crocker had given me an invitation on behalf of Mr. Hearst to visit San Simeon. I told Mother that I had accepted, and was very interested to see the man and the establishment.

"You will have a wonderful time, Stevie. Mr. Hearst is devoted to things that are beautiful. He has an immense collection of everything. I only wish I could come along."

I drove off, and some three hundred and forty miles from Los Angeles I turned off the highway, to the right, at a sign that read "San Simeon."

I came to a cottage where a gatekeeper checked my invitation—he was in dungarees and a cowboy hat. He took hold of a rope and pulled on it, and a gate of a peculiar construction, an immense gallows, swung up and over the car. I drove on, and the gate swung back down. I continued on, and a mile past the private airport I came to another gate. This was unattended and of different construction from the first. A long metal rod lay on the ground. At the end of it was a cradle onto which the left front wheel of the car is driven. This puts in motion a mechanism that swings the gate open.

I passed over an identical cradle at the exit from the gate, which shut it behind me. On this side of the gate, under a sign giving instructions for its use, was another sign warning visitors not to leave their automobiles on account of the presence of wild animals.

I passed two more of these gates as I drove toward San Simeon. I was now about a thousand feet above sea level, and on the hills, in the valleys, and on patches of sunlit grass appeared the wild animals.

There were wandering herds of zebra, of yaks, of water buffalo, springbok, and deer of every description in a landscape that must be as big as a county. The animals were used to cars, and as I went on, the heads of a dozen bison appeared a few feet from the windshield. It is strangely simple, like turning the pages of a children's book. "Look, look! A zebra. Look, a yak! Papa Buffalo, Baby Buffalo. See the horns on the gazelle—the stripes on the zebra!" This simplicity is part of the whole establishment and comes at you again and again.

At a turn in the road I found myself close to the top of the hill, and there stood the castle. It was best described by a child who was brought here late at night for a visit and saw the castle for the first time lit up. The child softly began to sing "Happy birthday to you."

It is a mixture of a cathedral and a Spanish hilltop city with a piece of California suburb placed at its feet. It has the feeling of a community built by a monastic order that says mass with castanets. It is extremely Catholic in feeling, like Mont St. Michel, but with a fat top to it instead of a sharp pencil-shaped church steeple. It has all the characteristics of monuments built by man to the glory of himself and God.

The car stops where Nature ends and the monument begins. You have the same tourist-like feeling as at the base of the pyramid of Gizeh, or at the entrance to the Taj Mahal.

The gatekeeper below had announced the approach of the car, and down from the castle came a plain, friendly woman such as might run a middle-class hotel. She is the housekeeper, and she assigns living quarters to the arriving guests. She said, "I'll send somebody for the bags." I climbed four terraces and entered a vast hall paneled with the ancient choir stalls of a Gothic cathedral.

One of the dark walnut choir stalls functions as a door. The seat has been removed. I passed through this and came out in a cement vault, cold, dark, and drafty. In this stands an octagonal cement tube that holds an elevator. The elevator is self-operating and has room for three people. The inside of the elevator is again disguised with the wormholed wood of old church furniture— perhaps the paneling of several confessionals. In this I rode up to the top, to the tower apartment assigned to me, which is called the Celestial North. It is composed of a bathroom on the first landing, and above this, via a winding stairway, a living room, and over this a bedroom. This is in the very top of the tower. The bedroom is octagonal and about twenty feet in diameter, with a heavy inlaid gold ceiling—as are all the ceilings here. Between the massive beams are recessed spaces decorated with the things one finds on tapestries and carpets: jewel-colored fragments of flowers and fishes, birds and heraldry. Some of these are the work of origi- nal artists of hundreds of years ago. But frequently, as in this apartment, they are supplemented by "antiqued" new painting. There is no undecorated space: doorposts, hinges, niches, bal- conies, and the accessories to them, the things that support them, are all decorated. The only vacant and airy spaces—and they come upon you suddenly as you open a door—are unfinished cor- ridors, lofts, stairs, and passages where the cement seems still to be wet and bears the grain of the wood mold in which it was poured. Sticking out everywhere are the iron staves, like walking sticks, that you see in unfinished concrete construction work.

The furniture in the bedroom of the Celestial North consisted of a bed and two cabinets. The bed stood in the center, a four- poster of tremendous weight, and again carved and painted. On the wall were curtains twenty feet in length, gold brocade, with draw cords so that you could pull all of them closed and find yourself in an octagonal tent of gold. The two old glass cabinets were to the left and right of the bed. But there was no place to hang your clothes, so I hung mine on the wire coat hangers that a former tenant had left hanging on the arms of two six-armed gold candelabra, five feet high, on either side of the bed. On these I hung almost everything; the rest I put on the floor. There was no chair, no closet.

The bath below was done with mirrors and golden fixtures. And while there would have been plenty of room for a bathtub, there was none—but again, a museum piece of woodcarving, another cabinet, and a shower stall. In this apartment the water was connected up wrong, so that hot water came out of both faucets. I never thought cold water important in the bath, as long as you have enough hot water. The cold you take for granted. In a tub you can let hot water cool, but not in a shower. With hot water from both faucets you are defeated.

I thought of calling up, but then I found there was no phone. So I only shaved; and, after soaking a towel in hot water, I let it cool and bathed in the wet towel.

You are all alone up here. You can scream as loud as you wish and make any other noises you please; nobody will hear you. You try to look out at the magnificent scenery, but there is golden stuff at the windows. They are dusty, blind with a historic patina. And outside the windows is heavy golden scrollwork. Besides, on each window there hangs a sign, printed by hand on a piece of cardboard like the ones in shirts from the laundry, that says: "Please do not open the window." These signs, tied to the handles of the windows with string, are on all four windows of the eight walls.

On the inside of the elaborately carved door hangs a carbon copy, on half a sheet of typewriter paper stuck there with a tack, of the hours at which meals are served:

> Breakfast—10:30 to 11:30
> Luncheon—1:30
> Dinner—8:00

It was around six when I left the Celestial North suite and tried to find my way back, first passing through the cement vault, then into the octagonal confessional that is the elevator, then through the dark cement vault below, coming out eventually through the choir stall, and finding myself in the living room. This is half of Grand Central Station. The stalls go up to a height of twenty feet. Above them hang tapestries—for two of which Michelangelo did the sketches, and four others of heroic dimensions. Phoebe Apperson Hearst paid two million dollars for those four alone. In the four corners of the room stand statues—marble women of the anonymous type of nude holding a piece of drapery to her lower abdomen, leaning forward, the arms pleasantly arranged. Three of them are just statues. In the fourth corner is a special one—a very fine Grecian woman, with eyes such as are set into stuffed animals, that came from some London palace and cost a hundred and twenty thousand dollars.

Looking with the eyes of Elsie, I wondered about her genie, Good Taste, and the three attendants, Simplicity, Suitability, and Proportion. Couches all over, and in one corner, hiding the lower half of the marble woman, a radio cabinet done to match the room—a bad Gothic imitation of such woodcutting as the Riemenschneider altars in southern Bavaria, with figures in a very foreshortened perspective, and characters too lachrymose or too much in motion and out of control, and with dark stuff smeared into the deep parts to make it antique.

In the center of the room was a fireplace that reached the sixty-foot ceiling, and this by contrast was superbly beautiful—perhaps the rarest fireplace in the world—of great tenderness, magnificent color, a breathless living monument, a perfect thing, big as the façade of a house.

A few feet away stood a dreadful rosewood piano with a carmine coverlet of the unhappiest texture and shade.

Next to the awful things and the beautiful things were the sad. There were two long boxes, polished old-fashioned stereopticons. I sat down on a high chair and twisted two black handles, adjusting the lenses to my eyes, and the machine lit up and showed a series of slides. As I turned there appeared scenes of travel—Mr. Hearst in Venice, in Bad Nauheim, in Nuremberg, in Switzerland, on a road in the Dolomites, and leaning on a fountain in a street in Rothenburg; sometimes alone, sometimes in a group, but in every picture he was like a stranger, not the person who was photographed, but somebody cut from another picture, always the same, and pasted into the setting.

I walked through the dining hall. It is formidably Gothic. Up above hang the old, torn battle flags of the city of Siena. Below is a table the length of the room, so big that whoever sits at the far end is very small. Here again is a fireplace that devours the trunks of trees. The flames, behind a glass screen, leap up to the height of a man. At the right is an armorer's anvil, arresting and beautiful, but the base of it is fixed to hold nuts, and on top of the anvil lies a hammer to crack the nuts. There are tall silver altar candlesticks all along the center of the long refectory table, and between them stand, in a straight line and in repeating pattern, bottles of catsup, chili sauce, pickled peaches, A-1 sauce, salt and pepper in shakers that are cute little five-and-ten-cent figures of Donald Duck with silvered porcelain feet, and glasses in which are stuck a handful of paper napkins.

The kitchen is immense. The large oven is operated by a blow-torch-like device that spouts oil. The smaller ovens work by electricity. (The entire castle is electrically heated—the bill is twenty-five hundred dollars a month.)

On a blackboard in the pantry I saw several notices tacked up—all written and signed by Mr. Hearst. One said: "Keep the meals simple. No meat for breakfast, except bacon; and for lunch, use stews; for dinner only, meat. The guests must be on time for meals. No trays in rooms. Try and keep the food for the staff as much like that of the guests as possible. Simplify and cut down whatever you can."

The kitchen was clean. The butler was a German, a small thin man. His wife, a curious creature, looked the way she should in this house—like a polychrome figure, also of the Nuremberg-altar period, with a round nest of golden hair; and she had that face which they must then have thought pretty. By our sense of design today, she had the look of a gargoylish cellar-and-moat beast with blinking eyes and a birdlike, hopping walk, just right among the choir stalls.

I wandered into a billiard room with the most beautiful tapestry of the lot, and then down to the kennels.

I had noticed a sign at one of the automatic gates: "Dogs not allowed, except in kennel." In these kennels, in long rows of runways, were about two hundred dachshunds of every shape and size and dachshund kind—black, brown, long-haired, short-haired, crossbred with soft long-haired. They all were yapping and running. As I looked at these dogs, which were born in these kennels and live and die in them, a visitor to the castle, who was about to leave and was making his last tour, joined me. The way one would leave a farmer friend's with a box of eggs, and debate whether it was worth the trouble, this departing guest looked at the dogs and said, "I wonder should I take along a dachshund?" But, a true lover of dogs, he answered himself, "No, I'm out too much. I don't want to make a dog lonesome."

I went back to the living room and found a group of people—

all business faces, executives. They were talking about "the Chief," exchanging polite stories that made him human, great, but with weaknesses that a great man could afford.

I had often heard that liquor at the castle was taboo. But the butler came in with a large silver tray and set up everything anybody wanted to drink.

Presently the huge glass and iron door, on which hung another laundry-cardboard sign, saying, "Keep this door closed," opened. Two dachshunds that had escaped the fate of the others in the kennels below flitted across the floor and jumped on one of the couches, and Mr. Hearst came into the room.

I have often observed that men who have to do with property walk with one shoulder held higher than the other. That is the way Mr. Hearst walked. The immense frame moving forward was curiously light on its feet. He walked as if to music, as if somewhere a band was playing, and he was advancing, reporting for a seat in a grandstand. He wore high-laced boots. All the weight was in the upper body and the shoulders. The legs were light beneath him.

The executives had arranged themselves in two groups, one at each end of the room, and Mr. Hearst approached first the left half-dozen men. As he went there, everyone in that area who was not in the group moved to another couch or chair, as small birds fly away at the approach of a big one.

Mr. Hearst talked in a high soft voice. The day's news was brought from tickers; copies of all the newspapers were spread out on a large table. The King was very polite and quiet, and after a while he march-danced past to the other end of the room. Again the small birds flew away.

His head deserved the attention of the best sculptors and painters. The expanse of his countenance was almost twice that of the ordinary man—just as his thumbs were three times the size of my own. The most commanding thing in his face were the eyes, which were as large as fifty-cent pieces, but pale, like dusty stones, or like two immense tunnels running through his head. The nose was formidable, straight and strong, and occupying half of the big face. In profile it continued the straight line of the forehead. The shape of the skull, if traced by a pencil from the top of the forehead to the back of the neck, was a simple line, slowly curving.

The cheeks sagged and were gray. The face was most curious

when he laughed. All its properties remained undisturbed—the sadness and the hollow eyes—but the strong jaw went down, the mouth split open, a relatively small and lipless mouth, and remained for a while like a half moon lying on its side. It was a melancholy lonesome laughter, but it belonged to the medieval man and was part of his design, like the instinct for moats, oubliettes, and towers, Gothic choir stalls, and battle flags. It was all as simple as the stripes on the zebras in the landscape below.

The meeting on both sides of the room took about an hour; then everybody left.

For dinner, refectory chairs for eighty people stood along the sides of the table. Most of them remained empty. Places for the guests were prepared near the middle of the huge banquet table. There were place cards: one size for the guests, plain with the name written on it in a fluid hand; and a larger one with a gilt edge, on which was written in scrollwork "Mr. William Randolph Hearst."

The Nuremberg-altar figure with the crown of yellow hair appeared, in black, with white starched apron. An old factotum, like a sacristan, lit the yellow candles in the twenty-five-pound silver candelabra down the length of the table. Two men put ten-foot logs on the fire. The catsup bottles were straightened out, and the condiments and the glasses of paper napkins. I thought of Elsie: there was nothing green-and-white-striped here. The servants did as they pleased. This was another form of builders' and collectors' paradise.

The door with the laundry sign opened, and, with a draft of cold evening mountain air, the two dachshunds streaked through the room again followed by Mr. Hearst. He passed through the hall into the dining room and the guests followed him. The group was lost in the immense structure. There was the usual talk. The food was mediocre and badly served. The Moselle wine was superb. Mr. Hearst drank beer from a very beautiful ancient glass mug. The executives sat with proper respect. Mr. Hearst talked little.

Toward the end of the meal a friend, who had traveled a great deal with him, made a short speech. The little half moon in Hearst's face began to shine. In this controlled smile of his, there were variations; for something that made him really happy—and it was always something back in the old days—he suddenly had eyes. It was as if a myopic man suddenly saw an object clearly in the middle distance and warmly admired it. This was a matter of seconds, then the gaze vanished.

The friend told old stories, and, just as a child will listen again and again with pleasure to every detail of an oft-told tale, the sad King laughed and looked at the storyteller. The stories were of voyages, of difficulties with chauffeurs in the Dolomites; scenes here and there, meaningful only to the people who had been in them. Occasionally a detail was wrong, a place not sufficiently identified, and then the storyteller was stopped and the facts re-established. It was the story of an innocent voyage, never an off-color joke, never an adventure in which everything did not come out right. Small misfortunes, mix-ups with happy endings, trouble that became immediately amusing when the traveler was identified or his generosity came into play.

Hearst's high voice piped an anecdote. His huge bison head wobbled. That again was uncomplicated, like the beer in front of him.

We got up when he did and followed him into the movie theater. This was as grandiose as the swimming pool and the hall and the dining room. Its ceiling supported by over-life-sized odalisques, the theater held about two hundred people. Mr. Hearst had a big armchair in the first row. The guests were seated around him, and the help nearby.

A newsreel of the Teheran Conference was shown, and when Mr. Roosevelt's lined face appeared the King remarked, "Looks like a plate of tired whitebait to me." A routine musical ran after that, and the evening ended with drinks in the living room.

The newly arrived visitor gets very sleepy up here. The air is brisk and thin. I walked out on the terrace and around outside the castle. It was like Monte Carlo, but it was icy cold. A thousand white alabaster lamps lit it up, some of them part of balustrades and balconies, others standing along paths, along marble benches, next to statuary, and beside the pool.

I went back in and walked through the hall. People were playing cards. Mr. Hearst sat with his eyes on the black peepholes of the stereopticon and turned the images of his happy times. I left. I opened the door in the choir stall, entered the confessional elevator, and rode up to the Celestial North. I put my clothes on the black wire coat hangers and hung them on the candelabrum. The mattress of the costly bed was hard and cold, and so was the pillow.

I could not find the place to turn out the light, and left it burning.

The next morning I soaked my towel again and waited for it to cool, and then rode down to breakfast.

New trees were brought to the fireplace. In the living room was a man with an immense aluminum pole at the end of which was a flexible wire cone. With practiced skill he slipped the cone over the burned-out electric bulbs in the ceiling, then turned the pole until the bulb came out, and replaced it with a new one. An average of sixty bulbs burned out a week.

The grounds are vast. "You really need a horse to see the place," said one of the executives, who also had got up early and was having breakfast at the banquet table.

I got a horse a little while later, with one of the cowboys to ride with me. He brought the horse into a wide courtyard whose walls were unfinished, with the cement again bare, and the plain surfaces broken only in one place where an exquisite Florentine loggia was installed. In this courtyard, building was to be resumed, and antique stone lay ready in crates, to be unpacked, to hide the ugliness.

We passed the herds of zebras and came to a grove of tall trees. "Those," explained the cowboy, "are for the giraffes. At one time we had a lot of trouble with them. We had two of them die on us and didn't know why. The local vet couldn't do anything about it, so the boss sent East for a specialist. A man in charge of the New York Zoo was flown out. He examined the dead giraffes' stomachs and found gravel in them. They had picked up the gravel as they fed, from the ground, and that was the trouble. Giraffes eat from treetops and can only swallow properly when the head is up high. So special trees had to be planted for them, but until those trees grew high enough we rigged up feeding troughs on stilts and pulleys that you can lower and then pull up filled with the leaves of those trees, and the giraffes are happy now."

We came to the bear pits, which he explained were emptied at the start of the Hearst depression. "They'll be back any day now," he said with hope.

The paths go along ridges. To the west is the view down to the ocean, and to the east, always in a contrasting light, is an immense valley that reaches to the next ridge of mountains. Down at the foot is the village of San Simeon, with a post office and a general store where they sell picture postcards of the castle. There, also, is a dock where the ocean-going ships discharged their cargoes of antiques. There were warehouses with crated stuff, a railroad track, and cranes.

We rode up the hill again.

I did the tour of the castle after this, going down to the cellars—cold, cement smell, huge iron doors, double doors of black steel, large tombs. One held a collection of three thousand lamps; another of beds, pictures, chairs; others of tapestries and silver—an auctioneer's paradise of magnificent pieces mixed with junk.

I saw the custodian of some of these things. "Oh, that fellow," he complained of Hearst. "I tried to get him to sell some of that stuff, and he promised me he would. Look—"

He took me to a refectory table on which stood a library of black-bound books, each made up of pages of photographs of antiques, their history, and the price Hearst had paid for them.

"I told him to sit down and mark what he wanted to sell. Well, he sat down here with the pencils I had sharpened for him, and he took the first book and opened to the first page, and then slowly he went through the whole book, smiling. I knew then that it was no use. He picked up the next volume, and he didn't mark a goddam thing in any of them, and sat there all day going through every one of them, always smiling. We needed money then, but now that fellow, he's richer than he ever was, and he won't sell a thing."

One of the executives, who also spoke of him as "that fellow," said, "Christ, for five years, every day there was a crisis. We almost went into receivership, but that fellow never batted an eye—never said anything. Well, by God, it's the other way now. He's twice as well off. Now he'll start buying again, and that's good for everybody."

The architect was one of the few happy people around Mr. Hearst. In his shack were new plans, and there the King sat among models and on packing cases and plotted new additions. "As long as he builds," said the architect, "he thinks he won't die."

I walked with Mr. Hearst and the architect along a two-mile

stretch of trellised columns, fruit trees, and grape arbors. At one point Mr. Hearst stopped. "I want a terrace here," he said.

It was a tough terrain, it would take a lot of underpinning and work, the architect explained, and he made the mistake of asking the King why he wanted a terrace there.

Mr. Hearst pointed to a scrubby tangerine tree growing across from where we stood and said in his high voice, "I might want to pick one of those tangerines."

"I'll never ask him again why he wants to do anything," said the architect later.

I went back into the house. There was a message. Lady Mendl's secretary had called. Would I hurry back as quickly as possible? I tried to get the house in Beverly Hills on the phone, but the line was constantly busy, and the phones at the castle were all in the hands of the various executives.

A little later in the day I received a wire asking me to hurry back and signed "Mother," and I was worried; but I decided to finish out the day.

I went back to the custodian. "These things, of course, I wouldn't sell myself," he said, pointing to the tapestries. "I know the history of all the things here, of every piece. Outside him and me, I guess nobody cares a damn—not a goddam—for anything here. Now, his boys, they don't care at all. They used to run around here throwing things at each other, playing roughhouse among all these beautiful things. One time they had a fight with flypaper right here where the fine Gobelins are. They'd have taken scissors and cut the figures out like paper dollies if I hadn't stopped them."

The telephone rang. The custodian answered. Shaking his head, he said, "It's no use—that fellow won't sell them. He won't sell anything. It's no use talking to him even."

He hung up and said to me, "There's a couple of Chippendale beds that somebody is after, offering ten thousand apiece, but that fellow won't part with anything. Ten thousand bucks is just a dime to him. He'll never sleep in them—nobody else ever will. They'll just stand down in the vaults, just stand there until he dies, and he won't even bother to say who should get them. He doesn't think he'll ever die."

An instrument of the very greatest epoch of clockmaking, its dial set in an elongated cartouche framed by acanthus leaves and marked "Causard Horloger du Roi," struck the time. On the desk stood an abominable combination inkwell and ashtray with a green nude, an arts-and-crafts objet d'art perhaps picked up in an auction room. "Nobody is allowed to mention death in this house, but one day he will die just the same," said the custodian; "and God knows what will become of all this stuff that he loves as if it was his children."

We stood at a window. The custodian pointed outside. "And who will weep for Willy? Well, maybe the lame Duc de Bourgogne who rides through the cold California night outside of the castle, magnificently cut in stone, a falcon on his arm, grateful for having been saved from destruction in the bombing of his native land. Yessir, maybe tears will roll down out of those eyes."

Early the next day, just before I left, Mr. Richard Berlin, an executive of the Hearst Corporation, arrived with his family. He didn't run away from the King, and he had his own opinions, but out in the park he said to one of his little children, "Now, dear, don't pick any fruit or flowers. Mr. Hearst doesn't like that." The child had an orange in his hand and explained that it was from the breakfast tray, and it was marked with the blue stamp of the grower. It was decided, however, that he'd better eat it right away. It was peeled, and we looked for a place to hide the skin. It was put inside a Grecian urn.

I took my leave, and drove off with many feelings, all of them low. I wanted to find a restaurant and console myself with the best bottle and a good dinner; but, alas, there is nothing of that kind in this latitude. I drove down the magnificent landscape, past the herds of animals silhouetted in the early sunlight, through the automatic gates, and it was like escaping from prison.

During the long drive in the blue haze of morning I came upon a truth, which, like all revelations, is simple as stone, and as heavy. I had met in Hearst the most lonesome man I have ever known, a man of vast intelligence, of ceaseless effort, and all he had done was to make of himself a scaffold in which a metronome ticked time away. Like Elsie, he had fled to objects. The revelation is that you cannot protect yourself, for you become desolate as the prairie. You must give yourself, you must take a chance on being hurt; you must take the chance to suffer from love, for the other is nil. In this visit Elsie was mirrored: the metronome ticked away inside a magnificent puppet. As lonely as Hearst.

I stopped for lunch at a modest place along the road. They had good dry martinis, and spaghetti and meatballs. Franz Werfel, describing a bad meal in *Class Reunion,* observed that even after the worst of meals a kind of contentment sets in. I drank a quart of California claret that was not bad, and some brandy that was awful. But by the time the coffee cup was removed, I was in a tolerable mood.

I put the top of the car down and rolled slowly along through the beautiful landscape. A sadness came over me, to the point of stopping my own metronome from ticking. I had a feeling that Elsie was dead—I saw her as someone whom in another life I had loved.

I saw her the way one sees the saints in gilded caskets, their bones enshrouded in silks and festoonery, made by nuns, of jewels and silver and gold. It wasn't anyone who had really lived; it was a gallant soul who had borne the burden of an experiment in evasion and nothingness. It had been a fine time, a wonderful party. I had loved it, and it would never be forgotten. But I remembered it now as a mirage. My own face is, like all faces, the mirror of the world, and I look at it searchingly. The American painter Alexander Brook once asked me to sit for him. He works ably and fast. He put a large canvas on his easel, looked at me, and then started to paint; and when he was through he turned the easel toward the wall so that I couldn't see it and said, "Come back again tomorrow." I came back the next day, and he looked at me and wiped off the canvas what he had done the day before. He started all over; he looked at me and painted, and the same thing happened again. Then I came a third day, and after ten minutes he threw his palette into a corner and said, "I can't paint you. The first day you looked like the messenger of God; the second day you looked like something out of hell; and today you look just stupid. What's the matter with your face?" I looked at myself, and I did look stupid; it was on account of a stupid day I had had.

During the time with the Hollywood crowd I looked like something out of hell most of the time. The only time I was satisfied with my own face was when I painted, when I gave myself wholly to my work in the shack.

While I was living at Elsie's, I read *The Theory of the Leisure Class*. I knocked together, or tried to, some kind of structure to explain it to myself. I said that not many people were needed to supply the necessities like shoes, coats, shelter, bread, and love, and the places and materials for those needs; and that it would leave a lot of people out of work if nothing else were called for. Were there not those who, by an extension of their needs, justified the talents and labors of artists, gardeners, embroiderers, pastry cooks, and milliners? All this thinking led into a domain in which I was stumbling through unfamiliar landscapes. At any rate, I could see a reason for the existence of the people who moved in Elsie's circle, if only because they made it possible for travel agencies and suppliers of wine and fine foods to pay their employees. The people themselves never had a very good time—they hated each other mostly, and, when one of the fine birds fell off its branch, none of the others dived down to chase away the foxes of misfortune that carried it off and ate it.

The egoist loses everything. You cannot live for yourself. The pursuit of pleasure does not bring it. But all this has been said, and better—for example, by Bert Brecht in *The Threepenny Opera*:

> *Ja, renn nur nach dem Glück,*
> *Da rennst Du nicht allein,*
> *Sie rennen alle nach dem Glück,*
> *Das Glück rennt hinten drein.* *

I am reasonably steady in moments of danger, but I am a coward when other people suffer or die. I got hungry from unhappiness again, and very thirsty, and tried to stretch out the return as much as I could. I came to a place with a restaurant that looked good; I ordered a big dinner, and it was very good. The plate was warm, and the wine was exceptional, a California dry white wine called Folle Blanche, a Schoonmaker wine, and it was clear, cold, and served in a decent glass. I found an excuse for further delay: I said a few kind words to the proprietor and I asked him where the chef was.

* Yes, go—run after happiness!
  You're not alone, you'll find.
  They all run after happiness—
  Which runs along behind.

"Second door to your right," he said.

It turned out to be the men's room; the proprietor had never heard the word "chef." I talked about cooks with him then, and he introduced me to the colored man who had prepared the meal; then we had brandy and I drove on.

I passed rows of lighted cabins in which happy people lived. I passed along stretches of sea to the right, with moonlight turning it to green silver. . . . I thought of the day when Elsie had made her will; she had become soft for a few moments, and I had forgotten it, because it didn't go with her portrait. Now it came back. In all the years of lonesomeness and discipline she had opened the curtains only once. She had dictated to West that day, when she thought she was going to die:

"When the spirit is gone, nothing remains. I want to be wrapped in a sheet and cremated."

"Stevie," she had said that day, "You know the big lonesomeness, as everyone does who is like ourselves outside, and to us applies what is so beautifully said on Oscar Wilde's tombstone:

> And alien tears will fill for him
> Pity's long-broken urn,
> For his mourners will be outcast men,
> And outcasts always mourn.

"We are like corals, we build and the sea washes over us, and we build again, and the shells of our bodies become structure, and a new reef rises. And the winds howl over it in the lonely night. Most people don't know it, and they live satisfied lives.

"You know, Stevie, if I had a tombstone, what I ought to put on it is, I suppose, what I put on Blue Blue's tombstone, and Mother wasn't original, it was Willy Maugham, another lost soul, who gave me the words 'To the one I love the best.' I have sacrificed my life and myself—and I end up empty-handed. What is called courage can also be despair.

"You at least have your art, and that is everything. Give, don't take."

It's too bad one cannot paint at night. I've never tried, but you'd have to light up your paintbox, or else flash a spot on the picture occasionally, to check. There is an American painter, little known, who lived in France and who painted very good night pictures. His name is Frank Boggs. I own several of them; one can buy them here and there in good galleries in Paris. I have an oil painting, a scene of the harbor of Honfleur, which has given me pleasure all the years I have had it. I look at it every day when I am in New York. It is in melancholy blues and browns, an old boat, a rope, nothing much and everything. There were the Boggs colors all about me now, and then came Santa Monica, and the road to Beverly Hills. I wished there were a few more miles. I did not want to drive up to the door. But when finally I got there, the house was gay, there were cars outside, and then I heard the sound of a decorative orchestra, playing quietly. Mother was having a party, that's why she had sent the telegram. I was happy, very happy. She made all the faces, kicked me in the ribs, and asked for a complete report on Willy Hearst, "that wonderful *chk-chk* man." I made him out as being as happy a man as Mother wanted him to be.

The music was gay. I went and looked at my face, to check my observations. I didn't look like something out of hell, I had had a good time, and I had miscalculated. Elsie was not as coral-reeflike as she herself thought; she was a tough old bird, but she had gallantry, courage, and, like Charles, the gift of friendship. I went down, happy to be back, and I drank until Mother said, "For God's sake, hasn't anybody here a home to go to?"—which was her way of ending a party.

Lust
For Gold

. . .

The right hand of Ludlow Mumm, the one he wrote with, was in
bandages as the result of a railroad accident some fifty miles out
of Los Angeles. The writer leaned forward with a painful move
and picked up the phone with his left hand.

"Good morning," said a cheery voice. "This is the Wildgans
Chase Agency. You're having lunch with Mr. Wildgans at Ro-
manoff's. Mr. Wildgans wants to discuss the contract with you.
We're sending a car for you. It will be there in fifteen minutes.
You will find it under the *porte-cochère* of your hotel."

Ludlow Mumm stepped out on the balcony of his suite and
looked down the front of the Beverly Hills Hotel.

"I would have called it a marquee," he said, and went back
into the room.

He took a dictionary out of his bag, and, holding it between his
legs and opening it with his good hand, he searched under the
letter P.

" 'Porte-cochère,' " he read, " 'a large gateway through which a
carriage may drive into a court; an extension of a porch; a roof
over a driveway.' "

He turned the pages and looked under M.

" 'Marquee,' " he read, " 'a tent; a window awning; an awning raised as a temporary shelter from the curb to the door of a dwelling or a public building.'

"She's absolutely right," said the writer, and put the book away.

He walked back out on the balcony, lifted himself on the toes of his small feet, leaned over the banister enjoying the scene, and scratched his soft brown beard. He had grown it to cover up at least part of a round face that was kind to the point of idiocy.

Ludlow Mumm would have been happiest as a lay brother of a religious order, one not too penitent. He would have fitted ideally into the cloth of that happy group of monks who brew sweet liqueurs to the glory of God in France.

He looked down again, smiling. On a balcony beneath him, stretched on a *chaise longue* which was covered with an immense bath towel, was all that is real and good in a sometimes lazily shifting female form, unclothed, inhaling and exhaling deeply, and occasionally running her fingers through her platinum-blond hair.

Women, in the life of Ludlow Mumm, took the roles of mothers, sweethearts, good wives, sisters, and little girls. Those that disturbed other men were regarded by him as remarkable adornments in that ever-beautiful green valley through whose dewy grass the padre in his sandals wandered with uplifted heart.

"*Porte-cochère*," repeated the conscientious scribe, looking once more down at the front of the hotel.

Then he went back into his suite again, picked up his hat with the unbandaged left hand, and walked to the elevator.

The happy first impression of the correctness and efficiency of the Wildgans Chase Agency was underlined when, exactly fifteen minutes after the telephone call, a black, polished Buick limousine purred up along the avenue of palm trees and stopped smoothly under the *porte-cochère*.

The alert, uniformed driver, who had never seen Mumm before this moment, touched his cap and smiled. The doorman opened the door and as Ludlow sat down, the driver said:

"Good morning, Mr. Mumm. Welcome to California."

As the car swung down and halted for the stop sign at the crossing of Sunset and Rodeo, the driver jumped from his seat and made Ludlow Mumm comfortable, suggesting that he move into the left corner of the car. He pulled down the arm rest for the injured member.

"Toni is my name," he said, and was back up front.

"You're in good hands, sir," he said, "when you're with Wildgans Chase. You'll get plenty for that accident. We had you insured from the moment you left New York."

The writer leaned back and smiled. The palm trees swam by and Toni identified the lovely homes of the stars along the route.

"I can get you anything you want in this town," said Toni.

By the time they arrived at Romanoff's, he had arranged for a car and chauffeur; for some color film for the writer's magazine Kodak; and he had promised to smooth out any difficulties and overcome all shortages and needs that would arise during the writer's stay.

Toni stopped the car and ran into the restaurant, announcing Ludlow Mumm to the head waiter, who at once took him to one of the good tables.

"Mr. Wildgans," said Joe, the maitre d'hôtel, "is up there now at the first table. He's expecting you. He'll be here in a little while."

Arty Wildgans, a portly, ruddy man, slowly came down the line; like a bucket in the hands of a fire brigade, he was handed on from one person to the next.

"The first thing I always say is 'Hello,' " he said cheerily as he finally arrived and sat down.

Looking over Mumm's head, he waved and smiled at several people in the rear of the room.

"And how are the folks back East?" he asked, picking up the menu.

Without waiting for the answer, he looked up at the waiter and said:

"How's the Vichyssoise today?"

"Well," said the waiter with indignation in his voice, "Joe Schenck just had some!"

"All right, all right," countered Wildgans, equally agitated, "Let's have that to start with—and what else did Joe Schenck have?"

"The boeuf à la mode with gnocchi," said the waiter bitterly.

"All right, we'll take the beef à la mode with the genukki, too," said Wildgans. "Or do you want something different? . . . Hello, Al," he said, with a wave of the hand to a man who approached the table. He made the introductions: "Al Leinwand—Ludlow Mumm, the great writer. You heard of him."

"Sure," said Al Leinwand.

Al Leinwand, a fierce man and rival agent, a birdlike creature with the head of a hawk on a sparrow's body, glared into the room over Ludlow Mumm's head, in that peculiar Hollywood restaurant manner in which one is never with the eyes where the ears are.

"Go on," said Wildgans, "about the accident."

Mumm recited the story of the derailment in which he had injured his hand, and Leinwand, who, like everyone here, was able to top any story, listened with an unhappy expression of impatience. Suddenly he cut the report short. Following the swaying rump of a girl in a Vertés print with his eyes, the small man said:

"I read all about your accident, Mumm. I could have been in that wreck too." He looked briefly at Wildgans, as if excusing himself for an omission, and added: "In fact, I almost was."

He nodded at a producer three tables away. "I had reservations on that same train. Only, at the last minute, I was held over in New York. Well, so long."

Wildgans salted his Vichyssoise.

"You made him very unhappy," he said to Mumm. "He's heartbroken he wasn't in that wreck. He's got to be in everything. Well," he said, stirring the cold soup, "how do you like it out here?"

The writer smiled and was about to say something when Arty Wildgans turned from his plate, looked up and said an indifferent "Hello" to a beautiful and exotic creature, a woman in her best years, who stretched out to him her carmine-gloved arms, pointed her lips, and made the sound of kissing several times as she sat down.

"Arty, mind if I sit down here for a minute?" she asked reproachfully, with a heavy foreign accent.

"Ludlow Mumm, the writer," said Wildgans and introduced the actress.

She talked into the small mirror of her compact, saying "Hello" with a quick glance at Mumm.

"Darling," she said, still reproachfully, "you promised as a favor to get me a test with Vashvily."

"I will," said Wildgans. "I'm crazy about that bit you did in *Jetsam*. I saw it yesterday. It was marvelous. Just a little more of that the next time and then Vanya Vashvily can't throw it in my face that you are nothing but a character woman and I can defeat him."

She purred and put her arm through his. A fourth person joined the group, a sagging individual in a pale blue sports coat, a musician, also with a heavy accent, who took a match from the table and relit his soggy cigar.

"You know Vogelsang," said Wildgans, and explained that the man was a famous composer of background music.

"You are Austrian?" asked the character woman, while Wildgans, whose client Vogelsang was, said to Mumm:

"Great talent. He did the score for *Magdalene*."

"*Ja, ja,*" said Vogelsang, or rather, "yoh, yoh."

"Ah, Austrians," she said with throaty laughter, "such gemütliche people, Austrians. Well, maybe not—nobody is *gemütlich* any more, except Arty here.

"You know Russians, kind, sing, dance, help everybody, suddenly turn into wild animals, beat innocents. Ach, prrrppzzt—man is terrible. Well, nice to have seen you."

Mr. Vogelsang, with the back of his trousers hanging sadly, stuck his wet cigar deep into his mouth, made a continental bow to the character woman, and left.

"I don't agree with what you said about the Russians at all," said Ludlow Mumm to the character woman. "I can't agree with you at all on that. I think they're a great people."

"I hope you are right," said the actress. "I am one of them."

She turned to Wildgans.

"Would you like to have a cheap thrill, Arty? I am going to have a massage and you can come and talk to me."

She was up and without waiting for the answer she sailed off, throwing kisses.

"I always inherit these dogs," said Wildgans, starting to cut the boeuf à la mode.

"Nobody else wants to have anything to do with them . . . just because I have a soft heart and can't say no. Of course, that dame will never be anything but a character woman, but I haven't the heart to tell her that. I could have told her five years ago when she came out here."

They both ate; Wildgans in haste, and Mumm with enjoyment of the sauce, which he mopped up with pieces of bread after he had eaten all the gnocchi.

"We have to get something blight-resisting for this table," remarked Wildgans as a tall, ascetic-looking man came up to the table with his hands in his coat pockets.

The unhappy-looking, pale individual stared at Wildgans, and without any change of expression in his face and tired voice he said:

"I'm still dazed. I fell off my filing cabinet last night when I got your note."

"What did you expect?" said Wildgans.

"I expected a check—money—for the difference between what they said they'd agree to and what I'm getting."

He stared at Wildgans and Wildgans said:

"You know, Ludlow Mumm, the writer."

Without taking his eyes off Wildgans, the tall, thin man said, "Hello, Mumm," and continued:

"Listen, Wildgans, I'm just a thin, tired Jew. I don't want anything for nothing. I only ask to be paid for my work, and when I'm not, I get unhappy and the fountain doesn't spurt."

"I'll see Moses Fable tomorrow," said Wildgans.

"Why not today?" said the man.

"Tomorrow is a better day. I'm a little dull today," said Wildgans.

"Did you hear that, Mumm?" asked the thin man. "He said, 'I'm a little dull today!' Why make an exception? Why not just say, 'I'm Arty'?"

Wildgans laughed and handed him a cigar. Jerome Hack rolled it in his long fingers, smelled it, and examined it with his unhappy black eyes.

"What are you staring at the cigar for? It's good. I gave it to you."

"Get busy, Wildgans, and do something," Jerome Hack said as he left.

"Great talent," said Wildgans after the departing writer. "On the same lot as you are—a mechanic, great on construction—

turns out rough-and-tumble musicals—cops-and-robbers—anything you want. Very dependable—great sense of humor—a very legitimate guy."

The waiter put the check down and Wildgans signed it.

He drove back to the hotel with Mumm.

"Well," he said, "I think we had a very fruitful talk. Good-by, Lud. I'll call you."

"How about the story? When do I start to work?" asked Mumm, leaning forward, ready to get out of the car.

"Oh, about the picture," said Wildgans. "Listen, Mumm, take it easy. Get settled first and don't worry about the picture. These days you can hang a sign outside a theater saying 'No Picture Today' and close up and they'll break down the doors. You don't have to show no picture—just turn out the lights and get a couple of guys to drag wet overcoats through the aisles and step on the feet of the audience.

"You need a rest, Mumm, after that shaking up you got," said Wildgans, and waved to him as he drove off, leaving the conscientious writer standing under the *porte-cochère* of his hotel.

Mumm scratched his soft beard for a while and looked after the car. He walked to the elevator, past the greetings of the assistant manager, room clerk, several bellhops, and the elevator operator, who all knew his name and pronounced it correctly. He came to his suite and opened the door.

An immaculately groomed young woman was in his living room. She smiled and went to the telephone.

"Operator," she said with gay inflection and smiling, "Mr. Mumm is back—just stepped in—but please announce everybody before you put them on.

"That will give you some protection," she said, and introduced herself as Miss Princip of the Wildgans Chase Agency.

"You're very popular, Mr. Mumm. You have three invitations for dinner tonight," she said.

"But I don't know anybody here," said Mumm.

"Miss Allbright's secretary was on the phone just now to ask you for dinner tonight. Betsy Allbright, you know, is a famous silent picture star. She's very nice. She has a magnificent home in Malibu and the food is excellent. I think it would make a lovely evening for you."

"Do you think I should go?" said Mumm.

"Well," said Miss Princip, "Miss Allbright is one of the un-crowned queens of Hollywood. It's a kind of command and I think Mr. Wildgans would say emphatically yes.

"Now," she said, opening a briefcase, "I'll explain to you about your salary check and how we handle that."

"Ah, yes," said Ludlow Mumm, whose funds were low, and moved toward her on the Modernage divan.

"We pick up your paycheck at the studio and deduct our ten percent commission and then we deposit the rest at the bank. We have opened an account at the bank for you and I brought a checkbook with me."

She pulled a large book from the briefcase with six checks to a page and "Ludlow Mumm" printed on each check.

"I can come here and make out checks and keep order in your account, and put things down so that we won't run into a tax situation. Is that all right with you, Mr. Mumm?"

"Oh, yes, yes, yes," said Mumm.

"Well, that's that," she said, and placed the checkbook and some papers on a small bamboo-and-ebony desk.

She reached into the briefcase again.

"I brought some cash," she said, "for current expenses. We thought you might find yourself short after the trip and the accident. Here is two thousand," she said and handed him the envelope, "and if you need more, just call me. Toni will bring it right over."

Mumm took the envelope and he said with elaborate, artificial calm:

"Thank you . . . and can you tell me about the studio—I mean, when do I start to work?"

"Your producer, Vanya Vashvily, is in the Cedars of Lebanon. He caught a cold and it turned into an infection of the middle ear—"

"I'm sorry to hear that," said Ludlow Mumm.

"Well, it's too bad," said the girl, "but it's all on Olympia time and he'll be back in the office again in a few weeks. You'll find that time passes very quickly out here, Mr. Mumm. Now, is there anything you want me to take care of? Any letters you want me to answer? Any bills you want me to pay?"

Ludlow Mumm went to his bags and dug up a pack of letters, all of them unopened, and handed them to Miss Princip.

He walked into his bedroom and carefully closed the door while the ambulatory secretary outside uncorked her fountain pen and began to settle his accounts.

Before he sat down on his bed, he made sure once more that the door was closed. Then he took the bills from the envelope and counted them, holding them like a deck of playing cards first and making a fan of them. Then, placing them neatly on the bed, side by side, the fifties, twenties, tens, and fives, he counted them that way again. He put them back into the envelope finally, and through the door that led directly from his bedroom to the corridor he went down to the lobby. He walked up and down for a while and then stopped at the cigar stand.

The fat white index finger of his left hand pointed through the glass of the showcase down to the old friend, the slim Robert Burns Panatela, which had been his faithful writing companion for years. But just as the girl was about to lift the box out of the case and bring it within his reach, Ludlow Mumm's finger, like the needle on a seismograph, began to waver and slowly slid across the glass to the opposite side—to the corner which was occupied by the exquisite products of the Republica de Cuba—by the Aroma Selecta; the thick, blunt Romeo and Juliet; the good Punch; the corpulent Upmann Double Claro, nine inches long and in a cedar box all by itself next to its smaller, slim sister.

After some indecision, Mumm pointed to a long Partagas.

"These just came in fresh today," said the girl and showed him an airtight glass jar of fifty Upmanns. She told him the price.

He hesitated for a moment, leaning on the glass case and cupping the bearded chin in his left hand, but then he suddenly shut heavy iron gates on the drab past and he held the bandaged hand over the glass jar as if blessing it.

"I'll take it," he said.

He reached for the envelope with the money but the girl was writing out a slip, spelling his name correctly, and she said:

"I'll just put it on the bill. That's simpler."

He picked up the jar and carried it across the lobby. Ludlow Mumm progressed in the fashion of a ball rolling softly over uneven terrain, taking advantage of depressions in the land. A shy creature, he walked at the sides of corridors, around people and behind potted plants and furniture rather than in front.

He always smiled first when he encountered somebody. He was

behind a big plant, on his way to the elevator, when he smiled again as an awkward-moving individual accosted him. A man in black gloves, carrying a cap in his hand, came toward him and in a hoarse voice said:

"I'm George, your driver. I'm down here whenever you want me. Got the car outside, boss."

Ludlow Mumm said, "That's fine," and rolled along the edge of the carpet to the elevator, where he stopped and turned to look back at the individual, who had resumed reading a moving-picture magazine and was leaning against the wall, awaiting his orders.

"I can do this just as well at the office if you want me to," said Miss Princip, looking up from her work as he came in and started opening his glass jar.

"That's all right," said Mumm. "You're not disturbing me in the least. Go right ahead."

"Lady Graveline wants you for dinner tomorrow," she said. "Shall I accept?"

It was remarkable with what speed the writer was accustoming himself to his new habitat. Without a trace of surprise, delight, or a hint that this was at all otherwise than as it should be, he took the lid off the jar, picked out a cigar, and said:

"I think so."

He went to his bedroom and put on a dressing gown and slippers. Then he walked through the living room, past the secretary, to his balcony—to a *chaise longue* upholstered in bright chintz.

As he placed the weight of his body on it, the intelligent piece of furniture made automatic adjustments in all its parts. The back rest sank away to rest his head and shoulders; the lower part lifted his knees and bedded them comfortably. Ludlow Mumm lay suspended in the comforts of a feather bed and as if he were floating in lukewarm water.

He lifted the cigar up over his face and balanced it in his hand. He looked at it closely and from all angles in the fashion in which a baby examines a new teething ring suspended over his crib. He stuck the cigar between his lips and was bothered for a second by the unpleasant prospect of having to get up again out of the *chaise longue* to look for a match.

As he was about to make the effort to rise, the meuble, whose trade name was the "King of Ease," adjusted itself again and put him in a sitting position so that he could see, on a wicker table at his left, a large onyx match stand, filled with kitchen matches, to which, as a cigar smoker, he was very partial.

The writer was about to reach for one of the matches when a voice said:

"Let me do it."

The valet, with a pair of his freshly pressed trousers over his arm, lighted the match, waited until the sulphur fumes had blown away, and then moved the flame carefully back and forth at the end of the cigar without haste, so that Ludlow got the cigar lit properly and without undue puffing.

The writer rewarded the servant with a raising of his eyebrows and leaned back. The "King of Ease" obliged, and, in great comfort again, Ludlow Mumm resumed drawing on his fine cigar.

The field of his vision was framed by night-blooming jasmine. The crowns of two high palm trees swayed with soft rustling of their dry leaves in the cloudless, dustless blue. He looked through the openwork of the banisters at the immaculate expanse of lawn, spread out like an immense green towel. A tropical garden crowded against the hotel with plants that were like animals rather than vegetation; some embracing one another, others holding large emerald umbrellas in their arms. There was the actuality of grapefruit hanging in trees; the thud of tennis balls; the shouting and splashing of children in the water of the hotel's pool; all mixed and far enough away not to disturb the siesta.

Miss Princip came tiptoeing out on the balcony. She looked anxiously at the writer. When she saw that he was awake, she held up a few bills, all of them stamped "past due," and she said with concern:

"I just wanted to find out from you, Mr. Mumm, whether I should keep up these subscriptions to the *Daily Worker* and the *American-Soviet Review,* or just pay them."

The otherwise mild Ludlow Mumm turned and sat up so abruptly that the "King of Ease" *chaise longue* for once was behind in its work and squeaked with anguish.

"Of course," said Mumm, and swallowed smoke in the excitement.

"Keep them up?" asked the frightened Miss Princip, with wide, questioning eyes.

Ludlow Mumm nodded violently through a coughing spell. He sat still after that. Under his beard and mustache, his mouth was a bitter line.

"I am sorry," said Miss Princip, as she came out once more with another bill. "The Hotel Wolff in New York—"

"Yes?" said Ludlow Mumm.

"Do we pay them—I mean, do we keep the apartment there?"

"No," he said, "just pay them."

He leaned back again. Now his mouth was clamped together like that of a turtle.

The poor scribe, whose view of the world up to now had always been from third-class accommodations, returned in unhappy memory for a while to the quarters that he had occupied in New York: the cell of a bedroom with the gritty window sill and faded velvet drapes, airless in summer's heat, off the soot-blown air-shaft of the Hotel Wolff; the living room whose three pieces of furniture changed forever from red to blue in the reflection of the alternating lights of the hotel's electric sign that hung out-side between its windows. He heard the ruthless bombardment of garbage cans and the explosion that awoke him every morn-ing when the cast iron covers of the sidewalk elevator fell shut. And he thought of the big ink spot on the brown carpet, unre-moved in all the years of his tenancy there. He had grown re-signed to it eventually, and fixed his eyes on it whenever he had to concentrate on the writing of the bittersweet, nostalgic pieces that were his specialty and that had finally released him from his debtor's prison.

He reached for one of the kitchen matches and relit his fine cigar. He blew a smoke ring up at the night-blooming jasmine and looked again at the palms. He was reassured. He regained some comfort from the chair as the "King of Ease" laid him out again, and contentment moved slowly back into his eyes.

There was one moment of concern—he thought he heard a downpour. But the sky was still blue, and his fears disappeared when he saw that the sound came from the hotel's rain machine, which sprayed a soft drizzle on the leaves from hidden nozzles.

"Good-by," said Miss Princip, softly.

"Tell George to take you home," he said, completely repaired and soothed.

He held on to his cigar as a sleeping bird does to the favorite branch of a tree, and then he fell away in the pleasant anesthesia, the dreamless, deathlike sleep, that is one of the many gifts that the glory land extends to the newly arrived.

Moses
Fable

. . .

After breakfast, Ludlow Mumm walked as usual, trailed by the aromatic thin blue ribbon of his morning cigar.

He was a new man, and rolled over the mimosa path with ease and freedom under the arms, around the waist, and in the crotch. Also, his neck was comfortable. He wore a low-collar batiste shirt made to his measure. On his feet were comfortable tan-and-white moccasin-type shoes. He wore a featherweight Harris-tweed jacket and fawn-colored flannels. His new cane of choice Malacca swung lightly on his arm and on his head was a fisherman-type zephyr canvas hat.

He stopped here and there, next to tangerine and orange trees, or mused a while, half-hidden by the leaf of an exotic plant. He smiled at children in the pool and at babies in carriages. He drank in the climate with deep drafts and unhindered expansions of his chest measurement.

He was in complete accord with his happy surroundings until Miss Princip appeared on the balcony of his suite and in unmelodious tones called out his name.

He turned his head, looked up, and answered.

"Don't forget, you've having luncheon with Moses Fable," she screamed, "at one. It's eleven-thirty now."

He stood still and looked at the ashes on the end of his cigar for a while, and then pulled himself together and walked to the hotel's porte-cochère.

He arrived at the Olympia Studios ahead of time and was immediately shown in by the reception clerk. A young woman in bobby socks and sweater took him up to the second floor of the immaculate building.

From the elevator he stepped on a battleship-gray linoleum floor along which are the offices of those writers who earn only one thousand dollars a week and have a common washroom to every six writers.

Passing this region, the girl led the way down a new, deeply-carpeted corridor off which were the suites reserved for the three-thousand-a-week writers.

The girl guide's golden mass of hair stopped bobbing up and down at a door on which "Ludlow Mumm" was lettered in bold golden capitals. She opened the door and let him in.

Except for the familiar manuscript of *Will You Marry Me?* which lay on the Sheraton desk in the first room, the suite looked like a roped-off, immaculate sample apartment in an expensive furniture shop.

The secretary came from her office. She was attractive without being disturbing, proper like the hostesses in restaurants frequented by women shoppers. She introduced herself, spoke a few complimentary phrases about the writer's work and her familiarity with it. Then, sliding past him, she showed Ludlow Mumm the various mechanical gadgets of the new office: The button which summoned her; how to get an outside number on the telephone; how to open the window; and how to turn on the air-conditioning apparatus. She took his hat and the cane and hung them on a tree in the small foyer. She asked him whether he wanted anything and when he said no, she departed in that curious disappearing act by which perfect secretaries leave a room. She was so prim there seemed to be no backside to her.

Mumm sat down as if he had just arrived in a strange town and were waiting for somebody in a suite in a new hotel. He washed his hand in the mauve-tiled private bathroom and sat down again.

He tried the leatherette swivel chair that stood at his desk, and almost fell over backward. It turned and leaned immediately in all directions without the comfortable, restrained movements of the "King of Ease." He had to grab for his desk and kick with his legs to regain balance.

He examined his desk. It was dustless, glass-covered, and provided with a large writing pad and fresh blotters. The glass inkstand was filled with ink as clean as if dark green wine had just been poured into a crystal goblet. There was a calendar and appointment pad, open at the right date, with his luncheon appointment entered in a neat hand over the line that was given to one P.M.

He opened one of the drawers and again found order. No dust in the corners, containers with paper clips and rubber bands. In the second drawer, the private telephone directory of the Olympia Studios and the directory of the extended area of Los Angeles.

In the large flat drawer, the one in the center, were reserve penholders, sharpened pencils, erasers, and blank paper in unlimited quantities and of the very best quality. It was white paper with a yellowish tint, neatly stacked. There were also envelopes and message pads with "Interoffice Memorandum from Ludlow Mumm to—" printed on them. Mumm had the impulse to put some of the paper and envelopes in his pocket. There was no typewriter.

He walked into the washroom again, and afterward took a cigar and lit it.

He sat for a while on the couch in the bright living room of the suite, and walked to the window, watching one gardener clipping a hedge below and another digging up dead blooms, replacing them with others that were flowering. He was warm.

He walked to the temperature control panel and pushed a button. There was a soft whirring sound, and presently the smoke of his cigar began to be drawn slowly upward.

The secretary came back and said:

"Is there anything you wish to dictate before I go to lunch, Mr. Mumm?"

He thanked her. She left him sitting on the couch, saying, as she was about to disappear:

"You know about the luncheon, Mr. Mumm?"

He asked where he had to go and she said:

"Don't worry, Mr. Mumm, just wait here. They'll come and get you."

At noon, the electricians on the various stages of the vast lot of Olympia Pictures threw their switches and the large family that worked on the Olympia lot began their leisurely trek toward the cafeterias and the commissary.

At one, the bells of the carillon with which Moses Fable had endowed a Methodist church that stood on a lot adjoining the studio began to ring their changes and the high executives in the administration building started to salivate.

A motherly woman known as Ma Gundel, in white with broad white shoes on her aching feet, would come out of the kitchen then, carrying a large wicker basket which contained various kinds of bread. In the basket were sourdough bread, sweet rye, Russian rye, matzoth, French bread, pumpernickel, Swedish crisp, potato bread, and Viennese rolls. She covered this with a napkin and put it in the center of the round table at which Moses Fable lunched and walked back through the commissary to get large kosher pickles, almost electric with their sharp, salty tang. She also brought red and green tomatoes, pickled; a dish with chopped chicken liver, Bismarck herring, sliced smoked salmon, sour cream, chives, scallions, immense sticks of Utah celery, radishes, and more pickles; and other good and salty delicatessen according to the day of the week.

Her last trip was for Dr. Brown's Celery Tonic, Pepsi-Cola, Coca-Cola, and bottles of milk and buttermilk.

All this done, she sat on a chair outside the executive dining room and looked into the large commissary at the assembled stars, bit actors, and extras, who, in the various costumes of the parts they played, sat there and ate and talked.

Nuns from religious spectacles sat next to gangsters; Gestapo captains ate in peace with the French Underground; and maharajahs were seated below untouchables at another table.

Ma Gundel could have retired years ago under the pension plan which enveloped all regular employees of Olympia. But she loved pictures and could not tear herself away from the forever-exciting scene of their making. She followed every production with interest. Moses Fable valued her criticism and had been known to consult with her seriously when casting important features. She was a person of consequence and everybody put his arms around her.

Ma Gundel rested her feet and awaited the arrival of Moses Fable and his guests.

Moses Fable and Olympia were made for each other. No player in Hollywood could have come near the perfect portrayal that he gave as president of the corporation. If he had limited his work to impersonating himself, his huge salary would have been earned.

There was a solid air about him as he walked through the pandemonium of the plant in his conservative gray suits. The thin veins on his massive cheeks were like the engraving on gilt-edged securities.

He moved with weight and deliberation, and when he wanted to look around he turned with the whole elliptical body, slowly and steadily, as a statue is moved.

"Here at Olympia," he was fond of saying, "we have both time and money in unlimited quantities!"

In his solid fashion, he was outstandingly different from his competitors, who always ran, and always seemed to suspect that someone was listening behind them.

A beneficiary of mankind in the mass, as he liked to think of himself, Moses Fable also richly rewarded those around him he thought worthy. He was interested in the last individual of his large family.

"Anyone can come and see me at any hour of the day and also the night, if it's important enough" was another of his favorite sayings.

But, if he was kind and human, he was not gullible, and while he spoke ordinarily with the rich organ of a psalm-singer holding himself in, once he was confronted with roguery, when he found lurking skimmers trying to dip their ladles in the rich Olympia broth, when his treasures were threatened, or he caught the competition trying to wander off with one of his stars, he became dangerously agile and emitted the sounds of a knife-grinder.

• • •

The procession of his virtues is not complete without citing his courage. He was envied and admired for the fortitude with which he regularly threw good money after bad and thereby regularly attained large grosses and fabulous successes with even his worst pictures.

With the same rare mixture of a peasant's cunning and an impressario's play of hunches, he chose people. If he saw talent and goodwill, he was generous with time and money, he forgave the beginner his mistakes, and allowed for occasional failure in old hands.

He read people through his sharp rimless glasses and he filed away what he found. The intricate cabinet in his head never mislaid information. It was a piece of occult furniture that belonged among the paraphernalia of stargazers and spiritualists; it was of paramount importance in his complicated industry, but would have wrecked any other kind of business, had it made use of it.

He was given to speeches. His winged words, uncensored, flew out over banquet tables and into the nation's press. He was upswept by his own words and believed everything he said.

The carillon was still ringing from the steeple of the church across the street when Ludlow Mumm followed another girl guide into the inner office of Moses Fable. She left the shy writer standing in the doorway.

The executives who stood in a group in the center of the room slowly moved toward him. They all talked: some to one another in the center of the circle; others shouted over the heads of people who stood between them; and some carried on conversations on the outside.

Vanya Vashvily was talking to a director.

"What is this, the emergency room?" asked Moses Fable, looking past Vashvily at the door, and pointing with slow, deliberate gesture at Ludlow Mumm, who stood there with his bandaged hand.

Vashvily turned around.

"Oh, hello," he said. "That's one of my boys, Mr. Fable. Ludlow Mumm, the great writer."

"I beg your pardon," said Fable, slowly approaching the writer. "It's a great pleasure to have you with us, Mr. Mumm. I want you to meet some of the people here. Wolfgang Liebestod, head of our musical department, Raoul de Bourggraff, head of the art department; John St. Clair; Sandor Thrilling, the director you've heard about."

Mumm shook hands without surprise. In a town that contains firms like Utter McKinley, the undertakers; a real estate firm of Read and Wright; two Prinzmetals; a LeRoy Prinz; a Jack Skirball; a Jerry Rothschild; a law firm by the name of Dull and Twist; and musicians called Amphitheatrof and Bakaleinakoff, he had become accustomed to unusual and distinctive names.

"Bob Evervess of the story department and Mr. Envelove of the legal end. Come on boys, let's go," said Moses Fable, and taking hold of the writer, he advanced with him through the door as the pealing of the carillon faded away.

"Mr. Mumm," said Fable, "you sit over there."

He indicated the chair opposite his own, but before he released him from the strong grip with which he had transported him from the executive suite, over the lawn and through the comissionary into the private dining room, he said:

"I hope you're feeling at home here. I hope you'll be with us a long time, Mr. Mumm, and I hope they're treating you right. If they don't, you come and see me. It's not like over at those windbags"—he nodded in the direction of another studio—"where you have to wade through fourteen secretaries before you can see anybody. Remember, here, you can see me any hour of the day, and, if it's important, any hour of the night."

Fresh
Paint

. . .

The faithful Ludlow Mumm was in his office every day. He sat at
the desk and he washed his hand and he thought about his work.
The fifth day, he had asked his secretary if he could have a typewriter. He said he was unable to dictate. His calendar was blank.
He left the door to the corridor slightly open because he felt more
a part of the living that way.

At the ringing of the carillon, he went to the cafeteria and ate.
Coming back, he found a large new typewriter beside his desk on
a small table. He put a piece of paper in it and typed with the
index finger of the left hand.

"Mr. Mumm," said the secretary, coming out of her small cubicle, "Mr. Vashvily's secretary is on the phone. She wants to
know if it's convenient for you to come up and see him for a few
minutes."

"Now?" asked Mumm, and he felt as he hadn't since he got out
of school.

"Yes, now," said the secretary. "Mr. Vashvily is leaving to re-
sume his rest in Palm Springs, and he wants to see you before he
goes."

Mumm stopped at the drinking fountain outside, although he

had the thermos bottle and glass in his office. Then he went into the producer's office.

Vashvily was in back of a partition where he kept a miniature haberdashery establishment. As he talked, he appeared first with a new soft shirt which he had half put on. Then, with a selection of ties, from which he chose the one that went best with his coat. Between his exits and his entrances, he said he just wanted to know how Ludlow Mumm was feeling. Vashvily's secretary packed for him and put papers, including a copy of *Will You Marry Me?* into his portfolio, and Vashvily spoke a few words about how he pictured the heroine. At the end he came out from his shop, felt in all his pockets, and said: "I think I've got everything."

He walked out of the room with Mumm at his side, and said good-by outside the office. A chauffeur carried his bag and danced attendance, running ahead to open the shining chromium door.

For a while Mumm stood in confusion watching the flashes of silver light that the door shot down the corridor as it swung in and out, activated by the chauffeur's energetic push. Then he rolled to the window and watched Vashvily's departure in a black limousine that was as large as a hearse, and finally he went to the fountain, drank, as all nervous writers do, and then into the washroom of the common crew, where he dabbed water at his face and looked into one of the three mirrors on the wall, as if it could tell him why he was here. He thought of all the things he wanted to be told, and the questions he had had ready for Vashvily. He dragged himself back to his office.

He turned the swivel chair and looked out. The gardener below had finished trimming the trees and was oiling his lawn mower. In the sky above was a passenger plane.

The pilot of the plane let down the wing flaps for a landing and then the wheels. Moses Fable, who was in the plane, looked down at his studio as he adjusted his safety belt. The psychic executive made a note to have a talk with Ludlow Mumm as soon as he came on the lot.

At four, Moses Fable knocked and came into the room. He looked at Ludlow Mumm.

"Stay where you are," he said. "Don't get up. Don't let me disturb you. I just thought you might be lonesome, so I came down to have a little talk with you."

"Thank you, Mr. Fable. I wanted to talk to you too," said Mumm. "I feel awful."

Without asking him to show his tongue or feeling his pulse, Moses Fable looked at Mumm with the searching eye of a great and practiced diagnostician who, standing at the foot of the patient's bed, can tell what's wrong with him by just looking at him.

"How are you getting along? How are they treating you?" he asked.

"Oh, everybody is nice to me," said Mumm. "The only thing that bothers me, Mr. Fable—I've come here almost for a week now and I haven't done anything."

There was nothing that made Fable happier than a man's throwing himself on his mercy. It warmed him all over. It brought, in some cases, tears to his eyes.

"How is the climate affecting you?"

"Oh, it's not the change of air. I love the climate. I sleep well. That is, I slept well until I tried to start to write."

"Well," said Fable, "it takes a while."

"I can't even read here," confessed Mumm.

"That's strange. What do you think it is?"

"I don't know what it is," answered Mumm.

"You dictate?"

"No, I can't dictate. I have to be alone when I write."

"You write in longhand?"

"No, sir, I type."

"Well, sure, it's the hand," said Fable, relieved. "As soon as you get that bandage off, you'll be able to write."

"That isn't it," said Mumm. "I can't even concentrate."

"Let's see, now," said Fable. "Maybe it's the room."

"Maybe," said Mumm.

"Have you tried to write at home? I mean in your hotel here?"

"I've tried everything," replied the hopeless Mumm.

"It's the room all right," said Fable, and walked to the window looking out on the lovely scene.

"When you write for yourself, Mr. Mumm, where do you write? Or, rather, where did you write?" he asked.

"Oh, I had a couple of rooms in New York. In a small hotel."

"And you were able to write there all right?"

"And I was able to write there all right," echoed Mumm.

"I wrote a lot at night," he added.

"What's the name of that hotel?" continued Fable.

"The Hotel Wolff on West Forty-fourth Street."

"You're homesick," said Fable. "Happens often. We had a writer here—great talent—and he got homesick for New York, so I told him to go a couple of hours a day and sit on Stage Eight.

"We were doing a picture about New York then and we had some sets of New York there. A couple of Fifth Avenue buses, a corner of Fifty-seventh street, and a piece of Central Park. He used to go there every day and walk around and sit on a bench and then he would come back feeling better. But we haven't got that set any more. Maybe that would have helped."

He walked slowly to the empty desk and then said:

"I have every confidence, Mr. Mumm, that you will write a great screen play for us, and I will do all in my power to help you.

"We have two things here at Olympia, Mr. Mumm, essential to the making of good pictures. They are Time and Money, and we don't care how much of each we spend to get the results we are after.

"Now, I tell you what you do. Take your hat, Mr. Mumm, and go to Romanoff's, and don't worry; do anything you want, and don't come back here until you hear from me."

With consideration for Mumm's hurt right hand, the kind president of Olympia held out his left, which the shy writer, who was crushed with gratitude, could shake without embarrassment or fumbling.

Mumm left the building reassured and uplifted. He resumed his walks in the hotel's park and he slept well.

A week later, he was summoned back to Olympia by Moses Fable.

"Now, to do a thing like that!" Mumm said, after entering his office.

"I can't believe my eyes," he stammered, and then looked at Moses Fable and Raoul de Bourggraff, the head of the scenic department, who had brought about the change, and who were waiting for him.

His old furniture from New York had been flown out to Hollywood. A few minor architectural adjustments had been made to change his office into an exact replica of Numbers 604–605 of the Hotel Wolff.

Mumm got up and walked into the bedroom. There was the old wallpaper, the faded velvet drapes. He touched the window sill and felt the grit. Outside was the sooty airshaft.

"Now, wait. Turn on the lights," said Moses Fable as a father does, instructing a child in how to work a new electric train at Christmastime.

He showed him how to make it dark.

"Remember, you told me you worked a lot at night," he said.

The room was in darkness. A dim light shone over the old type-writer that had replaced the new one, and the bad furniture changed from bluish hues to red in the reflection of the electric sign outside the window. In a drawer of the desk were reams of stationery with the crest of the Hotel Wolff.

"How do you like it?" asked Moses Fable.

"I don't know what to say."

"Everything in place?" asked the president.

"Yes," said Mumm, and then glanced at the carpet. A new carpet had been left on the floor.

"All except the carpet," he said. "My New York carpet had a large ink spot on it—it was in the exact center of the room. I used to look at it when I had to concentrate."

"Well, we want you to be happy," said Moses Fable.

He went to the desk, picked up the dirty brass inkstand and, bending slowly to the floor, he emptied it in the center of the new carpet.

"How's that?" he asked.

"That's fine," said Mumm.

"We had to board up the bathroom," said Fable, "on account of the layout."

"Oh, that's all right," said Mumm.

"Anything else?"

"No, I can't think of anything," said Mumm. It's perfect."

Fable turned to the building superintendent, who had joined the group.

"Keep the windows open and the fans going. Get that smell of fresh paint out of here so that Mr. Mumm can get to work." He stepped to the door. "Now, I'll leave you," said Fable, "and don't be afraid to call me. Anybody here can see me any time during the day and, if it's important enough, even during the night."

Ludlow Mumm stretched himself on the mangy black tufted leather couch, under the map of the world which was pinned on the dirty gray wall, and folded his hands under his head.

Presently he got up and walked out into the lobby. The Negro came toward his door. He stopped his wagon and took from it a towel.

"I'll take that, if you don't mind," said Mumm, and walked down to the common washroom of the cheap writers.

In this cubicle, which was tiled from floor to ceiling and contained three urinals, three wash basins, and three toilets behind swinging doors, he found Hack, who was washing his hands.

"You know what I think of Moses Fable?" asked Ludlow Mumm.

But Hack put his index finger to his lips, and with frightened eyes he turned and pointed with his long white finger at the center toilet behind them.

The bar-type swinging doors of this compartment were closed and only the tips of the shoes of the occupant were visible beneath them.

"Shhhh!" said Hack, and one of the rare kind words ever said about Moses Fable remained unspoken.

"This place is filled with Fable's spies. You have to learn to keep your mouth shut," said Hack, outside, as he ran to his office.

Adventures Abroad,
1950–1962

· · · · · ·

Cher Ami

. . .

To work for me, to live with me, is hard. I am composed of disorderly habits. I live the way William Saroyan thinks people live, and it's not so funny off the stage. Normally, I am filled with the greatest goodwill toward my fellow men, and I manifest this with generous gestures in all directions. I stop and smile at children, and I spread breadcrumbs for the pigeons on the stairs of Saint Patrick's, but the next day I would like to kick them all in the shins.

My habitat is mostly bars and restaurants, hotels and depots, and the lobbies and entrances thereof. In normal times I am found on the decks of steamships, and on the shores of tropic isles. I arrive suddenly, somewhere far away, and once there I haunt the piers and terminals and curse if there isn't a boat or plane to take me back immediately. I get homesick as soon as I am away from where I've gone—going it's for New York, coming back it's for where I've left. To share such a life, one needs a mobile servant, adaptable as a chameleon, shock- and surprise-proof, a person who gazes into your face as into a crystal ball and then knows whether to come close or stay away from you the rest of the day. The coin is not too good, either.

The ideal servant for me is a kind of Sancho Panza, a companion and friend with the melancholy kinship of an Irish setter. The run-of-the-mill retainer won't do at all; no Treacher type, no Admirable Crichton for me. I'd rather have him inept as far as service goes, but let him make it up with perfection in all the other departments. Above all, let him be someone curious and different. My ideal would be an ex-sergeant of the Foreign Legion, or a bankrupt banker, a retired road-company leading man who could mug Hamlet and Shylock, or a third-rate Karloff. Give me a burglar, or even a dismissed G-man, anything, but not the meek soul whose life is a monument to a million polished teapots.

My wishes are usually fulfilled with miraculous promptness, sometimes with such dispatch that I get scared at the prompt benevolence that hovers over me.

For example, I wished for this fol-de-rol butler, and not very hard either. I did not go to any employment agency to look for him; I did not even put an ad in the paper, nor did I ask anyone if they knew of such a man. I just wished, and he came.

I met him in Haiti after a trip to Panama, where I did an article for the June 1941 issue of *McCall's* magazine. In Haiti I stayed in the annex of a small hotel, the rooms of which were like the cells in an exquisitely run insane asylum. Every compartment had its own precise garden of tropical greenery. Planted in the exact center of each of these eight-by-twelve-foot gardens was a tree, not large enough for anyone to use it for climbing in or out of the garden, but with enough leaves to shade a rattan *chaise longue,* and with four branches for birds to sing on in the twilights of morning and evening. Each of the gardens was enclosed by a white high wall.

The floor of the bedroom was a mosaic of black and white tile, and in its center stood a bed with tortured cast-iron ornaments, small knobs, and buns, spirals and little brass blossoms stuck and twisted on its head- and foot-boards. During the day, the design of the bed was somewhat diffused under a tent made of mosquito netting, which was attached to the ceiling by a rope and pulley. At night, one was under the tent, and then the fancy ironwork was beautifully clear.

The morning after the night when I wished for the companion, I beheld on awakening the outline of a man outside the mosquito tent. It seemed that he had stood there for a long while. He was in a state of repose, leaning on the wall, and he threw the butt of a cigarette out into the garden when he saw me sit up. On his head was a Chevalier straw hat. I lifted the netting, and, leaning out of bed, I observed that my visitor was barefoot and sunburned, and that his hat was honored with the bright colors of a Racquet Club band. He had a lean, generous face, and looked somewhat like a skiing teacher or a derelict tennis pro. Over his lips lay a black mustache, and his shirt was without buttons. The sleeves were torn off halfway between the elbow and the shoulders, offering ventilation to his chest.

He sat down at the foot of the bed and told me that he was my friend. He told me his name and informed me that he was one of a group of escaped prisoners from Devil's Island, and that he was taken care of, with his companions, by the good *Soeurs de la Sagesse.* He and the boys lived at the convent. . . .

He corrected himself and explained that he and the others were not escaped criminals in the strict sense of the word, but that since the Vichy Government was unable or unwilling to pay the up-keep of the prison or the salaries of the administrators and guards at Guiana, the prison doors had simply been left open, and who-ever wanted to, left.

"I," he continued, "was a *doubleur;* that is, I had served my sen-tence, but had to stay on the Island. We left French Guiana, my friends and I, in a sixteen-foot *canot.* No one tried to stop us. We were twelve when we started. The hardest part was to get straight out to sea past the reef which is called the Frenchmen's Grave. To pass this, you have to go over sand-bars in a straight line for about thirty-five kilometers, and then you turn left.

"That takes courage. We did it all with the aid of a map, which we had copied, and with the aid of a Greek, a seaman who knew the stars. We also had a small compass with us, and we got as far as Trinidad. It was easy. A captain of a ship must find a port; we only tried to find the land. The Governor of Trinidad gave us eighty dollars to buy a bigger boat, and with that we got as far as Jamaica. Now we are here and thinking of going on to Cuba. We have a tolerably good life here. Twice a week we watch the plane come in, that is where I saw you arrive. We sit in the convent gar-den or along the water most of the time, and the *bonnes soeurs de la Sagesse* take care of us as if we were little birds, but it's not a life for a man.

"*Cher ami,*" he said, "do something for me. I am a pastry cook, I have been a hotel director. I know how to drive a car and how to fix it. I can write on the machine. I can steer a boat. I am ready to go anywhere, and I am afraid of nothing. Give me a little food and pocket money, and I am your man, your servant, your friend for life."

He lounged back on the bed, lit a cigarette, spread his toes fanwise, folded his hands in back of his head, and looked up at the ceiling, waiting for my answer.

"I wanted to talk to you last night," he added after a while. "I followed you from the cinema up to your hotel, but I thought you might get scared or nervous, so I came this morning."

He broke the few moments of silence, in which I thanked that particular department of Providence that concerns itself with me, by remarking that if I was worried about his past he could put me completely at ease. He confessed that when he was young, he had made a mistake—he had disemboweled his mistress. Ah, Simone was a very beautiful girl, but she had been unfaithful, and he was not sorry.

I told him he could start in right away. He could pack my trunk and take it to the ship; and as soon as he got to New York, there were several people I would like to have disemboweled, but nicely, and I would give him a list every Monday. I gave him a small advance, and then I said that the only thing I was worried about was how he would get to New York, past the immigration authorities, the police, and J. Edgar Hoover's sharp-eyed and resourceful young men.

"Bah! Leave that to me," he said. "I shall be in New York—let me see—it's the middle of August now; give me until the end of September. It's child's play. About the twenty-fifth of September, I would say. Where do you live?" I gave him my address, and that afternoon he arrived with a boy to carry my trunk, which he had neatly packed. On the way to the boat, he stopped the car at the *Magasin de Mille Cent Choses* and bought a pack of razor blades, which he said I needed; and then he said good-by and *au revoir*. He slowly shook my hand and lifted the Chevalier straw hat. He waved it so hard when the ship pulled out that the Racquet Club band came off and fell into the bay. A native boy dove after it, and he gave him a coin.

"Wonderful, wonderful," I said to myself and missed him im-

mediately. Stretched out in my deck-chair, I thought how very fortunate I was. When I got home, I was still gloating over the fact that I had found the perfect man.

One morning soon after my return, I found a letter. It started: "La Havane, Cuba. *Cher ami,* I have the honor to address these few words to you, to inform you that, after a sudden departure from Haiti in a boat which I and a few of the others who shared my idea procured along the waterfront, we proceeded for Cuba. The beginning of the voyage was without incident. One night, however, we had some difficulty holding our direction, as a violent wind caused our leaking shell to dance an infernal sarabande on the waves.

"Without the sail and the mast, and also without the man who steered the boat at the outset, without a rudder even, the wind delivered us to the eastern shore of Cuba, and, to make our *misère* perfect, into a nest of waiting gendarmes from whom we were too wet and exhausted to flee. My companions and I find ourselves detained at the *Centre D'Émigration,* and I regret to inform you that my departure from here can only be effected by the immediately-sent sum of one hundred dollars. I will consider the hundred dollars in lieu of six months of service."

I sent him the money. I have faith in such characters, and they have never failed me. Neither did *Cher Ami.*

In the middle of one night when I lay awake, I had one of my rare moments of worry again. Suppose, when he turns up, I said to myself, he's the perfect servant, butler, and companion, and besides, a good pastry cook. Suppose he's out in the pantry one day squeezing "Many Happy Returns" on my birthday cake when there is a knock at the door, and it's the police. Then follows the story of the body of a young woman, partly decomposed, found crammed into the luggage compartment of my convertible coupé . . . O.K., take him away; but he won't come quietly . . . smack, smack, *klunk;* I hold the door open while they carry him out. Then I have to get hold of Leibowitz, but Leibowitz has turned judge, and Arthur Garfield Hays is out of town. And then the trial and the conviction and the pictures in the paper, and then the visit up the river, and the last mile. It's all absorbing, stirring, and excellently done, but it's not much fun, riding back alone from Ossining with a cold friend up there.

The morning after the night that I wished he wouldn't come, he didn't come, but there was a letter from him, one of the nicest documents I have ever received and certainly worth a hundred dollars.

"*Cher ami,*" it said, "I have the honor to address these few words to you, wishing to keep you informed of my condition. I have the honor to inform you with my deep personal regret that I will not come to America. Dishonesty is not my game. The money you so generously sent to me is paid out in the most splendid of causes. I have used it to obtain for myself and for a friend who shares my idea, passage to Jamaica, from which isle this communication is addressed to you. We have come here to enlist in the forces of

General de Gaulle. This is attested by our pictures and the text which you will find under them in the accompanying clipping from the Kingston *Star*. It's not patriotism, *cher ami*, France has not been a good mother to me. . . . But it's the quickest way to become a man again. Please accept my respectful salutations.

André Pigueron."

My Favorite City

·   ·   ·

There are many ways of getting to know the cities of the world. For me, the best way is through the eye. I look at a city much as I look at the face of a person. Some cities, as with some people, I take a liking to instantly; others, it takes more time to know.

The problem of the first look at Europe is a grave one, and people who have planned the trip often say, "I have been advised to go to such and such a place, to get to know it thoroughly, instead of flitting all over."

My advice would be to the contrary. For one's first look, I advise the traveler to take the guided tour within his means and flit all over. First impressions are strongest; you will discover what you like most and you will have a point of comparison. Later you can go back to those places that have impressed themselves upon you most.

My first visit to Paris depressed me. I hated it. I was then a bus boy in a New York hotel and my mortal enemies were waiters, waiter captains, and headwaiters. I worked my way over on the old S. S. *Rotterdam* and dutifully made my way to Paris. It seemed filled with battalions of my enemies. I left after two days and swore never to return. (I even circled around it to get back to New York.) I fled to my native Tirol, got into buckskin shorts and a green hat with the shaving brush. A photograph taken of me at that time is referred to by my daughter Barbara as the "Bing Crosby picture of Poppy." The buckskin pants have got too tight for me, the mood has changed. I have developed a tolerance for hotel personnel, and now my favorite city is Paris.

• • •

The hum of the engine changes, and afterward there is that always reassuring whine of lowering flaps and landing gear. A few rain clouds hang in the sky, violet on the underside, mother-of-pearl above. The plane banks, and now it sinks down over small houses and their kitchen gardens framed in neat walls against which fruit trees have been trained to grow. The runway is watered down by showers, the grass stands up like the hair on little boys' heads, and the morning sun shines on it all.

The door opens and you breathe the air of France. You are saluted by two of her officials, men with small mustaches and little blue capes barely reaching beneath the seats of their pants. And beyond them, as in a worn mirror, stands the Eiffel Tower, the capricious symbol of the beloved city. This way, please. Through a mildly fogged glass door you follow into a room filled with fellow passengers. *Thump, thump*—we are passed by the police. *Thump, thump*—we are passed by health. *Merci, monsieur . . . merci, mademoiselle.* To the customs now—no bottleneck here merely the question. "You have nothing to declare?" and a chalk mark on each piece of baggage releases us to the bus.

The wind has done some brushwork on the sky and blown the clouds upward, and now we roll into the long avenue that leads to the Porte d'Italie, to the Esplanade des Invalides, where the Air Terminal is located. Sometimes one can wait an hour here before getting a taxi, so I always leave my baggage there and send for it later. For here Paris begins: the Pont Alexandre III is in front of you. It shines in emerald and gold now, a bridge decorated with the makings of bouillabaisse. Among its decorations are crabs, crayfish, conger eels, red mullet, hogfish, swordfish, sharks, pike, carp, and over a thousand scallops, together with seaweed and mermaids. One of its ornaments is a small crab that has become brightly polished because everyone tries to pick it off and take it home.

And in the next moment you see the Place de la Concorde, with its unbelievable vehicles and even more unbelievable congestion. Here also is the Obelisk whose hieroglyphs recount the glorious episodes in the life of Ramses II. It replaced the statue of Louis XV. Why do we take the time to stop to look at monuments? Because from their inscriptions Parisians learn their language and their history.

Turn around. There is the Eiffel Tower again, now close enough so that you can see the elevator climbing up to the first platform. It's a cockeyed kind of Toonerville trolley moving in a diagonal ascent. Has anyone written a song about the Eiffel Tower? Certainly—and there are songs about the heart of Paris, the wines of Paris, the streets and bus lines of Paris, the sidewalks of Paris, the bridges of Paris, the air of Paris, the rain of Paris, the girls of Paris, the skies of Paris, and the eyes of the women of Paris. It is the most sung of city in the world.

Every Parisian is an enthusiastic turntable for the long-playing records of praise and affection. This love of their home town is one of the ingredients of the glue that holds Parisians together. Penurious as they are, they are fully aware of the gift of beauty. The heavily jeweled finger of Louis XIV still points out what he has given them, and they enjoy it, whether they live in elegant quarters or under bridges. Another ingredient is their common love of pleasure.

Paris's love of pleasure is frigid at the top. The Parisienne of the *beau monde,* when seated at Maxim's close to a display of jewels better than her own, can lengthen her already long and fashionable nose into a dagger. The caviar in her mouth will turn to porridge, and the salesmen at her favorite *bijouterie* will jump the next day with trays of stones.

At the bottom, it is warm. What matters government, what matter the thousand and one chagrins of life on earth? Forgotten is the standing in line—have patience—the strike will end. Anyway, one is prepared—there is a little pot simmering on the back of the stove and a bottle standing in a cool place.

Paris is a city in which women outnumber men—hence you see them pulling carts in the street, washing cars in the railroad yards, doing menial work everywhere. From his imperial tomb, his power radiating as from an atomic pile, Napoléon still influences the lives of the French, and especially the conditions of Frenchwomen. He decreed under the Code Napoléon that no woman may have a bank account or a passport without her husband's permission; that adultery is of consequence only when committed by her husband in her own home, and so on and on.

Under the French system of education, girls become well-informed, but they are molded into a pattern of sweet women who sing off their lessons, believe them, and, although at times they are a little sad-eyed, in general they are happy.

Those in revolt fall into several classes. One is made up of the ambitious wives and mistresses of the *haut monde*. Another is a class peculiar to France—a monster in human form called the concierge. There is one to every apartment house. She lives on the ground floor near the entrance. She sits in what is called the *loge de la concierge*, which corresponds to the janitor's quarters in America, and she is installed there for life. "Beware of the concierge" would be a good sign to place on most apartment-house doors. She can answer for you the sometimes difficult question, "Where were you on the night of so-and-so?" She is ready to supply detailed answers to all other questions about you and the other tenants on her list. She has a dossier on the people of the neighborhood and adds to it by daily contact with the other concierges of the community. A cat and a snapping dog are always beside her. Her costume is never complete without a black knitted cape thrown over her shoulders. The loge smells the same, whether of food cooking or meals partaken.

If you are a Parisienne, young and beautiful, you will find a young man, also young and beautiful, and you will sit along the quais and dream of love—of marriage and children. That is the desire of most Parisiennes—and you see them in front of furniture stores, making their plans. The young man looks for a home, small and snug, which he and his bride will decorate, and in which they will install the comforts of life and where he will exercise a totalitarian regime of family and love. In Paris the young people do not share the American dream of ascending to a vice-presidential chair. Instead, they are happy in the domain of the small bourgeois. Great events to them are children, not many, and these are paraded on the streets in their Sunday best, like little dolls, with carefully tied shoelaces and clean white socks and gloves.

If you are a young and beautiful Parisienne, and this domesticity does not appeal to you, then one day you can take off all your clothes and pass in review before a director of one of the hundred institutions devoted to the gaiety of Paris; and if you pass muster, you may appear in your little skin on the stage, freezing in winter, and even in the best-paying shows you won't earn enough to take a vacation to get away from the summer heat.

If you are neither for marriage nor for the music hall, you can become one of the "little hands," as seamstresses are called, and work in an establishment of high fashion. What you are paid will help the family support you, but it is not enough to clothe, house, or feed you on your own. And you have to be very diligent, for there are so many.

And so, if you are young, and the old ones are eager to have you out of the crowded quarters, and you're not beautiful enough for the stage or the screen or the young man you love—then someday a man will speak to you, and you'll look at him and answer, and for once you'll get a full meal with champagne. Maybe the man is decent, and in this case he sees you again and he takes care of you. And things could be worse.

But maybe you're unlucky; maybe the stranger who speaks to you is kind only at first, and after a while you no longer go home, for somehow you find yourself providing him with clothes, silk shirts, perhaps a car—and although you may not feel gay about it, you also are adding to the gaiety of Paris.

Liberté, Egalité, Fraternité—the three words are written on almost all public buildings in France. *Liberté* Parisians do not want so much as the freedom to pursue a fanatically individual course. They have no desire to share either opinions or goods with anybody. The people of this ancient and restless city have a passionate interest in living, a constant renewal of ideas, and a vitality of optimism nonexistent elsewhere.

The mind of Paris is a split mind, constantly contradicting itself. You go into a shop and ask for something relatively simple, and the shopkeeper will start to argue and convince you with elaborate logic that what you ask for is impossible, and, even if it were possible, it would be of no benefit to you. You are content, you thank him and bid him good-by. Now he stops you, reverses himself, and with his index finger to his nose he pleads your case and convinces you and himself that what you asked for is the most important thing in this world. Similarly, the policeman who walks over to hand you a ticket ends up by helping you push your stalled car; he may even detect the defect and repair it.

The contrariness to a given issue, opinion, or condition of life is perhaps the most distinct and typical of Parisian traits.

The clearest example of this I found in the lowest quarters. I walked through the streets around the Place Blanche, in the company of a lawyer who had for a client a lady of the sidewalks who was over sixty. Her name was Gabrielle and she was of robust allure, starting out late at night when the clientele was dim-eyed and congenial. I wanted to interview her one Sunday morning, when she could usually be found drinking her coffee in a small place along the rue St.-Dominique.

"She's not here," said the woman behind the bar. "She left this morning—and I wish you could have seen her. She had on a white organdy dress with leg-o'-mutton sleeves, a cartwheel hat, also white, with blue cornflowers on it. And naturally, she had the little white sachet containing the white sugar almonds that one always brings, for she went to the First Communion of her niece. She went out to the suburbs, Marly-le-Roi. What a lovely day she has!"

A few of the girls came in.

"Ah, they love her so, she is like their *maman,*" said the woman, indicating the girls.

All the faces in the bar seemed to shine with the light of the First Communion lace. In Paris girls like these don't bother much with introspection.

"This is the world as it is—and I live in it. Too bad it is as it is, but let's not waste time. *Je suis très jolie, monsieur.*"

Yes, très jolie.

I talked to Gabrielle later, and she gave me an account of her niece's First Communion in Marly-le-Roi that had all eyes moist. Then she stopped. "But the prices, my dears," she went on. "What I paid for the car, and the little dress for my niece—and the small *déjeuner* in the local inn. It is no longer possible for ordinary people to live decently in Paris."

The Dog
of the World

.　　.　　.

The fact that one can go into a shop and buy a dog has always depressed me. The windows of pet shops, especially on holidays, when the animals are altogether abandoned, are among the saddest sights I know.

After losing a fine dog I promised myself never to own another, for if you really love dogs they change your life. You have to cross oceans on ships, for you can't conveniently take dogs on airplanes, and you must use particular ships, which don't require them to stay in the kennels. I often travel on freighters so that my dog will not be left alone. If you live in the city you feel guilty; if you let your dog off the leash in a park you get a ticket. Then the dog gets sick, the dog dies, and all those troubles are forgotten; all you know is that you miss him.

I was still grieving for a departed dog when my friend Armand said, "The only way to get over it is to get another dog. I shall get one for you—the dog of the world—the greatest dog. I will get you the champion of all dogs, for I am president of the Club National du Bouvier des Flandres."

"What is a Bouvier des Flandres?"

"*Alors,* the French have their poodles," said Armand, "the Germans the dachshund, the British the bulldog, the Swiss the St.

Bernard, the Arabians the Afghan, and so on. But the Flemish—
and you are half Flemish—have the Bouvier des Flandres.

"Hundreds of years ago, the counts of Flanders wanted a dog
of their own, and they found that the only distinctively native dogs
were working dogs—raw-boned, hard-working animals of no particular pedigree, accustomed to pulling carts and herding cattle in
dirty weather. There was one great advantage to these dogs. They
were simple, strong, intelligent, and healthy. There was nothing
inbred or nervous about them. They usually lived in the huts of
peasants as members of the family and were extremely pleasant
companions as well as good protectors."

We saw a Bouvier on the streets of Paris the next day. He was a
fearful-looking creature with a rough coat and reddish eyes. He
was black, gray, and sand-colored. There was nothing graceful
about him. He looked like the hound of the Baskervilles.

"You have never owned a dog until you've had one of these,"
said Armand, and a few days later he telephoned that he had
found the one for me and that we would drive out to see him.

Armand's car is usually being repaired, for he drives with slow
deliberation and other cars frequently run into him. The last
crash had taken off a rear fender, and on the day this was replaced we drove out of Paris in the direction of Reims. After
thirty-odd miles without mishap we came to a village and stopped
at a small stone house. A very old man opened the garden gate.
There was deep barking, and then I was presented to Madame, a
son, a daughter, the grandchildren, and visiting relatives. The entire troupe followed us to the kennels, and there was my *"fils."* In
France people refer to your dog as your "son." He was six weeks
old and blue-black; he had the shapelessness of a half-filled hot-
water bottle; he had an immense head, large opaque eyes, and a
long pedigree. We had immediate rapport with each other. He
gave me the first of many sad looks as I patted him and left to go
into the house, where a glass of wine was offered, and where I became officially the owner of Bosie. I wanted to take him along,
but Armand said, "He's only a baby. He must remain where
he is."

I returned to America, and every ten days or so I received a letter in the thinnest pen line. It gave me long reports about my *fils,*
how *sage* he was, what a lucky dog he was because he would eventually go to America. On one of these letters appeared his foot-

print by way of signature. He took on shape, and I looked forward to seeing him again and to having him with me.

Back in France, some months later, Armand drove me out to see Bosie. I had told the people at the good old hotel I stay at whenever I am in Paris that I was getting my dog, and I can highly recommend it as a dog-owner's hotel. Everybody there was happy, and a special dish with water was in a corner of the bathroom. The maid had changed the fancy rose-colored eiderdown for a less costly coverlet.

"For," she said, "he will want to sleep on your bed, monsieur. Also, don't be worried about the carpet—this one is old and will be replaced anyway." The tolerance for dogs at this hotel is due to the proprietress, who loves them dearly.

On the way Armand said, "You can't have him yet. You don't want an average dog, a dog that pulls on the leash, that gets into fights, jumps up on you, and misbehaves. I promised you the greatest dog in the world, and that is what you shall have. I know an old clown who had the most famous dog act at the Cirque Medrano. He trains dogs with patience and love. He is retired now, and has agreed to keep the dog for a year and train him. After that you shall have a companion who does all but speak. He will be gay or serious; he will console you in your lowest moods. He will be perfectly behaved and never leave your side. He will entertain your friends. He will rescue a child from a burning building or, if ever you are in danger of drowning, pull you from the water. He will watch your car, protect you against attack, carry your packages or umbrella, and refuse food from strangers. I have arranged for it all."

I enjoyed my "son" only briefly; we took him from his former owner, proceeded to Chartres, and I received the second sad look from Bosie, when he was handed over to the clown. When I returned to the hotel, everybody was disappointed. I completed my European assignments and left for America.

The clown did not write, but the time passed and I came back again to France. At the hotel I was again given a room with an expendable carpet, and the eiderdown was changed for a blanket. Again Armand drove me out to Chartres, and the old clown asked us to hide so that Bosie would not be distracted. We watched from the window of a small garden house. The clown leaned a ladder against an open window a floor above the ground. Then he went indoors and reappeared with Bosie. The dog was now big, and reminded one of medieval missals illustrated with devils, gargoyles, and things that knock in the night. His eyes were red, his hair bristly. He wore a large collar and he was very mannerly, respecting flower beds, looking at the old clown, and sitting at attention when told to.

The clown addressed Bosie by the respectful *vous* instead of the familiar *tu*, giving him a series of commands which were carried out with precision and eagerness. Next the dog did some tricks, and finally the clown informed him that there was a fire in the house and a little girl was in a room upstairs.

"*Allez*," he said to Bosie," be nice and rescue the little girl."

Bosie went up the ladder, vanished into the room, and returned with a large doll in his mouth. He carried it carefully, coming backward down the ladder, and put it on the grass ever so gently. Then he looked at the clown, who patted his head but reproached him softly.

"Isn't there someone you have forgotten, Bosie?"

I could almost hear the dog say, "Oh, yes," as he turned and climbed once more into the "burning" building. This time he returned with a large tiger cat in his fearful fangs. He held it the way cats carry kittens, and again he descended. The cat was put down, and it turned, sat up, and licked Bosie's large black nose.

"We have seen enough," Armand shouted with enthusiasm and congratulated the clown.

There was wine again, this time in the little garden house, and then the clown brought out a statement on lined paper. He had written with a pencil the cost of training and of boarding Bosie. It came to sixty thousand francs. I gave the money to the clown, who counted it. As he came to the last five-thousand-franc note his mouth got wobbly and his eyes filled with tears. He sat down on an upturned wooden washbasin. "Bosie," he said, "come here for the last time."

The dog sat down in front of him and looked into his face.

"I've been good to you, haven't I?" The clown could hardly speak. "I've never had one like him before, so gentle, so courageous, so understanding."

Both the clown and the dog turned their heads in my direction.

"You are tearing the heart out of me," said the clown. "You are taking my brother from me," he cried, "the only friend I have in this world!"

Close by was the tiger cat, and I have never seen a cat so close to tears. It was all so terribly sad and desolate. A steady stream of tears ran down the clown's face now, and his face, even without make-up, was the saddest clown's face I had ever seen. I cannot look at people in tears, and certainly not clowns. I was all for letting him have the dog. I started to walk away, but Armand, who understands his compatriots better than I, said, "Just a moment."

He turned to the clown. "We shall leave him with you, but give us back the money for his board and tuition."

"Ah?" said the clown. He dried his tears and pocketed the money. He got up and, in slow, bent motions, walked toward the door of his house, without turning. He said, "Adieu, Bosie, go with your new master." Bosie gave me the third sad look and silently followed me to the car.

La Colombe

. . .

During one of my sojourns in Paris I lived in a house that belonged once to the chef of Louis XIV. It was the color of cold salmon and stood on the left bank facing the Seine, on the Quai des Grands-Augustins, at the corner where the rue Gît-le-Coeur meets the quai. It had a two-person elevator, a statue by Rodin in the entrance hall, and the top floors were furnished like a country house in Westchester. It belonged to an American lady, Miss Alice de la Mar, who rented it to me. From its roof terrace you could see all that is most beautiful in Paris: the sweeping panorama of the city, the Cathedral of Notre Dame, Montmartre, the Seine, and even the Eiffel Tower. My dog, a Bouvier des Flandres, was with me.

At the time, I was working on an article on the Paris underworld for *Holiday* magazine. I spent a good part of the nights in the rough quarters around the Place Pigalle and La Chapelle. I found out what I wanted about crime and the police, for that is easy enough, both sets of actors in this drama being eager to explain why they are on this or that side of the heavy doors. A group of Parisians that are more difficult to know and live in the shadows are the antisocial people who are called *clochards*. A clochard is usually mistaken by non-Parisians for a begger. He is however intensely respectable, but wants to have nothing to do with life as it is lived by his fellow citizens in stations below or above him. He despises the beggar, the criminal, the police, the bourgeoisie high and low, the aristocracy, the civil servant, the religious, the good and righteous, conservative and radical and all other political parties, with equal vehemence. He lives a hard life, sleeping under bridges, collecting cigar or cigarette butts, which are sold at a special market. He also collects old paper, bottles and shoes, string, rags and other waste materials. In contrast to the people who are called *chiffoniers* and who do this regularly in day-to-day labor, he works only when he must have a meal or a bottle of the very cheapest wine.

There are married clochards and also a few women clochards. In the summer, they arrange themselves, leaning against trees along the Seine; in cold weather, they disappear into cellars or wander south. From one of the windows of the apartment in the house at Number 1, rue Gît-le-Coeur, I observed a clochard who lived under the Pont-Neuf. I watched him for weeks. He had a mattress on which he slept under the arch of the bridge that rests on the Left Bank. For his collection, he used an old baby carriage, and at night this baby carriage was the place where his small fox terrier slept. He was a clochard who shaved every day—most of them wear beards. After rising, he rolled up his mattress and tied it with a string; then he stuck into it the sack that covered the dog. He had an empty can, on a string, which he let down into the Seine and brought up filled. He heated the water on some sticks, then put a broken mirror on a small ledge formed by the stonework of the bridge and there he shaved. He had a box attached to the back of the baby carriage with dry pieces of bread and some wine in it—that was his breakfast. The preparation of his toilette, the eating of breakfast, the stowing away of the gear, all done in his own good time, took about two hours and were followed by playing with his dog, stretching, and, on bright days, by careful washing of his shirt, which he dried while the sun shone on his back.

Sometimes he sat in the sun and watched the patient fishermen, who never seem to catch anything. Or else he admired the women on the barges which are tied along that stretch of the quais. Not their beauty, for they are all hard-looking laboring women. What he admired with reserve was their forever cleaning the already shining boats, watering plants, painting, hanging up laundry, carrying things home from market. He never seemed bored.

Occasionally he was visited by a little girl, pale-faced and thin. She accompanied him on his walks when the weather was nice and played with the dog. Clochards don't like to be asked personal questions and I never found out who the little girl was.

Several days a week at about eleven in the forenoon, he decided to go and do that minimum of work that guaranteed his freedom. He slipped on a coat and a slouch hat with holes in it, and with the dog dancing ahead of him in his stilted fox terrier way, the clochard pushed the baby carriage up to the Quai des Grands-Augustins and disappeared into the street next to La Pérouse. The kitchen window of this restaurant is at street level and open except on the coldest days. The kitchen was his first stop. He inhaled the warm vapors of cooking and sometimes even stopped to inspect the luxurious garbage of this establishment.

The clochard then took various routes, his eyes mostly on the ground. He passed the markets, where he found overripe bananas, discarded greens, pieces of potatoes, and arrived eventually at a bistro, to rest, to listen to gossip, to read the paper and to drink one small glass of a cheap, drinkable red wine.

I observed him daily at his bridge with my binoculars, and I followed him at a distance to his bistro. I was too busy with crime and the police to stay always on his track. But during the day, around noon, I used to give my dog a run at the quai near the bridge below. I saw the mattress there every day and, when he was not there, got into the habit of sticking a half pack of American cigarettes, some once-used razor blades, a piece of soap, and some other small clochard's gift into the mattress. Then I watched him in the morning, trying out the new blade or smelling the soap. It was like befriending a squirrel in a park, a wildlife project.

Eventually, an overcoat was beyond its last dry cleaning; it was a warm, heavy dark blue coat become shiny. I took it down one autumn day, when it was getting cold, and left it toward evening, before his habitual hour of return.

I was amused by seeing my coat walking over the bridge the

next day, topped by a hat I had given him. This was a bowler, a new hat, which made my face even rounder than it already is. He seemed to enjoy these acquisitions and nothing happened until a little man who sold gasoline along the Quai des Grands-Augustins told the clochard that the coat and hat he wore came from the fifth floor of Number 1, rue Gît-le-Coeur.

He appeared there one day and acknowledged the receipt of the coat, the hat, and the smaller gifts without exactly thanking me for them. He offered instead to do something for me in return.

"I have a vast store of information about this part of the city, it is my *quartier*. I know every house around here and across on the Island. If you are interested in anything, present or past, ask me. I know the quartier inside out; I was born a few houses from here."

He told me that he had been what is called a respectable citizen at one time, in so-called good circumstances, a teacher of history in a lycée for young ladies of good family.

"Oh, not what you think happened—God forbid! It was just that I was in steady conflict with the director. The maniacal principal of this institute almost drove me to suicide. I had to leave or I would have killed him."

One day he had decided that he was unhappy and had had enough and that he could no longer bear the burden of his bourgeois existence. He lived on the top floor of an apartment house on the Boulevard St. Michel. He opened the window and let out a bird he had kept in a cage, a finch. Then he threw the cage out of the window and all the papers of his pupils which he was correcting; they fluttered away like happy little sails, this way and that.

"I had the most beautiful sensation watching them. Finally I threw out all the rest of my possessions. Below in the street a vast throng formed as the things came down, photograph albums, shoe trees, lamp shades, bills, letters, all things that complicate life, and the old typewriter. I looked down first, for I did not want to give cause for trouble or hurt anyone. I only wanted to get rid of my personal belongings, of my tiresome identity.

"The eyes of the people below were alight with envy at this performance and some took the things and carried them away. Finally the police came, but there was nothing except a little explaining to do at the commissariat, and I was free—and so I shall stay. But what can I do for you?"

I said that I, too, envied him but that I had not yet reached his state of independence and still chose to remain imprisoned within my bourgeois walls.

"One must respect the ideas of others," he simply said. "I am not a fanatic. I do not try to change anything in this world, except I did change my own life, and for the better. But tell me, what is there I can do for you?"

I told him that like him and everyone else I had a desire to change my environment. My problem was that I, all my life, had passionately wanted to paint, and never found the right place and the time. Now I had the time. At long last I wanted to give myself to painting alone and was looking for a place in which to live and work.

I wanted to own an old house like the one I lived in—because where I resided was a place merely rented to me by a good friend I was in need of a place, facing north, in which I could have my studio and do nothing but paint.

"It may take time. I will try and find an old house for you," he said simply and, putting on my hat, he left.

I saw him occasionally in the years that followed, and one day in the spring of 1953 he said that he had found the house, and that I was to come right along.

"When we get there, walk past it, but don't go in yourself, for that would raise the price; I shall arrange everything. I have a friend who is an advocate, a decent one who defends prostitutes and the unfortunates of the underworld. I have told him of you and he will attend to the business part of the transaction. For a while you will not be able to live in the house as it is; it has no water, no electricity, no gas, no plumbing, but it is exactly what you are looking for."

We walked to the front of Notre Dame, turned left, walked down to the Seine, turned right, came to a blue-painted laundry, turned right again, and there it was.

At Number 4, rue de la Colombe. It was precisely what I had been looking for—a lovely house, half palace, half ruin, an old house covered partly with vine. It had a bistro on the ground floor frequented by clochards and a small garden in front in which people sat. The professor said:

"If you look over the door, you will see the ancient name of this street cut into a stone. It was called at one time 'rue d'Enfer'—the street of hell—and if ever you want to get rid of the clochards, just let someone clean up the bistro, or paint a wall; they will flee as if from a blinding flash. Then you can do with the place as you wish."

We sat down in the garden and he said: " 'This is the head, the heart, and the marrow of Paris,' as Gui de Bazoches wrote in the twelfth century of the Île de la Cité. It was also compared to the prow of a ship that got stuck in the Seine. It is the most medieval part of Paris and retains its original aspect, especially on the corner where this old house faces its small private square. It was built in 1225 and later became the hôtel particulier of the mistress of François Premier, 'la belle Ferronnière.' In the adjoining street lived Héloïse and Abélard. The house became a tavern later and the hangout of François Villon. It was built in part from boulders which formed the ramparts of Lutetia, as Paris was then known when it consisted only of this island. The old house became a hotel eventually and was known as the Hôtel St.-Julien-le-Pauvre, named after a saint whose church stands across the Seine on the Left Bank."

With the help of the underworld advocate, I bought the house. I found a quaint architect with a beard and a pipe, which was mostly cold. He had a great feeling for what I had in mind.

"Touching—touching," he said between sucks on his cold pipe. "One would not expect such understanding from an American. Very touching."

Of the old house, the shell was to be left undisturbed, but the inside completely rebuilt. The bistro would remain as it was, above this would be my apartment, above this I would break through a floor and make a duplex studio overlooking the Seine. I wanted to install steam heat, an elevator, move the kitchen to the basement and, on the roof, build a garden and a hothouse. The architect made plans, and said that it would be difficult, but that he had great friends among the officials on whose goodwill one was dependent. He lit his pipe and looked at me through his sharp glasses. "Besides, for a foreigner, distingushed as you are, monsieur, and a great *ami de la France,* exceptions will most certainly be made." He bowed. I looked at my house and saw it as it would be, filled with music, gaiety, and life, twenty-four hours a day.

Paris is a village. Soon everybody knew about the Colombe and people came every day to inspect the house. They looked at me with envy, and wives said to their husbands: "Why don't you ever think of anything like this?" or they said to me: "How clever of you, what a brilliant idea, how did you ever find this wonderful house? And to think of having one's own bistro and sidewalk café in Paris—and to get your liquor and wine wholesale and all your meals free—open day and night—no entertainment worries, five for dinner or fifty—and no servant problems. Do you know of any other such place for sale?" To this I could shake my head wisely and say "No," and all the people who stood around, neighbors, clochards and workingmen, also shook their heads, and murmured that this kind of thing happened only once. Several offers were made then to buy the house, and I could have sold it at great profit.

My friend Jean is the owner of the restaurant La Méditerranée. Sitting at my usual table there, every night, on the back of menus I had drawn and revised the plans for the old house and finally arrived at what it eventually would be like. Jean came to the Colombe every day; he would say, "It always takes an outsider to find a good thing like this. You know, whenever I am worried, in unhappy times, I come down here to get away. I promenade up and down, in these streets and on this little square. Oh, how often have I sat here—in this lovely green tunnel quietly drinking a *petite coupe* of the wine, which isn't bad at all. How stupid of me! I must have passed here a thousand times; I saw it—why didn't I buy it! However, I am glad it's yours now." He shook my hand and wished me luck. "Not that you need it, a house like this, a palace. You will live like a prince. And how quiet it is, no traffic, only the bells of Notre Dame. What poetry in this corner, what beauty, and how practical! You even have a private place to park your car—and the little garden covered with vine. I have a friend who is the head gardener at the Luxembourg; I will bring him, and he will look at the vine and have it properly taken care of." He started off on his long legs and then came back again.

"Would you consider selling me a half interest in the bistro? We'll get rid of the clochards, we'll make a terrace here, I will relieve you of all the worry. I am sure, mark my words, this will be a gold mine."

I like Jean very much, but I did not want a gold mine. I merely wanted to have this house as it was, and its spell unbroken, and that could not be done, with Jean. He is a good restaurateur, but he loves business and worships money. I go to his restaurant some-times, and he sits there and looks as if he were about to cry. I ask him why and he says: "Look at the empty tables." Then a half hour after when the place is filled, he still looks sad, and I ask him: "What's wrong now?" and he says. "Yes, yes, it's full now, but re-member how it looked half an hour ago!"

So I told him. "No, thank you, but stay my friend and help me."

"Ah, yes," he said. "I have been thinking of the opening. Let me do the opening. I will take care of everything; we shall invite the most important people in Paris and have the best wines, a memorable menu—*une fête,* a celebration. Music, flowers, it will be wonderful."

I said that perhaps we could ask everyone to dress in the cos-tumes of the period. People could come as François Ier, as la belle Ferronnière, as Héloïse and Abélard, as Quasimodo and Es-meralda. There was a role for everyone.

"We must get busy with the invitations," said Jean. "This will be the Paris party of the year." We sat down under the vine with the architect. The date was set for the opening. Plenty of time for engraved invitations—almost a year. And more people came, and stood about and said: "How wonderful," and some said: "How is it that such things only happen to him?" And Jean observed: "It's very simple—because he makes them happen! That's how any-thing happens in this world."

The architect came one morning, sat down in the garden, took the pipe out of his mouth, and announced that we had to make the first démarche to the authorities, to obtain a permit. He inter-rupted himself, saying that he would explain on the way to the commissariat—there were some papers to fill out, and did I have my birth certificate with me?

I said: "No, I'm not even sure when I was born. It says in my passport April 27, 1898, but my mother said it was at 3 A.M. the last day of April."

"But has this uncertainty never troubled you?" asked the ar-chitect.

"No, on the contrary," I said.

"That will make it complicated as far as the authorities go," he said, sucking in air. He then departed to inquire what to do.

Jean came, as he did every day on his way back from market.

"Is there anything I can do for you?" he asked, as he always did.

I told him that it was time to think of a staff. Did he know of any nice people to work for the Colombe?

"I have exactly the person for you. She is sent from heaven. She is the equivalent of the entire staff of a house. She will cook, clean, inside, outside, do everything. You won't need anyone else. She will save you her salary in repairs alone." He referred to her as *la mère machine.* This extraordinary person presented herself on the afternoon of that same day. She was as old as the stone of the house, a little woman, dressed in black, a working monster with hands and a face as if cut from tree root. She attached herself to the building immediately and knocked about in cellar, in attic, and on the stairs. Her head was in the position of the beak of a pitcher from which one pours water, and by stiffness of joint confined to one movement, to the left or right, as are the heads of puppets. My dog Bosie shied from her at first sight and always squeezed past her on the stairs to avoid touch or caress. Her voice rasped; her eyes blinked like those of an owl. She held things as in a vise and she was never seated; she never leaned on anything or was in repose. With a broom she would start to clear the small garden and then to inspect the doors for security. On the door that led from the street into the dining room was an ancient lock, from which the key was missing. The place had been closed every night by putting in front of it a weighty iron grille and keeping this in place with a heavy chain. I did away with the grille and the chain and told la mère machine to go and get a locksmith and have a key made for the door. She twisted her head so that she could give me a quick glance. "You will never get anywhere if for every little thing you call in plumbers, electricians, mechanics, who are all robbers, crooks, and wasters of time," she croaked. "I will take off this lock and find a key. No use throwing away money!"

There was then near the Bastille, spread over the length of the sidewalks there, a junk and old iron market, an annual affair called la Foire à la Ferraille.

La mère machine took the lock off the door and, with it in her hands, tried several hundred keys, rusty and of all kinds of design;

going from one heap of old iron to the other, after a search that took hours, she finally found a key that fitted this lock. This gave her immense satisfaction.

The salary of la mère machine was fifty dollars a month. Like the clochard she had a mattress; she had it in the house, I don't know where she put it at night to sleep on. She marketed and, like the clochard, looked under the stands for vegetables that had dropped, or been discarded, and put these into her shopping net along with the things she bought, after smelling, feeling, and berating the article in question, often tasting it. There were small tangerines called *clémentines,* overripe and discolored. Of these la mére machine bought half a dozen, at about one cent apiece, but not before one had been given her to taste. The same with any reduced pâté, or sausage and cheeses recommended for quick sale. The small shopkeepers of the neighborhood, as avaricious as she was, were anxious to keep her miserable trade, and treated her with great respect. "Bonjour, madame," they would sing and point out the day's special, half-rotten bargain.

At one time, the architect and the underworld advocate and I were sitting in the small garden over the plans and we wanted to go to lunch. La mère machine came out protesting, wringing her hands and twisting her head left and right. Why waste money by going to a restaurant? She would serve luncheon in the garden— *une blanquette de veau à l'ancienne.* She must have found some ancient mushrooms under the stands that day, for she was not normally given to spending money for anything above wilted carrots, leeks, and potatoes. She set the table and brought out wine. It was the only meal I ever ate in this house. It was very good and, if I had left things as they were—the clochards in the bistro, who brought a profit of $15 a day, la mère machine as the general factotum— everything would have been fine.

On a lovely morning, Jean came and with him a chef of the proper weight, face, voice and authority, beard and mustache. A good man. The chef sat down, and Jean spoke:

"Monsieur Tingaud is looking for you, as desperately as you are looking for him; he is of the grande cuisine; he will make your table famous. He is retired but the way things go in France, the uncertainty about the future . . . anyway, to make a long story short, we met, we talked, and then I told him about the little palace here—La Colombe—and Monsieur Tingaud said, 'It sounds like exactly what I am looking for.' " The chef nodded and I told him how lucky that he had come before the final plans for the kitchen were drawn up; we could now benefit from his experience. The plans were inspected and some details changed; he found them in general very practical. The matter of salary was settled to mutual satisfaction. We drank a glass of Jupon and congratulated each other.

"I have never in my life seen anything like it," said Jean. "Everything falls into place as if by magic—the gods love you."

One day, Jean came and brought with him the head gardener of the Jardins du Luxembourg to look at our vine, or, as it is called in France, "the green tunnel." He pronounced the vine healthy and identified it as a Virginia creeper. He suggested that it be replanted in a new box, with earth which he would order. He had the box made, and the earth came, and two gardeners who replanted the vine and trimmed it. La mère machine looked at all this with suspicion and jabbered about the needless waste of money.

The two big gardeners not only were paid, but sat in the green tunnel after the work was done, and ate and drank, and the officials from the commissariat who had closed an eye and accepted the uncertain date of my birth, and various other advisers and official personages also came, ate, and drank. For the wine, which we had inherited from the former owner, la mère disappeared down the steps of a steep ladder into the cave, where she drew it from the barrel, and came up again to serve it. The business of the bar increased and we had steady income from the clochards, which la mère machine kept in a dreadful lead canister. This she shook with great energy and a bitter, contented smile when I came to the bistro toward evening.

After shaking the canister, she poked me with her outstretched index finger and said: "Leave this place as it is; listen to the advice of an old woman. This is a good affaire; you can live off it for the rest of your life."

Alas, I did not listen to her. The plans were going forward, and all that can go wrong with owning property, with building, with making alterations, with city ordinances, city architects, workmen, and materials went wrong.

The dear little house, the poetic corner, turned into a cathedral-sized nightmare. We had difficulties at every step with the government, with the Beaux Arts, with the architects of the city of Paris. With the prefecture of the police, the neighbors, the officials of the telephone monopoly, the water authority, and most with the sewage authorities. When I speak of "we," I mean the clochard, the architect, and I. What I attempted to do in a year takes in France normally five years of contemplation. There was never a "yes" or a "no," but grave doubting all along. All the people who had the power to make decisions warned us, with a finger to their noses, that all this would have to be carefully studied, weighed, passed on to others, considered, and was most probably in the end impossible.

One who has never filled out forms in France, who has never sat on a chair in a bureau of French officialdom has no idea of the might of functionaries. Nor of the time they have on hand, of the many people who can lengthen this time and stretch it beyond the point where anything made of rubber, hemp, or steel would snap. One problem, that of moving a stairway or a doorpost, can engage an entire floor of French bureaucrats for a month. In the case of Number 4, rue de la Colombe, there was a magnificent opportunity for them to procrastinate, to detour, block and hamper, that could keep them busy until retirement, when fresh replacements would take over. Not only does the code, the law, the statute, ancient precedent, and the opinion of the last judge enter into each minute decision; there is, moreover, the matter of the attitude of the officials on various levels toward you and your project, and the mood each one is in on a particular day. Does the official like you? Does he like your necktie, your nose? Does he feel that what you are doing is sensible? Will France be benefited by it? He will, as a judge and magistrate, examine you carefully; the lower his office the more weighty his manner. He will argue about the most abstract matter, the most remote, adverse possibilities of it. You will go through this rigmarole over and over again, and since I have no patience and am disinclined to humor defeatists and black-seers, we made snail's progress.

The patient architect, who sucked his cold pipe, wiped his glasses and his forehead and tried to establish a tolerable mood between the petitioner and the authority in a hundred offices. Eventually he said: "I think it is better I go alone, for this way we will never, never come to terms. You ask too much at once—an elevator, a roof garden, a cellar, a floor broken through, windows unbricked, gas, water, electricity. All this at once renders them dizzy. They detest you, in spite of my repeating every five minutes that you are *'un grand ami de la France,'* and that your project will enhance the appearance of the rue de la Colombe, and bring additional glory to Paris; they do not wish to see it in this light, at all. It is to them as if the money came out of their own pockets; it hurts them to see it, so to say, thrown away. You must not forget that to them the purchase of a pack of the cheapest cigarettes is a major decision. That you can, without reflection and concern, decide on all these things, and with impatience wave your hand over their objections, doesn't endear you to them. I must confess, dear friend, it sometimes upsets me too. I wish we had more time to sit and ponder this or that, but evidently yours is the American way of doing things, and I have been trying to adjust myself to it. I have had nightmares doing it. I dream of the skyline of New York and high buildings falling on me, and when I wake up I say to myself, 'Well, that's the way they do things in America. Evidently no one worries over there, especially not about money.' "

I was worried too, but I didn't want to upset the architect any more than he already was, and I suggested that from now on he go alone to deal with the officials.

Playwrights always have difficulties in eliminating a character when the person is no longer needed, and inventing a logical exit. But life itself is direct and brutally simple. One evening la mère machine went out; she had locked the bistro. In the rue de la Colombe, fifty feet toward Notre Dame, an Arab hit her over the head and ran off with her purse, which contained the canister. She remembered all that in the Hôtel Dieu, the hospital which fortunately is right across the street, when she regained consciousness.

We took flowers to her and Jean sent her strong soup in bottles from the Méditerranée, and she lay in bed looking horrible, like a Buffet drawing, and with a Van Gogh kind of bandage around her head and fists tightly balled. She reproached herself for the time she was wasting.

She replaced herself with two young girls, her nieces. They were of the group of sweet, underprivileged "little hands" that make up the largest body of the women of Paris. Of these, one who had no family was a part-time usher in a cinema and, unable to support herself that way, wanted to earn some extra money.

The other came from a family where, with two little sisters, she had to share one bed. They owned one dress each and a pair of shoes. Both were eighteen.

"Get to work," commanded Jean.

He was a thorough man. He had had the stove going and on it a large pail with water, another waiting to be heated, and a third standing beside the girls, who had their sleeves rolled up and were scrubbing the floor of the dining room of the bistro. They emptied one pail in the street and a gray, greasy lukewarm soup ran down the gutter; a sick-making stench rose from it. The bistro stank awfully of the smells of sweat, of excrement, of unwashed people and of their filthy clothes. Bosie soaked up all the fleas in the house. The clochards, men and women, all drunk, stood around and gave me their dirty hands, paid in cash, and left.

"They will never come back again—they are very polite people. They said good-by to you for good," remarked the professor.

"But why?"

"Because you're cleaning it up. That stench and stink of soap and hot water frightens them. Let's go out and get some fresh air—the dirt of centuries is being disturbed and it makes me ill."

The girls also came out for air. They looked awful, pale and thin, with dirty hands and arms, and they stank like the bistro. On the third day of cleaning, one of them said:

"You can't wash it off; it stays dirty. Everything is dirty. We have cleaned every day and washed the windows—there were windows suddenly where nobody thought there were windows. First we thought it was a board, then we washed and washed, and a gray light came in and a large rat jumped over the chair from a table. He must have eaten off the table and lived behind the closet."

They were rolling up their sleeves again.

"We excuse ourselves for speaking like this," said the one who had a family, sadly; and the other added cheerfully: "Oh, it will be better after today; it will be like living in the country."

"What makes you say that?"

"Oh, the beautiful green vine, the little garden. Excuse us, we must continue."

The house grew on me, in spite of all the difficulties or because of them. Although it was far from finished and I could not move into a room of it as yet, the joy of owning property covered me like a warm mantle. Even Bosie was delighted; at last he had a house to guard. I would meet the professor toward evening and we would walk across the Pont-Neuf, turn right at the statue of the Vert-galant, which is my favorite monument in Paris, and then walk along the Seine, through the flower market, finally coming to the house.

"The girls are right. Everything around here is like a dirty board; when you wash it long enough it becomes a window through which you see the past. As you know, I spend most of the cold days in the Louvre—it belongs to me now—and the very cold days I spend in the National Archives, which are better heated. There is one good thing about the French, say what you please: they respect what they call your quality. When I pull out of your old suit the card which entitles me to entrance to various places, they are respectful, and when I sit down for my researches I am left undisturbed. Alors, here—I will explain to you why there is space in back of this house, and why this was called 'the street of hell.'

"There was a friseur and wigmaker shop here, where this gar den is. It belonged to a man known in this neighborhood for his kindness and his devotion to Notre Dame. He shaved the priests and cut their tonsures. Back to back with the house that stood here, and facing Notre Dame, on the spot where you can park your car today, stood the house of his brother, who was a charcutier, famous for a marvelous pâté maison which the prelates of Notre Dame fancied, and which was exclusively sold to them. The priests lived in a row of houses close to the cathedral. The two houses of the brothers that stood here were linked by an underground passage. They prospered for many years, until by accident a dog digging for a bone led to the discovery of heinous crimes committed over a period of many years.

"You see, men wore wigs in those days and the friseur and wigmaker was in need of human hair. When someone, man or woman, with a likely head of hair entered his shop—and of course the best and loveliest hair was on the heads of the young—then, in the case of a man, he would start to shave him, after which he would cut his throat. In the case of a woman, he strangled her. The hair was then shorn off and used for wigs. The next step was to drag the body through the underground passage, over to the delicatessen shop, where the brother made it into sausages and famous pâté, so beloved by the priests of Notre Dame that there never was enough of it.

"When the dog had found the bone and the terrible butchery was discovered, the brothers were tried and executed—there across the river, in front of the Hôtel de Ville. They were torn into quarters by horses after torture. The houses were burned down. The Pope was in Avignon then, and a deputation of priests of Notre Dame went there, for, having eaten this unholy pâté for years, they felt impure and in need of special dispensation, which the Pope granted, with the proviso that no building should ever stand again where these two evil brothers had lived. In consequence of this, your little garden, your private square, and your parking place. Alas, every foot of this ground is storied."

I proposed to the professor that he write a book about it.

"You write it," he said. "I will tell you all about the place, and you write it. But I thought you were going to paint, which I am afraid you never will, because something will always come in between, like this pâté." He looked strange for he had cut my overcoat off at an angle, which he said allowed him to walk more freely. He had done it simply with shears, clipping it like a hedge. The piece cut off had been made into a shawl and cap for the little girl.

The professor left. The girls were still scrubbing, and the place now smelled of insecticide and chlorine. The water was carried in a pitcher from a pump as it had been for hundreds of years. It was Sunday evening and I told them if they wanted to they could come to the rue Gît-le-Coeur and take a bath. Afterward I would take them to dinner at the Méditerranée.

As we were eating, they explained: "We had no appetite at the Colombe—we could not even eat an apple there, it was so dirty." They drank some wine and then started to tell stories about the Colombe, about the architect and, with their hands held over their faces, about me, and what the neighbors said and thought. They laughed so hard that tears ran down their cheeks.

"Oh, it's wonderful," they said. "Like a theater—we learn so much—it has given us a new life—and freed us. We are like birds now. The wonderful people one meets—Claude Dauphin comes every day and has a glass of wine, and yesterday a Mister Buster Keaton was there and asked for you and he drank wine and gave each of us a thousand francs. Last week we divided sixteen thousand francs between ourselves. Such good fortune doesn't come to everyone. We are so grateful."

I then had to go to New York but rushed back as soon as I could with the impatience that is part of my make-up. I had announced the opening of the house—much too soon. Not even the rooms were done. The architect had become imaginative and had got students of the Beaux Arts to come one weekend to paint the two lower floors. I painted décor on the wet walls. More students got the rest of the house in order. Music and food were arranged for. The housewarming was imminent.

At this point Jean appeared and with him the chef, Monsieur Tingaud. "Don't let what this one has to say upset you," started Jean unhappily, raising his hands. "Quelle catastrophe!" he wailed, looking with disgust at the chef.

The chef broke in: "I hope monsieur will understand. First of all I must say that I regret the matter, that is, I am in a way sorry. For I am certain that I would have been happy here, and that we would have understood each other. But I cannot come and cook here. Why not? Because, monsieur, I cannot afford it. Do you understand?"

"Please come to the point, monsieur," said Jean.

"The world is vastly changing and everything with it," he went on.

Jean became impatient. "We know, we know. Tell what has happened."

"One day I was walking down the rue du Bac," started the chef, but Jean let out a moan and ran his fingers through his hair and said: "He has taken a job in a factory, can you understand that?"

The chef was now in a temper and, pushing Jean aside, said: "I have been offered the position of executive director of the kitchens of the Renault factory."

Jean put his fists on his hips and said: "He is in charge of a mess hall for mechanics; he has *la folie des grandeurs*."

The chef answered: "Perhaps, perhaps, but neither of you could afford to pay my salary—and the conditions, the conditions—you could not offer me those in a thousand years." He held up one finger and pointed: "One meal a day, one dish to cook. I come to work at nine, I go home at five. Two weeks' holiday with pay. Pension, medical and dental and other benefits. My kitchen of ten electric stoves looks very much like an operating room."

Jean shook his head: "And you are proud of this? Tell me how many of this one dish you serve a day?"

"Seven thousand and some hundreds."

Well, bon appétit, monsieur."

"I am sorry, I did not mean to brag," said the chef.

"Oh, don't be sorry," said Jean. "There are still cooks in France with some pride!"

Now they came close to each other and the chef yelled: "Pride for what? Pride to stand fourteen hours behind a stove, pride for being underpaid, and to cook a hundred things and listen to complaints and to have a miserable proprietor watch every gram of butter and cry in your ear? No thank you." Without saying good-by and in haste, Monsieur Tingaud stalked off in the direction of Notre Dame.

"Don't worry," said Jean to me. "We are going to save ourselves. I will cook myself if all else fails." He left muttering.

I had invited for the housewarming about fifty people, who had accepted, when the architect with pipe in hand came running and informed me that it would be impossible to give the party, because we would have no toilet.

"The final permission has not been granted," he said sadly. "It will not ready."

In agony of mind I wrote a letter to Air France, to TWA, to BOAC, and Pan-Am, asking if they would lend us mobile equipment necessary for the comfort of guests. Air France as well as all the other airlines sent their regrets; it was the height of the tourist season and they were in need of all their ambulatory conveniences.

I finally settled the matter by buying an old taxi. On the right door I had neatly lettered MESSIEURS and on the left MESDAMES and made an arrangment with Jean, so that the taxi would go back and forth from my place to the Méditerranée whenever the need arose.

The party was a great success. I said to the architect as I left for America again the next day, "Finish the bathrooms first, no matter what it costs. I give you carte blanche." He brought a paper to the plane at Orly Airport, which I shall forever be sorry I signed.

The house had by now eaten immense sums. I had to go back to America and do some work quickly to earn more money.

When I returned, I rushed to the house to see how far things had progressed. It was toward evening, the lamps were lit, and in back of my house stood Notre Dame, floodlit. The effect was grandiose and exciting, and as I surveyed the scene I was glad that I had done it all. It was perfect. As I went down the short way to the small square where the house stood, I saw that there was a large hill inside the garden. It was of earth. Children were playing on top of it. Through a large hole in the street I saw a man below filling the stuff into sacks with a shovel; about a hundred such sacks were neatly tied and stacked on the steps against the side of the house to the right of mine. The street was barred and a red lantern hung on the barrier. I asked the man what he was doing. "An American millionaire is putting bathrooms into this house," he said and kept on shoveling. A truck came and loaded the sacks and took them away.

At the time I had bought the house, some forty people lived in it and all shared one toilet, consisting of a large square stone with a hole in its center. It stood in a recess under the circular stone stairs. A door of a few painted planks nailed together, hung on iron hinges, gave it privacy. The stone was a historic memento, having been visited by François Villon, François Ier, and la belle Ferronnière. The venerable black stone stood under the special protection of the Beaux Arts and nobody could move it.

But, because I was "un grand ami de la France," the august body charged with the care of national monuments extended me their tolerance to the extent that I was allowed to install sanitary facilities elsewhere in the building.

When this work began in my absence, the worst happened. It was discovered that the sewers of Paris were some two hundred yards away from the rue de la Colombe. It was also discovered that the foundation of Number 4 was the same as that on which Notre Dame stands, the Roman wall of the ancient Lutetia. If a pneumatic drill were used, the disturbance caused would, like an earth tremor, carry from boulder to boulder to the Cathedral, and saints, stone ornaments, or gargoyles might fall off the edifice. Therefore, it was necessary to do this work by hand. All day there were two men with an acetylene lamp, busy carefully chipping through the ancient stone and tunneling toward the sewers of

Paris. The underworld lawyer calculated that each sack of debris cost me a hundred dollars. He had so far counted 260 sacks.

The next day, the clochard stood in horror, fascinated, when he saw me. I had lost some ten pounds. He also had changed. It was getting cold, he had stopped shaving and grown a beard. He was wearing the blue coat and the bowler; the little girl held his hand.

"I am sorry I had anything to do with this," he said, pointing with his cane at the house, the sacks of white dust and chips of the Roman wall.

I reflected, which I rarely do, and always too late. The clochard said: "Take my advice, turn your back on it. Do the way I did and throw everything out of the window. If you don't, this house will eat you. You will never be through with its difficulties. This is a cursed and haunted building and it doesn't want anyone to touch it." I followed his advice.

Bosie performs for me the functions of the picture of Dorian Gray. When we left, when I had gotten rid of the old house, he looked as awful as I felt inside.

Ship-Owner

· · ·

One of the spots on the Riviera I like best is the harbor of old Antibes. I had ordered some of my large canvases made into little ones—for this a place for small pictures filled with happy objects—and when these came, I went down there to paint. You see much more when you paint than when you just look. I found a scene of warmth and color, composed of a very old cutter with Fort Carré in the background, and set up my easel. As I painted, the old boat began to speak to me. I went on board and knocked on the cabin bulkhead. A man, older than the boat, emerged and I asked if, by chance, the boat was for sale. He motioned me to come below; it was very simple, very honest and homey—a rough work boat.

"This old boat?" said the man. "It's been for sale for twenty years—it's fifty years old. It once was a pilot boat in Bristol—that's in England—and when they changed to motorboats, they retired it, and also its captain. He bought it, rebuilt it, and lived on it until he died. The English know how to build boats—this one could go to sea when no other dared. I bought it—my name is Glorieux—when the old pilot passed on. I named it *Arche de Noé*."

"Why did you call it *Noah's Ark*?"

"I have five sons and twelve grandchildren," M. Glorieux replied, "and they used to go sailing with me when I first bought this boat. It had an English name then that meant nothing to me—the people in Honfleur, where I got her, called her *The Old Lady*. My grandchildren had wonderful times—diving, swimming, fishing all day—there's nothing like a sailboat for kids. Toward evening, though, they'd get tired and unruly. The smallest boy had a pointed face, and the others called him 'the little rat,' and he'd say, 'If I look like a rat, you look like pig, and you, there, have a face like a hippo, and Matilda is a monkey.' To put an end to this, I said, 'Quiet—if you all are animals, I will grow a beard and be Noah, and this boat shall be known as Noah's Ark.' That's how it became *Arche de Noé.*"

I bought her for the price M. Glorieux asked.

When you become the owner of a boat it's almost as if you had inherited a boundless gift. The expanse of the sea, with its ever-changing seascapes, is yours, as well as landscapes seen from the water which terrestrial creatures never behold. The deck you stand on is your floating wooden island, your house like a turtle's shell that goes to sea with you. Even when it is moored to a stout iron ring, swaying, everything is changed. The water, the stars, the moon, the clouds—all take on new meaning. You join the great company of discoverers, adenturers, and restless men. More than that, you find yourself a member of the large body of small mariners, owners of boats like your own: individualists and escapists. They form a devoted brotherhood, a society that makes sense. Its members depend on each other for help, night and day, rain or shine, wind or calm. Without knowing you, they run to make a rope fast, reach out a hand to help you onto the dock, pass you an oar, and go on from that to any assistance you need, even at great risk.

A Dutch canal boat is moored to our right—its name is *Mariyke*—and from it comes organ music. I was asked aboard and there is a real old organ. Its owner was a Dutch minister, and when they pulled his old church down to replace it with a modern one he took the old benches and beams and aged doors and the woodwork from the sacristy, and knocked them together into one of the most unusual ship's interiors ever made. On our left is an English family with three children, a cat, a dog, and several flower boxes; and each of the kids has a bike.

The flags along the dock are of all colors and many countries:

BAROMETER

DECK

BENCH

FUEL TANK

DRAWING MATERIAL & PAINTS

DRAWING PAPER

CANVASES FOR PAINTING

Space for Drawing board

FLARES— FIRST AID EMERGENCY EQUIPMENT.

Australia, Canada, United States, Greece, Egypt—everywhere—
even Switzerland. It's astonishing how such small boats get here
from so far away. The *Arche de Noé* flies the French flag.

The whole scene outside is gay and bright. Inside I find rope
ladders, spare anchors, an instrument to trail along behind to tell
how fast or far you are going, portfolios of charts, including the
South Sea Islands and the Bering Sea, a locker with flags, extra
lamps, and a lot of junk. Sorting that out is one of the best pas-
times; it's like making garden furniture, good occupational ther-
apy. A boat is never done. When you end up at the stern, there is
still the dinghy. It should have the boat's name on it, an old sailor
tells me. Yes, you will paint it one day.

The old sailor asks if he can come aboard, he has something to
tell me: he knows this boat and he doesn't like the new name. He
knew her when she was known as *The Old Lady* and he knew her
owner, the retired British pilot. For years she was in Honfleur; she
had been around the world, and she was known all along the
coast of Normandie. The old pilot had loved her. He had a shack
where he lived ashore, and there was an old stone stable nearby.
When the Germans came, he pulled *The Old Lady* out of the water,

took down the mast and rigging, and put the hull inside the stable. Then he built a wall and a small door, and it never occurred to the Germans to look inside. So there *The Old Lady* sat all through the war; that's why she is in such good condition. "You know she is fifty years old," the sailor said, "and she's good for another five hundred; these boats aren't built any more. Now you must have a captain, and a good one. This fellow going by is a good sailor, but not for this boat because he is too big." (He was some six feet tall and very heavy.) "You want a small man. Also you must become a member of the Yacht Club de France; it makes things much easier all around."

Captain Richardson, who had rented me a villa and also sold boats and other happy dreams, agreed with the sailor. "Yes, yes, I know. In America you would handle this boat yourself, but here in France you must have a captain. Now it is July and most men that are any good have their ships under them, but we shall see what we can find."

And so there came a captain—we shall call him the Barometer, for he was concerned with the weather. He was a nice, orderly man about fifty years old, small and with iron-gray hair. He was a good sailor, knew motors, and was honest. My old sailor friend recommended him. His name was Charlie, pronounced Sharlee.

The *Arche de Noé* was tugging at her lines ready to go to sea.

Sharlee was aboard early and late, he put all the ropes in order and I was convinced that I couldn't have taken her out alone; handling the four sails was too intricate. He explained everything carefully—this goes here, that goes there. Very important advice: wear sneakers, and in the beginning wear a pillow on your head, or a stout cap, for—*bang!* and you have a bump from the swinging boom or from forgetting the sliding hatch.

Sharlee smoked a pipe and was the picture of a French salt, the old wolf of the sea, especially when he crossed his arms and squinted in the directions of the four winds. Unfortunately, he was a landlocked mariner who liked to sit on a ship tied to the dock. He contemplated the sea and sky, and when the heaven was purest azure blue without a cloud and I suggested going out, he would shake his head. He had a way of heaving up his small belly, not with his hands, but with his inner arms. He would remove the pipe from a gap caused by several missing teeth, and say, *"Non, monsieur*—I cannot let you go out."

The *Barometer* heaving up his stomach

"But look at the sky, Sharlee!"

"*Oui, oui, oui*—look at the sky. Let me tell you something—it is just when the sky looks like that, monsieur, that the worst happens. Look, come with me and look at the water. I will tell you, monsieur, the sea, she is a *grande dame;* the wind, however, is the king and he whips the *grande dame* around as if she were a harlot—and she gets into a fury. There, look, you see—at Point de la Garoupe—how the water changes from green to deep blue and to almost black. That is what we call a running sea and I don't like it."

On that running sea there were several *pedalos,* on which people in bathing suits propelled themselves with their feet.

"Look, Sharlee—those people out there playing with *pedalos*—"

"Yes, yes, I see."

"Well?"

"Do you want me to tell you a story, monsieur? One day, just like this one, sunshine, running sea, I took out a boat. A running sea can be caused by wind, by a disturbance from the Golfe du Lion or the Golfe de Genoa, there is no warning—suddenly there are whitecaps near the Island of Sainte-Marguerite. I see a small boat in trouble. I come to its aid, but it is empty. I see a man in the water, he swims towards land, I think he will make it. Suddenly a wave dashes him against the rocks and I see a hand—reaching out of the water. When I get there it is too late. That hand, monsieur, I will never forget."

The Barometer had told this story so vividly that I was surprised the sun was still shining. He lifted his stomach with his thin arms and said, "Perhaps monsieur would like a little pot of wine and we see how things are towards evening. The sea always calms down towards evening, and we could take a sail toward the Island of Sainte-Marguerite, and I will show monsieur the place where the man went down."

He went down to the cabin, where there was an icebox, and arranged a lunch of cold beer, *salade nicoise,* a veal cutlet, cheese, and coffee. You save a lot of money in one way, owning a boat. When we had eaten, he washed the dishes, cleaned up everything, tied the ropes, and looked up at the sky. Even when the sea was the most forget-me-not blue and as calm as the floor of a library, he could make thunder, lightning, and storm appear in his face, in the wrinkles around his eyes; and he always had a good new story of disaster. He had a warning system better than all the meteorological stations along the coast. He could foretell a storm months ahead. His favorite words were the names of the winds, the Tramontane and the Sirocco.

Luckily for such captains there are owners who also hate to leave port. They sit with them, talking, giving orders, supervising, while the sailor goes on sandpapering, painting, varnishing, and caulking. All summer the boat gets more and more beautiful, shiny and clean, and then when it is perfect the season is ended— the fun is over and it is put away. When such an owner finds such a captain as Sharlee, all is well. They esteem each other. But I am not one of them. I wanted to sail. So when he said once too often, "Monsieur, I am sorry but I cannot let you drown yourself," Sharlee and myself parted company. With some regret, I must say, and in friendship.

Came the second captain, on August seventeenth. He was a man of action who looked like Spencer Tracy, with able hands and few words and the will to go. He went into the cabin, cranked the motor, listened, and said, "Aha. *Le moteur* wants adjustment. Listen—hear that *clac, clac, clac?* Allow me to tell you why marine tragedies occur; at the critical moment *le moteur*—she fails. Now this is a stout boat. When I have adjusted *le moteur* she will go any- where. Monsieur can rest assured."

"What would that cost?"

"Monsieur pays me as a captain, and my time is his for twelve hours a day. One hundred sixty dollars a month in summer and one hundred dollars in winter. In the winter months I will redo the entire wiring and the plumbing. Also you need an auxiliary tank for long voyages. This is another cause of marine disasters— running out of fuel."

Next day the boat was filled with pieces of machinery, grease, and tools. The new captain was not there. He had dismantled the motor and taken parts of it home to clean them. Then he would rebuild the engine. He also had ripped open the cockpit to install the new fuel tank.

Meanwhile the boats on either side of us left. The *Arche de Noé* was still at her old place and new boats came and moored next to us. There was a stately ancient ship, ocean-liner style, with a large funnel painted red above the white hull, named the *Iphigenia.* It was a remarkable marine object, its deck like the terrace of a club under a vast awning lined with flowered chintz, the deck furni- ture covered with antique pink velvet. There were children and a Great Dane on board. The owners were an unusually handsome young American woman and her husband, an Italian who looked like the Great Lover out of an opera. This boat flew the pennant of the Royal Italian Yacht Club, the Italian flag, and a string of diapers on the rear deck. We suffered from the aromas of excellent cooking that came from a porthole at the height of our noses when we stood on deck; but we benefited by the shelter from the wind that the yacht's immense bulk gave us. Its captain was uncommunicative, but there were arguments on board between husband and wife—in English—and occasional yells from the baby, whose nurse seemed to be the Great Dane.

The dog, whose name was Amanda, kept an eye on the three children; her special care was the little boy. He wore rubber baby pants, and whenever he came near the rail of the *Iphigenia,* or the steep stairs at the stern that led down to the afterdeck, or the gangplank when the boat was made fast, Amanda gently took hold of his panties from behind and pulled him back—letting go softly so that the elastic would not snap back and hurt him. The little boy rode the dog like a pony, put his hands and arms in her mouth, and sometimes stuck his fingers in her eyes. When the play got too rough, the Great Dane just moved her head and let out a sound like a bass fiddle being stroked. Sometimes, when his mother called, she picked him up by the seat of his pants and carried him, helplessly rowing in the air, to wherever the mother was.

On the *Arche de Noé* the new captain came with pipes and faucets. He looked at the beautiful lady on the *Iphigenia* drying her russet hair in the sun. "As a rule, women do not like boats," he said to me. "The usual female, *la vraie femme,* is a creature with her roots in the earth." He went on ripping out more planks. "When they are very young girls, they may like to go out for a sail, and of course when they are in love, then they don't mind. But from my experience, honeymoons on water are rarely happy, and marriage on the water—except for some Scandinavians, and the English— is a disaster. Boats are for men alone. My wife has never set foot on any of the ships I've owned or worked on. If a man loves a boat, the boat becomes sort of his wife. There is no reason to have women on board; they are superfluous. The sailor is also a wife: he does the cooking, washes the dishes, does the laundry and the rest of the housekeeping. Especially on a small boat like this, where quarters are close and you are constantly in each other's way; you cannot get away from each other. The happiest boat is a boat without women on board. Now, would you give me a hand?" There was a pause while we moved the old fuel tank into the open. In this silence came some sharp words in English from the

Iphigenia. A determined female voice said, "Every time I open my mouth about this gosh-darn boat, you go into one of your Italian rages. I said I'd come, and here I am. The children haven't had a proper bath for weeks, there's no hot water, the plumbing doesn't work. Now all that is to be expected, but I reserve my right to complain about it."

The two small girls, wearing life jackets in case they fell overboard, played with their toddling little brother. They seemed used to arguments between their parents. The Great Dane lay on a sofa on the upper deck, head and feet hanging down relaxed. The argument had started on account of the dog. The husband had complained that he would have to have the sofa recovered— the dog made a mess of it and was more important than he. Now he answered in Italian *sotto voce* and walked off.

As we carried the tank ashore the captain said that children were happy on ships, being savages and liking to move about, and as for dogs, small dogs were happy too. For big dogs it was not the place. He put the tank in back of him on his motorbike and started off. He said he had to flush it out because, if the boat got to pitching in a storm, sediment could block the carburetor and sink you.

This captain lived in a house he built himself that had a great deal of character. It stood on the shore between Cap d'Antibes and the Nice airport, in a very lively scene, alongside an open strip of pebbly beach with pale green water plants and tall marsh-grass. It was painted cadmium yellow; there were flowers everywhere, and old anchors, ships's lamps, and several used outboard motors for sale, and also a rowboat.

I painted the yellow house while he cleaned the old tank and welded the connections for the new auxiliary tank. From the small balcony you could see down to Monaco and up to Cannes, and watch every airliner coming and going. Back of the house the trains passed all day and night. The cooking was excellent and the hospitality was complete, including wine, and a bed when it got too late to drive back. It was one of the gifts of the boat, for without the *Arche de Noé* I would never have stopped there. And later I was grateful for this man's thoroughness, which eventually saved the lives of all on board.

The *Iphigenia* moved on with her children and dog. The *Arche de Noé* was ready to go to sea by September fifteenth. Unfortunately,

I had to leave for America. The mechanical captain found another job. I sailed for New York on the S.S. *United States*. I had never before properly appreciated the departure of a boat on time. That all was in working order on this colossus—that people were fed, walked the decks, and lay unconcerned in deck chairs while the ship ticked off its quota of sea miles and reached New York on schedule—had a new meaning for me.

Before I sailed, however, the *Arche de Noé*, after much paperwork, had been designated an American boat while retaining its French name; and I, as a member of the Yacht Club de France, was her captain—empowered to baptize babies, perform marriages on board, and read sermons committing bodies to the deep. I also could order people to abandon ship, or put them in irons. But I hadn't been able to get the *Arche de Noé* out of Antibes Harbor.

I spent the winter thinking about the *Ark* and looking at its picture over the fireplace in my New York studio. I had good memories of the work that had been done on it—not only to make it a floating studio for my comfort, but also to make it shipshape and fit for long voyages in all weathers. I read manuals, studied the Mediterranean's tides, bought charts, and learned navigation. I looked forward to spring and the first cruise. But I still needed a skipper willing to go to sea.

I wrote a friend in Naples who was once in the Italian Navy and asked if he could recommend a sailor. He answered that he had the very man for me, and by good fortune he was free for the coming season. He knew the sea, sails, motors; he cooked the most wonderful spaghetti and played the guitar. When did I want him?

And so, one day at the Antibes railroad station, two men alighted. I pride myself on my judgment of people—I have an eye for the right man. At long last, these two were the ones. They had two duffel bags and a guitar and they walked softly with incredible elegance. The captain said he had brought his sailor along because, from the description of the boat and the voyages, two seemed needed; but I was assured that I would never be sorry, and, with Italian pay, two would cost no more than one Frenchman.

They installed themselves on board, doing everything soundlessly; apparently they had been together a long time, for never was an order issued. Silently, they pulled in the gangplank, started the engine, cast off the lines, moved away from the dock, their noble faces turned toward the lighthouse, toward Monte Carlo, toward Italy.

I looked with relief at where we had been docked so long, and as the sun set I waved at the *confrérie* of old salts hanging around the harbor and the land-locked owners, of whom I knew every one. Slowly the white lighthouse turned the pale rose sheen of evening. Colors you see only along water—deep purples and glowing carmines—sank from the Maritime Alps into the sea; the beacon of the Cap d'Antibes lighthouse became a white plume sweeping the Mediterranean. We were on our way at last.

I smiled. "How far tonight?"

The captain said, "If agreeable, signore, as far as Monte Carlo—to try out the boat, to get the feel—and not too much the first day. Then tomorrow we shall get the tanks filled in Monte Carlo where the facilities are better. There is a gasoline pump on the dock, and we can also fill the water tank with clean water and provision the boat with the things you will want to take from France and which are not obtainable in Italy. If you permit, I will make a list. I suggest that tomorrow we sail toward evening. There is always a good wind, but I am at your orders if you prefer day sailing."

"I am in full agreement with you."

We arrived at the rock of Monaco, turned into the harbor, and made fast, and there was the *Iphigenia*, and the Onassis yacht, *Christina*. My men did their elegant silent chores of putting the gangplank ashore, and getting the boat ready for its overnight stay. I was astonished anew to find that the second had even laid out my dinner clothes.

·   ·   ·

The next day as we cast off, the owner of the *Iphigenia*, his beautiful wife, and the children waved from the high deck of their ship, and the Great Dane wagged its tail. We passed the *Christina* and, as the sun set, started on the voyage proper, going out into the calm Mediterranean between the two lighthouses of the port of Monaco, which is as neat and clean as a pastry shop.

The icebox door opened and closed quietly several times, and wonderful aromas filled the air. Then dinner was served. Light faded, the mate went below. Presently I heard his soft voice and the guitar. How often had I thought it folly—buying this boat. And now—how glad I was! Dear *Old Lady,* dear *Arche de Noé.*

A good wind pushed us along. Where the bow parted the waves, a million pearls of light danced on the water. The captain brought me a pillow, a cigar, a drink, tuned the radio to classical music, and silently disappeared. We passed Menton. The mate came aft and hoisted a small Italian flag, for we were passing Ventimiglia. I had started on the long voyage. We went as far as San Remo.

Mayday

. . .

The glory lasted all the next day. I have never been able to figure out the mechanism of what followed; but after that a rapid deterioration took place in my two men. The *noblesse* left their faces; they stopped shaving. In port they frequently vanished, walking away in their elegant, floating fashion, to stagger back late at night and rummage noisily in the icebox. The gas and oil purchases doubled, something was always needed—rope, black paint, white paint, brushes, tools. They begged for money constantly— for food, drink, cigarettes, advances on salary. When I gave them money they counted it, shrugged their shoulders without saying thank you, and one turned back to steering the ship while the other went to the icebox and got himself a drink. Perhaps I had two murderers on board. For who would know what happened on a boat out of sight of land, at night? I spun at this scenario for a while, then reassured myself that if this were true they would not bother to ask for money but would just take it.

We made frequent stops now. At Savona, a port where repairs are made, they reported propeller trouble and advised that the boat be hauled. They made arrangements and said the price would be two hundred thousand lire. The boat had been hauled in France, and it cost thirty-five thousand francs, including painting the bottom. Marine work was supposed to be cheaper in Italy.

I went to the shipyard, where the owner agreed to pull the boat, scrape it, and paint it for thirty-five thousand lire. I also had the propeller examined; nothing was wrong with it. When I confronted the crew with this information, they mumbled among themselves in Italian, saying that they had fallen on a very bad *padrone*. They consoled themselves in a bar. When they sobered up, we proceeded toward Portofino.

There is a German proverb that says that a good conscience is the best pillow. This doesn't hold true at all. My crew of thieves, who had drunk all my whisky and gin, and whose hearts were filled with larceny, lay on deck and slept like babies. They were always barefoot, although I had bought them new sneakers. They could sleep anywhere, on the blade of an oar, or up in the bow with an anchor for a pillow. To wake them up took shaking, and like young dogs they only slowly focused their eyes and then collected themselves.

We sailed into Genoa, where I called my Italian friend in Naples and told him about my bandits. He said they had served him many years and never stolen a thing. "I used to kick them around," he said. "Maybe you treat them too well. By the way, what flag do you sail under?"

"American."

"Oh—no wonder. I advise you to fire them. If you don't they will take your eyes out and eat them."

They started wailing that the season had advanced and they would be without work all summer. After an hour's dispute, we came to an agreement. I gave them two months' pay and transportation home. Carrying their duffel bags, they walked off the ship as softly as they had come.

The *Arche de Noé* was now abandoned in Genoa, hometown of Christopher Columbus. People and animals have moods, and so do boats. The icebox was empty, the forecastle dirty; the dinghy needed bailing. I sat gloomily on deck and asked myself why I had ever got into this mess. The best thing would be to sell the old tub to the first fool to come along—for anything—and forget it.

In desperation I called Captain Richardson in Cap d'Antibes.

By happy coincidence the right man was available. "A captain who is perfect for you," he said. "A Yugoslav, but a French citizen with a French temperament. Ready to go at a moment's notice, and his mate is his father."

At last, two honest, simple people came aboard and said, *"Bonjour,* monsieur." The boat was in order quickly, gas and oil came on board, also water. René started the motor, listened to it a moment, examined the sails, and said he was ready to go.

Along the coast before one gets to Portofino there is a small harbor which is easily missed, but worth a visit. One becomes aware of it only because small excursion ships that go toward it suddenly seem to vanish into the rock. As you follow one of them, you see an opening, and you enter through a narrow, high cleft in the stone, as through a portal, and come upon a small circular lagoon of deep green water.

The place is called San Fruttuoso, and the space on land is so limited that the fishermen, instead of spreading out their nets to dry, must hang them up on ropes stretched overhead between the high walls of the fiordlike scenery. Thus suspended, they give the place the air of an outdoor theater. There is a monastery or cloister forming the background, and to the left a very good restaurant. We anchored there.

Everything here is done, as in a circus, with trapeze wiring and ropes. The fishboxes, suspended in the water, are worked with a pulley by a chef who wades into the water, pulls out the box, opens it, and lets you pick out a lobster, which he cooks in memorable fashion. There are also excellent salad, good pasta, good wine, and reasonable prices.

Half an hour's sailing from San Fruttuoso is the entrance to the harbor of Portofino. There René proceeded across the harbor and gave the command, *"Mouille,* Papa." *Mouille* means wet and is sailor lingo for drop the anchor. René was a careful captain; he gave the anchor plenty of play. When the hook was dropped, he reversed the engine and went to the opposite side of the harbor, where small boats dock.

I had recovered from my black mood. These seemed to be the boatmen I had been waiting for. It was homey again to sit in the cabin or aft in the cockpit, cool, comfortable, and snug. The Neapolitans had not disturbed my floating office or my typewriter, papers, paints, or brushes. I did some painting. Papa went ashore and returned carrying a net filled with food and red wine. All was fine. Good thing I bought this boat, I reflected; from now on it would be a joy. (Or so I thought.)

Last Visit
to Regensburg

. . .

I decide to drive to Regensburg.

I have had a report that my brother's grave is in disrepair. Personally, it doesn't matter to me, for I have no feeling for cemeteries, except the romantic ones like Arlington and Père Lachaise in Paris.

But my brother Oscar was always in my care and looked to me as to his father, and so I drive there—to the doubly hateful place to which my roots are attached like those of moss to a stone.

Easter Sunday—rain and snow. Gray lead in the sky, a snow cloud over an onion-topped church. Munich is very empty with no obstruction, no work, no people promenading.

I sit up front with the driver, Herr Durreman, who speaks the Bavarian patois. He is of well-fed form and pleasant. His black hair and dark brown eyes are reminders of the Roman invasion of Bavaria.

The Mercedes rides hard. It has no feeling of going on its own momentum but is exactly tied to the revolutions of the motor; stop giving gas, and it slows down.

The pleasant, rich farm landscape passes. The Autobahn goes on—no cars—102 kilometers to Regensburg—68 kilometers to Regensburg—triangle, left to Nuremberg—right to Regensburg—

center to a place in the memory album of childhood—Bad Aibling, the Saratoga of this region, to which my grandfather drove with his landau and horses for the cure.

We get off the Autobahn and go along winding roads. The peasant houses are neat. This is the hops section; the hops are raised like beans, but on telegraph-size poles, held together by strong wire.

We come to the Danube.

"That is the Danube," Herr Durreman informs me. "It flows seven thousand kilometers to the Black Sea, from here to Austria, Hungary, Romania.'

I see a sign on the right: Two kilometers to Hohengebraching. This belonged to my grandmother's family—church, brewery, forests—a castlelike, big-walled estate.

We pass an ox and a cow. On the cow sits a chicken; all is as it was.

"On the next hill you will see the towers of the Cathedral, Herr Bemelmans." And there we are.

"Das ist Karthaus on the right, the insane asylum."

Everyone was afraid of eventually ending up in Karthaus, including my mother.

"Herr Durreman, please slow down—at the bottom of the hill, turn right—there—now go up all the way."

"To the cemetery?"

"Yes."

"To the upper katholischen cemetery?"

(The Protestant one is somewhat below, closer to the railroad tracks.)

"Ja, ja, Herr Durreman, you know Regensburg."

In my childhood this cemetery was out of town. Barren, immense, and ugly, I went there first for the funeral of my grandfather, when I was nine years old, and then for my brother's when I brought him back from America. (He was killed in a fall down an elevator shaft in the Ritz Hotel.) Now it is surrounded by houses, the trees are old, and it is less ugly. Durreman parks the car, runs to open the door, and helps me out.

"Can I go with you?"

"Nein, danke. Just wait for me—I won't be too long."

Everywhere are the friends of the dead—the little old ladies, called Cemetery Flies, who attend all funerals. On Sundays, on holidays, they resent the intrusion into their domain, which is theirs alone all week, of running children, gaily dressed young married people, and large families.

I thought the family plot was on the right as you come out of the church. It is on the left.

A set of stone slabs. An ugly black marble cross. A faded everlasting wreath, left perhaps from All Saints' Day.

The grave is not in need of repair. It's three o'clock. I turn. There is a grave half hidden by a cypress tree. A distance away stands Herr Durreman. He comes as if to offer condolences.

He points at Oscar's name. "So you too are a Regensburger."

"My brother was. I just came to see that the grave is in order."

"You are an Amerikaner?"

"I live in New York. Let's go."

"Herr Bemelmans, do we stop in town—do we have some relatives or friends to visit here?"

"No, we will just drive—just drive through the town."

Now we go down the hill, past the Palace of Justice and the *Augustenschule* and past the Dornberg villa with a beautiful garden.

In that house, next to the Church of the Minorites, lived the Deacon, who gave us religious instruction in school. At the beginning he took a great liking to me and made me sit on his knee, facing the class, as he spoke his few phrases of French. Once I carried the schoolbooks for a little girl I liked. Then I skated with her. I was seven. The next day a boy in school lifted his hand and told the Herr Katechet, as he was called, that I and the little girl kissed each other and that I was married to her. I grabbed the boy and banged his head. The Herr Katechet took his cane, asked me to hold out my hand, and brought it down ten times until it seemed that it was on fire.

Next, on the right, the Pustet villa—publishers of religious textbooks, with a shop in New York. Another villa, with a Greek façade, shaded by large plantains. Here lived Helma, the girl Oscar was in love with.

In a park, the villa of Uncle Wallner, pretentious little miser and merchant, who was called in to administer a beating to me when I was strong enough to hold my mother's hands, whose top hat I kicked down the stairs and threatened to kick him down after it.

And here, to the right, in the ivy-green building, the first floor was the office of my grandfather's lawyer, Herr Commerzienrat Doktor Emanuel Heidecker, the Disraeli of Regensburg, with a nose like a pince-nez'd lizard, and quick steps and mind, who had the great fortune to die when people of his race were still treated with respect in Germany.

We come to the *Neupfarrplatz,* with a massive church in the center, a good place for playing. It had a wide, high walk about it, like a promenade deck on a ship. It is all there as it was on a very cold winter evening, with a chain between the heavy stone posts. The Ordinarius, the teacher who was the most mortal enemy, the Professor of French I had dared to correct once and who hated me from then on, slipped here, on what is called *"Glatteis,"* very smooth ice. He lost his balance and fell into the chain and knocked out his upper front teeth. The snow was stained with his blood.

We hadn't pushed him, although we were suspected of it because we had been seen playing around there. We were always suspected. It did us no good, except inwardly. I can see the snow now, and the stain—its exact color—still after more than fifty years, and the house in back of the chain, a mustard-colored Baroque building, which was one of the few I liked.

We come to the Dom (Cathedral). Here on this spot, I received two slaps on the face from my great uncle, the Bishop, who otherwise loved me.

Pleyer, Pfannenstiel, and I called him the Fischkopf—our humor of those days on account of the mitre, which looked like a fish head, and because it sounded like Bischof.

I had been in an inquiring mood and I looked up at the spires of the Cathedral and saw that attached to them were lightning rods.

"Uncle," I said, "if there is a God and he believes in the Catholic religion, why do you have to put lightning rods up there?"

That is when I got those two smacks and thought my head would snap off.

Across the river to the Spitalgarden—place of the most beautiful view of the Danube. The same old chestnut trees, not yet in bloom—it's cold—but all the tables and chairs painted new in case the sun would shine.

Farther on is a large, empty field. In May there is the annual fair, called "Dult," where my friend Richard Pleyer and I disgraced our families by hiring ourselves out to push a merry-go-round.

"Shall I turn around, Herr Bemelmans?"

"No, go to the hill there—to the cave, Herr Durreman."

My grandfather lagered his beer over here. It was pulled in a typical beer wagon by heavy horses, who were overfed and always showed their impatience by pawing, usually with the left foreleg, striking sparks, scraping the stone. The cave is still used, the stones are still scraped. The horses standing there shook their heads, making the sleighbells ring like the Indians do in America in their war dances. The beer rested here for six months in wooden casks.

We drive to the end of the island, where the Danube splits in two. Here we had constructed a float like the Indians do in Peru, tying bundles of bullrushes together, ready to go wherever it carried us—Pleyer, myself, and Pfannenstiel. We had provisions and money, but the raft sank where I now stand. We made a tent of bullrushes but were found and taken home again by the Police.

We three—what held us together?

I was an outsider because I couldn't speak German when I started school and on account of my different clothes; Pleyer, because he came to my defense and hated all the others; Pfannenstiel, because he had carrot-red hair and was cross-eyed. Both are dead.

"And now, Herr Durreman, we go back to the city, over the bridge."

"Excuse me, Herr Bemelmans, here we must turn right. This is a one-way street now."

This was a no-way street when I was in the charge of a very religious nursemaid, the *heilige* Anna. We never entered here, for in the middle of this block, on the right, was the butcher shop of Abraham Hekscher, and in back of it he butchered small children in ritual fashion and sold the sausages he made of them to the Christians. Anna knew that and crossed herself.

At the end of the street stood a Protestant church and in that lived the Devil himself. Any good Catholic knew that, and if by accident one passed the Pastor, whose cursed name was

Pürkhauer, or his wife or children, one crossed himself and went into the nearest Catholic church to dip into the vessel with holy water.

On our way to the *Arnulfsplatz* the car faces the Portal of the *Neue Münster* (the new Cathedral). Our First Communion took place here, Pleyer's and mine. Pfannenstiel was a Protestant.

On the left is Saltner's Konditorei—my first ice cream. At the right there was a Cinema, where to the music of a piano that sounded like a *piano mécanique* I saw my first film, a flickering comedy made by Pathé Frères and played by Max Linder.

Now through a narrow street, and at last the *Arnulfsplatz* and my grandfather's Brewery. My uncle's business was across the Square. The same lettering, the same houses, the same windows. I walk into the Brewery, the tables the same, the chairs the same. In the hall it is cold. There is the same smell of latrine, beer, and heavy cooking. Nothing is changed.

The big dining room of the *Wirtshaus*. The same menu at the side of the door; the big pine top table at which Grandfather sat, close to the green, tiled stove.

The waitresses passed here from the kitchen with the platters of food. My grandfather looked at everything, not to inspect it, but in case there was something he liked. Then he would say, "Frau Breissle," or whatever the waitress's name was and point at the table in front of him. This meant that whatever she was about to serve had to be put there for him to eat.

If the waitress said, "But, Herr Fischer, that is for the Assessor So and So, and it's the last portion—and it's his favorite dish," Opapa said in the Bavarian dialect, "Put it down, let him order something else."

On Sundays we went over the bridge to Stadamhof and over another bridge across the river Regen. Here there was a little landscape—open sky, and the radish fields of the village of Weichs. Here was a neat place, a house with saintly pictures and a crucifix, and at every door a vessel with blessed water. Here Anna was raised in the most holy fashion, with a large, ugly church across the road, the priest a daily visitor. This was her home; here she labored. She was an illegal child and adopted by the two old sisters who spent several hours a day on top of a curiously constructed pump, seesawing back and forth, pumping water, like all

the others did, for their famous radishes, which are the most famous in all Bavaria.

These people, these two old women and their pump, and their
brother, an old man, I put into a book called *The Blue Danube*.
There was no place to run or play, only to sit, with quietly folded
hands, and listen to one of them reading the lives of the Saints or
to conversations free of all interest for me or for anyone living. Towards evening we would return in time for vespers at the St.
Jacob's Church or a litany at the Carmelites

Herr Durreman drove through a side street, where an old man
gave lessons to pupils who did not do well in school. His three
sons, all honor students, also gave lessons. The old man walked up
and down, looked over shoulders.

I spent most of the time sitting in the toilet and reading cut up
newspapers—mostly feuilletons, without the beginnings or ends
of stories. I was dismissed from there after three months. The sons
all became important men, and each one was killed in the war.

We drive on, over the railroad bridge. The unchanged train
station—sad and heartless. In these rails was my Fate—my escape. Here I left for Rothenburg, to be put into a Pensionat. Here
I left for my uncle's hotels in Tyrol when I was thrown out of
school. Here I left for America.

Some of the selections in this book were first published in periodicals as follows: "Little Bit and the *America*" (as "The Dog That Travelled Incognito") in *Collier's*; "My Favorite City" (in different form as "Paris, City of Rogues," and "Bemelmans' Magic Cities") and "The Dog of the World" in *Holiday*; "The Ballet Visits the Magician" (as "The Ballet Visits the Splendide's Magician"), "The Homesick Bus Boy" (as "The Homesick Bus Boy of the Splendide"), and "The Isle of God" in *The New Yorker*; "My First Actress" in *Stage*; "The Splendide"(as "Monsieur Victor"), "Herr Otto Brauhaus," "Mr. Sigsag" (as "Bus Boy's Holiday"), "The Old Ritz" (a portion of which appeared as "A Gemutliche Christmas"), "Camp Nomopo" (as "Little Girl with a Headache [Camp No Mo Pie]"), and "Lust for Gold" (as part of "Servant Trouble") in *Town and Country*; "Swan Country" (in a different form as "When You Lunch with the Emperor"), "Bavaria" (as "Seven Hundred Brides"), "The Footstool of Madame Pompadour" (in slightly different form as "The One I Love Best—Lady Mendl"), and "Cher Ami" in *Vogue*.

Some of the selections in this book also appeared in the following books by Ludwig Bemelmans published by Viking Penguin Inc.: *Dirty Eddie*, 1947; *Father, Dear Father*, 1953; *Hotel Splendide*, 1941; *I Love You, I Love You, I Love You*, 1942; *Life Class*, 1938; *My War with the United States*, 1937; *On Board Noah's Ark*, 1962; *Small Beer*, 1939; *To the One I Love the Best*, 1955; and *The World of Bemelmans: An Omnibus*, 1955. One selection first appeared in *My Life in Art*, published by Harper and Brothers, 1958.